CRAWSHANKS GUIDE TO THE RECENTLY DEPARTED

CASE #2: MRS DELORES ABERNATHY

VAWN CASSIDY

Tristan

The *tip tap* of the rain against the panes of glass wakes me slowly. I swim up through the layers of consciousness reluctantly, feeling a pleasant warmth plastered against my back and the dead weight of an arm slung over my waist. There's a very loud, distinctly feline purring next to my ear in direct contradiction to the very human appendage pinning me to the bed.

I turn my head carefully and look over my shoulder to find my cat, Jacob Marley, currently curled up on the side of my boyfriend's head, his tail curling around Danny's neck like a facehugger from the film *Alien*. I can barely see Danny's face, just a nose and mouth, and I suppose I should be grateful my cat is allowing him to breathe at least. Although, saying that, I know he'd never do anything to harm Danny. Jacob Marley has made his preference very clear; Danny is his prince and the rest of us mere mortals are nothing more than peasants.

I watch as Jacob Marley opens one sleepy eye and stares at me lazily as if to say, *Yeah? What are you gonna do about it, peasant...*

I suppose I should also be grateful Danny doesn't have any

allergies or his head would be the size of a watermelon by now. Turning away from the territorial glare of my cat, I snuggle back down into Danny's warm embrace and sigh in contentment.

The rain has risen to a clatter as the heavens open outside. I'd forgotten to close the curtains again last night when I crawled into bed to wait for Danny. I must've fallen asleep by the time he got in. We've barely had time to see each other lately between my job at the mortuary and his job as a detective. It's frustrating when our schedules don't align for weeks on end. Most of the time he's at his flat and I'm at mine. If we do manage to see each other we don't always get the chance to do more than sleep and occasionally have breakfast together.

But not today. I grin to myself.

Today is one of those rare days when serendipity has aligned to give Danny and me twenty-four glorious hours together with no interruptions.

I glance back at the window again. Who said April showers were a pain? I can't think of anything better than snuggling in bed all day, preferably naked, while watching TV and snacking in between bouts of really hot sex.

My eyes drift closed again and I'm floating away, surrounded by Danny's warm scent and the lulling rhythm of his even breaths. I feel like I'm wrapped up in pure bliss, as if contentment were something tangible I could wrap around myself like a blanket.

I don't know how much time has passed when I notice a loud and persistent dripping above the pitter-patter of the rain against the window. Cranking open one eye, I lock on the source of the sound and sigh inwardly. There's a large wet spot on the ceiling directly above what looks to be a small lake pooling on the floor.

Lifting Danny's arm gently so as not to disturb him, I slide out of the bed and flop onto the floor gracelessly. Fumbling for my glasses on the bedside table, I shove them onto my face, almost poking myself in the eye.

Climbing to my feet and scratching my belly absently, I let out a jaw-cracking yawn and stumble out of the bedroom, stopping briefly in the bathroom to pee.

I resume my sleepy amble to the kitchen, almost tripping when Jacob Marley appears from nowhere and twines himself around my legs, trying to take me down like a furry ninja.

As I enter the kitchen, I do my best to ignore him as he leaps up onto the counter with the kind of agility an overweight ten-year-old cat probably shouldn't have. He plants himself imperiously beside me, tail twitching as he starts up a purr so loud it sounds like a rusty tractor.

"Oh, now you want my attention." I roll my eyes. "Honestly, I don't know why I let you treat me like this," I bemoan as I pick up his bowl from the floor and then automatically reach into the cupboard for his food. "You treat me badly and I still do everything you want." I place his food bowl on the floor and watch as he nimbly drops down beside it and sniffs at it disdainfully. I place the fresh water bowl down next to it, and he lets out an indignant yowl.

"Oh, for god's sake," I sigh as I reach for a clean bowl and open the fridge to pour him a small amount of milk. "There." I set it beside him. "That's all you're getting. It's no wonder you're getting tubby."

He gives a snooty sniff and turns to lap daintily at the milk while lifting his tail and showing me his bum hole.

"You're a dick," I tell him with great conviction. "Get a cat, they said," I mutter under my breath. "It'll be great company." I snort as I reach into another cupboard and pull out several large saucepans and pots. "Next time I'm getting a dog," I tell Jacob Marley, who is flat out ignoring me. "It may drool all over everything and chew my shoes, but at least it will love me unconditionally, unlike you, you spiteful little Jezebel."

I swear he would've flipped me the finger while nonchalantly drinking his milk if he could've. Turning away, I spy another rebellious drip from the ceiling. With a sigh of resignation, I place a pot underneath it and head out into the living room. Finding the other leak I know is there, I set another pot beneath it, then listen to the tinkling sound of the dripping for a moment before heading back into the bedroom and locking the door behind me with a perverse little snigger. Jacob Marley won't be able to get back in and stake his claim on my boyfriend now.

Setting the last pan under the leak in the bedroom, I lift the covers and slide back into bed beside Danny, who automatically wraps his arm around me and pulls me in close, nuzzling into my neck with a hum of contentment.

"Your feet are cold," he mumbles.

"You know those are some finely honed observational skills. Have you ever thought of a career in law enforcement?" I grin.

I yelp and laugh loudly as he whips me underneath him, rolling and pinning my body to the bed. I can feel his morning glory press against me, making my dick wake up and take interest as he buries his face in the crook of my neck and breathes deeply before kissing my warm skin.

"Want me to read you your rights?" He chuckles as he rolls his hips against me, and I let out a burst of laughter.

"Oh my god, that was terrible."

"I've only just woken up, this is what I have to work with." He lifts his head and takes my lips as I wrap my arms around his neck and grind my dick against him, trying to get some desperate friction.

"I could handcuff you to the bed again." His voice rumbles against my lips in amusement. "You know you liked it."

"Need I remind you what happened last time," I gasp out as his hand slides into my PJs and fists my cock lazily.

"That wasn't my fault." He smiles against my mouth, his

voice deliciously gravelly as he continues to stroke me slowly. "I could've sworn I put the key on the bedside table."

My eyes roll back in my head and my toes curl as he adds that little twist he does with his palm when he reaches the head of my cock. His tongue slides back in to tangle with mine as his fist tightens, and I moan obscenely into his mouth. A shiver rolls down my spine, and I can feel my balls tightening.

"Hold that thought." He pecks a quick kiss to my lips and jumps out of bed, leaving me splayed out like a starfish with my rock-hard dick poking out of my PJs.

"What?" I blink through a haze of lust as Danny shoots me a grin and disappears into the bathroom.

"Sorry, my bladder was about to explode," he calls through the open door to the accompaniment of a thin stream hitting the water.

"And they say romance is dead." I drop my head back against the pillow and stare up at the ceiling morosely.

"Don't worry, I'll make it up to you," he replies as he flushes the toilet and washes his hands. "Repeatedly." He chuckles as he clicks the light off and leaves the bathroom.

"Be careful of the"—I glance across and watch as Danny steps in the saucepan of rainwater—"pot," I finish with an apologetic snigger.

The look on his face is absolutely priceless as he lifts his dripping foot and stares at it before turning his gaze back to me.

"I thought you were going to speak to the landlord about that?" He grabs a nearby towel from the laundry pile and dries his foot before hopping back into bed and snuggling down under the covers with me.

"I spoke to him last time it rained and the roof leaked." I climb onto Danny, plastering myself to him and kissing his lips with a hum of pleasure.

"And what did he say?" Danny's hands snake down my spine to cup my buttocks, pulling me in closer.

"I think we've come to an understanding." I roll my hips against him.

"What's that?" Danny snorts. "You complain and he does nothing?"

"Pretty much." I shrug and take his mouth again.

"Tris..."

"Danny," I huff indignantly. "I'm trying to entice you to get naked here, I really don't want to discuss Mr Ahmed."

"Noted." He grins as he unceremoniously shoves my PJs down past my hips and fists my cock once more, and I let out a strangled moan.

He rolls me back underneath his body. I knock my glasses lopsided in my haste to get him naked as I grab at his t-shirt and yank it over his head, making his blonde hair stick up and crackle with static. I skim my hands down his sides, reaching for his boxers, and slide my hands in to cup the hard muscles of his gorgeous arse.

"You're all mine for the next twenty-hours, no interruptions," he gasps between frantic kisses.

Suddenly the shrill ringing of a phone breaks the lust-filled stupor we're both immersed in.

"It's like the universe hates me," I sigh as he releases my mouth. "My balls feel like they're about to fall off."

"Your balls are perfectly fine, sweetheart. Would you feel better if I hold them for you?" Danny grins and leans over to glance at the phone.

"I'd feel better if your lips were wrapped around them," I reply sulkily. "What is it?" I ask at the sight of a slight frown marring his brows.

"It's yours." He picks up my phone and hands it to me. "You'd better take this, it's Sunrise Care Home."

My heart thuds erratically in my chest as I fumble to

connect to the call from the care home that looks after my dad, a mixture of dread and worry lodged in my throat like a hot, hard ball.

"Hello, this is Tristan," I answer abruptly. "What's wrong?"

I listen for a few moments to the familiar voice on the other end of the line, my chest fluttering with a mixture of emotions.

"Okay, thank you for letting me know," I reply before hanging up.

"What is it? What's wrong? Is your dad okay?" Danny asks, watching me in concern as he props himself up on one elbow.

"It's nothing bad." I shake my head, swallowing tightly. "It's the opposite, actually. He's having one of his rare good days, and they wanted to let me know in case I wanted to spend the day with him."

"That's a good thing though, right?" He studies my face as if trying to gauge my mood.

"It is." I nod. "I'm sorry," I murmur despondently.

"For what?" He tilts his head as he watches me.

"We haven't seen each other properly in weeks." I let out a frustrated breath. "We were supposed to spend the day together."

"We'll still be spending the day together, just with your dad," he says easily. "Unless you don't want me to? If you'd rather go on your own, I can catch up on some of my case notes. I'll just wait for you later. We'll still have this evening after your dad's gone to bed."

"Danny." I cup his face softly as he settles me back onto the bed, our earlier passion banked. He wraps his arms around me and holds me comfortingly. "I definitely want you with me, are you sure you don't mind?"

"Of course not." He runs his fingers through my thick dark curls, raking his fingers soothingly against my scalp. "Tris, it's important you have this with your dad, especially on his good days. There'll be time for us. I'm not going anywhere."

"Danny," I whisper, unsure what else to say as he leans in and takes my lips. It's deep and drugging and seems to say all the things I can't articulate right now.

After a moment, he pulls away and strokes my face gently. "We should get up and get dressed if we're going to drive to Shadwell."

I glance across at the clock, biting my lip as I stare at him. "You know, if we were to leave now we'd probably hit traffic. It might be best to give it another ten minutes."

"That's true." A smile tugs at his lips. "Probably should make it fifteen just to be on the safe side."

"Seems sensible," I agree with a nod.

I yelp and follow it up with a giggle as he grabs my hips and yanks me down the bed, pulling the covers over us and sealing us in an intimate little cocoon. His lips find mine once more and we devour each other, trying to avoid elbows and knees as we strip our clothes off. His hot mouth trails down my neck, then my chest, skimming across my belly before the hot wet heat of his mouth envelopes my cock.

My hips arch and a groan spills from my lips as my fingers tangle in his hair. His tongue swirls around the head and my eyes cross. God damn it, he's good at that. He bobs up and down on my dick, the delicious friction sending little sparks dancing down my spine and lighting up every inch of my skin.

I feel his fingertips skim over my balls and down between my legs before a gentle finger rubs maddeningly slow circles over my opening. I pull the covers off my head, dragging in a gulp of cooling air as I fumble for the bottle of lube on the bedside table.

Suddenly, he swallows me deep, my cock hitting the back of his throat. I arch back on a gasp, my arm flailing as I knock the lamp on the floor, along with my phone and a tatty paperback. Grasping desperately, I manage to lock my grip around the lube bottle. I thrust it under the covers, accidentally smacking Danny in the head.

"Oops, sorry," I pant, feeling him chuckle around a mouthful of my dick. Seconds later, I feel the silken glide of his slick fingers pushing inside me.

I let out another long drawn-out groan as he crooks his fingers inside me and rubs over my prostate. I reach blindly behind me, my fingers grasping around the spindles of the headboard and gripping tightly as I unconsciously draw up my knees and ride his hand shamelessly.

"Danny, please," I breathe as he pulls free and climbs my body, slicks the hard length of his cock, and slides into me.

Releasing the headboard, I wrap my arms and legs around him, pulling him in as close as I can. He slips his arms under my back until I feel surrounded by him.

"Danny," I gasp desperately, my breath puffing against his ear as he rolls his hips sinuously, rocking deeper inside me with every thrust.

Our mouths are fused together as I chase the sweet oblivion of surrender I've never experienced with anyone but him. Every molecule of my body is attuned to him alone.

The tension in my body builds. I'm shaking with the intensity of it, feeling the thick heavy drag of his cock over that bundle of nerves deep inside me, and I need more. I need him to push me over the edge.

"Harder," I whisper harshly, my fingers gripping his back so tightly they're almost bruising.

His hands cup my buttocks, pulling my pelvis in tighter as he thrusts impossibly deep. My cock ruts against his abdomen, trailing precum.

"Danny... I can't..." My voice breaks desperately, and my orgasm rips through me with such intensity it leaves me dizzy, with swirling lights dancing in front of my eyes.

While I lie there panting, my heart thundering against

Danny's chest, I feel his cock pulse inside of me as he orgasms on a low moan. I trail my fingers along his spine, laying my head contentedly on his shoulder as he kisses my neck, and I feel sleepy and sated.

This right here... is pretty close to perfect, but I can't ignore the feeling fluttering at the edges of my mind... the feeling that things are about to inexplicably change.

2

Tristan

Dad looks across the table and smiles at me and it's everything. He no longer truly speaks, mostly just mumbled nonsense. He can't say my name, and I don't think he knows who I am anymore, just that I was once someone special to him. It's hard watching the man I love slowly disappearing in front of my eyes. Most days it's so painful to be here it takes everything in me to sit and just be here for him.

It's like Danny knows somehow. I don't even have to explain it to him. He just gets it, gets how draining it is for me. He's extra careful with me on those days, gives me little things: a cup of tea, a foot rub, a hug, and Netflix.

I stare at Danny seated comfortably on the opposite side of the table as he patiently removes a Scrabble tile from my dad's mouth and hands it to him.

"The G's don't taste as good as the Q's," he tells him and my dad smiles at him, actually beams at him as if he knows it's a joke. "Now, where are we putting these?" Danny asks. He slowly hands the tiles to my dad one by one and watches as he sets them on the board.

"Ha! Z on a triple word score. We are cleaning up, Martin!"

"I don't think"—I lean across the table and look—"ZYWQBCCKDDGHYYG is actually a word."

"It's a Welsh word, note the lack of vowels." He counts up the score and scribbles it in his police notebook, which is never far from his breast pocket, even on his day off. "So that's 62 on a triple word score, which makes 186, which brings our grand total to 489."

"I think you two are cheating." My mouth twitches.

Danny turns to my dad and grins. "He's such a sore loser."

My heart throbs in my chest as I watch my dad lean his head on Danny's shoulder. Danny wraps his arm around him without even thinking about it as he gathers up the Scrabble tiles with his other hand.

"Well, I don't know about you, Martin," he remarks conversationally to my dad, "but I think we've embarrassed Tris enough for one day over his appalling spelling skills. How about Jenga?"

"They banned Jenga," I lament ruefully. "There was nearly bloodshed last time between Mr Peterson and Mrs Phelps."

"Ok, no Jenga then. What do you want to do, Martin?" Danny asks him, like it's the most natural thing in the world, and in response my dad picks up a puzzle box and nudges it into my hands.

"You want to do a jigsaw?" I ask as I open the box and scoot my chair in closer.

I don't bother looking at the picture, it makes no difference. Dad can't do puzzles anymore, not properly anyway. He just kind of fits all the pieces together haphazardly so the finished article somewhat resembles a brightly printed cardboard spiderweb, but it keeps him focused for a little while and makes him happy. Danny and I sit companionably taking turns to hand him random puzzle pieces.

I'm so focused on Dad I almost miss the cool trickle down my spine followed by a small shudder. I shift my shoulders uncomfortably and glance behind me, but nothing seems amiss. Just the regular residents milling around with the carers and various visitors and family members.

But I can't shake the strange feeling. For just a moment, I could have sworn a cold shadow had passed over me.

"Hello there, Tristan." One of the familiar nurses stops by the table to check in. "Danny." She smiles at him.

I shake my head lightly to clear the strange thoughts swirling in my mind and greet her warmly. "Hi, Lois." She's been caring for my dad ever since he was brought here nearly four years ago.

She nods at my dad. "It's nice to see Martin so relaxed."

"Yeah." I smile softly as I watch Danny handing him another puzzle piece.

"It's nearly lunchtime," she says. "I doubt you'd want what the residents are having since most of them are on soft food and liquids to avoid choking, but I can get cook to rustle you up a couple of sandwiches if you'd like."

"That would be perfect, thank you." I smile up at her and Danny does the same as she wanders off towards the kitchen.

We pack up the puzzle and help Dad into the dining room, settling him at a table between us. Danny sits and holds Dad's hand, chatting about random things, knowing he's not really taking it in, as I feed him slowly, stopping now and then to wipe the mashed potato from his chin. Danny takes over spooning him some sort of pink gooey pudding so I can eat my sandwich from a plastic plate and sip my juice from a plastic beaker.

The rest of the day passes much the same. We sit with Dad while he scribbles in a colouring book with brightly coloured felt-tip pens, getting more on himself than the page, but then again, art is in the eye of the beholder. We sit curled up on a sofa and watch some old episodes of *Supermarket Sweep* for a while as the rain continues to pelt the wide steamed-up windows of the dayroom, the sound comforting over the muted volume of the TV.

We help him with his dinner and then after, we sit in the kitchen eating Chinese takeaway with some of the staff while Lois and one of the other carers bathe Dad and get him ready for bed. Usually, I'd sit by his bed and read to him, but tonight Danny surprises me by pulling out loads of extra blankets and pillows Lois has provided and building a blanket fort on the floor in Dad's room. He places the small nightlight we brought with us on a previous visit inside so it casts stars and constellations across the roof of the tent.

It feels like my lungs are too small as I suck in a breath and stare at his finished fort with tears burning my eyes. It's just like the one my dad built for me after Mum died. Dad and I slept inside it every night for six months because I was afraid he was going to die, too, and leave me all alone.

"I thought that"—Danny's hand slips into mine and grips warmly—"as he's having a good day, this might feel familiar to him and help him connect with you, even if it's on a level we can't see. I like to think that some part of him deep inside will know."

I can't speak, my throat is aching. Just when I think it's not possible to fall even more in love with this man, he goes and does something like this.

My watery gaze falls on Dad as he crawls slowly into the fort and flops on his back, patting the pillows and blankets around him before staring up at the stars cast above by the rotating nightlight.

"Come on," Danny says, grasping my hand and picking up the battered copy of *The Voyage of the Dawn Treader* from the bookshelf.

He tugs me forward and we crawl into the snug fort, one on either side of Dad. We burrow down into the blankets as Danny opens the book and begins to read in that delicious low

Northern burr of his and holy cow, why don't I get him to read to me more often? His voice is all kinds of delicious.

I glance over to the open door of the bedroom and see Lois leaning against the doorframe, watching us, a soft smile playing across her lips. She sends me a wink and disappears down the corridor, leaving me to settle back and let Danny's voice wash over me. After a moment, Dad turns over onto his side and burrows into me. Wrapping my arms around him, I pull him in close, close my eyes, and breathe in the familiar scent of him with a painful pang. For just a brief second, I'm once again that small boy in his fort with his dad. Now, in many ways I'm the adult and he's the child, but we're still together, and that's all that matters.

Dad reaches up unconsciously and twirls a curling lock of my dark hair, listening to the story even though he's not really taking it in.

Surrounded by the warmth and comfort of the two who mean the most to me in the entire world, I lose myself in the story as Lucy and Edmund join Prince Caspian onboard the Dawn Treader for a high seas adventure.

Slowly, Danny's voice trails off, replaced with Dad's deep exhausted snore. I glance over his frail body and my eyes lock on Danny. He gives me a small smile and I nod. Ever so carefully, we slide out of the fort and remove the blankets so we can reach Dad easily. I cross the room and pull back the bedding, watching as Danny effortlessly lifts Dad's slight form from the floor and settles him in bed.

I lift the nightlight and set it on his bedside table so it casts starlight on the ceiling for him even in his sleep while Danny puts the chairs back in place and folds the blankets neatly. I'm just tucking Dad in as he joins me.

"Night, Martin. Sweet dreams." He pats one frail hand gently so as not to wake him.

Leaning forward, I kiss my dad's forehead. "Night, Dad.

Love you lots like Jelly Tots," I mutter. Admittedly, it would probably sound childish to anyone on the outside looking in, but it was always our thing. It was what Mum always used to say to me when she tucked me into bed at night.

Taking Danny's hand, I step out into the empty corridor and close the door behind us with a quiet click. I release the breath I didn't realise I was holding, my head folding into Danny's broad chest as his arms come around me, and I feel him drop a kiss on my head.

He rubs my arms comfortingly. "Are you okay, love?"

"Yeah," I sigh.

I am, it's been a good day, but I feel absolutely drained. Suddenly I shiver as a cold draught blasts down the still corridor, rippling my hair and sending shivers down my spine. I look up sharply and turn my head to glance down the hall, the feeling from earlier in the day returning full force.

"Did you–" I frown, looking up as the fluorescent tube lighting flickers with an insect-like hum.

"What is it?" Danny asks.

I'm about to answer when I see a dark shadow rush past the end of the corridor and disappear into the adjacent one. My stomach jolts sharply and my heart pounds. There's no way I just saw what I thought I saw.

Without thinking, I hurry past several rooms and turn the corner, then draw up so sharply Danny almost crashes into the back of me. My mouth falls open at the sight of the shadow in a doorway, hovering a couple of feet above the ground for a moment before drifting into the room and disappearing.

I dash forward to the doorway, but the shadow is gone. The softly lit room is only occupied by a couple of sombre-looking staff members, including Lois.

"Lois, what's going on?"

"Mrs Abernathy just passed away," she says sadly, moving aside to reveal a little old lady laying serenely on her bed.

I recognise the tiny woman, she often sat beside my dad in the dayroom. They didn't talk, given that my dad has vascular dementia and Delores has Alzheimer's, but they often gravitated to each other for some unknown reason.

Delores Abernathy had been a sweet little old lady. At over ninety-five years old, she was tiny but not as frail as you might think. She still went out twice a week to meet with her friends at the community hall in Clapham, under the watchful eye of one of the carers, of course. Delores had advanced Alzheimer's and was quiet more often than not, but on the rare occasions she did speak, she was trapped in the past, remembering family and friends that were long since gone and a war that most of us are too young to remember.

She's laying out on top of her neatly made bed, fully dressed and wearing sensible laced shoes over mismatched argyle socks, one red and one blue, which are pulled all the way up her skinny ankles. Her skirt is a thick pleated charcoal grey, and her white blouse is neatly tucked into the waistband and covered by a pale pink cardigan decorated with embroidered rosebuds that is buttoned all the way up to the collar. Her cloud of silver white hair is combed neatly into waves beneath a brightly coloured pink hat which looks like a tea cosy.

She's lying on her back, feet together, her face in calm repose and her hands tucked neatly over the clutch of her black leather handbag, which she was never without. I wish I'd known more about the little old woman who always seemed to keep silent company with my father.

"Why is she dressed?" I ask as I look up at Lois. It's way past the residents' bedtime and yet she looks like she's dressed to go out and is simply waiting to be picked up.

"It wasn't unusual for her." Lois plucks a tissue from her uniform pocket and wipes her eyes, sniffling quietly. "She would get confused; she couldn't keep time. If she woke up, she would decide it was time to get up and would get herself dressed. Quite often, we'd find her wandering the corridors in her shoes and socks with her heavy winter coat buttoned over her nightdress."

"I'm so sorry, Lois," I whisper as I glance down at the old lady.

"It's part of the job," she sighs. "It doesn't get any easier, but it was obviously just her time."

"Is there anything I can do?" I ask, aware Danny is hovering quietly behind me.

"No, love." She shakes her head and gives a teary smile. "Thank you, but we have the on-call doctor stopping by to call time of death, and we've called Delores' niece in."

I'm just about to open my mouth when a large brusque man jostles into the room wearing evening dress and looking quite put out beneath his bushy eyebrows and moustache.

"Dr Carroll." Lois nods, her demeanour cooling slightly, indicating she obviously doesn't much care for the on-call doctor, and when he opens his mouth, I can see why.

He flips on the main light and marches over to the bed, all business. "Right then, shall we get on with it? I have dinner reservations at The Savoy." He glances at his watch in annoyance. Leaning over the bed, he pinches the inside of Delores' wrist to check for a pulse. Satisfied there's nothing going on, he slowly peels her eyelids back before nodding to himself. "Time of death, 8.47 pm. Do you have the papers for me to sign?"

He takes the clipboard Lois hands him with a pinched expression.

"Just a minute!" I snatch the clipboard out of his hand.

Lois blinks. "Tristan! What are you doing?"

"His job for him, obviously." I narrow my eyes and glare at the intruder. "You might as well run along to your reservation. I doubt you'd want to miss the starter course." I eye his vast paunch tucked ruthlessly into his tightly notched leather belt.

"Well I never," he sputters indignantly.

"Run along now, and you can expect a call from your practice supervisor, as I can assure you I will be putting in a very strenuous complaint. I've never witnessed such a callous lack of regard for the dead, not to mention your utter incompetence."

Deciding his dinner plans are obviously far more important than arguing with me, he turns on his shiny buffed shoes and sails out of the room, muttering under his breath.

"I assume there was a reason for that?" Danny's brow quirks curiously.

"Tristan, what did you do?" Lois' eyes widen in shock. "He's a pompous, self-important prick, but we need someone to sign off on the death certificate."

"It's okay," I tell her solemnly. "I'm fully qualified to call time of death and sign off on her death certificate, but you might want to hold off on the whole natural causes thing for a minute."

"What? Why?" Lois frowns. "She was ninety-seven years old. She slipped away in her sleep."

"She may have slipped away in her sleep"—I shake my head—"but it wasn't because of old age."

"What's going on, Tris?" Danny steps in closer.

"Look." I lift Mrs Abernathy's hand carefully.

"What am I looking at?" he asks in confusion, and that's when he sees it, the dark brown banding horizontally across all of her nails. "What's that?"

"They're Mees' lines, they're indicative of heavy metal poisoning. They usually present between three and six weeks after the initial poisoning." I turn to Lois, who's looking faintly ashen. "Last week, you mentioned Delores hadn't been well. Stomach problems, I think it was?"

Lois nods slowly. "Stomach cramps, some diarrhoea, but the last few days she's had some seizures. We just assumed it was the natural progression for her and were just about to start discussing palliative care."

"What are you thinking, Tris?" Danny asks.

"She'll need a full post-mortem and blood tests to be sure, but I'm almost certain we're looking at arsenic poisoning."

"Arsenic?" Danny swears under his breath.

"Yes…" I nod slowly. "I hate to say it but I think Mrs Abernathy might have been murdered."

3

Tristan

The care home is a hive of muted activity, the police having arrived along with forensics, the carers and staff trying frantically to stop them all from waking the residents and causing chaos.

"We're going to need to get all the residents tested for heavy metal poisoning." Danny scratches the stubble along his jaw thoughtfully.

"I went back to Dad's room and checked his hands. He looks clear, as do most of the others that I've seen, but if the poisoning occurred here, we can't rule out cross contamination."

"We'll get to the bottom of this, Tris." He gives my arm a comforting stroke before he looks up and sees the flaming red hair of his partner.

"Detective Wilkes," I say with a warm smile as she stops in front of us. I've gotten to know Maddie and her wife Sonia well since Danny and I have been going over to their place for dinner when all our schedules allow it.

"Tristan," she greets. "They said arsenic poisoning. Arsenic? Really?"

"Looks like, but we still need to confirm."

"It's like an Agatha Christie novel."

A throat clears behind us, and we all turn to see a thin middle-aged woman with ash-brown hair wearing a Sainsbury's uniform and looking tired and sad.

"Maddie, this is Clarissa, Mrs Abernathy's niece," I tell her pointedly as I move to stand next to the tearful woman.

"Very sorry for your loss," Maddie says contritely, offering her hand. "I'm Detective Wilkes, and this is Detective Hayes."

"I've met Danny," she sniffles. "Call me Larry."

"Larry?" Maddie blinks.

"Clarissa... Larry..." She shrugs. "It kind of stuck when I was a kid, and now it's just what everyone calls me."

"Larry!" Lois appears from nowhere, exclaiming loudly as if to make Larry's point. "I'm so sorry, darling. Your aunt is going to be missed terribly."

"What happened? I heard someone say something about her being poisoned?"

"Larry," Danny says gently, "we don't know what happened yet so we can't make any assumptions, but it's looking as if your aunt died from some kind of heavy metal poisoning, most likely arsenic."

Larry gasps, her red-rimmed eyes widening in shock. "Arsenic? I thought that went out in the 1800s. Isn't that what little old Victorian ladies used to bump off their husbands?"

"It's still around, just not widely used," Danny replies.

"I can't believe this." Larry presses her palm to her forehead. "Who would want to hurt her? She was just a sweet, harmless old lady who didn't even know what day of the week it was."

"I don't know but we're going to find out, I promise," Danny says.

Lois puts a comforting arm around her. "You look like you've had a long, hard shift, and this has all been a terrible shock." She gives Larry a little squeeze and releases her as she turns to look at me. "Tristan, why don't you take Larry down to the dayroom, and I'll bring you both some tea while the police do their work."

I nod and head towards the dayroom, Larry walking along companionably beside me.

"How's your dad?" she asks as we enter the room.

I flip on the lights and approach one of the tables. "He's..." I give a helpless little huff as I take a seat.

"I get it." She nods and sits down, shifting a stack of board games out of the way.

"He had a good day today," I say softly.

"You take them when you can." She pulls out her phone, staring at the screen with a frown.

"I know it's a stupid question, but are you okay?"

She places her phone face down on the table with a huff of frustration. "I've been trying to get hold of my mum. Aunt Delores is... was her older sister."

"You haven't been able to reach her?"

"She's on a cruise with number 32." Larry rolls her eyes.

"Number 32?" I ask, my interest piqued.

"That would be lover number 32, husband number 8." Larry offers a small smile. "You'd think at her age, she'd slow down some. When I was growing up, there was an ever-revolving door of men in Mum's life. She fell in love as often as some women change their knickers. Fortunately, she didn't marry all of them, but there were enough of them that it was just easier to assign them a number rather than bother learning their names."

"Wow."

"Yeah." Larry looks up when Lois wanders into the room with a tea tray laden with a plate of biscuits, a teapot, two sturdy mugs, and several pots of milk and sachets of sugar.

"Thanks, Lois." She smiles tiredly as she reaches for a mug and pours herself a strong cup of tea.

"So Delores was her sister?" I ask as Lois slips back out of the room. Larry nods.

"They're not close, there was a big age gap. I think Aunt Delores was nearly twenty by the time my mum came along. Their mum remarried after the war when Delores' father was killed in action. New marriage, new baby. I was always the one who looked after Aunt Delores as she got older. She was really good to me when I was a kid, tried to give me the stability my mum couldn't, or rather wouldn't." Sighing deeply, she stares into her mud-coloured tea as she absently stirs it. "I can't imagine Mum will cut her cruise short, she's too selfish for that. She's never bothered with her sister before; I doubt she'll start now."

"Danny and I will help you, whatever you need." I reach out and lay my hand on hers comfortingly,

"Thanks." She squeezes my hand and manages another small smile even as an errant tear runs down her cheek and she quickly wipes it away. "So what happens now?"

"She'll need to have a post-mortem to confirm my suspicions," I say gently.

"And will you be doing that?"

I shake my head. "Probably not. She'll be transferred to a local mortuary."

"What if I want you to do it?" she asks. "It's just that..." She swallows hard. "She's so tiny and... and I know you'll be kind, that you'll give her her dignity."

"I don't know," I tell her honestly. "I can see if Danny can pull some strings and get her transferred to Hackney, but I can't make any promises."

"Thank you." She snuffles as she reaches for a tissue from a nearby box and accidentally knocks a sealed pot of milk onto the floor, but as she bends down and reaches for it, my eyes widen at the familiar-looking little old lady hovering behind her.

Mrs Delores Abernathy looks no different in death than she had in life with her strange tea-cosy hat, buttoned-up cardigan, and pleated skirt. She's still clutching her handbag in front of her chest, both frail hands wrapped around the leather handle, as she hums absently to herself.

I can feel the frown tugging at my lips as I study her. She seems lost in her own world, exactly as she had before. Once she was free of her physical body and the disease which had kept her trapped in the prison of her mind, I would have expected her to be more coherent, but she seems just as lost and confused.

A death cycle, I muse silently, just like Dusty. After her murder, the drag artist Dusty Le Frey had been trapped, frozen as she had been at the point of death. Which is why for the first few months she always appeared to me in the gold dress she'd died in, wearing a blood-stained wig, ruined makeup, and only one shoe.

Evangeline Crawshanks, the old lady who haunts the Whitechapel Occult Books & Curiosities shop, had said it was because she was locked in a death cycle, unable to move forward until her murder had been solved. No, I think suddenly. It wasn't her murder that needed to be solved, it was her unfinished business with her father that had been stopping her from moving on.

Shit. I stare back at the old lady, who once again disappears from view as Larry sits up and places the disposable milk pot back on the table. How the hell am I supposed to figure out what Delores' unfinished business is when she is still suffering from the ghost version of Alzheimer's?

Damn it, where's Dusty when I need her?

"I just can't believe this is happening," Larry says miserably. "Do you really think someone murdered Aunt Delores?"

I open my mouth to say I don't know what. On the one hand, I wish I could give her the peace of telling her Delores just slipped away from natural causes and went skipping off into the light. On the other, I'm staring at the proof that Delores had been shuffled off the mortal coil before her expiry date.

Before I can confirm one way or the other, Larry lets out a distraught sob and shoves her mug of tea out of the way, folding her arms on the table as she buries her face in them and cries. I watch as Delores shuffles up behind her, patting her niece awkwardly even though Larry can't feel it and is completely unaware of her presence.

It's sort of sweet in a weird, surreal kind of way, right up until the moment the tissue box flies off the table and slaps Larry in the side of the head. I snatch it up quickly with a grimace just as Larry looks up at me with swollen, tear-stained eyes.

"Tissue?" I hold up the box with an awkward smile.

She plucks a tissue from the box and holds it up to her face, closing her eyes to blow her nose, and just as she does the tea pot levitates off the table and floats toward her cup.

With a mortifying squeak, I reach out and grab it as Larry opens her eyes.

"Um, refill?" I jiggle the teapot in one hand while still grasping the tissues in the other one.

"Uh, no thanks." She frowns, reaching down to pick up her phone and glance at the blank screen once again.

"STOP IT!" I mouth silently at Delores, smiling at Larry innocently as she turns her attention back to me.

"Still no response from your mum?" I ask, setting the tissues and the teapot down.

"No, I..."

"Whoa... ah." I leap out of my chair as I see Delores amble toward Larry, holding the board game she liked to play with her every time she visited. I grab it quickly before Larry can see it levitating seemingly by itself across the room, shoving it behind my back as I grab Larry's arm and pull her up from the table.

"You know what we should do?" I tell her in a rush, turning her toward the door as I slip the board game onto the table behind us. "We should go see Danny... Yes, that's exactly what we should do. It's been a long night, and you should probably get some rest. So we'll check in with Danny and then we'll get someone to give you a lift home."

I steer her toward the corridor, the ghost trailing along behind us, once again humming to herself.

We catch up with Danny and Maddie outside Delores' room, but there's really nothing more that can be done tonight. They've organised for Delores' body to be removed and delivered to the Hackney Mortuary tomorrow. Danny, god bless that man, he knew I'd want to see this through and had pulled those strings to allow me to perform the post-mortem despite the death occurring just outside my area.

Larry, almost dead on her feet, heads home, leaving me her phone number and address so I can stay in touch with her throughout the investigation.

When the rest of the police have finally left, Danny turns to me, looking as exhausted as I feel.

"Well, that day was not what I was expecting," he chuckles.

"You're telling me," I mutter under my breath.

"I tell you what." He wraps his arms around me and pulls me in closer.

"What?" I smile up at him.

"Why don't we head back to your place? We could slide into the bath together." He drops a teasing kiss on my upturned lips. "I'll wash your back if you wash mine."

I snort quietly in amusement, groaning when I feel a presence hovering beside me. I turn my head to the side a fraction to see Delores staring at me. There is no way I'm getting naked in the tub with Danny while Delores is on the loose unsupervised.

What's really worrying is how she is able to move solid objects with such ease. It took Dusty weeks to manage even just the small stuff, but Delores doesn't seem to think twice about it. Which can only spell trouble for yours truly. How the hell am I going to explain this?

"Actually," I begin reluctantly.

How am I supposed to tell him that, as much as I desperately want to get all wet and soapy with him, we have to babysit a ghost with dementia who just happens to be able to move physical objects? Fuck, I inwardly groan. I haven't even worked up the courage to tell him I can see dead people yet.

"What is it, Tris?" He cards his fingers through my hair, and I want to arch into his touch like Jacob Marley does. Damn Danny and his magic hands.

"Actually, I'm shattered," I reply and I'm not lying. I feel like I've just run a twenty-mile marathon in flip-flops. "I really just want to crawl into bed with you and snuggle."

"A plan I can fully get on board with." He grins as he takes my hand.

Winding his fingers through mine, he steers me down the corridor, but the whole time I'm painfully aware of the tiny dead lady following along in my wake like a baby duck.

4

Tristan

My eyes are barely open as the stingy dribble of water from the shower tickles my face. It's like being lightly rained on, and yet another thing I need to speak to the landlord about. As if having to complain about the cheese grater I have for a roof isn't bad enough, now I have nonexistent water pressure.

After washing my body as best I can, I shove my hair under the pathetic stream of water. Rinsing the shampoo from my thick hair takes twice as long as usual, and by the time I'm done the water is freezing cold and I'm shivering like a half-drowned Chihuahua.

Shoving the shower curtain aside roughly, I let loose a rather unmanly scream as my nearsighted eyes land on a blurry figure standing in front of the closed door of the bathroom. I grab the shower curtain as my feet slip out from under me in the wet ceramic bathtub. I roll into the shower curtain, clutching on tightly as I lose my balance and go down, sending the plastic clips pinging off in all directions like tiny missiles knocking bottles off shelves and cracking the corner of the bathroom mirror. Pain clangs through my elbow and vibrates up my arm as, cocooned in clear plastic, I slide into the bath, breathing heavily and looking like I've been gift-wrapped by a serial killer.

"Owwww," I croak slowly to no one in particular.

Reaching one arm over the edge of the bath, my body follows and I flop ungraciously onto the rug like a newborn baby seal. Squinting without my glasses on, I can just about make out the still person clutching a handbag.

Mrs Abernathy, I realise with a groan of resignation. What is it with ghosts? First Dusty and now the old lady. What part of 'the bathroom is off limits' do they not understand? Is nothing sacred anymore?

I'm about to open my mouth when the bathroom door swings open and Danny strides in, passing straight through Mrs Abernathy and making her disappear into a thin vaporous mist.

"I heard a crash." Danny's eyes land on me sprawled out on the floor. "You okay?" His brow quirks as he takes in the assortment of displaced bottles and small plastic shower curtain clips everywhere.

"Slight shower malfunction." I release a winded breath. "A little help, please."

He strides toward me and effortlessly scoops me off the floor. His hands are gentle, his eyes filled with worry.

"Did you hurt yourself? Maybe we should get you looked at, you might have a concussion."

"I'm fine," I manage.

"We could call 111." He turns me slowly, peeling me out of the shower curtain like he's un-bandaging the Mummy in one of those Lon Chaney Jr movies.

"I wouldn't even call 111 for advice on how to remove a splinter." I wrinkle my nose. "Honestly, I'm fine."

He wraps the towel around me, pinning my arms to my sides as he drops a kiss on my nose. "Be more careful, I have plans for this gorgeous body later." He smiles, kissing my lips softly.

"It doesn't involve us both utilising the shower or the bath, does it? Because the water pressure's just packed up again, and last time it took three days to get a plumber out."

"For fuck's sake," Danny mutters with a frown. "I take it Mr Ahmed hasn't got back to you yet?"

"Are you kidding? The flat could burn to the ground and he probably still wouldn't return my calls." I snort. "My lease is up for renewal though," I muse. "Maybe I should start looking for something else. There's not much around here in my price range, which is why I've put up with the amazingly invisible Mr Ahmed, but I guess I could get something further out and just get the tube to work instead of walking."

"About that." Danny tilts his head as he studies me. "I was thinking, maybe we should…"

Whatever he was about to say is cut off by the loud and insistent blare of his phone. He pulls it out of his pocket and mutters under his breath. "I have to take this, it's Maddie."

"It's fine, we'll talk later." My mouth curves. "I'm at least eighty percent certain I can get myself dressed without injuring myself."

He chuckles as he hits connect and lifts the phone to his ear. "Hayes," he states by way of a greeting as he strides out of the room.

Drying off quickly and tossing the towel into the laundry basket, I pull on my boxers and skinny jeans, followed by my socks and my faithful Doc Martens. I've just chosen a clean t-shirt from my drawer when I turn around and yelp.

Directly in front of me, practically pressed up against my chest, is Mrs Abernathy.

"Er." I clutch my t-shirt to my nipples and try to take an awkward step back, but she simply steps into the space as if she

31

doesn't want to be parted from me. "Mrs Abernathy, you're violating my personal bubble."

"Bow," she says decisively.

"Uh.... okaaay," I reply slowly as I edge away from her, but she follows me like a puppy with boundary issues.

"Bow," she repeats with a smile.

"Right... sure, why not." I sigh resignedly as I pull the t-shirt over my head and scoop my hoodie up on my way out of the room, pulling it on haphazardly.

Danny turns and hands me a mug of coffee as I enter the kitchen. Taking it gratefully, I lean against the counter and watch him sip his own coffee while listening avidly to his partner. I love to watch him in hyperfocused cop mode, it's seriously hot. Although my blatant ogling is somewhat marred by the little old lady plastered to my side, staring silently up at my face.

"Okay, thanks, Maddie. I'll see you shortly." He hangs up the phone and turns his attention to me. "Maddie's confirmed that Mrs Abernathy's remains have arrived at the mortuary safely, and her post-mortem has been bumped up to first on your schedule this morning. I know she's probably on your mind."

I glance down at the wrinkly face next to mine surreptitiously. "You have no idea," I murmur.

"Poison Control has marked it as urgent. They're worried in case anyone else has been exposed, so we need to find the source of the poisoning as soon as possible." He turns and rinses his cup out, setting it on the draining board. "I'm heading back to Sunrise now. Maddie's going to meet me there."

"Check on my dad, will you?" I set my half-full cup on the counter, my stomach churning with unease.

"Of course I will, you don't even need to ask." He cups my face and drops a kiss on my lips. "I'll see you tonight, okay?"

I nod slowly as he heads out of the kitchen. "Oh"—he stops

and turns back to me, but my gaze is already locked thought-fully on Mrs Abernathy—"maybe we could finish that conversation later?"

"Yeah, sure," I murmur absently, wondering what conversation he's referring to.

Moments later, I hear the front door open and close but I barely pay any attention. I can't imagine who'd want to poison Mrs Abernathy, and why arsenic? It's so dated. If you want to kill someone there are far easier ways to do it. Of all the people at Sunrise Care Home, I can't think of anyone there who'd be capable of such an awful thing. Which begs the question, who else had access and motive?

"Okay, I'm here." A familiar voice splits the silence so abruptly it even makes Mrs Abernathy jolt in shock. "What did I miss?"

I glance across the kitchen to Dusty as she smooths down her skirt, rearranges her slightly lopsided wig, and produces a small compact from her cleavage to repair her smudged lipstick.

"How's Bruce?" My mouth curves as I take in her ruffled appearance.

"Vigorous." She grins.

"I'm sorry I asked." I shake my head in amusement.

Dusty looks over at me and does a double take, blinking slowly and tilting her head. "Er, Tristan, you've got something stuck to you, did you know?"

"Dusty, this is Delores Abernathy. She came home with me and Danny last night."

"You two are all kinds of freaky." Dusty clucks her tongue, staring at the spectral barnacle currently attached to me.

"Gross, but no." I pick up my now cold coffee and take a sip with a grimace before tossing it down the sink and rinsing the cup. "We went to the care home yesterday."

"That wasn't the plan." She frowns. "You said, and I quote,

'make yourself scarce so I can spend the next twenty-four hours nailing my incredibly hot boyfriend.'"

"I'm pretty sure I didn't use those exact words."

"So I'm paraphrasing a smidge." She purses her lips as her gaze once again deviates to the little old lady who is still attached to my side and is once again humming to herself. "So what's with Old Mother Hubbard?"

"Danny and I went to the care home yesterday to spend the day with my dad because he was having one of his good days. While we were there, Mrs Abernathy passed away, only I'm pretty sure she didn't pass of natural causes."

"Murdered?"

I nod. "Looks like. She has markings on her nails that indicate heavy metal poisoning, most likely arsenic."

"Jesus, what is this? 1842? No one uses arsenic anymore, darling, it's so passé."

"Tell that to Mrs Abernathy's murderer," I reply. "Anyway, Mrs Abernathy followed me home, and I'm pretty sure she's not going anywhere until we either solve her murder or resolve her unfinished business."

"Can't you just ask her?" She turns to the old lady. "Delores, honey? What do you need to go into the light?"

"You can't just ask her," I interject. "She probably doesn't know who killed her and besides, she's got Alzheimer's."

"What? Still?" Dusty blinks and I nod. "She's locked in a death cycle?"

"That would be my guess."

"I guess that's one more tick in the probably murdered column," Dusty ponders.

"There's one more thing." I chew my bottom lip. "When I was in the care home yesterday, I had the strangest feeling I was being watched."

"Tris, darling, you probably were being watched, and by at least twenty different people. It's a dementia home."

"No, that's not what I meant." I shake my head, trying to figure out how to explain the cold trickling feeling down my spine. "Just before we discovered Mrs Abernathy had died, I saw a... a shadow."

"A shadow?" Dusty repeats slowly. "I'm guessing you don't mean Hank Marvin."

"No, a shadow, a blacky smudgy thing." I make a weird indecipherable gesture with my hands. "It was hovering above the ground and looked like a kind of weird cloak hovering in the air. I couldn't see its face because it had a hood drawn up and it was thin... insubstantial. Like smoke. It hovered outside Mrs Abernathy's room and then floated inside and disappeared."

"That is some freaky-arse shit right there." Dusty's eyes widen.

"Have you ever seen anything like that before?" I ask.

"No, thank god." She shakes her head. "We could always ask Bruce or Evangeline Crawshanks, though. When she's feeling helpful, she's a goldmine of spiritual information. It's catching her in the right mood that's the trick."

"It might be worth a shot. But first I have to get to the mortuary so I can do Mrs Abernathy's post-mortem."

"Oh fun," Dusty says dryly. "I'll just wait here for you, or better still, I'll meet you at the bookshop."

"Stop thinking with your dick." I roll my eyes. "Bruce has a job to do too, you know."

"I am aware of that," she answers primly. "I'll be helping him out."

"With what?" My eyes narrow.

"His job... thingy." She smiles.

"Nice try, Dusty, but I need you to keep an eye on Mrs Abernathy for me. The last thing I need is for her to be looking over my shoulder while I'm dissecting her corpse."

"In fairness, she probably wouldn't even reach your shoulder. It's like someone put her on a spin dry and shrunk her," she remarks.

"Dusty..."

"Oh, come on. Why do I have to babysit Grandma Coco?" she whines.

"Because that's the job," I decide. "You chose to come back and help me, this is how you help me right now."

"Fine," she huffs as she rolls her eyes. "Come on, Delores, honey," she says in a loud and exaggerated tone as she holds out her hand.

"She's dead, Dusty, not deaf," I say dryly.

"As far as you know," she mumbles, and I'm surprised when Mrs Abernathy obediently crosses the kitchen and takes Dusty's hand, smiling up at her sweetly.

The morning is grey and dreary, as April mornings often are, but everything feels crisp and clean. It's not cold and I find myself deeply breathing in the clear air. My head is a maelstrom of thoughts ranging from my dad to Danny and back again. Pushing it all aside, I try to focus. Right now the best thing I can do is complete Mrs Abernathy's post-mortem and get the samples off to the lab. Once we've confirmed my hypothesis regarding the cause of death, we can try to figure out how to get the old lady into the light.

It's not far to the mortuary and regardless of the weather, come rain or shine, I always enjoy the walk. I can't say I'm thrilled about the prospect of having to search for a new flat, but really, Mr Ahmed is just too unreliable and the building is over a hundred years old. With how bad the leaks have got, it's only a matter of time before I have to deal with a black mould problem.

Aware of Dusty and Mrs Abernathy walking along hand in hand behind me, I push the door to the mortuary open, waving to my colleagues as I head back to dump my stuff in my office and pull on my lab coat. After grabbing the correct paperwork, I head into the main room to start setting up everything I need.

"Morning, Tristan," a chirpy voice greets me as the doors swing open.

"Morning, Ted," I nod to the orderly.

"They said you wanted the old bird from the care home." He heads over to the bank of refrigerators and pulls up a trolley, then opens the small square door and slides out the drawer with a steely hiss.

"If you mean Mrs Abernathy, then yes," I clarify.

"Sorry, Doc, didn't mean no disrespect." He swiftly transfers the petite remains to the metal table in the middle of the room. "Henrietta had her prepped last night, and they've bagged and tagged all her clothes, so she's good to go."

"Thank you." I lean over and start laying out tools on the rolling trolley.

"Give a yell if you need anything." He slides the trolley back against the wall and shoots me a mock salute.

"Will do." I watch as he disappears back through the swinging doors as abruptly as he arrived.

Dusty and Mrs Abernathy are hovering at the edge of the room while I clip the papers I need to my clipboard and set them down along with a pen.

"Morning, Tristan!" A jolly Scottish voice booms through the cavernous tiled room. I look up and see a tall skinny man walk directly through the wall, giving Dusty and Mrs Abernathy a jolt of surprise.

"Morning, Dave." I greet the pale Scot with chalky white skin and black hair. His clothes are soaked and wherever he walks a small patch of water appears below him.

"Lovely morning to... LICK MY HAIRY BALL SACK... have a stroll in the fresh air," he remarks pleasantly.

I nod. "Isn't it."

"I was just thinking I might take a little walk down to Camden market today and... BIG DICK BIG DICK BIG DICK... people watch for a while."

"Have fun." I smile.

Dave saunters past an open-mouthed Dusty and nods in her direction. "Morning," he greets her with a charming smile. "COCKWAFFLE!"

Dusty blinks as he disappears through the opposite wall. "Who on earth was that?" she asks incredulously.

"Oh that." I shrug. "That's just Dave. Don't mind him, he has Tourette's."

"I noticed."

"He's such a lovely guy," I muse. "Shame."

"What happened?"

"He showed up about six weeks ago. Apparently, he was well known for having one too many Jägerbombs and doing stupid shit. He took a dare that went a bit awry, resulting in a rather spectacular head dive into the Thames from what I hear. They fished him out two days later," I tell her. "Lovely funeral though. I've always liked bagpipes."

"But what's he still doing here?"

"Oh," I purse my lips thoughtfully. "We haven't quite figured out what his unfinished business is yet. He wasn't murdered, it was a case of death by being a prat, but he's such a sweet, happy-go-lucky guy. Doesn't hold a grudge against anyone. In fact, he's taken being dead completely in his stride."

"Just when I think I've seen it all." Dusty shakes her head.

"Dusty, I have a feeling we've barely scraped the surface." My lips twitch as I pick up a pair of blue latex gloves and snap them on, glancing at the shroud-covered corpse on the table and then back at Mrs Abernathy.

"Come on, Delores." Dusty tows her to the other end of the room. "You don't need to watch that gruesome mess, but lucky for you"—she flicks her fingers, and a chair slides across the room, stopping in front of them—"for one night only"—she seats the tiny lady in the chair, facing away from the table— "the Fabulous Miz Dusty Le Frey floor show is returning just for you."

I cross the room and slip my phone into the docking station alongside a small Bluetooth speaker. "Try and keep it down," I whisper to her. "We don't want to wake the dead."

"I can't make any promises, boo," she snorts.

I cross back to the table as I hear my phone start to cycle through my playlists until the opening chords of Abba's *Waterloo* blare out, accompanied by Dusty's incredible voice. I glance back and chuckle. She's gone full-on showgirl in a brightly coloured skin-tight sequined jump-suit with matching knee-high platform boots. The shoulder pads are so enormous I don't know how she fits sideways through a doorway in them, let alone dances like she is. Still, I suppose she doesn't have to sweat the technicalities now she's dead and can pretty much do what she wants.

I watch for a moment, smiling as she dances through the first number, while Mrs Abernathy claps along in delight. Shaking my head with a quiet laugh, I pull the rolling screen across, blocking them from my view as I step up to the table. Pulling the sheet back slowly, I sigh at the sight of Mrs Abernathy's grey skin and slack features.

"I am so sorry about this," I whisper as I pick up the scalpel and begin.

5

Tristan

I glance down at the almost illegible scrawl on the piece of paper in my hand and check the address once again.

"Okay, this is the one," I announce.

"Why are we here again?" Dusty leans against the fence, Mrs Abernathy still clutching her hand like an obedient child.

"Because we need to find out as much about Mrs Abernathy as we can." I unlatch the rickety gate and shove it open awkwardly, wiping the flakes of old white paint from my hand. "Even if Danny manages to solve her death, there's no guarantee that will be enough to get her into the light. If she has unfinished business, we need to try and figure out what that is."

I head up the path and ring the doorbell, conscious of the fact Dusty and Mrs Abernathy are both trailing behind me but no one else can see them. I guess it's just as well. The three of us standing aimlessly on the doorstep with me looking like a slightly scruffy student, Dusty wearing tiny sparkly pink hotpants and five-inch platform stilettos, and Mrs Abernathy in her tea-cosy hat clutching her handbag like she was about to be mugged, we look like a really odd bunch of Jehovah's Witnesses.

I'm about to lift my hand and ring the bell again when the door finally opens and Mrs Abernathy's niece appears, once more in her Sainsbury's uniform, looking exhausted.

"Hello, Tristan," she greets me in surprise, as if she wasn't actually expecting me to use the address she gave me.

I smile. "Hi, Larry. Is this a bad time? I just wanted to stop by and see how you're doing."

"Oh, um no, it's fine. I just got in from work, and I'm about to put the kettle on. Would you like a cup of tea?"

"That would be lovely." I step over the threshold as she moves aside to allow me in.

"Sweet of you to come out of your way." Larry closes the door behind me. "You live in Hackney, don't you?"

"I do, but Stepney's really not that far." I follow her along the dark narrow hallway to the kitchen at the back.

Much like me, she seems to live in a narrow Victorian terrace which has been converted into one-up one-down flats. Unlike me though, she's on the ground floor, causing my thoughts to momentarily flick back to my leaky roof which my landlord is still dodging.

"Tea?" Larry asks as we enter a small well-kept kitchen. "Or would you prefer coffee?"

"Tea would be great, thanks. Milk with one, please." She nods and reaches for two cups on the mug tree, setting them on the counter. "How are you doing, Larry?" I ask as she flips the switch on the kettle.

"Honestly," she sighs, "tired, a little sad... confused." She looks over at me as I lean back against the counter.

"That's understandable."

"Have you heard anything yet?" She drops a tea bag into each of the cups.

"Nothing definitive. They've put a rush on all the results, but it may be another day or so yet."

"And you still think she was deliberately poisoned?" She retrieves the milk from the fridge.

"Nothing is certain. Danny and his partner Maddie are still investigating," I reply carefully. "All I can tell you is it's likely she died from fatal arsenic poisoning and that the poisoning probably occurred over a matter of weeks. If it was accidental exposure more people at the home would be showing symptoms."

I am not about to share with her what I discovered during the post-mortem. Although I'm still waiting on the results of the blood, urine, and tissue samples, the condition of her lungs and kidneys, not to mention the discolouration of her skin and nails, was enough to confirm my suspicions. Well, that and the fact Mrs Abernathy's ghost is currently sitting at the kitchen table with her handbag resting on her knees, looking as if she's waiting patiently for the number 7 bus.

"I still can't believe this is happening." Larry hands me a cup and indicates for me to follow her.

"I know it's a lot to take in, but we'll get to the bottom of this, I promise." I follow her through to the small sitting room and take a seat on a worn armchair. "Did you hear back from your mum?"

"Yes, eventually." She takes a sip of her tea and lets out another sigh. "She's not coming home. I don't know why I expected any different. She said number 32 spent too much money on the cruise for her to cut it short, plus it would cost extra to fly home. She said to just do whatever I think is best and if she's back in time, she'll go to the funeral. I guess it depends when they release Aunt Delores' body."

"Oh my god!" Dusty squeals loudly, which thankfully Larry can't hear. "Have you seen this vinyl collection! Oh sweet baby Jesus, are these originals?"

I surreptitiously glance over to where she's standing beside a highly polished old-fashioned record player and several storage boxes of records. "That's an interesting collection of records." I take a sip of my tea. "Are you a fan of vinyl? I hear they're coming back in."

Larry looks over toward the neatly organised collection and a small nostalgic smile tugs at her lips. "I love records. I guess it's a carry-over from my childhood." She turns back to me. "That whole collection and the record player belonged to Auntie Delores. Mum used to just drop me off at her house whenever she was off with a new fella. Auntie and I would sit for hours listening to her collection."

"That sounds like a lovely memory."

"When Auntie had to go into the care home, Mum cleared her house, and all I managed to save was an old box of photos and personal effects, the record player, and the vinyl collection. It's just as well Mum had no idea what it was really worth, or she probably would've sold that too."

Christ, her mother sounds charming. I glance at Mrs Abernathy as she hovers determinedly over her record collection. I jolt in alarm as she reaches out and I see a specific record slide upwards out of the pack.

"Oh no, Delores, honey," Dusty admonishes her with a tut, tucking the record back in before Larry notices. "We don't move things in front of the normies unless we want to scare the shit out of them."

Mrs Abernathy frowns and reaches for the record again, and I have the uncomfortable feeling she's not going to take no for an answer.

"Did she have a favourite record?" I ask quickly.

"She did," Larry nods with a smile, setting her cup down on the coffee table. "Do you want to hear it?"

"I'd love to," I reply fervently, hoping it's enough to placate the dead woman, who, I'm certain, is about to throw a spectral temper tantrum.

Larry crosses the small space and flicks through one of the

sections while Mrs Abernathy stands beside her, smiling widely when her niece selects, presumably, the correct one.

A framed black and white photograph sitting on the shelf above the record player catches my eye. Setting my cup down on the coffee table, I cross the room as Larry carefully slides a record from its sleeve, blows on it to remove any dust, and tilts it into the light so she can scrutinise it for non-existent scratches. Seemingly satisfied, she reverently places the record on the turntable and sets the needle down.

After a brief crackle, the unmistakable dulcet tones of Ella Fitzgerald fill the air. Mrs Abernathy smiles serenely and sways on the spot, humming to herself, and I realise that this is the song she's been humming ever since she died and appeared at my side.

"Bow," she says happily and resumes her swaying.

"What is this song?" I ask Larry.

"It's Ella Fitzgerald's *Every Time We Say Goodbye*," she says with a sad smile. "I'm going to have them play it at her funeral, along with Glenn Miller's *Moonlight Serenade*. They were both her favourites."

"Was this your aunt when she was young?" I point to the framed photo. I'm pretty certain it's Mrs Abernathy, but it must have been taken a long time ago. The young woman in the picture is soft and pretty and can't be more than twenty. She's wearing some kind of military uniform and a cap with the letters *H.M.S.* on it.

"Yes." Larry reaches up and takes the picture down, tracing her fingers across the glass affectionately. "Auntie was a Wren during the war."

"A wren?"

"Women's Royal Navy," she clarifies, her voice filled with pride. "She worked, amongst other places, at Bletchley Park."

Now that I had heard of, and I suck in a little gasp of

surprise. How did I not know this about her, I wonder. "She was a code-breaker?"

Larry nods. "One of the youngest, barely eighteen at the time." She passes the photo to me so I can get a better look. "She had such a brilliant mind, it was cruel to see what she became in the end. She burned so brightly, and for all that fire and intelligence to be slowly eaten away by her disease..." She shakes her head sadly.

"I know," I murmur.

"I'm sorry, Tristan," she apologises when she realises what she's said. "That was insensitive of me."

"No, it's the truth." My stomach aches at the thought. "My dad was brilliant too, so clever and passionate. He loved history and science so much, to watch him disappearing by inches is excruciating."

Suddenly, I hear Dusty's clear voice singing word for word over the top of Ella's and I glance over. She's dancing with Mrs Abernathy and it's quite a sight to behold. A six-foot drag queen in glittery pink hot pants, five-inch platforms, and a wig Dolly Parton would be proud of, hunched over a tiny little woman in her pleated skirt with her socks falling down. She looks up into Dusty's eyes as Dusty croons her song to her, both of them turning in a small slow circle on the carpet, and I can't help the small smile tugging my lips at the picture they make.

"Tristan, are you alright?" Larry asks, drawing my attention back to her. "You look like you zoned out there for a moment."

"Just thinking, I guess." I place the photo back on the shelf. "You said you saved a box of your aunt's photos and personal effects?"

"That's right."

"I'd love to see them," I say. "I just feel like I should have known her a little better."

"Are you sure? You don't have somewhere to be?" she asks.

"It's sweet you stopped by to check on me, but I'm sure you don't want to sit and listen to me reminisce over my late aunt."

"I actually can't think of anything I'd like more," I reply honestly. Even though I'm determined to figure out if Mrs Abernathy has any unfinished business that would keep her potentially haunting my flat and cramping my sex life, I find I actually really would like to know about the sweet little woman following Dusty around like she's her mother duck.

"If you're sure." Larry beams. "I'll just go and fetch the box. Why don't you finish your tea before it goes cold? I'll be back in a jiffy."

I settle myself once again in the armchair, sipping my luke-warm tea, but as I glance across at Dusty I almost accidentally snort it up my nostrils. The record now finished, she's currently dressed in a tiny little military-style hot-pant jumpsuit a la Christina Aguilera and is performing a rather enthusiastic version of *The Boogie Woogie Bugle Boy from Company B*.

"Here we go." Larry re-enters the room holding a battered old cardboard box, the open flaps curling with age and 'Fox's Assorted Biscuits' printed across the sides.

She scoots a glass fruit bowl filled with potpourri out of the way, sets the box on the table, and settles herself back onto the sofa. Reaching in and grabbing a handful of photos, she goes through them one at a time and explains what each one is. There are a surprising amount of Larry and Mrs Abernathy, confirming how close they were. There are also a lot of pictures of a younger Mrs Abernathy in the post-war years.

"Did she ever marry?" I ask.

"She did, but it didn't stick." Larry rummages through the box and plucks out a picture. "Here it is." She passes it over to me and there's a picture in soft tones reminiscent of photography from the seventies. Mrs Abernathy is wearing a floral summer dress and sandals, standing propped up against an orange Ford Cortina parked on a residential street. Beside her is a tall man sporting sparse curly hair and glasses and wearing casual slacks and a paisley short-sleeved shirt . I turn it over and see, scribbled on the back in blue biro, the words *Delores & Doug - Bristol 1972.*

"Is this her husband?"

She nods slowly. "His name was Douglas Abernathy." Larry stares down at the photo in my hand. "I vaguely remember him, but the marriage only lasted six months. By that point, Auntie was about forty-seven. She said she was too set in her ways to put up with a man disrupting her life."

"You think that was the real reason it didn't last?" I ask, wondering if he could be her unfinished business. It's possible something about their relationship was never resolved.

"I couldn't say." Larry shrugs. "Like I said, I barely remember him. I was really young at the time, hardly more than a toddler. But on the rare occasions she mentioned him as I got older, I got the feeling the real reason was because she didn't love him. I think she wanted to but there was something holding her back, something she wouldn't talk about."

"Is he still alive?"

Larry shakes her head. "From what I hear, he died back in the nineties."

"Oh." I frown. I'm screwed if he is part of her unfinished business then.

Sensing a shadow beside me, I look up to find Mrs Abernathy peering into the box in agitation. She doesn't even glance at the photo in my hand, so I decide Douglas Abernathy is most likely not important and set the picture down on top of another stack.

"Bow?" Mrs Abernathy says, impatient.

Suddenly the box topples over, sending the remaining contents skidding across the carpet.

"Oh god, I'm really sorry," I apologise to Larry as I drop down to the floor. I right the box and scoop handfuls of photos up, hoping she thinks it was me who knocked the box over and not the dead woman in her living room.

"No harm done." She kneels down to help.

From the corner of my eye, I see a photo slide across the floor toward me while Larry's not looking.

"Bow," Mrs Abernathy says, and it sounds more like a statement than a question.

It's an old, dog-eared, black and white photo of a handsome young man in a military uniform and not a British one. American, I think. He's reclining on a patch of grass and smiling into the lens. I turn the picture over to see if there's anything written on the back.

Beau - Hyde Park, London 1944.

"Not Bow, Beau," I mutter.

"What's that?" Larry looks up as she scoops the last of the photos into the box and sets it back on top of the table.

"Do you know who this is?" I ask, handing her the photo.

"Oh." She blinks. "Where did this come from? I've never seen this before." She turns it over and reads the name and date written on the back. "How strange. I must've gone through this box a dozen times over the years and I've never seen this photo, but that's definitely Auntie's handwriting on the back. I wonder who he was?"

"She never mentioned someone called Beau? Or an American G.I. she met during the war?" I ask as she hands the photo back to me.

"No." She shakes her head with a small frown.

The sudden ringing of the doorbell has Larry climbing to her feet, wincing when her knees protest with a creak.

"Sorry, that'll be my neighbour. She had an Amazon package dropped off here earlier. I'll just be a minute."

"Good for you, Delores." Dusty whistles as she leans over me and eyes the picture in my hand. "That is one hot piece of man candy. I do love a guy in uniform." She winks at the old woman, who beams up at her happily.

"She's been trying to tell us since the moment she died," I whisper to Dusty once Larry is out of the room. "The song she's been humming, the name Beau, this is it!" I wave the piece of paper. "This is her unfinished business."

"Huh." Dusty leans over my shoulder and takes a closer look at the photo. "He looks a little like you."

I turn my attention back to the photo and study it intensely. There is a passing resemblance. Beau has dark wavy hair and the shape of his face, the line of his nose, the curve of his smile are similar to me and also... my dad.

"Oh," I breathe with a sudden clarity. "That's why she always gravitated toward my dad. He must've reminded her of Beau." I bite my lip thoughtfully. "I wonder if he's still alive."

"I doubt it." Perched on the arm of the chair beside me, Dusty purses her lips. "That was taken in what? 1944? And he looks like he's in his late twenties, possibly early thirties? That would make him well over a hundred, and that's if he survived the war."

"That's true," I muse. "In all likelihood, he may have been killed in action. That would explain the unfinished business, especially if she was in love with him. It would also explain why her marriage never worked out."

Dusty stares consideringly at Delores, who is smiling at the photo in my hand and has once again resumed humming. "We need to find someone who knew her from before her illness. Either someone who knew her when she was younger or someone she confided in."

I hear muffled voices in the hallway quieten, followed by the sound of the front door closing. I quickly shove the photo into my back pocket as Larry heads back into the room.

"Sorry about that." She smiles tiredly.

"It's okay. I've kept you long enough, you must be tired after work."

"It's been a rough few days, I won't lie." She releases a long slow breath.

"Well, I won't keep you." I rise from the chair. "But can I just ask, did your aunt have any other friends, old friends? Anyone who might have visited her or known her before her illness?"

"Sure," Larry shrugs. "She went out every week to the community centre in Clapham to meet up with her friends, and Trudy has known her since they were kids. They were always so good with Auntie even after her Alzheimer's got really bad. Trudy organised a private carer who would collect Auntie every week from Sunrise and take her to meet up with the ladies."

"Clapham?"

She nodded. "Northwold Community Centre. I expect most of the ladies will be at the funeral once I get it arranged."

"If you need any help at all, you only have to ask." I follow her to the front door. "Danny and I are happy to help however we can."

"Thank you, Tristan." She smiles warmly as she opens the door and I step out. "I really appreciate you stopping by."

"Anytime." I give a small wave and head back out the gate and onto the pavement. I'm almost to the end of the road with Dusty and Mrs Abernathy ambling along companionably beside me when my phone rings in my pocket. I pull it free and notice it's Danny calling.

"Hey." I smile as I answer even though he can't see me.

"Tristan," he rumbles in response, and I feel the familiar warmth spreading in my belly. "I've just got the toxicology reports for Mrs Abernathy."

"And?"

"And it's confirmed, she died from acute arsenic poisoning," he replies. "Poison Control has also finished with Sunrise. They've concluded there was no cross contamination and that, although they can't be a hundred percent sure, it's most likely the poisoning didn't occur while she was there."

"So my dad and the others are okay?" I breathe a sigh of relief.

"Yes, but it begs the question, if she wasn't poisoned at the home, then where? Lois tells me Mrs Abernathy went to a social club once a week in Clapham."

"Larry told me the same thing," I reply. "I was just thinking about heading over there."

"What? Why?"

"I stopped by to visit with Larry just now and–"

"Tristan." Danny sounds exasperated. "As much as I like Larry, she hasn't officially been cleared from the suspect list yet."

"Oh come on," I scoff. "Larry adored her aunt. In fact, she was the only one in her family who bothered with Mrs Abernathy at all. I just don't see her being a murderer."

"As much as I might be inclined to agree with you, your gut feeling doesn't exclude her from the suspect pool. Please stay away from her until I have a better handle on what we're dealing with."

"I'm really in no danger, Danny, so will you stop worrying?" I say softly, touched at his protectiveness. I've spent so long on my own. It's nice having someone to worry about me, even if it is unwarranted.

"Do I need to remind you what happened last time you got caught up in a murder investigation?" he replies pointedly. "If I recall correctly, you were kidnapped, held at gunpoint, shot at, and almost killed."

"I was not almost killed." I roll my eyes with a smile. "But I'll give you the kidnapping and being held at gunpoint. Kaitlin Fletcher was definitely one sandwich short of a picnic basket. Seriously though, what are the actual chances of something like that happening again?"

"A lot less if you'll just stay away from the bloody suspects," Danny grumbles.

"How about a compromise? Why don't you meet me at Clapham so we can both talk to Mrs Abernathy's friends? And then you can protect me from a bunch of potentially murderous old ladies."

"You joke," he snorts, "but statistically–"

"Oh my god. Seriously, Danny," I laugh, "stop worrying. I'm in Stepney at the moment, but I can be in Clapham in an hour. I'll meet you at the Northwold Community Centre and once we're done, you can give me a ride home and then"—I lower my voice, aware of how close Dusty and Mrs Abernathy are— "maybe I'll ride you."

"You're not playing fair," he says after a moment's silence, and I chuckle loudly.

"I'll meet you in Clapham in about an hour." I hang up the phone before he can argue further.

I mean really, what are the chances of lightning striking the same place twice?

6

Tristan

It's raining again by the time I reach the community hall, great pelting shards slashing down dramatically as I make a dash for it inside. Standing in the entrance foyer, dripping on the rug and smelling of the rain, I push the hood of my parka back and shake like a dog.

"My goodness, is it raining?" A small, neat woman in a lilac pantsuit and pearls asks.

I glance down at the puddle of water pooling around my soggy Converse and back up at her. "Just a tad."

"Yes, well." She frowns. "Can I help you?"

I wipe my wet palms against my damp jeans and hold out my hand. "I'm Tristan Everett. I'm looking for someone named Trudy? I'm sorry, I don't know her surname."

"Oh well, you found her." She shakes my hand, then reaches out and plucks a wet leaf from my jacket, dropping it to the ground.

"Trudy?"

"Wells." She fluffs her perfectly coiffed grey hair, more from a nervous habit, I suspect, than from any concerns about her pristine appearance.

"Excuse me?"

"Trudy Wells. Now, what is it I can do for you, Mr Everett?"

"Tristan, please," I reply. "I knew Delores Abernathy. Her niece Larry told me I could find her friend Trudy here."

"You knew Delores?" She tilts her head as she studies me.

"I knew her from Sunrise," I clarify.

Her eyes narrow. "You work at the care home? I haven't seen you there before."

"No, I don't work there." I shake my head. "My father, Martin Everett, is a resident."

"Ah, Martin." She nods, her expression softening a little at the edges. "Delores was fond of him in her own way."

"She was," I murmur as I watch Mrs Abernathy stand next to Trudy and stare at her. Despite the poor woman being trapped in a death cycle, struggling in death with the same disease that took so much from her in life, I wonder how much of her mind is trying to break through and remember.

"I'm sorry, Mr Everett–"

"Tristan," I correct again.

"Tristan," she concedes. "What exactly is it that you want from me? Delores is gone now and as much as I'm relieved she's no longer suffering, the grief is still very new."

"I appreciate that," I say. "I just... I wondered if I could ask you some questions about her... about when she was younger."

"Why?"

"Ooh, she's a tough nut to crack." Dusty smirks.

"I... uh–"

Boy, this is going to be a tough one to explain. It's not like I can exactly tell her that her dead bestie is eyeballing her from two feet away and I need to figure out her unfinished business so I can pack her off into the light. I feel a sudden gust of wind and rain as the door opens behind me and someone else is blown in.

"Tristan." A familiar voice trickles down my spine, causing me to smile and turn.

"Danny," I greet him as he steps up beside me. "Mrs Wells, this is–"

"Tristan's boyfriend, Danny." He offers his hand, and I notice he deliberately omitted the part about him being a detective.

I glance up at him, tilting my head slightly, and his eyes widen a fraction in warning. I can only assume it's because he doesn't want it to be public knowledge that Mrs Abernathy's death was under suspicious circumstances. I guess it stands to reason that, if she hadn't been poisoned at the home, it had to be someone else she knew, possibly even one of her friends.

"Trudy." She reaches out and shakes Danny's hand, studying him suspiciously before turning her attention back to me.

"As I was saying," I continue, picking up on Danny's cue and trying not to give too much away, "we both knew Delores." I switch to her first name and soften my tone. "She was very fond of my dad, and we often saw her when we visited him. Unfortunately, due to her illness, we didn't know her as well as we would've liked, and I know it sounds strange, but I suppose I just want to know her a little better... know the woman she was. Larry told me she was a code-breaker during the war, and it fascinates me, I guess."

"She was a fascinating woman." Trudy sighs.

"Perhaps you could tell us a little about her," Danny says smoothly. "We'd love to meet her friends and hear their stories about her."

"I suppose so." She glances down at her watch. "Come on, Bingo Bonanza is starting in ten minutes."

"Bingo Bonanza?" Dusty shoots me a dry look. "This is what my afterlife has been reduced to? Babysitting senior citizens and bingo?" I shoot her a warning glare, unable to answer her directly with Danny standing right next to me. With a tut and an eye roll, Dusty takes Mrs Abernathy's hand and swaggers off on her heels behind Trudy.

"Don't tell them I'm a detective," Danny mutters under his breath as we follow behind Trudy. "People tend to clam up around the police. Let's see if we can shake anything loose before they find out about the investigation."

"How do you know Larry hasn't already said something?" I whisper back.

"I'm hoping she hasn't," he replies, pasting on an affable smile as Trudy holds the door open for us to enter the hall.

The scent that hits me is like every other community hall in the UK—the dry, stale smell of old wood, rather like a church. The space is filled with random tables, each one surrounded by plastic chairs filled with an eclectic assortment of people ranging from pensioners to young mums with buggies parked beside them. Up on the makeshift stage is a microphone and a cage of numbered ping-pong balls, beside which stands a portly man wearing a tracksuit and with a massive bald patch in the back of his salt and pepper hair.

"Testing, testing, one two three," he shouts into the microphone, causing it to squeal loudly. He winces. "Sorry." His Somerset accent makes him sound like a pirate. He blows into the microphone, making it sound like a typhoon blowing through the noisy room, before tapping it several more times. "Ten minutes, folks. Make sure you've grabbed your cuppa and bingo cards and found a seat."

I follow along, listening to the chinking of cups and teaspoons, all blanketed by a loud hum of chatter. Trudy weaves effortlessly through the crowd, greeting people and smiling in welcome. Finally, she approaches a large round table in the centre of the room where several ladies who look to be at least in their eighties, at least, sit.

"Ladies." Trudy claps her hands together loudly. "We have

some guests today." She indicates two free seats at the table for Danny and me to slide into before she tucks her skirt under and sits regally. "This is Danny and Tristan," she introduces us, "friends of Delores."

Every eye at the table turns towards us, and I fight the urge to squirm under the intense scrutiny.

"It looks like Delores was holding out on us," the woman sitting directly to Danny's left states in a querulous voice. Her face is heavily made up with snowdrifts of facial powder sitting in the deep grooves and lines. Her lips are painted with a bright pop of bubblegum pink lipstick that settles into the wrinkles around her mouth, and her sparse eyelashes are liberally coated with black mascara. When she smiles coyly at my boyfriend and winks, it looks more like she has a tic in her right eyelid than a seductive overture.

"Oh for heaven's sake, Ivy, do control yourself." Trudy sighs. "Don't mind her, she still thinks she's got hormones."

Another woman with an enormous wiry hair growing out of a chin mole cackles. "Only hormones she's got have dried up like a week-old slice of bread."

"Be nice, Birdie," Trudy tuts. "What will our guests think?" She turns back to us and gives us a smile. "Danny, Tristan, welcome to the Clapham Senior Ladies Social Circle and Jam Tart Society."

Dusty snorts loudly.

"Uh, it's nice to meet you all," I say hesitantly.

"Likewise." Danny looks uncomfortable as he shoots a wary look at Ivy sitting next to him and scoots his chair closer to mine.

"You might want to watch out for Barbara Cartland over there." Dusty nods in Ivy's direction. "I think she might have her hands on your fella's goodies."

Danny gives a squeak and edges even closer to me. Honestly, if he gets any closer he's going to be sitting in my lap.

I glance across at Dusty who winks at me. "Don't worry, boo, I gotcha back."

Suddenly Ivy gives a yelp, and her chair shoots back a few paces. She glances around a little wildly before dropping her gaze to the floor.

"Did someone spill something?" She frowns in confusion. "The floor seems to be awfully slippery around here."

"Anyway"—Trudy rolls her eyes—"that's Ivy, next to her is Vera, then Maeve. Over there is Birdie, Phyllis, and Violet." She finishes the introductions with a little wave of her hand.

"Good god," Dusty mutters. "It's like the cast of Cocoon."

"Ladies." I offer a smile, ignoring Dusty's snarky commentary. "What exactly is a Jam Tart Society?"

"It was a tradition we started years ago," Trudy explains. "Just a little bit of fun."

"A little bit of fun?" Maeve retorts indignantly. "It's an integral part of our community spirit. Everyone looks forward all year to the JTSS."

"The JTSS?" I repeat slowly.

"The Jam Tart Society Social." Maeve folds her hands neatly in her lap primly.

I'm really trying to keep a straight face but all I can hear is Dusty laughing loudly behind me. "The Jam Tart Society Social?" I repeat faintly. "You don't say."

"That sounds... interesting. What exactly does a Jam Tart Society Social entail?" Danny asks politely.

"On the first of May every year, we gather for the tart social," Maeve replies primly, and I desperately try to ignore Dusty who's practically wheezing behind me she's laughing so hard. "Everyone enters their own tart."

I covertly cast my eyes to the side and widen them, hopefully conveying the message that Dusty needs to shut up right now and keep an eye on Delores, who's randomly wandered off. Ordinarily, I wouldn't have worried, but given that she seems to move things quite easily, I can only imagine the chaos she could cause in a place like this.

Giving one last unladylike snort, Dusty wipes a tear from beneath her eye and saunters off in search of the wayward old lady. "I swear we need to put a bell on her..." Dusty mutters as she disappears.

"So it's like a bake off, then?" Danny tries to look interested while edging further away from Ivy.

"I win every year," Maeve says smugly.

"Except last year," Birdie cackles, her wiry chin hair vibrating.

Maeve sniffs. "You're just jealous because no one is interested in your crusty old tart."

"And you're just sour because Delores won last year and she didn't even have all her marbles fully intact," Birdie smirks back.

Maeve sucks in such a loud and dramatic breath as she clutches the small golden cross at her neck, I'm surprised there's any oxygen left in the vicinity.

"Ladies," Trudy warns them both.

"Delores baked a pie and entered it in last year's competition?" Danny asks.

Maeve huffs. "Cheating."

"Hush now, it was not cheating," Trudy tuts. "Delores baked one every year and yes, it's true, her carers had to help a lot, but the recipe was hers. It was the one she used to make with her mum when she was a girl. It was one of the only things she retained with her Alzheimer's. She couldn't remember the day of the week or what she'd had for lunch, but she could remember that recipe right down to a teaspoon of sugar and I tell you what." Trudy smiles softly in remembrance. "It tasted just like her mum's did."

"You knew her for a long time then?" Danny asks.

Trudy nods, blowing out a slow breath laced with grief.

"Since we were about five years old. Our families lived on the same street, three doors apart."

"Who are they and what are they doing here?" The one called Vera pipes up.

"Vera." Trudy rolls her eyes. "This is Danny and Tristan."

"Franny and Crispin?" She squints, leaning closer.

"Danny and... oh for god's sake, turn your hearing aids up, you daft old bat," Ivy yells at her friend as she points to her own ear.

"Ladies." A young man in his twenties swings by the table. He's wearing plain jeans and a hoodie, and his scraggly hair is tied back in a messy ponytail at the nape of his neck. He leans over the table and collects some of the empty teacups. His smile is friendly enough, but there is no mistaking the scent that hangs around him like a shroud, a fact that's not lost on Danny. I glance over at him as he lifts a brow, his mouth curving into an amused grin.

"Hello, Kevin." Ivy fluffs her hair and bats her thickly caked lashes at him.

"Hello, Ivy." He chuckles as he stacks the empties on a tray and moves onto the next table.

Ivy beams. "Such a lovely young man, and he always smells so lovely, like a fresh herb garden."

"Herb garden? Its bloody weed, you stupid woman, he's one of them hippies." Birdie shakes her head.

"I don't think they're called hippies anymore," Phyllis interrupts.

"I saw a hippo once at the London Zoo," Vera yells loudly.

"Not hippos," Phyllis explains slowly. "Hippies... and besides I think they're called stoners now." She says it so loudly Kevin turns around at the next table, flushing pink and shaking his head with a laugh.

I can barely keep up with the chaotic conversation of these old ladies as I share an amused look with Danny. I don't think

I'm going to be able to ask Trudy about the photo that's burning a hole in my pocket, or the man Delores calls Beau. I'm pretty sure I'm going to have to come back when it's quieter.

"I heard Delores used to come down to the community centre regularly," Danny remarks casually.

"She did," Violet pipes up. Up until now, the sweet little lilac-haired old lady seemed content to concentrate on the brightly coloured woollen blob she was creating, the click clack of her knitting needles lost amidst the noise of the room. "Delores used to come twice a week, regular as clockwork, never missed a Bingo Bonanza, enjoyed a Macmillan's coffee morning too."

"Did she always meet up with your group, or did she have other friends?" Danny asks and I sit back, watching him with a small smile playing on my lips. Although I still need to have a conversation with Trudy, it's easier for me to just let Danny ask his questions.

"She always stayed with us," Trudy answers. "We kept her safe. She had a tendency to wander off the minute you weren't watching." She shakes her head. "Her carers always had their hands full with her."

"Were they always the same carers?"

"Usually the same three," Trudy replies. "That sweet girl, Jane, and Derek, of course, and–"

"Polina," Violet finishes for her.

"That's right, Polina." Trudy turns back to Danny. "Everyone adored Delores. That's not to say she wasn't hard work, but it was her illness, not her. Delores was always the kindest, sweetest person you could ever know. Her sister, on the other hand, is as selfish as they come."

"I heard her sister was out of the country."

"Is she? Again?" Trudy rolls her eyes. "It doesn't surprise me. Now I don't like to speak ill of anyone, but she's always hopped from one man to the next to fund her lifestyle." Her voice drops as she leans in closer. "Did you know that when Delores was first diagnosed, her sister tried to get power of attorney so she could access her money?"

"Did she?" Danny tilts his head. "Did she stand to inherit much when Delores passed?"

"Oh heavens, no." Trudy shakes her head. "I doubt there's a single penny left. Delores wasn't a rich woman by any means, and what little she did have was taken by the government to pay for her care. At that point, her sister didn't even bother to pretend she cared."

"Unlike Larry," Danny prompts.

"Ah, Larry." Trudy smiles. "She loved Delores more than she did her own mother, I imagine. Delores doted on her from the moment she was born, while her mother ignored her in favour of her men."

"She never wanted children of her own?" I pipe up, seeing an opportunity. "Delores, I mean."

"It just wasn't in the cards, I suppose," Trudy replies, lost in thought. "She was very close to my children too. I think she'd have made an incredible mother, but her marriage didn't last, and I think they both thought they were too old by that point anyway."

"Larry said her marriage didn't work out," I say, subtly fishing for information. "Was there never anyone else?"

"Not that I know of," she answers carefully, and I watch as her mouth tightens into a sharp line. Oh yeah, she definitely knows something.

"Shame," I mutter.

"Found her." Dusty reappears, holding onto Delores tightly. "What did I miss?" I don't know why she asks, and I have to fight the urge to roll my eyes. It's not like I can answer her in front of everyone without them thinking I'm crazy.

"Ladies and gents," the man on the platform calls out, wincing as the microphone squeals again loudly. "Sorry for the small delay. The cage got stuck and I couldn't turn my balls."

I don't need to look to know that snort came from Dusty.

"Right then." The man on the stage smiles widely. "Everyone got your dabbers and cards at the ready?"

I turn to see several of the old ladies reaching in their purses and setting out in front of them an impressive array of bingo daubers in a myriad of bright colours and glitter.

"Wow," Danny mutters under his breath. "They take it very seriously, don't they?"

"Like an Olympic sport," I agree.

I only know because my friend Henrietta from work has dragged me along several times with some of the rest of the staff from the mortuary. She says it's a fun team-building experience, but I now know it can go from light-hearted fun to cat fight in seconds.

"Okay then, here we go," the man on the platform announces. I watch in amusement as he grasps the handle of the small barrel-shaped wire cage and turns it slowly. The numbered ping-pong balls tumble around for a moment or two until he's sure everyone's primed and then he stops and pops the door open, pulling out a ball at random as he clears his throat.

"All the threes... thirty-three," he announces.

Suddenly everyone's heads are bent over their cards, blotting out the numbers with their brightly coloured felt-tip daubers.

"Knock at the door... number four."

The whole room quiets down and I get the feeling we're not going to get much more out of them. I have no doubt Danny will find out who killed Delores, but deep down in my gut I get the feeling that's not what's keeping her here. It may be what's keeping her locked in a death cycle and unable to effectively communicate with me, but I think she's trying. The same song she keeps humming and the name Beau, the only word she's spoken. Not to mention the photo. I know I'm onto something. I just need to figure out how to get Trudy on her own and get her to open up.

"Danny La Rue... Fifty-two."

I glance absently across the room at all the bowed heads worshipping at the altar of Bingo Bonanza and wonder if Danny and I should just excuse ourselves and head back to my place. After all, I did make certain promises that I'm eager to make good on.

"Clean the floor... fifty-four."

I'm just about to turn to Danny when I feel a strange yet familiar shiver roll down my spine, and I shudder hard. I could swear it was the same odd feeling I had that night at Sunrise Care Home.

I turn sharply and glance around the busy room. It's only when my gaze falls on the double doors leading from the hall that I see a dark shadow rush past the glass. I stand abruptly, barely noticing the loud scraping noise of my chair legs across the battered hardwood floor. Ignoring everyone around me, I hustle through the maze of tables and chairs, buggies and walking frames, and push my way through the doors into the small quiet foyer.

I skid to a halt, my still-wet shoes squeaking as I freeze, wide-eyed and open-mouthed. There's a dark black shadow hovering two feet above the ground, and I can see right through it to the door of the gents' toilet. Although it has no face, just a deep-cowled hood surrounding its head, I get the distinct impression it's staring at me.

My mouth is dry, and my heart is trying to pound straight out of my chest.

"Tristan, wha—" I feel Dusty appear beside me. "Holy fuck! What the fucking fuck is that fucking thing?"

The door behind us bangs open and I hear Danny's calm

voice. "Tris, are you alright?" The moment he speaks the dark-shrouded apparition shoots upward and disappears through the ceiling.

"Tris." I feel Danny's hands cup my face and turn me toward him. "You're all cold and clammy."

"I uh..." I clear my throat, shaking my head slightly to try and make some sort of sense while my brain is still clearly stuck in *What the fuck did I just witness?* mode.

"You rushed out so quickly," Danny says in concern. "Are you feeling okay?"

I latch onto the excuse. "Actually, I'm not feeling that well."

"Well, your clothes are all damp." He frowns as he looks down at me properly.

"It's left over from getting caught in the rain earlier." I offer him a small shaky smile.

"We should get you home." He rubs my arms in a soothing manner. "Don't want you to catch a chill."

"Yeah," I mutter, and my gaze drifts across to the patch of ceiling that thing had disappeared through. Suddenly, I just want to get as far away from this place as possible. I have no idea what the hell that thing is, but it can't be a coincidence that I'd seen it twice now. All I know is I want to be cocooned back home, warm and safe, with Danny's arms wrapped around me.

I turn back to him and draw in a shaky breath. "Take me home, Danny."

7

Tristan

I jolt violently, startling myself out of sleep with the same kind of abruptness as if I'd dreamt of falling. For several long seconds, my mind is confused, trying to recall the details of a dream that are fading fast. I shiver and pull the covers up to my chin, then reach out to grasp my glasses and fumble them onto my face so I can read the time on my phone.

Urgh, five thirty.

I toss my glasses back onto the bedside table. Rolling over, I burrow down into the bed, feeling the chill right down to my bones. With a strange sinking feeling in my chest, I reach out and run my hand over the empty space next to me. I can't quite recall the details of the dream that had awoken me, but it's left me feeling unsettled. I wish Danny was here. Usually I don't mind being alone, but something about the day before and the dream has left every nerve in my body frayed. I grasp the pillow on Danny's side of the bed and hug it close, burying my face in the cool cotton and breathing in the lingering scent of him.

It sucks when he has to go home. It's crazy, we've only been together six months, but now I just can't imagine my life without him in it. I feel like at some point I should be panicking, but I'm not so far.

Holding the pillow a little tighter, I rub my cheek against it and wish I was cuddled up next to his warm, hairy chest instead as the wind howls outside. The windowpane rattles loudly as the aged frame lets in a draught. No wonder it's so cold in here. I'm sick of trying to get my landlord Mr Ahmed to fix anything in the flat. I really am going to have to look for a new place, not that I want to.

My gaze locks on the nearly full saucepan of water in the corner of the room and then tracks upward to the expanding brown stain on the ceiling. Yeah, it's definitely time to move on. I've been here for almost four years now, having moved in when my dad went into Sunrise Care Home and we needed to sell my childhood home. I'd spent years, even through school and Uni, looking after Dad as his condition worsened until he needed full-time nursing care.

Moving into my little flat had been lonely in the beginning, which is why I'd ended up with Jacob Marley, and even though he's a contrary little shit, I do love him. In fact, I honestly don't know what I would've done without his company those first six months. My default setting has always been shy and introverted, even at school, but after losing Mum and dealing with my dad's illness, it became even harder to make friends or build relationships.

Then came Danny. My gorgeous, sweet, kind, sexy-as-hell dream man from the North. Sometimes I wonder if he's even real, he's so perfectly in tune with me... so perfect for me. It was like he was custom made and my name was on the order form.

Right now, though, I want nothing more than his warm body wrapped around me, holding on tight. I want his voice rumbling against my ear as we talk about silly random things. In fact, I want him with me all the time, I want him here, not going back to his flat and leaving me in this draughty old flat that leaks like an old barge.

Lately, I've had this little voice in my head, and it just keeps getting louder and more insistent.

What if Danny and I moved in together?

I've never done this before. Is there a rule about how long you're supposed to date before moving in together? I mean, how do I know when it's the right time? I've never had a serious boyfriend before Danny, just a string of disastrous dates. Is this going too fast? Would he even want to live with me? I guess it's a conversation we really should have sooner rather than later, but there's this little part of me that's worried he'll think I'm getting too clingy. After all, this is my first proper relationship, what do I know?

From the moment I met him, all my good intentions about not getting too close to anyone flew straight out the window. Danny snuck under every single defence I had and just held tight. I guess I thought any serious boyfriend wouldn't understand my responsibilities to Dad, but Danny is so patient and understanding with him and with me. I can't help but wonder what I did to deserve him.

Should I ask him to move in with me?

Well, not in with me, at least not here. We'd have to look for something else obviously, a new place that would be ours from the start. The more I think about it, the more appealing it is. The thought of going hand in hand, viewing flats, arguing over parking, heading down to Ikea to pick out new furniture, spending every evening and morning together. The whole cosy fantasy gives me a lovely warm feeling in my belly. I'd never really given much thought to domesticity before, but now I'm imagining it, I want it so bad it's making me ache. There's just one problem.

Dusty.

It's hard enough trying to communicate with her now when

Danny's around. If we lived together it'd be nearly impossible. We won't even think about all the times I inadvertently end up with lost spirits wandering up and attaching themselves to me. So far, Danny's just thought I was talking to myself whenever he caught my side of the conversations. He thinks it's cute and quirky. But if he sees me doing it all the time, how long until he just plain thinks I'm nuts?

A dumpy fur ball launches himself up onto the bed and lands next to me, startling me out of my thoughts.

I huff a startled laugh. "Christ, Jacob Marley, give me a little warning, will you?"

He lifts his tail in the air and sashays across the bed, then treads onto my balls before walking up my body and to my chest, where he sits and squints at me in judgement.

I can almost hear his thoughts. *Where's my Prince Danny?*

"I miss him too." I sigh loudly, feeling just as pathetic and needy.

This is ridiculous. I just saw him last night after we got back from Bingo Bonanza, but he got unexpectedly called back into work last night and wouldn't be done until late so decided to head home to his place.

I wish I could say this was all tied to that weird encounter at the community hall and not how I feel every morning he isn't here, but I would be kidding myself or Jacob.

Jacob Marley lets out a loud, indignant mewl and begins to knead my upper chest and neck with his paws.

I pout in sympathy. "I agree, this all sucks." He continues to knead his paws against me and I wince. I appreciate the solidarity and all, but it's reminding me that I really need to get his claws trimmed. "What do you think, Jacob Marley? Should we ask him to move in with us?"

As if understanding every word, he suddenly softens and rubs his head against my cheeks and under my jaw, purring loudly. I take this as agreement and lift my hand to stroke his head, feeling the delicate bones of his skull under my palm.

"We're a right old pair, aren't we?" I sigh.

He lifts his head, climbing further up my body and pressing his head right between my eyes as he stares at me unsettlingly, then lets out a loud meow, and I swear to god it sounds just like the word hungry.

"That's not very subtle." I roll my eyes and blow out a breath. "Fine." Scooping him into my arms, I climb awkwardly out of bed and head out of the bedroom, but as I reach the living room I'm brought up short. A familiar figure is perched on the edge of the sofa with her ever-present handbag balanced on her knees, the tatty handle gripped tightly in her bony hands.

"Delores?" I frown as I glance around. "Where's Dusty?"

The little old lady looks over and smiles widely at me before getting to her feet and scurrying over to me, then pressing up against my side and startling Jacob Marley. He gives a shrill yowl and leaps out of my arms, then streaks through the flat and back toward the bedroom.

"Beau?" Delores says hopefully, and I'm almost certain it sounds more like a question than her mistaking me for someone else. After all, no matter how loose her marbles are, there's no way you can mistake a skinny bespectacled mortician for a gorgeous strapping American G.I.

"Delores." I stare down at her and try to look stern. "I thought we talked about personal boundaries."

She doesn't seem to hear me as she stays plastered to my side. Giving up, I let out another sigh and turn toward the kitchen, the tiny ghost following in my wake.

"Dusty?" I call out loudly, but there's no other sound in the flat at all. Dusty is very clearly not here.

I shouldn't be surprised—I mean, it's not like she's with me all the time. She comes and goes as she pleases, a habit that I'm pretty sure she perfected in life, not just in death. There's no making Dusty do anything she doesn't want to. But I thought she'd stick around after what we saw yesterday. Maybe she's as freaked out about it as I am.

I grab myself a bowl of cereal and a cup of tea and settle on the sofa with Delores right next to me. As I flip through the channels, she makes a sound of delight as I land on the shopping channel.

"QVC?" I wrinkle my nose, turning to look at her. "Really?"

When she doesn't answer, I shrug and set down the TV remote on the coffee table. Her eyes are already glued to the screen, watching some guy in cycling shorts who is wearing so much fake tan he looks like he's been rolled in Dorito seasoning. He seems to be trying to sell something that looks suspiciously like a 1980s ThighMaster to anyone who's dumb enough to be awake at this hour.

"There's no way he got those thighs with that thing," I remark to Delores as I prop my feet on the coffee table and scoop a spoonful of cornflakes into my mouth. "It looks like it was made out of paperclips and a rubber band." I chew thoughtfully before muttering, "Oh would you look at that? For only three instalments of twenty-nine ninety-five, plus postage, you get the Pec Buster 3000 free."

I munch my breakfast as the guy in the Mr Motivator unitard disappears and the screen cuts to a woman standing next to a display of gaudy gold earrings. With her tawny-coloured hair extensions, thick dark fake eyelashes, and ridiculously long spiky acrylic nails, she resembles a sloth.

"There's no way she's getting those earrings in with those nails." I shove another spoonful into my mouth. "And I bet those earrings aren't even cubic zirconia. They look like they've robbed them off a Barbie doll. I bet they say *Made by Mattel* on the box. What do you think, Delores?" She makes a little humming sound in the back of her throat. I nod. "Just what I thought."

I glance across at Delores transfixed by the screen, and I feel something in my chest uncoil slightly. It's true she's not particularly good company seeing as she doesn't talk, stalks me obsessively, and is... well... dead, but I find myself grateful for the companionship. I don't feel quite so alone now.

I've just lifted the spoon to my mouth when something sails across the room and smacks me in the side of the head.

"Ow," I hiss loudly as the bowl in my hand jolts, sending a small tsunami of cold milk over the rim and soaking the t-shirt of Danny's I slept in. Picking a couple of wet soggy cornflakes off my chest, I drop them back in the bowl and set it down on the coffee table.

I rub the back of my head, looking around to see what hit me, and frown as I catch sight of a rather familiar book which, up until a couple of seconds ago, was tucked neatly on a bookshelf... in the other room.

My life is so weird these days.

I reach down to pick it up, but my hand freezes when I see the illustration on the page where it's fallen open. My lips part in a silent gasp as I stare at the picture before picking it up slowly. My gaze skims down the page quickly as I read the accompanying text.

"There you are." A familiar voice breaks the silence in the room, and I see Dusty literally skid into the room and come to an abrupt halt. She's wearing a fedora set at an angle, her signature blonde curls spilling over one shoulder. She also has on a beige belted raincoat and black leather gloves, and her eyes are covered by dark, oversized sunglasses.

"Where else would I be? I live here," I reply, watching her in confusion as she keeps looking behind her. "What's with the outfit, Inspector Clouseau?"

"Nothing." She shakes her head. "I'm in disguise."

"You don't say," I murmur.

"I'm just checking I wasn't followed." She checks behind herself again.

I frown. "Dusty, where have you been, and who would be following you?"

"I went back... you know..." She points toward the ceiling. "I asked Upstairs Management about that shadowy thing from yesterday."

"And what did they say?"

"Well that's where it gets even weirder," she replies.

"Weirder than you dressed as Peter Sellers?" I blink, momentarily forgetting the book in my hand and the cold milk seeping through my t-shirt.

"Funny." She rolls her eyes. "Do you want to hear this or not?"

"Sorry," I reply contritely as I pull the clammy material of my damp t-shirt away from my skin.

"When I first started asking questions they seemed really surprised, but then they got cagey, really fast. They flat out shut me down and told me to stop asking questions." She slips off the ridiculously huge sunglasses and her concerned gaze lands on me. "Tris, I get the distinct impression that whatever the hell that thing was, you weren't supposed to see it, and up there?" She points to the brown leaky patch on the ceiling. "They are not at all happy you did."

I break her gaze and glance down to the open book in my hand.

"As much as it pains me to say it," I murmur, "I think you might be onto something." I lift the book so she can see it. "Something just flung this book at me."

"Something?" she repeats slowly.

I shake my head. "Or someone."

"Is that what I think it is?"

I nod my head in confirmation. *"Crawshanks Guide to the Recently Departed."*

"Great, because that's just what we need. A hundred-year-old book of spiritual nonsense written by a drug addict." Dusty fists her hand on her cocked hip and purses her lips, lifting her perfectly sculpted brows.

Okay, admittedly, she may have a slight point once again. The book came into my possession six months ago when a ghost threw it at my head in an occult bookshop in Whitechapel and was written by the Victorian spiritualist Cornelius Crawshanks, who also more often than not happened to be riding the crazy train whilst high on opium. The problem is, Cornelius did actually know his stuff and had incredible knowledge of life after death. Unfortunately, he was nearly always heavily under the influence while writing his how-to guide, and sifting through pages of drug-addled rambling to find the hidden gems of wisdom is not for the faint of heart.

"You can't take anything that crackpot says seriously," Dusty huffs.

"Maybe not, but sometimes he gets it right." I hold up the open pages for her to see.

"Well I'll be damned," she mutters, her eyes widening as her gaze locks on the illustration.

It's almost a perfect representation of what we saw the previous day, a dark-shrouded wraith-like creature hovering above the ground, its face concealed beneath a heavy hood.

"What does the book say?" Dusty inches closer.

I turn the book back toward me and begin to read aloud. "The dark angel will appear to those upon the precipice of transversing the pathway between life and death. It is not to be taken lightly but rather as an ominous portend of great danger, for only those bound for the spirit realms are able to look upon its shadowy countenance without inviting madness. Beware the angel of death if you can see it, you are courting trouble beyond measure."

"Well, that's cheery." Dusty purses her lips thoughtfully. "So what he's basically saying is, if you see the angel of death you're screwed... good to know."

"I've seen it twice now," I say quietly. "In two separate locations, first at Sunrise Care Home, then at Northwold Community Centre, and the only common denominators in both instances are Danny, Delores, and me."

"Sounds like a cheesy rom-com title."

"Sounds like trouble, more like." I frown as I look down at the book. "I haven't got a clue what to do."

"I do," Dusty says suddenly. "We need to go to the bookshop."

"This is not the time for you to get freaky with Bruce," I reply dryly.

"No—well, I mean, yes." She smirks. "I fully intend to do that later, but I mean not right now. Right now, I think there's only one person we can go to. Evangeline."

Evangeline Crawshanks not only happens to be the dead great, great... several number of greats grandmother of the current owner of Whitechapel Occult Books, she is also the great-niece of none other than Cornelius Crawshanks himself, author of the book I'm currently holding. Dusty may be right. If there's anyone who might know something about this, it's Evangeline.

"Go get dressed. Hold it, are those cornflakes stuck to your t-shirt?" Her eyes narrow on the splattered stain on my chest. "Never mind." She shakes her head. "We'll head over to the bookshop as soon as it opens."

"I can't," I argue. "I do have an actual job to go to, you know. I can't just run around solving mysteries and only showing up to work when I feel like it. This isn't an episode of Baywatch."

"I should hope not. You'd catch your death running around in a skimpy little red swimsuit in that draughty old mortuary."

"I'm serious, Dusty."

"So am I. Do you know how much waxing it would take to get into one of those swimsuits? They ride up so high, I'm surprised those girls didn't get haemorrhoids."

I sigh. "Dusty, focus."

"Right, sorry." She shakes her head. "Look, sweetie, I know you're all responsible and whatever, but this is important." Her gaze flicks over to Delores. "Somehow, this goes beyond one old lady's unfinished business. I think there's something much bigger going on. That you've seen that weird thing twice now coupled with the fact that Upstairs Management actually seemed really shocked that you did? I think you need to ask Evangeline about it. After all, she was the one who threw the book at your head last time."

"Fine... but I really wish people would stop throwing things at me," I lament sulkily. "I'm going to need a crash helmet soon."

8

Danny

I yawn again as I raise my cup to my lips, disappointed to find nothing but the cold dregs of my third cup of coffee. Setting the cup down on my desk and trying to avoid the over-spilling towers of paperwork, I blink in an effort to focus on the report in front of me, which might as well be written in Sanskrit for all the sense it makes.

I really need some sleep. I had to leave Tristan's flat late last night and head back to work when all I really wanted to do was crawl into bed with him and hold him. He wouldn't say what was wrong, but something was definitely up. After he'd rushed out of the community hall so abruptly, I'd caught up with him in the foyer. He was pale and shaky, and his skin when I'd grabbed his hand was cold and clammy.

I'm still not convinced Delores Abernathy hadn't been poisoned at the community hall. After all, it was the only place she visited frequently, other than the care home where she'd lived. At first I'd been worried that Tris might've been exposed to something. I was halfway to taking him to the nearest hospital to be checked out—which, in hindsight, probably would've been a bit of an overreaction on my part, but I can't help it. After that crazy murderer Kaitlin Fletcher kidnapped him at gunpoint last year, I've been a little over-protective, but it's something I'm working on. I love Tristan and I want to build a life with him, a future, and the last thing I want is for him to think I'm some over-possessive boyfriend.

By the time we'd arrived back at his flat, he'd almost returned to normal, although he'd stayed quiet the rest of the evening, lost in his own head. I'd asked what was wrong, but he wouldn't say, and I don't want to push him, but I know there's something bothering him. I feel it in my gut.

"So have you asked him yet?" A denim-clad bottom plonks down on my desk, displacing more errant reports.

I look up at my partner Maddie and see her smiling widely.

"What?" I blink, my brain not quite catching up.

"Uh oh, someone hasn't had enough coffee yet this morning," she tuts.

"Someone only got a couple of hours sleep on the tiny sofa in the staff room," I reply tiredly.

"Danny," she sighs. "You don't have to try so hard. You've been here six months already and have the highest closed case stats. Trust me, your work ethic more than speaks for itself. You're allowed to have a life outside of this place. I know we're short-handed but that's nothing unusual, and it's not going to change anytime soon. Don't run yourself into the ground. You'll burn out and then Tris will end up looking after you as well as his dad."

"I'm fine, honest." I yawn again, my jaw cracking loudly.

"Really?" She rolls her eyes and hands me her own coffee mug, which is mercifully hot and full to the brim.

"Thanks." I take a grateful sip.

"So, did you ask him?" she prompts again.

"Who?"

"Tristan." She snorts. "God, you really aren't with it this

morning, are you? You said you were thinking about asking Tristan to move in with you."

I take a slow sip of coffee as Maddie watches me suspiciously.

"You haven't asked him yet, have you?"

I shake my head.

"Why not?" she whines. "Sonia is messaging me every five minutes and asking."

"I don't know why you and your wife are so invested in my love life."

"Because we love you and Tristan, and we want you to be happy."

"No, I haven't asked him yet." I blow out a tired breath and set the mug down on the desk. "There hasn't been a good time to bring up the subject."

"Pft," she snorts. "Never a good time. Danny, it's really not that hard. Just send him a text saying, 'Tris, I know your lease is almost up and your flat's falling apart, wanna move in together?'"

"Very romantic," I say flatly.

"Then send him a bunch of flowers from the shop around the corner with a card saying, 'Wanna be my roomie?'"

I shake my head incredulously. "How the hell did you ever convince Sonia to marry you?"

"I didn't." She smiles widely. "She asked me. She's the romantic in our relationship. I get too caught up in work and forget all the little things."

"And you say I'm a workaholic," I reply pointedly.

"That's why we get on so well, you're like the male version of me." She grins. "And Tris... he's the Sonia in this equation. That's how we know you two are perfect for each other, so can you step up the timetable on your happily ever after? Because Sonia says she has the perfect hat to wear to your wedding."

"Wedding? Hang on a minute. I haven't even worked up the

courage to ask him to move in with me yet, marriage is a ways off."

Her eyes narrow. "Are you seriously telling me you don't want to marry him?"

"Are you kidding? I'd march him down to the registry office and marry him tomorrow if I could."

"Then what's holding you back? You two love each other, you've already exchanged the L-word, I don't see what the problem is."

"The problem is he's too important to me to mess this up," I admit. "I mean, we've only been together six months. Isn't it a bit soon to be thinking about cohabitating and marriage?"

"Oh, I'm sorry," she replies. "I wasn't aware there was an official timetable."

"You know what I mean." I roll my eyes. "I don't want him to think I'm pressuring him or being... I don't know... too demanding."

"Oh my god, Danny Hayes, you are the least demanding person I know." Maddie releases an exasperated breath. "You need to get out of your head. You're overthinking this, and I know that for a fact because it's exactly what I'd do. So, I'm going to tell you what my wife told me: stop being an idiot. You love him, right?"

I nod.

"And he loves you?"

I nod again.

"Then just ask him. What's the worst that can happen? If he says he's not ready, you give him a little more time until he is. It's not like you two have to go sign leases tomorrow or pick out duvet covers from Dunelm, but you do need to at least have a conversation. There is no right time, the progression of a relationship is different for everyone. You and Tristan have to figure it out for yourselves, but you won't be able to do that if you can't even talk about it."

"Okay, fine." I pull out my phone and shoot Tristan a quick message.

Dinner at Bella Vita, 7pm?

It only takes him a moment to message back with a simple, *Love to see you at 7 x.* I lift the screen for Maddie to see.

"Satisfied?" I ask as she lifts a brow. "I'll ask him tonight."

"Aww." She wipes a mock tear from the corner of her eye. "My little man's all grown up and asking his boyfriend to move in with him."

"Shut up." I huff out a fond laugh as I shove her unceremoniously off the side of the desk. "Are you going to do any work today? Or did you just stop by to dissect my private life?"

"A little of both, if I'm being honest." She slides onto a chair and scoots back toward me. "How did it go interrogating all the murderous little old ladies yesterday? Any suspects?"

"I have a list of names of the women Mrs Abernathy was closest to, those who had access to her, but honestly, most of them are in their eighties. I can't see them murdering each other over whose strawberry tart wins the blue ribbon at the May Day social."

"You'd be surprised." Maddie snorts. "Those things can get brutally competitive."

"Maybe." I chuckle. "We'll check their backgrounds anyway."

"Oh, by the way, Polina Ogarkov is back in the country," Maddie says as she leans back in her chair.

"Polina," I murmur as I cast my mind back. "She was one of Mrs Abernathy's carers, wasn't she?"

"Yep." Maddie pops the word in her mouth as she nods her head. "Although she's actually Polina Porter now. Got married, just back from her honeymoon, left just before Mrs Abernathy's death."

"Not being in the country at the time of the murder doesn't

preclude her from the list of suspects. She could've been poisoning her for weeks leading up to her death."

Maddie nods. "I know, which is why I checked with the home. She's working a shift this afternoon and into this evening." She glances down at her watch. "She should be there by now."

I stand abruptly, still feeling the tiredness dragging at me, and know I need to get up and move. I unhook my jacket from the back of my chair and slide it on. "Well, no time like the present. We might as well head over there now and question her."

"Fine, but I'm driving. I'm not having you fall asleep at the wheel." Maddie stands and holds out her hand. "Keys."

"Fine." I hand them over reluctantly. "But we're stopping at Starbucks on the way. I see a triple espresso in my very near future."

"Deal." She grins.

By the time we arrive at the care home, the sky has once again turned a threatening grey and the clouds boil across the sky, dark and heavy.

"Looks like we're in for more rain," Maddie remarks as we climb out of the car.

"You know, I expected more sunshine when I moved South," I mutter as we cross the carpark.

"Dream on." Maddie looks up again as an unexpected rumble of thunder ripples across the sky. "You know the drill, it's the same as up North. We get approximately one week of blazing sunshine, at which point we reserve the right to strenuously complain about it being too hot, before the weather flakes on us again."

"Come on, best get inside." I start trotting in the direction of the entrance as the heavens open and the first fat droplets of rain begin to fall.

The main doors slide open smoothly as we hurry into the reception.

"Danny," I hear my name called before we even have a chance to check in with the receptionist.

I turn and greet Martin's carer. "Hello, Lois."

"I wasn't expecting you today." She peers around me. "No Tristan?"

"He's working." I brush my damp hair back from my face. "As am I, unfortunately. You remember my partner, Detective Wilkes?"

"Of course." She nods at Maddie. "Detective."

"We're here to see Polina Ogarkov."

"Porter," Maddie interjects.

"Polina Porter," I correct myself. "I believe she's working today?"

"She's in the dayroom," Lois replies. "You know where it is."

"I do. Thank you, Lois." I smile politely as I set off in the direction of the dayroom, Maddie beside me.

As we enter the room, it's uncharacteristically quiet. The first thing I hear is the rain pelting against the window and the unmistakable tones of Del Boy and Rodney in a random episode of *Only Fools and Horses* coming from the TV in the corner.

I scan the room until my gaze comes to rest on a slim young woman with ivory skin and jet-black hair tied back in a long ponytail. She's wearing a lilac-coloured tunic and black trousers, the standard uniform for the home. Crossing the room toward her, I notice that the name badge on her breast pocket has the name *Polly* written across it.

"Polina Porter?" I call to her in a soft tone of voice so as not to startle any of the residents dotted around the room.

She looks up from where she's leaning over a table tidying a stack of games and puzzles and smiles. "It is still strange to me when people call me my husband's name," she answers, her accent belying her Eastern European roots. "How may I help you?"

"Detective Hayes." I show my badge. "And this is Detective Wilkes." I nod to Maddie and she flashes her badge too.

"Is this about Delores?" Polina asks softly and I nod. She sighs, slipping the last few pieces of a puzzle into a box and setting it down. Sliding onto a chair at the table, she then motions to two empty chairs. "Please, have a seat. What would you like to know?"

Maddie and I sit down as well, and I take out my notebook.

"You were Mrs Abernathy's carer, correct?" Maddie asks, and I let her take the lead on the questions as I make notes.

"One of them, yes," Polina replies. "It's so sad. I know that we are not supposed to have favourites in this job, but she was one of mine. It's hard not to get attached, and Delores was so sweet."

"Could you please clarify your duties when it came to Mrs Abernathy?" Maddie continues.

"The same as the others." Polina shrugged. "Depending on the shift, I would help her in and out of bed and get washed and dressed, make sure she ate. During the week, we would take turns driving Delores to visit her friends at Northwold Community Centre."

"So you helped her with her eating and drinking?" Maddie clarifies.

"Yes," Polina replies.

"Did you ever prepare any of her food?"

"No." She shakes her head. "That's not my job. Delores was mostly able to feed herself, but every now and then she'd get frustrated or distracted, so we made sure she'd eaten and drunk enough. So many of them end up suffering from dehydration if we don't keep a close eye on them."

"But there would've been many times when you had access to her food and drink unsupervised," Maddie confirms.

"I'm going to stop you right there, Detective, because I know where this is going and I'm going to save you some trouble," Polina says calmly. "Yes, I and many of the other carers have more than enough access to cause harm to Delores or any of our patients. They are very vulnerable, and we hold positions of great trust. I'm not naïve enough to think that people in my position have not abused that trust before, but I would never harm Delores. Like I said, I was more than fond of her. I cannot prove beyond a shadow of a doubt that I am innocent, however the substance used, this... what do you call it?"

"Arsenic," I answer.

"Arsenic." Polina shakes her head. "I am not familiar with this, and I would not know where to find it. Anyone working in the care environment has full access to many lethal drugs which are quick and undetectable. From what I have heard, someone was giving this substance to Delores over some time. Believe me, if I'd wanted to harm Delores, I could've made her death look completely natural."

"Well that's blunt." Maddie raises her brows.

"That is not a confession." Polina's mouth curves slightly. "I am simply trying to make you understand that if it had been one of us, you most likely would never have known about it."

"When was the last time you saw Mrs Abernathy?" I ask.

"About a week and a half before my wedding." Polina frowns. "I was supposed to work right up until the day before because I'd saved all my holiday for my honeymoon, but I was very sick for about a week."

"Sick?" I tilt my head as I study her. "What kind of sickness?"

"Severe stomach cramps, vomiting. I was very ill, so much so that my husband wondered if we would have to delay the wedding. Fortunately, I recovered enough for the wedding to go ahead, and it was a beautiful day, even though I was still not at my best."

"What had you done the day before you became ill?" I ask.

"My usual duties." She cast her eyes to the ceiling as if trying to remember. "I'd worked the afternoon and evening shifts. I'd taken Delores to the community centre to meet with her friends for a craft session followed by afternoon tea. I brought her back to the home, but by the evening I'd begun to feel very unwell. I left work early and once I got home, I started vomiting. After a few days, my husband called the doctor, and they said it was most likely a virus of some sort."

"Did you eat or drink anything at the community centre that afternoon?"

"I had a cup of tea as usual." Polina frowns. "Actually, Delores was feeling fussy that afternoon. She had a scone she didn't want so I ate it instead. Scones with cream and strawberry jam is something I have discovered a love for since I've lived in the UK."

Maddie and I share a concerned look.

"Polina, I don't want to alarm you," I say carefully, an uncomfortable suspicion occurring to me. "But you really should go back to your doctor for a follow-up appointment. I think it's possible you may have been poisoned by eating something intended for Delores."

"Poisoned?" Her eyes widen as her hand unconsciously drifts to her stomach. "But I discovered a few days ago that I'm pregnant."

"Congratulations," I offer, although the words seem hollow. I glance down at her hands, looking for the telltale Mees' lines Tristan had pointed out to me on Mrs Abernathy's body, but her nails are painted a pale pink, concealing any potential markings.

"We don't want to scare you," Maddie says. "The chances are you're fine if you were only exposed once. But I really think you shouldn't take any chances since you're pregnant. Try to get in to see your GP today and if you can't, go to the nearest hospital and let them know what to check for."

Polina looks very pale so I reach out and grasp her hand. "I'm sure it will be fine."

"I have to speak with my manager and call my husband." She rises shakily, her hand still resting on her belly. "If there's nothing else?"

"Actually just one more thing, if you don't mind," I say. "You said they were hosting an afternoon tea at the community centre that day." She nods. "I don't suppose there's any chance you remember who made the scones?"

She shakes her head. "I'm sorry, I don't."

"Okay. Well, thank you for your time," I say gently. "I hope everything is well with the baby."

"Thank you," she mutters, her eyes filling with tears as turns and heads toward the door.

"Well fuck, I feel shitty." Maddie rubs her face and breathes deeply.

"You and me both," I agree. "I think we can probably exclude her from the suspect list."

"Everything does seem to be pointing to the community centre, doesn't it?" Maddie rises from her seat, and I follow.

"She also had a valid point." I scratch my chin thoughtfully as we cross the room and head out into the corridor. "If it was anyone at the home, they'd have access to much more efficient and undetectable medications. Hell, they could have smothered her with a pillow and still make it look like she passed away in her sleep."

"Fuck, that's a scary thought." Maddie grimaces as she pulls out her phone and taps out a quick message. "Just telling Sonia to never put me in a home," she says after seeing my curious glance. I shake my head.

"We need to contact the community centre and find out

who organised and who catered the afternoon tea that day," I muse as we head back toward the reception.

"Danny!" I hear someone call my name and I stop and turn to see Lois hurrying down the corridor toward me. "Oh, I'm so glad I caught you. I know you're technically working right now, but Martin is very unsettled. I think it's the storm."

Her words are suddenly punctuated by a roll of thunder and a crack of lightning, both so loud the glass doors slightly shake. I glance across to Maddie, who smiles sympathetically.

"Go on, Danny, it's fine." Maddie pats my arm. "You're owed so many hours anyway. Why don't you finish up early? I'll head back and see if I can contact the community centre. You go and settle Tristan's dad, then for god's sake, go home and get a few hours' sleep before your date tonight, or you'll be falling asleep and face-planting in the starter. Then you'll end up tragically drowning in your soup and won't have the conversation with Tristan, which in turn will mean Sonia will be unhappy because she won't get the chance to wear her new hat to your wedding."

"I'm not bloody proposing." I roll my eyes. "But thank you anyway. I'm not going to lie, I could do with a couple of hours' kip to recharge my batteries."

She nods and heads out the door into the storm as I turn back to Lois, who is eyeing me with a barely concealed smile.

"I'm not proposing," I insist.

"I heard nothing." She smiles like the Cheshire Cat and turns away, leaving me no choice but to follow her.

As we enter Martin's room, we find him pacing agitatedly, but as soon as he sees me, he rushes forward and grabs hold of me, burying his face in my chest.

"Hey," I say softly as I wrap my arms around him, sharing a concerned look with Lois. He's never done this before. "It's okay, Martin, it's just a storm." He lifts his head slowly and peeks around me. "Tris isn't here. I'm afraid you're stuck with me today."

He grips onto me for dear life as I manoeuvre him to the small secondhand two-seater sofa we found and crammed into his room so he and Tristan have somewhere to snuggle up when Tris reads to him.

I gently pull him down to the worn plush cushions and wrap my arm around him as he snuggles into my body like a child afraid of monsters under the bed.

"I know Tris likes to read you the Narnia books, but how about something different?" I ask Martin even though I don't expect an answer. I look up to find Lois already browsing the bookcase Tristan has filled with children's books.

"How about something a bit more modern? Harry Potter?" She slides a colourful book from the shelf. It's a special illustrated version Tris and I bought Martin for his birthday because, although he can't really follow the story, he likes to focus on the pictures as he listens to our voices.

"I'll leave you to it." Lois hands me the book. "Cup of tea?"

"That would be lovely." I smile up at her tiredly. "Just the thing for a rainy day, eh, Martin?"

"I'll be right back." She smiles and disappears from the room.

There's another sudden loud boom from outside the window behind us and the rain pelts harder against the glass. I stare down at Martin. He didn't so much as flinch from the thunder nor the crack of lightning that follows. In fact, his gaze is fixed on the corner of the room by the open door that leads out into the empty hallway.

He's shaking like a leaf as he reaches for my hand and grips on for dear life. I watch him as his gaze tracks slowly across the room as if it's following something. I look again, but there's nothing there.

"Martin," I say softly, rubbing his back gently with my other hand, feeling the soft wool of his cardigan beneath my palm. "It's okay, nothing will hurt you. I'm here."

He turns his head and looks directly at me, and I could swear for a second there is something in his eyes, something awake, before he turns back to stare at the corner of the room and the moment is lost.

Opening the book and laying it in my lap, I tap the page to draw Martin's attention to the pictures, but as I begin to read, and he slowly relaxes against me, I can't help but glance up at the empty corner shrouded in shadows from the storm lashed window, and a shiver trickles down my spine.

9

Tristan

It's late into the afternoon by the time I finish work and find myself wandering down the rabbit warren of back alleys in Whitechapel toward the little hidden Victorian-era building that houses The Whitechapel Occult Books & Curiosities, founded by a descendant of none other than Cornelius Crawshanks, the absolute headcase who wrote the actual book on spirits.

Of course, these days it's run by Madame Vivienne, or just plain Viv, according to Dusty, who seems to spend an inordinate amount of her afterlife there. I'm pretty sure that has more to do with the hot former-rugby-playing ghost of Bruce Reyes, with whom Dusty happens to be very intimately acquainted, than any interest in the merchandise. Still, I guess it's nice to know there's sex after death.

I sigh and shake my head at that thought. My life is so... I hesitate to use the word weird... unexpected, maybe? Six months ago, if anyone had told me I'd have a full-time boyfriend I'm madly in love with and I'd be best friends with a ghost who helps me help other ghosts find their happily ever after, I'd have flat out laughed in their face. Guess you really can't see what's around the corner.

I walk around the corner and collide with a slim body about my height. I stumble back and begin to lose my balance, only to have a pair of hands shoot out and grab my upper arms to steady me. I find myself staring into the face of a man about my age, maybe slightly older. He has the fiery red hair of a Celt, parted sharply at the side and combed into ruthlessly neat waves, along with cornflower blue eyes and pale skin.

A quick scan reveals an outfit of slim-fitting trousers and tightly laced brogues, a pale blue checked shirt and burgundy bow tie, all completed by a smart blazer. The whole look just screams hot, twinky professor.

I open my mouth to apologise, and those summery blue eyes narrow before flashing in irritation. Seeing that I have my balance, he releases his firm grip and steps back.

"Be more careful where you're going next time," he says sharply, his cut-glass accent surprising me. With his colouring, I wouldn't have been surprised to hear him sound Irish... or possibly Scottish.

"Sorry," I mutter as he huffs and brushes abruptly past me, leaving a vague hint of sage dancing on the air. Trying not to bristle at his rudeness, I notice something fall from his pocket and flutter to the ground.

I reach down to pick it up and turn it over in my hand. At first glance, it looks like a business card, but a strange shimmer ripples across its surface when the sunlight hits it just so, and I realise it's blank.

"Hey! You dropped your... weird... shimmery... " my voice trails off as I look up and the stranger is nowhere in sight. "Okay then," I murmur, tucking the card into my pocket. I hate littering, so there's no way I'm just going to chuck it back on the ground. I'll just hang onto it until I get to the book shop and can dispose of it.

"Tristan, come on!" Dusty calls from up ahead, holding onto Delores' hand as she taps her foot. She's abandoned her trench coat, fedora, and dark glasses, and is now dressed like one of Charlie's Angels in a skintight zip-up bodysuit and go-go boots, and with her wig styled into Farrah Fawcett flicks. I shake my head with a small laugh escaping my lips; never knowing what she's going to be wearing next is one of my favourite things about her.

I jog along the rest of the alley to join them under the old wooden sign which reads, 'Whitechapel Occult Books & Curiosities.' It creaks alarmingly on hinges that look like they're held together by rust and hopeful intentions.

"I really hope no one throws anything at me this time, it's really getting old." I reach for the handle and reluctantly open the door to step through onto the battered old floor, then close the door firmly behind me.

"Welcome! Welcome, seekers of spectral and occult wis– oh, it's you." Madame Vivienne breaks off her rather theatrical greeting as her gaze narrows. "Come to destroy more of my birthright?"

"Birthright," Dusty snorts. "Viv, you offer fake readings to fleece unsuspecting strangers of their hard-earned cash."

"Everyone's got to earn an honest living." She folds her arms across her chest, the rows and rows of silvery bangles lining her wrists chiming merrily.

"Honest being the operative word," Dusty claps back. "There's really nothing honest about what you do."

"Doesn't mean I don't have bills to pay. What good is being able to see the ghosts when I can't control which ones I see? Every time I try to do a reading for a customer, I can't seem to tune into their relatives. I just keep getting random spirits showing up."

"As much as I sympathise, Vivienne"—I glance down at my watch, knowing I need to leave enough time to get back to

Hackney for my date with Danny—"I really need to speak with Evangeline. Is she here?"

"Oh... her." Vivienne's mouth puckers like she's sucked something sour. "She's the worst of all of them."

"She's your relative, Viv," I remind her.

"She's so judgey. All she does is criticise how I run my own shop, and she keeps hiding the gin!" she exclaims. "I found it in the washing machine last time."

"Um... well... sorry to hear that," I say diplomatically. "But I really do need to speak to her."

"Fine. I'm going to watch Eastenders, they're streaming all the classic episodes on BritBox and Den's about to serve Angie with divorce papers. Call me if there are any real customers." She huffs as she sweeps through the beaded curtain to the back, leaving the strands swinging and clattering together in her wake.

"Got a liver like a jar of pickled eggs, that one," a quiet voice tuts.

"Hello, Evangeline." I glance over at the little old lady who's appeared on the sofa, her knitting needles clicking softly in the quiet of the room.

She looks up and the needles slow. "Hello, Tristan, Dusty," she greets us, then she notices the little old lady clutching Dusty's hand. "And who do we have here?"

"This is Delores Abernathy," I say as she lets go of Dusty's hand and shuffles across the room toward the sofa.

Evangeline smiles and her demeanour softens. "Hello, Delores. Would you like to sit, dear?" Mrs Abernathy obediently slides in beside her and eyes the pale pink knitting in Evangeline's bony hands.

She offers the needles to Mrs Abernathy, who hooks her handbag over one wrist in order to hold them properly as she looks at Evangeline.

"There you go, dear." Evangeline pats her wrist kindly. "You just finish that one up."

Delores starts looping the pale yarn over the needles, although not quite as fluidly as Evangeline, who settles herself back into the cushions and begins knitting again with a second set of needles and a blue ball of yarn that have appeared from somewhere.

"Um... so I was hoping I could ask you something," I begin awkwardly as I hover next to them.

"Take a seat, Tristan." Evangeline is once again all business as a chair slides across the wooden floor with a loud scraping sound. "I may be dead, but it doesn't mean I want to crane my neck to look at you."

"Sorry." I drop onto the chair as I fumble in my messenger bag, pull out Crawshanks Guide, and open it to the page marked with a neon pink post-it note. "Um, I was wondering if you knew anything about this?"

I lift the book to show her the illustration of the shadowy creature Cornelius Crawshanks referred to as an angel of death.

"I know enough to stay away from them. Why do you ask?" She sets her knitting in her lap and folds her hands neatly as she gives me her full attention, and it's slightly unnerving being under that direct gaze.

"Because I've seen it, twice now."

"I saw it too," Dusty adds as she leans against one of the bookcases. "Creepy as hell, looked just like one of the bloody dementors from Harry Potter."

"I'm sure it was, dear, but I have no idea what these dementors are that you're referring to." Evangeline turns her serious gaze back to me. "You saw them? The reapers, I mean."

"Them?" I blink slowly.

She nods, lips pursed. "There are many of them." She stares at me, contemplatively. "I'm not surprised Dusty saw one but you, Tristan? The living aren't supposed to be able to."

"What are they?" I whisper.

"Exactly what Uncle Cornelius called them, angels of death," she replies. "They're reapers."

"Reapers?" I repeat.

"They have one purpose," Evangeline explains. "They're here to collect souls."

"That sounds a little dark." I swallow tightly, my stomach swooping slightly at the thought.

Evangeline shakes her head. "You misunderstand. Everything has an order to it, a series of checks and balances. Souls that die at their designated time are ready to move on, and are usually greeted by friends and family who guide them into the light. Those who go before their time—murder victims mostly, like Dusty and, I suspect, Delores here— are still tied to their former existence and require a guide, such as yourself, to help them resolve their unfinished business so they can cross into the light. The reapers come for those who have to be pulled from their bodies quickly, accident victims more often than not. They possess the power to separate a soul from its body and lead it into the light."

"So why can I see these reapers all of a sudden?" I frown. "I've been able to see ghosts for over six months, but this is the first time I've seen these guys, so why now?"

"I can't answer that for you, Tristan. I don't know what their plan is for you."

"Their?" I swallow my mouth suddenly dry.

She points to the ceiling.

"Evangeline," Dusty interrupts with a wave of her hand. "I was just up there and I'm telling you now, the Executive Level has no clue. Trust me, I didn't spend most of my life up on a stage in sequins and five-inch heels without learning how to read a room, and those guys up there were shocked to learn Tris can see the dementors."

"Reapers."

"Whatever." Dusty flicks her hand dismissively. "If someone has a plan, it sure as hell isn't theirs."

Evangeline stares at Dusty, brows furrowed, then turns her attention back toward me. "And you said you've seen them twice?" I nod. "In all my time I've only ever known of one other person who could see them."

I glance down at the book in my hands. "Cornelius?"

"So he wasn't just hallucinating while on a drug-fuelled bender." Dusty raises her brow.

"You've got completely the wrong idea about Uncle Cornelius, just like everyone else. He spent so much of his life being ridiculed but he truly was an exceptional man, and a very kind one. You have to understand he didn't see the reapers because of the drugs." She sighs. "He saw them despite the drugs."

"He was using the drugs to cope with the things he saw, wasn't he?" I say.

"He was a man ahead of his time. He didn't understand many of the things he saw, and some of them were equally frightening and fascinating to him. He had no one to talk to, no one to guide him. He used the laudanum, the opium, and the cocaine to soften all the hard edges of his world and to shield himself from the hard words of his peers," Evangeline explained. "It was a very different time back then."

"Poor man," I mutter, seeing Cornelius Crawshanks in a new light for the first time. "It must have been so isolating for him."

"I think that's what writing the book was about for him." Evangeline even shrugs with elegance. "It was his way of trying to make sense of it all."

"Wow, who died?" A new voice intrudes, and I look up to see Bruce emerge from a bookcase.

Dusty gives a little squeak of pleasure and practically skips across the room to throw herself into Bruce's thickly muscled arms, wrapping her arms around his neck as she plants a rather thorough kiss on his lips, kicking her back foot up like a 1930s movie starlet.

Bruce pinches Dusty's bum and winks at her cheekily as he pulls back to study us all. "So what's with all the morose faces?"

"Tristan saw a couple of dementors," Dusty says, remaining plastered to Bruce's side, his arm wrapped around her waist.

"A what now?" He blinks.

"Reapers," I reply as I absently stare at his thickly muscled thighs framed by the tiniest pair of rugby shorts I've ever seen.

"Reapers?" Bruce frowns. "But I didn't think the living could see them?"

"Well, aren't I just the lucky one?" I mutter sourly.

"Tristan," Evangeline muses, "where did you say you were when you saw them?"

"The first time was at the care home where Delores died. It led me to her room, then disappeared inside. When I got there, it was gone... Come to think of it, her room is in the opposite direction to my dad's. If I hadn't seen the reaper and followed it, Danny and I would've just gone out the main entrance. If I'd gone straight home, I never would have seen the Mees' lines on Delores' nails and her death would've just been ruled natural causes."

"That's interesting." Evangeline's eyes narrow. "Go on."

"The second time was at the community centre miles away in Clapham, where Delores used to go to meet up with her friends. I saw it and followed it, then it..."

"It what?" Evangeline asks, her eyes lit with curiosity.

"I could've sworn it turned and looked right at me."

"But that's not possible." Evangeline frowns. "From what I know of reapers, they are only cognisant of the person they've been assigned to reap. It shouldn't have been aware of your presence at all."

"You don't think..." I swallow nervously. "You don't think it's come for me, do you? Am I going to end up dying in some freak accident?"

"Honey, you did that already and they sent you back," Dusty reminds me.

"Dusty's right, dear," Evangeline says. "If they wanted you dead, you'd be dead. But I have to say, I'm at a total loss, I've never heard of reapers acting like this.... Bruce?" She looks to him for confirmation.

"I'm stumped too." He lifts the hand not currently wrapped around Dusty and strokes his jaw. "Unless..."

"Unless?" I repeat, certain I probably don't want to hear the answer.

"Unless you saw the same one both times?"

"A rogue reaper?" Evangeline blinks. "I've never heard of such a thing."

"I've never heard of them behaving like this, either." Bruce shakes his head as he looks at me sympathetically. "It may not be here for your soul, but even I can tell this doesn't sound good, mate."

"Thanks a lot, really comforting," I say flatly. "What am I supposed to do now?"

"Carry on as normal," Evangeline replies.

"I hate to break it to you, Evangeline, but there's nothing normal about this. In fact, my life is so far from normal these days I don't even recognise it." I frown.

"I know, but since it first appeared the night Delores died, I say help her unravel her unfinished business, get her crossed into the light, and by finding the answers for her, you might just find answers for yourself."

"You think the two are connected?"

"I don't think it can be discounted without more information." Evangeline tilts her head slightly as if she's listening to something we can't hear. "I'm sorry," she says suddenly, "but I have to go now. I'm needed elsewhere. Good luck, dear."

Before I can say anything else, she's gone between one blink and the next, leaving Mrs Abernathy on the sofa, still knitting with her pink ball of yarn.

I glance down at my watch. "We should get going too," I tell Dusty. She plants another kiss on Bruce's lips, leaving a bright red print from her lipstick.

"We're going now, Vivienne," I call out toward the back of the shop.

"Go then, and bring gin next time you stop by, the good stuff, not that tap water from Tesco," she yells back as I roll my eyes.

Dusty helps Delores up from the sofa as I wave goodbye to Bruce and turn toward the door.

"Tristan, wait a moment." Bruce jogs over to me. "I know you've got a lot on your plate right now, but Dusty said she'd mentioned to you about..." He drops his voice. "You know... my unfinished business."

Dusty had mentioned it to me months ago after Bruce had taken her on a wild Valentine's date to the land of the dead, a place he could only visit for short periods of time because he's anchored to our world and will stay until his remains are found and his murder solved.

I nod. "She did mention it, yes. And I really want to help you, I just haven't figured out how yet. Your murder happened over forty years ago, your remains were never recovered, it's a cold case, and you may even still be a missing persons case if they had no cause to suspect foul play back in the day. Danny doesn't know about me—I mean, about the whole ghost thing. I'm still trying to figure out how to get him to reopen a cold case without having to explain why."

"It's okay." Bruce nods slowly. "I get it. It was always going to be a long shot and to be honest, I've kind of gotten used to being stuck here with the portal."

That's the key reason the bookshop exists and has for so

long. It's a crossing point, an in-between place where the world of the living meets the world of the dead. Concealed behind one of the walls is a portal into the spirit world, and somehow Bruce has found himself responsible for that portal.

"I will help you," I tell Bruce earnestly, "I promise. I just need to figure out how."

"It's okay, really."

I glance down at my watch again. "I'm really sorry, but I have to go."

"Sure." Bruce smiles and he's so sweet and so handsome, I can see why Dusty ended up getting attached to him. "I'll see you soon."

"Go on." Dusty smiles as she waves me off. She knows exactly why I'm in such a hurry. "Have fun. I'll babysit Delores."

"Thanks." I throw her a heartfelt grin as I head for the door.

Despite the stress headache I have brewing over my left eye and the potentially horrifying reaper that may or may not want to collect my soul, I have a date with Danny, a beautiful, romantic candlelit meal at our favourite local restaurant, just the two of us... and it's going to be perfect.

10

Tristan

"Oh my god, Danny, I am so sorry. That was such a disaster." I trip through the front door of the flat and toss my keys at the bowl on the table. They miss entirely and skid across the polished wood, landing on the floor. "We'll be lucky if they don't ban us for life, and I really liked that restaurant too." I kick off my boots and stomp into the living room with a pout.

Danny calmly hangs his jacket up by the door and takes his shoes off, setting them neatly by the front door before wandering into the living room with an amused smile.

"Well, that was an interesting evening." He chuckles. "It's never boring with you, Tris."

My eyes skim over the large red wine stain spreading from his chest all the way to his groin and then take in his tie, which is blackened and singed on the end, before travelling up to the clump of butter in his usually pristine blonde hair.

"Oh yeah, it's all fun and games until someone loses a limb," I huff.

"Well, you needn't worry." He wanders over and runs his

hands down my arms comfortingly. "All my limbs are still intact."

He leans in and brushes his lips across mine, and I sigh loudly.

"Sometimes I don't know why you put up with me."

"No putting up required." He slips his fingers under my chin and tilts my face up so my eyes meet his. "Tris, you're perfect just the way you are." His lips curve slowly. "Even when you're trying to set fire to our favourite restaurant."

"Oh god." I close my eyes briefly as my cheeks heat with embarrassment. "Clearly, I cannot be trusted with candles."

"I'm only disappointed that they didn't need to call the fire department. A bunch of hot firefighters would have just set the night off perfectly." He grins as he gives me a little playful tug.

"I'll try and organise some for your birthday then." I can't help the smile hovering at my lips. "You know"—I reach up and loosen the wreck of his tie, sliding it from his collar and dropping it to the floor—"we never did get to have dessert." I unbutton his soaked shirt slowly.

"We barely got a main course, to be fair," he murmurs, his eyes dancing as he watches me.

"And I feel I should make that up to you." I push his wine-stained shirt from his shoulders, skimming my palms over his pecs, and my fingers drag through his hairy chest and downward while I inhale the scent of the wine on his skin. "I bet you taste yummy." I unbuckle his belt and lower the zip on his trousers.

"I have it on good authority that the wine was an excellent vintage," Danny gasps as I trail my tongue down his torso and hook my thumbs into his trousers, dragging them and his boxers down his thighs.

I pause long enough to press my nose into the hair nestled at the base of his cock, breathing in the arousing scent of him. Before he has a chance to get hard, I slide my lips over his soft cock, fully engulfing him in my mouth. I don't know why, but I love the feel of him growing in my mouth, it turns me on.

He lets out a quiet gasp of pleasure and leans his head back as I begin to slide my lips up and down the length of him with a hum of happiness in my throat. God, he tastes so good. My hands slide around to squeeze his bum cheeks, encouraging him to fuck into my mouth as I suck enthusiastically.

Suddenly a shrill scream splits the air, and I jolt abruptly. Danny seems completely unaware. I freeze, my eyes widening. If Danny didn't hear that scream, that can mean only one thing.

My mouth falls open and his dick falls from my lips. I swallow tightly as I slowly lean to the side, peering around Danny's hip. My gaze lands on Dusty as she holds her hand over Mrs Abernathy's eyes while trying and failing to hide a smirk.

I squeak loudly and grab two cushions from the sofa, using one to cover Danny's naked arse and one to cover his erect cock.

"Er, Tris, what are you doing?" Danny looks down at me in bewilderment.

I stand quickly, still holding the cushions against his body. "There's a draught and I wouldn't want you to catch a cold in your extremities."

"Actually, my extremities were quite warm and snuggly where they were," he replies as I start towing him out of the living room.

"Well you know, Jacob Marley is skulking around here somewhere, and I wouldn't want him to get jealous and scratch anything important." I shuffle him toward the bedroom, his trousers still pooled around his ankles.

"I'm sure he won't care." Danny frowns as we pass Dusty and Mrs Abernathy.

"Tris, honey," Dusty calls out wickedly. "You've got a little something right here." She taps the corner of her lip, and I swear I'd flip her the finger if I wasn't still clutching the two sofa cushions to my boyfriend's naked parts.

I shove Danny unceremoniously into the bedroom and slam the door behind us to the ringing of Dusty's throaty laughter. Slumping against the door, I risk a glance at my confused boyfriend standing at the foot of the bed, completely naked but for the cushion he's taken over holding in front of his dick and the trousers pooling around his ankles.

"Okay, what is going on?" he asks.

I literally don't have any kind of answer for him that won't sound completely bonkers, so I go with plan B... Strip immediately.

My clothes go flying and Danny's brows rise, his hot blue gaze dragging over my naked skin. I launch myself at him, wrapping my legs around his waist and toppling him back onto the bed as he drops the cushion.

My mouth lands on his as my fingers slide into his hair and grip tightly. I may have catapulted myself at him as a distraction, but, as always, the taste of him is utterly addictive. I moan deeply into his mouth and grind my aching cock against his.

I feel his arms wrap around me and drag me even closer as we rut against each other, moaning loudly. I completely forget about my dead houseguests in the other room. I don't care if they hear as long as they're not looking at my boyfriend's goodies.

"Danny." I pull my mouth from his, panting heavily as I flip myself around to lay against his stomach and plant my head between his spread thighs. I dive in and swallow his cock, devouring him like I need the taste of him more than oxygen.

A moment later he lifts my hips and plants my knees on either side of his head, and I feel his hot wet mouth close around my dick as he groans. Then he tilts his head back and slides my cock deeper, and I can't help the cry that tears from my throat, rippling around the mouthful of hot flesh I'm trying to inhale.

Hell, I am not going to last long. Danny is far too good at deep throating, which is why we don't sixty-nine often. I get too distracted by his talented mouth. Unable to help myself, I rock my hips, finding the perfect rhythm to fuck his mouth while I enjoy his cock in my mine. I reach down to cup and massage his balls.

Lightning races down my spine as I suddenly tense up and let go, coming so hard I'm practically seeing stars. Seconds later, Danny's cock is pulsing, filling my mouth as I swallow. I flop onto my side next to him and breathe heavily, my heart still pounding in my chest as he absently traces shapes on my thigh with his fingertips.

"Wow," I whisper in awe. "Your mouth, Danny... my balls are still tingling."

He chuckles softly. "You have a pretty talented mouth yourself."

"Well, aren't we just the perfect power couple." I grin and look down the length of the bed to see him smiling back at me.

He sits up, displacing me slightly as he kicks his trousers and boxers off his feet, and reaches to flip me around and pull me up beside him. We settle back onto the bed butt naked, our bodies and legs tangled intimately as he wraps his arms around me, and I run my fingers through his chest hair.

He hums contentedly, closing his eyes.

"Are you tired?" I murmur as I reach up and trace his brow. "I can't imagine you got much sleep last night with work."

"Actually I had a nap earlier," he admits sheepishly as he opens his eyes, his cheeks flushed as he looks down at me. "With your dad."

"My dad?" I choke out a laugh. "Should I be jealous?"

A warm laugh rumbles through his chest. "I had to go to the home earlier with Maddie because we had a member of staff we needed to interview. There was a thunderstorm at the time, and Lois found me, said the storm was scaring your dad, so I went in to check on him. We ended up curled up on the sofa reading Harry Potter, but I must have been more tired than I thought because the next thing I knew I was out for the count."

"You fell asleep hugging my dad while trying to comfort him during a thunderstorm?" I smile widely. "You're too cute."

"I'm not." He frowns. "I thought we'd had this conversation. I'm very rugged and manly."

"Like I said… cute." I lean in and kiss him softly. "Thank you for taking care of him."

He nods and we once again lapse into a comfortable silence as we naked-snuggle.

"Tris?" Danny mumbles after a while.

"Yes?" I shift my head against his chest to look up into his eyes.

"Does Martin's dementia usually include hallucinations?" he asks.

I frown. "Not that I know of, why?"

"It's just… nothing… never mind."

"No"—I prop myself up on one elbow and gaze down at him—"What?"

"It's just, when we were sitting on the sofa, the thunder was so loud it sounded like it was almost on top of us, but your dad didn't even flinch. He was really unsettled, scared even, but I don't think it was the storm frightening him."

"What else could it have been?" I ask.

"He was watching the corner of the room, and I could've sworn he was seeing something I couldn't. I wondered if maybe his condition sometimes means he sees things that aren't there."

"I don't think so, but maybe we should keep an eye on him."

"Who knows, maybe he was looking at a ghost." He chuckles.

"Imagine that," I murmur awkwardly.

"Tris?" He trails his fingers lightly up and down my back.

"Yes?"

"What's going on with you?" he asks. "You've been out of sorts lately."

I settle back against his chest, remaining quiet for a moment, twirling imaginary circles through his chest hair while I contemplate how much I can actually tell him. Obviously, telling him a dead lady is wandering around my flat or that I seem to keep running into a scary dementor-shaped soul collector is out of the question.

"Tris?" he says and I feel his heartbeat under my cheek. "You can talk to me if something's bothering you."

"I don't know," I reply. "I've got a lot of stuff rattling around my brain lately. I guess Mrs Abernathy dying kind of reminded me I'm on borrowed time with Dad. I also can't believe someone would deliberately poison her. She was a harmless little old lady who didn't deserve what happened to her."

"No, she didn't." Danny strokes my back contemplatively. "There are some bad people out there."

"I had a bad dream last night." I glance up at him. "At least, I think it was a bad dream. I don't remember what it was about, I just remember how it made me feel."

"How was that?"

"Unsettled... This is probably going to sound pathetic and I'm undoubtedly going to regret saying it, but when I woke up... all I wanted was you." I huff slightly. "That sounds really childish when I say it out loud."

"Hey." His arms tighten around me. "I'm sorry I wasn't here."

"Oh, don't pay any attention to me. I'm just in a weird head-space today," I brush it off, suddenly embarrassed at sounding so needy. I guess seeing that reaper shook me more than I thought, but I can't tell Danny that. I'm probably sounding like a whiney, clingy boyfriend right now.

"Tristan," he says suddenly. "I wanted... there's something I've been meaning to talk to you about... to ask you."

"What?" I bite my lip, wondering if I've been a bit too Tristan for him lately. I know I'm a lot to deal with, even for his practically limitless patience.

"I was just thinking, I don't know if it might be too soon, or you might not want to... but I was wondering–"

He's cut off when my phone rings loudly from the pocket of my jeans.

"I should get that," I say uncertainly. I want to know what it is that has him looking so nervous, but I can't ignore my phone in case it's something to do with my dad.

"It's fine." Danny releases his hold on me, and I roll out of bed. Grabbing my briefs off the floor, I slide them on, then pick up my skinny jeans, which are currently inside out and half balled-up. Fumbling in the pocket, I manage to retrieve my phone before it rings off. Glancing at the screen, I realise it's not the home. It's Mrs Abernathy's niece, Larry. I note the time on my phone and I'm a little concerned as to why she's calling so late.

I hit connect. "Hey, Larry."

"Hi, Tristan," she replies a little uncertainly. "I hope you don't mind me calling."

"Of course I don't." I sit on the edge of the bed as Danny watches me. He grabs the covers and pulls them over himself as if she can somehow see he's naked. It's kind of cute, actually. "What can I do for you?"

"I... well, it's about Aunt Delores. I don't really have anyone to talk to about her."

"Is your mother still on her cruise?" I ask, wondering how it's possible that Larry's mother doesn't seem to care that her sister was murdered.

"Yes," Larry replies with a sigh. "She's somewhere in the Baltics, I think." She goes quiet for a moment. "Oh god, I've just realised what the time is. I'm sorry for calling you so late. I've been doing so many shifts at weird hours lately, I've lost track of my days. I can call you back tomorrow."

"No, it's fine," I assure her.

"The reason I'm calling is because Mum isn't coming back for the funeral, so I'm just going to go ahead with it because I don't like the idea of Aunt Delores lying in some funeral home somewhere."

"Of course you don't," I say gently. "You need closure."

"Yes, I guess that's it." She blows out a breath. "I feel like she's in limbo, that she can't be at rest until she's had a funeral."

I wish it was that simple. Thank goodness Larry doesn't actually know the truth about her aunt being trapped here until she resolves her unfinished business.

"Do you need some help organising the funeral?"

"That's very kind of you, but actually it's already organised. It's going to be just a small gathering, and I was just wondering if you would come, maybe bring Martin?"

"Dad doesn't do well with a change of environment, so I won't be able to bring him, but I'll come."

"You will?" She breathes out in relief and I get the distinct impression there aren't going to be many people there.

"Of course I will," I tell her sincerely.

"It's the day after tomorrow. I'll send you the details," she says, her voice a little lighter now.

"Okay then," I reply. "Call me if I can help with anything."

"I will."

After we exchange goodbyes and hang up, I turn to Danny. "Larry asked if I could go to Mrs Abernathy's funeral. I get the feeling there aren't going to be many people there."

"Do you want me to go with you?" he asks.

"You wouldn't mind?"

"Not at all. It's not the first time I've attended the funeral for a murder victim."

"Oh... right... the investigation." I don't know why I suddenly feel disappointed. What is wrong with me? My moods are just all over the place at the moment.

"I didn't mean it like that." Danny reaches for my hand. "I just—" he breaks off and my worry returns full force. It's never this awkward between us.

"You wanted to ask me something before we were interrupted?" My stomach gives a nervous roll as I remind him of our conversation.

"Yes, I did." He draws in a deep breath. "I don't know if you want to, or you think it might be too soon, but when you started talking about your lease on your flat expiring and finding a new place to live... well I wondered if you might... maybe want to move in... with me... together.. the both of us."

My heart skips a beat. This wasn't what I was expecting him to say, but a lovely warmth starts spreading through me until I'm sure I'm glowing like a Roman candle. "You want me to move into your flat?"

"No... I mean yes, I want us to move in together, but not in my flat. I thought we could get somewhere new, somewhere that would be ours," he explains hurriedly. "I know we've only been together for six months and some people might think that's too soon." He continues to speak quickly, as if the faster he talks the less chance I have to say no. Like that's going to happen. Something exciting is dancing in my stomach as he offers me everything I've been thinking about for the past several days. Of course, it might just be hunger pangs because we didn't get to actually eat dinner, but regardless, I can't stop the slow grin spreading across my face.

"What do you think?" he asks nervously, which is adorable.

"Just to clarify," I say as I feel the tension seep out of my body and confidence replace it. "You want to live with me even though I almost set fire to you, practically drowned you in red wine, and accidentally flung a butter knife at your head."

He shrugs. "I'm willing to take my chances. So..."

"So?" I toss my phone down and launch myself at him, kissing him wildly as we fall back on the bed. "I... think... it's... perfect." I punctuate each word with a kiss as he laughs against my mouth. I pull back to stare into those deep blue eyes. "I'd love to live with you."

His smile is like the sun dawning after an endless night and it's everything.

"How did I get so lucky?" I murmur as I study his face.

"I believe some things are just meant to be, Tristan." He pulls me close. "I don't know that I've ever believed in fate, but I think you and I were meant to find each other because nothing else in my life has ever felt this right. I don't think we have to question it, we only need to feel it."

His hand slides up my back, grasping the nape of my neck as I lean in and press my lips to his. This time, the kiss is slow and deep, filled with promise and such an innate sense of rightness. I could kiss him for hours like this, until the end of time even, but eventually I pull back with a sigh and press my forehead to his.

"I love you," I whisper.

"I love you too," he replies in a low sleepy rumble as I slide down and rest my face on his chest so I can once again listen to his steady heartbeat.

The tension is all but gone, replaced with the excitement and knowledge of what Danny and I are building together, but somewhere, deep down beneath it all, a restless thought stirs.

How on earth am I going to explain to him that I see dead people?

11

Tristan

I stand staring at my reflection as I carefully adjust my skinny black tie to the right length and smooth down my blazer. I'm still wearing my black skinny jeans but given the formal and sombre nature of the occasion, I've switched out my beloved Doc Martens for black shoes. I've tried to tame my wild hair somewhat, but the dark curls just like to do their own thing, so I've given up.

"Well don't you look handsome, boo," I hear Dusty behind me and turn.

"Why do you look like Bette Midler?" I stare at her. "It's like the funeral scene from *Beaches*."

She's wearing a tight-fitting pencil skirt that ends below under her knees, with skinny heeled black Louboutins like Chan would wear. She has a matching fitted jacket with black gloves. On her head is the widest brimmed black hat I've ever seen, it's like a sombrero on steroids. Seriously, it should come with its own postcode. She's pulled a lacy black net over her face and is holding a pristine white handkerchief pressed into a neat triangle.

"What?" she asks innocently.

"How on earth do you fit through doorways with that thing? It's like the whole top section of the Space Needle in Seattle."

I shouldn't really be surprised, it's relatively tame considering some of the outrageous hats and outfits I'd seen at Dusty's funeral.

"Darling, I can walk through walls. I really don't think it's going to be a problem." Dusty flips her blonde curls over her shoulder.

"Just try not to knock Mrs Abernathy out with that thing." My gaze lands on the little old lady hovering at Dusty's side.

"Where's Detective Hot and Handsome?" Dusty asks, looking for Danny.

"Working." I check my phone before slipping it in my pocket. "He said both him and Maddie would meet me there."

"I suppose it makes sense they'd go to Delores' funeral given that they're in charge of the investigation."

"Larry's afraid there won't be many people there," I say quietly as I watch Mrs Abernathy stare aimlessly at my bedside lamp while she hums to herself.

Dusty opens her mouth to say something but stops abruptly when the doorbell rings out loudly throughout the flat. "Are you expecting anyone?"

"No." I shake my head in confusion as I head out of my bedroom toward the front door.

I don't usually get any visitors unless it's Danny or the deceased, and they tend to just wander straight in. Although, saying that, I remember one other person who stops by and that's–

"Chan," I exclaim in surprise as I open the door.

This is the first time I've seen her looking... well... not like herself. In fact, this is the first time I've seen Chan looking more like a he than a she—a very pretty he, but a he nonetheless.

Usually, when Chan's up on stage, she's in full drag persona and looks incredible, but all the other times we've met, she's been in a fitted dress and heels with immaculate makeup, looking impossibly elegant and very feminine.

Now Chan stands on my doorstep in slim black trousers and shiny black patent loafers, wearing a black t-shirt with a silver design on the front and a black jacquard blazer. That gorgeous hair, usually spilling down her back in an inky water-fall is tied up on top of her head in a messy bun and she's wearing no make-up except for a little mascara and lip gloss.

"Uh-oh." Dusty winces. "If Chan's wearing trousers and"— she glances at those shiny black loafers—"flats, that can only mean he's feeling out of sorts. Chan is genderfluid, but I could always tell where his head's at by whether he's looking more masc or fem."

I nod slightly so Dusty knows I understand. "Chan, is every-thing okay?" I ask in concern.

He sails through the door and into the living room like he's walking the catwalk and throws himself onto the sofa with a huff.

I glance down at my watch. I don't want to be late for the funeral when Larry specifically asked me to come, but it's clear something's going on with Chan.

"Chan?" I ask tentatively.

"It's my birthday today," he declares with a huff, and I glance up sharply at Dusty, who just looks sad.

"Why didn't you say your birthday was coming up? We had coffee last week," I ask Chan with a frown.

He shrugs, picking a piece of imaginary lint from his trousers. "I swear I woke up this morning with several new grey hairs and two new wrinkles."

"Chan..." I take a seat next to him. "You don't have any grey, and I can't see a single wrinkle, you know you look amazing. What's really wrong?"

He lets out a slow breath. "This is the first time in twenty years I've not celebrated with Dusty." Chan's words mirror the sadness in Dusty's eyes. "Last year we both turned thirty and we had a blast and I just..." He breaks off and swallows tightly, his eyes glossy as he shakes his head. "We always make a big deal of birthdays at The Rainbow Room, but I just wasn't in the mood for it this year, so I got Ruby to cover my numbers later and I took the day off. I need some time to wallow, and I thought of you."

"Er... thanks?"

"You know what I mean." He sighs as he drops his head against the back of the sofa. "I miss Dusty."

I watch as Dusty kneels down in front of him, reaching out and touching his face lightly. Chan lifts his fingers to his face, lightly tracing the skin Dusty had just caressed.

"I know you're here," Chan whispers. "I wish I could see you... I would give anything to be able to hear your voice again."

"Me too," Dusty replies and I can see the longing in her eyes. "I miss holding you."

"She says she misses holding you."

"God, this is killing me, Tris." Chan blinks back the tears.

"Give yourself a break, Chan. It's only been six months, you and Dusty spent most of your lives together. I can only imagine how hard it is adjusting to losing the most important person in your life."

"It's even worse because I know she's right next to me, but I can't see or hear her," he laments.

"I know." I nod sympathetically, once again glancing down at my watch. "I'm really sorry, but I have somewhere I have to be, and I can't cancel, but I don't want to leave you like this."

"Where are you going?"

"To a funeral, the one for that old lady I told you about last week. Mrs Abernathy? It's her funeral today, and her niece, Larry–"

"Larry?"

"Clarissa," I explain. "But everyone calls her Larry. She asked if I would go because she's worried there won't be many people there, but I kinda feel like I should be going anyway, considering her aunt has been my houseguest since she died."

Chan shrugs. "Okay. Then I'll come."

"Where?"

"To the funeral."

"You want to come with me to the funeral of someone you've never met?" I blink slowly.

He shrugs again. "Wouldn't be the first time."

"I'm almost afraid to ask." I shake my head. "But you can't go to a funeral for your birthday."

"Sounds like it perfectly suits my mood."

"I really don't think you're in the right emotional headspace to go to a funeral right now."

"It's not like I could feel much worse than I already do," Chan replies nonchalantly. "Besides, I need a distraction."

"It's not just the funeral though. The wake after is being held at the community hall Mrs Abernathy used to frequent and where she was most likely poisoned."

"Oooh." Chan's eyes light up. "Then the murder suspect might be there!"

"It's possible," I muse. "But I'm totally staying out of it this time. Being shot at once was enough for me. I'm leaving the catching the killer part to Danny and his partner, Detective Wilkes. I'm just going to support Larry and hopefully figure out what Mrs Abernathy's unfinished business is so I can get her packed straight into the light on next day delivery."

"Oh come on, Tris!" Chan sits up. "We made such a good team last time."

"We almost got killed last time," I remind him.

"Pft." He waves his hand dismissively. "That nutjob had the aim of an Imperial stormtrooper, I doubt she'd have hit either one of us. Besides, what are the actual chances of that happening again? It's a community centre, it's full of pensioners."

"Whoa. Hold up there, Jessica Fletcher. It's not our job to run around randomly solving crimes."

"Come on, Tris. Please?" He gives me his most appealing smile.

He's perked up a bit since he first walked through the door, especially at the thought of playing junior detective, and I just don't have it in me to burst his bubble.

"Urgh... fine." I roll my eyes. "But only because I'm going to be late." I stand up and pull my phone from my pocket to order an Uber.

"Yes!" Chan jumps to his feet. "This is just what I need as a distraction. We'll figure out who the murderer is, just like a game of Cluedo but real life. I feel like I need a cover story... ooh, you could tell them I'm one of your colleagues at the mortuary. I can be Dr Chan. "

"No," I reply.

"But it's my birthday," he says winsomely, fluttering his eyelashes at me again.

"I feel like you're enjoying this way too much, Dr Chan." I sigh as I head toward the door with him following behind me triumphantly.

Larry was right, there are barely a handful of people scattered throughout the first couple of rows of the crematorium. The officiant drones on as he stands at the little podium to the side of Mrs Abernathy's coffin, which is mounted on a platform and framed by heavy velvet curtains. They are the most unattractive shade of pink ever, a kind of mauve, the bastard child of pink and grey, and depressing as hell. We are supposed to be in a chapel of rest but all that colour is doing is making me more anxious.

I feel a strange prickling at the back of my neck and turn to look at the rows of empty seats behind me. There's no one there, just sprays of plastic flowers mounted either side of the closed doors. I feel Danny's hand on my thigh as he gives a comforting little squeeze, drawing my attention to him.

"Are you okay?" he whispers and I nod. "Tell me again what Chan is doing here?"

"He stopped by this morning and decided to tag along," I say as quietly as possible. Danny raises a brow, possibly at my choice of pronoun as, like me, he's only ever seen Chan looking very fem, but this isn't really the time or place to explain.

Even though the officiant at the front is tied up in a rather long-winded soliloquy on God working in mysterious ways and how he called Mrs Abernathy home to walk in his light or something—I don't know, I'm really not paying attention because in actual fact he hasn't called her anywhere. She's still wandering around the chapel clutching her handbag in her bony hands and randomly staring at people.

"Decided to tag along?" Danny repeats slowly.

I shrug. "You know what they say, the more the merrier."

"I'm not sure that applies to funerals." Danny fights a smile.

Chan leans over and whispers in my ear. "Hey, what's up with Barbara Cartland over there?" He nods toward the second row of seats on the opposite side of the room. "Is she having a stroke or something?"

I glance across to see Ivy, one of Mrs Abernathy's friends from the community centre, fluttering her heavy fake lashes as she winks at Danny and puckers her neon pink lips. She's wearing a lilac monstrosity of a dress with chiffon ruffles around the neck and wrists, and her hair is backcombed so high it makes her head look like a stick of candy floss.

"I think you've got an admirer." Maddie elbows Danny in amusement from where she sits on the other side of him at the end of the pew, having also caught sight of Ivy's interest.

Danny glances over and gives Ivy a strained smile, but I know I'm not imagining him sliding closer to me on the wooden bench.

Ivy's eyes slide over to Maddie, giving the fiery red-haired detective a thorough appraisal before pouting sourly, and I wonder if she actually remembers Danny is not only gay but also my boyfriend.

My gaze tracks along the bench on the opposite side of the room, cataloguing the motley crew of potentially murderous old ladies, and I just can't see it. They're quirky, there's no doubting that, but I just don't think any of them would murder their friend. I mean, there doesn't even seem to be a motive as far as I can tell.

Nope. Not my circus, not my monkeys. I'm here to support Larry and figure out Mrs Abernathy's unfinished business. I am not getting drawn into another murder investigation. That's my boyfriend's department.

I'm randomly staring at the coffin when I see Mrs Abernathy cross my field of vision and head for the pine box decorated with a spray of white carnations and lilies. She stops at the end of the coffin, probably not even realising her earthly remains are inside and about to be toasted like a marshmallow. Leaning in closer, she studies the framed photograph Larry had chosen. Instead of one taken later on in life, it's the beautiful black and white portrait taken during the war that I saw of her at Larry's house, with Mrs Abernathy not much older than eighteen and wearing her WRN uniform.

She studies it for a moment before turning and calling out. "Beau?" She shuffles around the coffin. "Beau?"

"Please rise as our dear departed sister is received into the loving arms of Christ," the officiant says sombrely, and we all stand, accompanied by the sound of creaking benches.

I realise that, while I was distracted, we've reached the part of the service where the coffin will slide through the curtain behind it, bound for the furnace, and the last thing I want is Mrs Abernathy following it. I glance across to Dusty in alarm, but she's already on her feet and heading towards the old lady.

"No, Delores, honey." Dusty firmly takes her hand, using the same tone of voice one uses when dealing with a toddler. "Why don't we go and have a look at the pretty flowers outside?"

"Beau?" Mrs Abernathy asks hopefully.

"Uh, sure." Dusty throws me a look and shrugs.

As Dusty takes the old woman and disappears through the wall in the direction of the remembrance garden, I'm more convinced than ever that the mysterious Beau is Mrs Abernathy's unfinished business somehow. I look across to Trudy, the ringleader of the Clapham Senior Ladies Social Circle. I'm sure she knows more than she's letting on. If she's known Mrs Abernathy for as long as she says she has, I'm hoping she can at least give me a second name for the handsome G.I. Mrs Abernathy met, and I suspect fell in love with, during the war.

Although, even if he's by some miracle still alive, he's probably in the States, which presents a whole new set of problems. I really am not sure how I'm going to get Mrs Abernathy's unfinished business resolved at all.

The gloomy notes of the hymn Abide with Me begin to spill through the speakers surrounding us as Larry sobs into her hankie. I see Trudy wrap her arm around the devastated woman's shoulders and my heart breaks for her, not just that she's grieving her beloved aunt's passing, but that her mother couldn't be bothered to cut her holiday short to attend.

The coffin slowly begins to slide backwards, disappearing through the discreet curtained alcove while the curtains close in front. There's a few moments of standing awkwardly before the funeral assistant opens the doors which lead out onto a covered patio, where the few wreaths and flower arrangements sent for Mrs Abernathy have been arranged for viewing.

We all solemnly shuffle through the doors and out into the fresh air.

"Tristan!"

I turn around to see Larry making her way over to me, her nose red and her eyes watery, but she manages a weak smile as she stops in front of me.

"Hello, Larry." I smile in sympathy. "How are you holding up?"

"Better." She blows out a breath and wipes her nose on a scruffy piece of tissue. "It was hard, you know, saying goodbye, but I feel like I have some kind of closure. I know that we still don't know who killed her or why, and of course I want to know, I want justice for her, but it's nice to know she's no longer locked inside her mind. That she's free now."

My gaze momentarily flicks to the dead old lady about to wander into the brick boundary wall and disappear from sight until Dusty stops her and turns her around, letting her meander off in the opposite direction.

Yeah not so much, I think to myself, but of course, I can't say that to Larry. I'm glad that thinking Mrs Abernathy has moved on to a better place is giving her peace of mind amidst a murder investigation, even if it isn't true.

"Hmmm." I watch as Larry turns her attention to Danny and Maddie.

"Detective Wilkes, Detective Hayes." She smiles. "Thank you for taking the time to come."

"Of course," Danny says politely. "And I'd like to assure you we're doing everything we can with regards to the investigation."

Larry nods as her gaze falls on Chan. "I don't think we've met," she says. "Did you know my aunt?"

"Unfortunately, no." Chan dazzles Larry with his smile and offers his hand. "Dr Chan. I work with Tristan at the mortuary."

I chance a quick glance in Danny's direction as he lifts his brow at the blatant lie.

"Oh well." Larry blushes as she takes his hand, and I don't blame her. However he identifies on any given day, Chan is stunningly gorgeous. "Thank you for coming."

"My deepest condolences," Chan replies.

"Are you all joining us at the community centre?" she asks.

"Yes." I nod, trying to keep an eye on Dusty and Mrs Abernathy, who've disappeared from view again. "Um... did you need a lift to Clapham?" I turn my attention back to Larry.

She shakes her head. "No need. I'm going with Trudy and the other ladies, we're going to split a couple of taxis." She excuses herself and hurries away.

"Dr Chan?" Danny turns toward Chan. "You do know it's illegal to impersonate a doctor? And that you're standing in front of two police officers?"

"What can I say?" He gives an impish smirk. "I like to live life on the edge. Besides, it's only illegal if you're offering medical services. Anyone can call themselves doctor. It's not like I'm performing surgeries or giving medical advice unless it's how to treat personal itching in your downstairs department. Which I'd like to add, is not from personal experience, but let's just say some of the ladies at The Rainbow Room are not as discerning as I am when it comes to their choice of bed partners, naming no names... Brandy..." He coughs into his fist on the last word.

"I don't even want to know." I shake my head and roll my eyes as he links his arm through mine. "Feeling better?"

"Actually, yes. Thank you for asking," Chan says. "Who knew all it would take is a funeral?"

"I think it's less the funeral and more the company," Danny rumbles, watching Chan fondly. I know he has a massive soft spot for the beautiful drag queen. "Tristan is always good at cheering people up, even if he doesn't realise he's doing it."

"That's because he's such a sweetie." Chan squeezes my arm. "And you're right. I just don't think I could deal with all the bitchiness and drama at the club today. I needed to be around people who are less high maintenance."

"Well, I'm glad we were here to bore you." I snort quietly. "Come on, let's get to Clapham before one of the old ladies asks you to look at their bunions, Dr Chan."

Chan gags and I chuckle as we head toward the cars, even as I wonder where on earth Dusty and Mrs Abernathy have disappeared to.

12

Tristan

The community centre is actually much busier than I thought it would be given the limited number of people who actually attended the funeral, but as Danny, Chan, and I weave through the tables after Maddie begged off with more work, I realise why.

Larry hasn't hired out the whole of the community hall for her aunt's wake. Instead, it's still open to the public but with a small corner sectioned off and labeled private.

They've made an effort, bless them. The Formica tables with folding legs are covered with white tablecloths—okay, they're paper, but they hide the worst of the scratches and dents, and there are about five tables out for them, all set with afternoon tea.

On each table is a little ceramic vase with plastic daisies in it from Home Bargains, and I know that for certain because as we take a seat at the nearest table, I can see someone has left the label on. There are also tiered china cake stands filled with plump scones, slices of Victoria sponge, prettily iced fairy cakes, and rich-looking chunks of chocolate brownies.

"Oh yes, now you're talking." Chan rubs his hands together gleefully. "I see a chocolate brownie with my name on it."

"No," Danny whispers. "Don't eat anything, just in case."

"Seriously?" Chan whines, eyeing up the brownies.

"It's probably fine, but I'd prefer if you both didn't risk it," he says firmly.

"What about tea?" I turn to Danny. "Can we at least have a cup of tea?"

He glances over at the large metal urn of hot water and the teacups lined up in a military-like fashion.

"Okay, but only as long as you've made it yourself," Danny concedes.

"Christ, I never thought I'd have to worry about my drink being spiked by a bunch of OAPs. It's like a bloody Agatha Christie novel," Chan mutters. "I'm going to grab something from the vending machine in the foyer."

He slides out of his chair and disappears back through the doors. I'm still busy scanning the room to see if Dusty and Mrs Abernathy are here, but I can't see them anywhere. In fact, I haven't seen them since the garden of remembrance at the crematorium.

"Here you go." I look up as Danny sets a cup of tea in front of me and places his own down next to it as he takes a seat.

A few seconds later, Chan sits down on the opposite side of me and cracks open a can of Diet Coke. "Okay, there wasn't a lot to choose from, the machine needs refilling... pick one." He holds up a pack of individually wrapped biscuits in one hand and a Mars bar in the other.

"Thanks." I reach for the biscuits and set them next to my tea.

"Do you really think one of those old ladies poisoned the old girl? What's her name again?" Chan mumbles around a mouthful of chocolate and caramel.

"Delores Abernathy." Danny stirs his tea thoughtfully. "And

no, not necessarily. We're just taking precautions. All we know right now is that the poisoning most likely occurred during her visits here. We've more or less ruled out her carers and anyone at the home, but here it could be anyone. Staff, visitors... even one of her so-called friends."

"It's a bit weird though, isn't it?" Chan wrinkles his nose. "Poison... I mean why would you? If you want someone dead, there's loads of easier ways to kill someone."

"Why do people even kill in the first place?" Danny shrugs. "Sometimes we never get to understand the thought process behind why someone commits murder and even less why they choose a certain method."

"But no one else has been affected though?" I turn to look at Danny. "So far it's only Mrs Abernathy that was showing signs of poisoning?"

He nods. "That's right. Other than one other person we suspect may have been poisoned by accident when she ate something that was intended for Delores. There's been no other cases of arsenic poisoning."

"That means it had to be someone she knew, doesn't it?"

"Most likely."

"Oh good, you're already here," a loud voice exclaims, followed by the chatter of several others, and I turn in my seat to see Trudy and Larry approaching the table, followed by the Clapham Senior Ladies Social Circle.

"Sorry it took us so long to get here, we had to wait for Aunt Delores," Larry says slightly out of breath.

"You had to wait for–" I stop mid-sentence when Larry sets an urn down in the middle of the table.

Chan pauses with his Coke halfway to his mouth and blinks slowly. "Is that what I think it is?"

"Aunt Delores." Larry pats the lid of the urn with a sad sigh of affection. "We thought she'd like one more afternoon tea with the ladies before we scatter her ashes over the rosebushes."

Chan shoots me a look and I shrug.

"Uh, that's... nice," I manage, eyeing the urn sandwiched between the vase of plastic daisies and the fairy cakes.

"Oh for heaven's sake, move out of the way, Violet," Ivy huffs. "I swear you're slower than a snail."

"What's that? You've spotted a whale?" Violet yells back. "But we're nowhere near the sea!"

Ivy rolls her eyes and shoves Phyllis aside in order to plant herself firmly in the seat next to Danny, giving him a coy flutter of her eyelashes.

I watch as Vera settles into the seat beside Chan and retrieves her knitting from a large Sainsbury's shopping bag. The fat wooden knitting needles start clicking together almost immediately as she continues to add to the giant multicoloured and shapeless lump she's creating.

"What is that?" Chan whispers to me. "It looks like she's knitting a full-body condom." I snort softly into my tea as I raise it to my lips and sip. "Bloody hell, it's the Trunchbull from Matilda." Chan's eyes widen as they land on Birdie, who has taken a seat beside Vera and is trying to avoid being accidentally impaled on her clacking needles. Birdie casts a steely eye in Chan's direction, whose eyes are fixed grimly on the old woman's ginormous mole which is sprouting several long wiry hairs.

"Jesus, has she never heard of tweezers," Chan mutters.

As Phyllis and Maeve take their seats, Trudy nods in approval. "Make yourselves comfortable, ladies. I'll organise the tea."

"Where's the redhead who was with you at the funeral, handsome?" Ivy leans over and purrs.

"She had to return to work," Danny says politely.

"Her loss." Ivy winks. "I wouldn't ever leave my man unattended if he looked like you."

Danny shakes his head. "We're not involved like that. Tristan here is my boyfriend." He reaches for my hand.

"Funny name, isn't it? Princeton," Violet shouts across the table at me. "Are you American?"

"Tristan," I yell, correcting her.

"There's no need to shout, dear," Violet huffs.

"The red-haired lady is Detective Hayes' partner, Detective Wilkes," Larry says to Ivy. "They're both running the investigation into Aunt Delores' murder."

"Old Bill, eh?" Birdie eyes him suspiciously.

"That's right," Danny replies.

Last time we were here, he wanted to fly under the radar to see if he could get a handle on who Delores' friends were and how they interacted, but now I see him studying each of their faces carefully. He seems to have changed his strategy.

"Poor Delores," Maeve says primly, folding her hands in her lap. "It's all very sad."

"It was a blessing if you ask me," Birdie huffs. "Don't get me wrong. I liked her, but it's no kind of life, is it? Being locked inside your mind. It was a mercy killing if you ask me. At least now she's at rest. No offence, Larry."

Larry looks at her miserably.

"For goodness sake, Birdie," Phyllis snaps. "Keep your opinions to yourself. Have a little tact, will you? She's sitting right there."

I, of course, glance around, expecting to see Mrs Abernathy come wandering along, one hand clutched in Dusty's, until I realise Phyllis isn't some sort of psychic but is actually talking about the creepy-looking urn on the table.

"Here we go, ladies." Trudy sets a large teapot down on the table as one of the community centre helpers adds plates and teacups, a sugar bowl, and a small jug of milk. "Help yourselves."

There's a slight lull in the conversation and the subtle chink of china as teacups are filled and brownies and scones devoured.

"If you'll excuse me for a moment," Larry says as she spots someone trying to get her attention. "I really should say thank you to the others who came."

"So, had you all known Delores long?" Danny asks as Larry heads toward another table.

"Years," Ivy declares. "She wasn't always like that. The dementia got a lot worse in those last few years, didn't it?"

Trudy nods as she bites into a brownie.

"She was such a clever thing," Phyllis muses while sipping her tea. "And always had a kind word for everyone. That is, until she deteriorated so much she couldn't really hold a conversation. Just kind of sat there, had to have a carer with her at all times or she'd just wander off."

"Yes, very sad," Vera murmurs to the *click clack* of her knitting needles.

"So she didn't have any enemies? Anyone who might wish her harm?" Danny inquires conversationally.

"Good lord, no." Trudy wipes the crumbs from her fingers on a paper napkin. "Everyone loved Delores."

"Clearly not everyone"—Chan raises a brow—"or she wouldn't be dead."

I give him a discreet elbow.

"What?" He mouths silently.

"Honestly"—Trudy waves her hand—"I can't imagine anyone wanting to kill Delores."

"Maybe it was the government," Birdie says, tapping the side of her nose and winking.

"The what?" I stare at her in disbelief.

"The government." Ivy nods sagely. "Delores was one of

those code-breakers when she was younger, wasn't she? Then after the war, she worked for the Ministry of Defence... never did say what it was she did for them."

"That was because she'd signed the Official Secrets Act," Trudy replies as she leans back in her chair.

"Exactly!" Ivy exclaims in triumph. "I bet she was a spy."

"Did someone say pie?" Violet looks up hopefully. "Yes, please, with custard. Tastes bloody awful with ice cream."

"I bet someone bumped her off because she knew too many secrets," Ivy says to Danny, ignoring Violet. She sidles up closer to him and he, in turn, edges towards me.

"Don't be ridiculous." Trudy snorts, sliding further down in her chair. "She hasn't worked for the government in nearly thirty years. Why on earth would they want to finish her off now?"

"Because she was losing her marbles." Ivy blinks owlishly and leans in closer like she can't quite focus. "Never know what secrets she might've accidentally spilled."

"Losing?" Birdie cackles. "Lost her marbles, more like." She smacks her lips. "I'm hungry. Is anyone else hungry?"

Danny tries to interject some sense into the conversation. "I really don't think the government was responsible for Delores' death. Besides, I hardly think they'd use something as dated as arsenic."

There's a rustling sound beside me as Chan opens a packet of cheese and onion crisps, popping one in his mouth and grinning as his head bounces back and forth between everyone like he's watching a tennis match.

"That's exactly what they'd use to throw you off the scent," Birdie declares as her gaze lands on the crisp packet in Chan's hand.

"Hey!" Chan cries out, indignant, when Birdie plucks them out of his grasp and starts munching her way through the bag.

Danny shifts as his phone starts ringing in his pocket. "It's Maddie," he tells me. "I'd better take this."

I nod as he makes his way back through the room to the exit where it's quieter.

"Trudy," I call out to the woman now slumped down in her chair so far she's practically taking a nap.

"Hmm, yes?" She smiles beatifically.

I see my chance and I'm not about to let it pass me by. "Can I ask you a question about Delores during the war?"

"What do you want to know?" she replies. "I worked in one of the munitions factories because I wasn't as smart as Delores, so I don't know much about what she did, only that she moved around a lot." There almost seemed to be a hint of resentment in her tone, or maybe envy, but it's gone almost as soon as I notice it.

"It's not about that." I'm about to elaborate when Danny appears back at the table and leans over my shoulder.

"Tris," he whispers. "I'm really sorry but I need to go. Do you want me to give you a lift home?"

I glance at Trudy, who's still watching me.

"No, I'll stay a while." I pat his hand where it rests on my shoulder. "I'll head back with Chan."

"Are you sure you'll be alright here on your own?" He frowns in concern.

"Excuse me?" Chan wrinkles his nose in indignation. "And what am I? Just here for decoration?"

"No." Danny's mouth twitches. "Just try not to get into too much trouble, you two. I'm still traumatised from last time."

"Oh my god, are we never going to be allowed to live that down?" I roll my eyes. "It was hardly our fault."

"Fine. Call me if you need me." He drops a kiss on my cheek and from the corner of my eye, I see Ivy's gaze narrow in my direction. "And stay out of trouble."

"I make no promises," Chan replies breezily as Danny leaves.

"Trudy," I call out to her again, and for some reason she's now staring at her hands as if they're the most fascinating things in the world. "Er... Trudy?"

"Hmm." She blinks. "Sorry, dear. What were you saying?"

"I was just wondering, did Delores ever mention a man she met during the war? He would have been American, tall, handsome, dark hair. Someone she might have been involved with."

"How do you know about Beau?" She frowns in confusion. "Beau... Beau..." she makes an exaggerated 'o' shape with her mouth. "Such a pretty name for a man, don't you think?"

She's acting very strangely. Trudy is usually so eloquent and poised, but now her speech sounds a little slurred and she appears distracted, like her mind keeps wandering off on a tangent.

"Trudy?" I try to draw her attention back. "Can you tell me about Beau?"

"Delores was so in love with him... Beaumont Olsen, a gorgeous hunk of an American." Trudy sighs. "All the ladies had stars in their eyes for him, but he only had eyes for Delores."

"So they were in love?" I ask. That certainly explains a lot.

"Very much so." She sighs dramatically. "It's sooooo sad." Her bottom lip sticks out. "So very terribly sad."

"What's wrong with her?" Chan whispers and I shrug.

"I don't know," I mouth back, a bit perplexed.

"They were supposed to meet up after the war, you see, but they never did," Trudy says pensively.

Well, that would certainly explain the unfinished business.

"Trudy, why didn't they meet up?" I ask, afraid I already know the answer.

"He was killed," Trudy adds.

Shit.

How the hell am I supposed to help Delores resolve her unfinished business if Beau's already dead? Should I take her to his grave? Would that even work?

"They never recovered his body," Trudy continues.

Double shit.

"They wouldn't even tell us what happened." She blinks in my direction, and I don't think it's my imagination that her fucking pupils look huge. "Both he and Delores worked in intelligence for their respective countries, but every now and then there would be a joint intelligence-gathering task, that's how they met. They fell in love and promised to find each other after the war ended, but that never happened. After he was killed, many years after, Delores tried to petition the war office for information, but all they would say is that the plane he was on was shot down over the ocean. They wouldn't even say which ocean."

"That's so sad," I mutter. "She never knew what happened to him?"

"No." Trudy shakes her head. "So sad... so very terribly sad."

"Tristan?" Chan looks around at the other women at the table. "Do they look a bit... stoned?" He sniffs the air. "Can you smell weed?"

"Who peed?" Violet blinks and looks down. "Was it me?"

"God, I hope not." Chan wrinkles his nose as Kevin scurries over, looking decidedly harried and holding a Tupperware container that's empty but for a couple of brownie crumbs.

"Oh crap. Please tell me they didn't eat the brownies." He looks in horror at the brownie crumbs scattered across their empty plates.

"Well, no need to ask were the smell of weed's coming from." Chan blinks rapidly, pressing his fingers delicately to his nose.

"Are you okay?" I ask Chan. "Your eyes are watering."

"I'll be fine." He turns to look at Kevin, one of the community centre's regular helpers. "Please tell me you didn't just feed a load of OAPs pot brownies?"

"Not on purpose," Kevin hisses as he looks around nervously. "My friend gave them to me, and I left them in the kitchen in a bag to take home, but somehow they got mixed up with the cakes from the bakery and put out by mistake. Oh my god, I'm so sorry. If it helps, it's a really mild strain. They might get the munchies a bit, but they'll be fine after they sleep it off. I'll make sure someone keeps an eye on them."

"Jesus Christ," Chan snorts. "And I thought this was going to be a boring birthday."

Kevin hastily shoves the couple of remaining brownies from the cake stand into the box and hurries away.

"Oh! Sorry it took so long." I look across to see Dusty standing by the table breathing heavily and holding onto Delores for dear life, presumably to stop her wandering off again. "She's remarkably quick for someone so small. I had to chase her all the way to Hyde bloody Park." Dusty holds her stomach as if to catch her breath, even though technically she doesn't breathe.

I want to ask her what on earth they were doing in Hyde Park, miles away from where we were, but I can't with so many people about.

"I think I need one of those human dog lead things," Dusty decides.

"What?" I mouth discreetly in her direction.

"You know, those things they put on children to stop them wandering off." She fists her hand on her cocked hip as she glances down at Delores. "Honestly, you can't take your eye off her for a second. Now I know why she had three carers." She stops and leans in, looking closer at the pack of old ladies.

Vera is no longer furiously clacking away at her knitting and instead seems to be hyperfocused on just trying to wrap the yarn around one needle and hook it into a stitch. Birdie and Maeve are fighting over Chan's bag of crisps. Trudy is back to staring aimlessly at her hands. Phyllis has upended the sugar bowl onto the table and is sifting through it like she's looking for buried treasure, and Ivy seems to be taking a nap judging by the snores coming from her brightly painted but lax mouth.

"Holy fucking shit, are they stoned?" Dusty frowns. "I miss all the good stuff," she laments. "We're really going to have a long talk about this. I did not sign up for Nanny McPhee when I agreed to be a spirit guide."

Bollocks, this is not going well. I look up at Delores as she stands at Dusty's side. How the hell am I supposed to help her resolve her unfinished business? I literally don't have a clue. Beau's body is at the bottom of some ocean somewhere, and his spirit, I would hope, is somewhere in the light. If he's not, what are the actual chances of his disembodied spirit wandering aimlessly around Clapham? It's far more likely he's haunting his old stomping grounds somewhere in America. Meanwhile, I'm stuck with Mrs Abernathy who, even dead, requires more supervision than a hyperactive two-year-old.

My stomach gives a loud growl, and I absently reach for the sealed packet of biscuits Chan got me from the vending machine. Ripping it open, I shove one in my mouth and start chewing, regretting it the second I realise how dry they are.

"Well, I think this is an excellent time for me to go and powder my nose." Chan rises gracefully. "Do you know where the loos are?"

I can't swallow enough to make actual words, so I wave in the direction of the door leading out into the entrance foyer.

"Thanks, honey." Chan slaps me on the back as he walks past. Unfortunately, it has the unintended side effect of me drawing in a breath and inhaling dry biscuit crumbs.

I cough sharply, accidentally spraying biscuit crumbs over the table, not that anyone notices. No matter how much I try to catch my breath, I keep coughing and coughing until I feel like I'm going to hurl up a lung. Fumbling for any kind of liquid, my hand wraps around a cup—mine or Danny's, I'm not sure which and I don't really care. I gulp down the cold tea until the cup is almost empty, dragging in a loud breath with tears running down my cheeks as the coughing fit finally subsides.

"Are you alright, boo?" Dusty asks in amusement.

"Fine," I croak, realising a moment too late that it was Dusty who'd asked me, and I'd answered her out loud. I glance around the table, but no one seems to have noticed my faux pas.

I take a couple of slow breaths, but after a couple of moments I become aware of a strange taste in my mouth. "That didn't taste right." I frown as I stare into the almost empty cup. "It tasted bitter."

I tilt the cup and to my horror notice a grainy residue sliding along the bottom of the cup that I'm pretty certain isn't sugar. "Oh shit." I blink as my head begins to buzz. "Dusty... I think... I think... something was in that tea," I slur.

But the last thing I hear is a loud thunk as my head hits the table...

13

Dusty

"Tristan!" I shriek, letting go of Delores' hand in the hopes that she doesn't stray again. "Tristan... oh my god... oh my god... Tristan, wake up!" I flap my hands uselessly in panic.

"Oh look," Violet announces. "Princeton has fallen over."

"It's Tristan," Trudy corrects as she looks down at Tristan passed out cold on the table. "What's wrong with him?"

"Do you think he's tired?" Maeve asks. "He looks tired. Is he taking a nap?"

"Young ones today," Birdie sniffs. "No stamina. Just leave him there." She waves her hand dismissively.

"Do you think he needs a blanket?" Trudy muses.

"He needs a bloody ambulance, you daft old bat," I yell, but they can't hear me or see me. Fuck... this is one of those times when being dead is really fucking inconvenient. I can't even check his pulse.

Oh god, what if he's dead?

"Tristan!" I yell in his ear before looking up at the old ladies who've gone back into their own little worlds and are ignoring him. "Help him!" I yell at them even though I know it's pointless.

I'm panicking now. I don't know what to do until a really crazy and very stupid idea occurs to me. I hesitate for only a second, knowing Tristan needs help.

"Oh, this is probably a really bad idea." I wince as I brace myself and dive toward Tristan and into his body.

It's the strangest feeling, a curious melting sensation, then warmth, like I've been wrapped in the warmest, softest blanket I could imagine, but that feeling lasts for only a fleeting second before I'm overwhelmed. Everything feels so heavy and loud. It's grating on all my senses—or should I say, Tristan's senses. From inside his body, I can feel his heart beating good and strong. He's not dead, just knocked out by whatever he's been dosed with, but that still doesn't mean he's out of danger. I need to get him to a hospital as quickly as possible.

I try to lift my head—or rather, Tristan's head—but it's weird being back in a mortal body after six months as a disembodied spirit. It's like trying to drive a car on the wrong side of the fucking road when you haven't been behind the wheel for ages.

"Tristan!" I hear Chan's beautiful voice in my ear and feel the warmth of his hand on my ba—Tristan's back. Wow, this is going to take some getting used to. "What have they done to you? I was only gone five minutes," he says in a panic. "Oh my god, Danny is going to kill me."

I lift my head slowly, and once again everything feels really heavy. "Tris, honey?" He cradles my face, but I can't seem to get my mouth working. Wearing someone else's body is like trying to figure out how to work a really complicated marionette.

"Got. To. Get. Out. Of. Here..." I say, pushing myself to my feet and stumbling forward against the table as Chan reaches out to steady me.

The table legs grind loudly against the floor as it moves against my weight, with the unfortunate side effect of setting the urn containing Delores ashes to a precarious swaying.

Chan's gaze widens and he reaches out to grab it but it's too late. It capsizes and rolls off the edge of the table, hitting the floor with a loud thunk.

Thank god it's made from something hardy and doesn't break, but thanks to its rounded shape, it continues to roll across the floor. Larry gives a cry of dismay and chases after it, with people scattering out of their seats and tripping over each other to get out of her way. Tables are shoved aside, causing cake stands to topple and sending cakes flying everywhere. It's absolute bedlam.

"Er... Time to go," Chan decides prudently and wraps my arm around his neck so he can drag me from the chair.

We stumble through the tables towards the door, and the more we move the more I get the hang of being back inside a corporeal body. The heaviness begins to recede slightly and I'm able to move my legs. We burst into the entrance foyer, and I stumble to a stop.

"Wait... wait..." I croak and my voice sounds really strange to my ears until I realise it's because it's not my voice, it's Tristan's. A wave of dizziness washes over me and I lean forward, resting my hands on my knees as I breathe heavily.

"Are you okay, sweetheart?" Chan rubs my back again in a soothing circular motion.

"I'm fine, there's just one problem..." I whisper as I look up, meeting those familiar dark eyes as I straighten. "I'm not Tristan."

His eyes cloud with confusion for a moment as he studies my face, then they widen and when he speaks, his voice is barely more than a whisper, one I have to strain to hear.

"Dusty?" I nod and his hands cover his mouth in shock.

"Hello, princess." I smile slowly, and his eyes fill with tears. It's what I've called him since we were thirteen and I'm the only one who ever has.

He releases his mouth and gasps, "Oh my god. Dusty?"

I nod again and he reaches out and grabs me, yanking me into his body and holding me so tight I shouldn't be able to breathe, but astonishingly, it has the opposite effect. It feels like the first time I can breathe properly in a very long time.

"I missed you so much," he breathes against my neck on a whispered sob.

"I missed you too." I swallow past the burning knot of emotion in my throat. "It's been hell being so close to you and being unable to talk to you."

"Wait a minute." He pulls back suddenly, holding my shoulders as if he's afraid I'm going to disappear any moment. "If you're here... I mean, in there"—he releases one shoulder and indicates Tristan's body—"then where the hell is Tristan?"

"I don't know," I reply, worried. "In here somewhere too? I think."

"What the fuck happened?" he asks.

"Someone drugged him."

Chan gasps. "What?"

"He drank a cup of tea and when he was done, he said it tasted funny... bitter. Then he just conked out like a sixteen-year-old in a field after their first two-litre bottle of cider."

"Well fuck, what do we do?"

"Get him to a hospital," I say urgently.

"I'll call an ambulance." Chan pulls out his phone.

"Don't bother, it'll take too long. I've got this. Call an Uber. I'll get his body to the hospital and then jump back out once they've got him."

"Okay, if you say so." Chan switches apps. "We're in luck, there's an Uber just round the corner. They'll be here in a minute. We need to get outside."

"Delores, come with me," I call out to the old lady hovering beside us as I turn and head toward the exit. But I can't seem to get my coordination, so what happens instead of a quick walk is a kind of jerky zombie-like stomp across the room. I intend to lift my hands, but they don't move in time, and I end up crashing into the door.

"Oh my Christ, it's like watching bloody Frankenstein," Chan mutters.

"You try driving someone else's body." I frown. "His legs are shorter than mine and my centre of gravity's all off. You know when you get into a small sports car that's really low to the ground? That's what this feels like."

Chan snorts as he grabs my arm and loops it around his neck. "Come on, I think I see the Uber pulling up."

He reaches out with the other hand and pushes open the door. A quick glance behind me tells me Delores is at least doing as she's told and staying close to me, although she's the least of my problems at the moment.

Chan helps me into an Uber and a short time later we're pulling up outside St George's and being dumped out next to the ambulance bay.

"Now what?" Chan says as the car pulls away.

"We go in and let them fix Tristan." I lurch toward the entrance.

"No, wait!" Chan says and I pause. "If we go in there with Tris walking and talking like normal, they're not going to take us seriously... wait here." He disappears inside the entrance and reappears moments later with a wheelchair. "Get in." He shoves me into the chair. "You need to be unconscious."

"Oh right, gotcha." I wink and close my eyes, letting Tristan's body go limp.

"Perfect." He starts wheeling me toward the doors. "Show time!"

It's so tempting to open my eyes and see what's going on but I can't. I concentrate on pretending I'm unconscious so that as soon as the doctors have got Tristan I can slip back out of his body—which sounds a lot dirtier than it actually is—and leave him in good hands.

"Hey!" I hear Chan call out. "I need a little help!"

There's a flurry of activity around me, and I feel Tristan's slight body lifted by several pairs of hands and set down on what I assume is a gurney or a bed. I can hear Chan giving Tristan's details in the background.

I'm poked and prodded to within an inch of my life, or rather Tristan's life. He's quickly and efficiently stripped down and covered with a thin cotton hospital gown as I try not to squirm and giggle. Who knew Tristan had so many ticklish spots? They attach monitors and stick in needles, then some sadist cranks open my eyelid and shines a light so bright directly into Tristan's eyes that I'm surprised it doesn't disintegrate his retinas.

Someone close by starts talking. "I see from his notes he had an accident about six months ago, a choking episode during which he stopped breathing. Do you know if he's suffered any headaches, seizures, or blacking out since then?"

"No, not as far as I know," Chan replies. "But this is unrelated to that. I'm pretty sure his drink was spiked."

"Was he drinking alcohol?"

"No, he was drinking tea with a bunch of old ladies," Chan replies.

"This is no laughing matter Mr...?" A disapproving voice admonishes.

"Chan, just Chan, and I was being serious," he answers. "He was drinking tea, he said it didn't taste right, that it had a bitter taste, and then he passed out quicker than Ruby on a weekend bender to Margate."

"I'm sorry?"

"Never mind," Chan says impatiently. "I'm pretty sure he was drugged... is he going to be okay?"

"His vitals look good, he didn't stop breathing, and he's got a good strong pulse, but we'll monitor him closely until he regains consciousness. In the meantime, we'll run blood tests to see if there are any drugs in his system. If he was drugged, however, it will have to be reported to the police."

"Already way ahead of you," Chan replies. "His boyfriend is a detective with the Metropolitan Police."

I hear a person exit the room while someone else fusses over me. I still don't dare open my eyes, but I do hear Chan's voice.

"Hey, Danny. Okay, please don't be mad at me but, um... I'm at St George's with Tristan. It looks like he might have been drugged."

I don't have to look to know Chan's face is probably displaying a pained wince. I can hear Danny's reaction halfway across the room and he's not even on speaker.

"No... no! He's fine! Well, okay, he's not fine, but they don't think he's in immediate danger. His stats are good, and they're keeping an eye on him and running blood tests." He listens for a moment and Danny seems to have calmed somewhat because his voice has lowered to the point I can no longer hear it. "Okay, I'll see you soon." He hangs up the phone.

A few more seconds pass and I hear a lot of shuffling about, then silence.

"Dusty," Chan whispers and I crank open an eye to see that we're alone in a cubicle in A&E.

I pull down the oxygen mask. "What's going on?" I whisper back.

"They're waiting on the results of the blood tests, and Danny's on his way."

"Okay, time for me to vacate, I think. The last thing I need is Danny holding my hand and telling me he loves me. That would just be super awkward," I decide. "Tris is in good hands."

"I wish we had more time," Chan says miserably. "I hate that this has happened to Tris, but I never thought I'd get the chance to see you again, although it is a bit weird what with you wearing Tristan like a Halloween costume."

"Hey." I glance around the cubicle quickly to make sure no one can see me as I'm supposed to be unconscious. I prop myself up on my elbow and reach for Chan, cupping his chin and bringing him in close so I can press my lips to his. "You're my best friend, Chan," I whisper. "My forever, my ride or die."

"But you did die." His mouth turns down and his lip pokes out.

"But I never left you," I say softly, "and I never will. I'll be waiting for you right there at the very end. We will see each other again, I promise."

Chan tilts his head and blinks back the tears. "Okay," he breathes out heavily. "I'm not going to say goodbye, but you better get out of there before Danny shows up."

I nod and lie back down on the bed, replacing the oxygen mask so Tristan's set once I exit his body. Closing my eyes, I take a deep breath and try to sit up, but instead of leaving Tristan's body lying on the bed behind me, he rises up with me. I blink a couple of times and frown. Okay that wasn't supposed to happen.

I lay back down and try again, but the same thing happens.

"Uh, Dusty, what are you doing?" Chan asks, uncertain.

"Shit," I mutter as I lay back down and look at Chan. "I think I'm stuck."

"What?" he whispers as he hears voices outside the curtains.

"I can't get out of Tristan's body," I say in panic.

14

Dusty

I come to slowly, rising up through layers of sleep, my brain gradually waking up. When Danny showed up at the hospital yesterday, I immediately faked unconsciousness. In fact, I spent so long pretending I was unconscious that I actually fell asleep. After spending the last six months as a spirit, I'd almost forgotten what it was like to get tired or hungry.

My stomach gives a loud growl as if responding to my random thoughts, and I frown even though my eyes are still closed. My body still feels heavy, and my stomach is obviously empty, which means I must still be trapped in...

Oh god, even as the horrifying thought occurs to me, I have the strangest feeling of being watched. I crank my eyes open and see a very familiar face leaning in inches from mine.

"Give me back my body," he says very succinctly.

I inhale sharply. "Tristan!" I shoot upright in bed, blinking a couple of times to clear the sleep from my eyes.

I then become aware of two things. One, I am definitely still in a hospital bed and not only am I still wearing Tristan's body but also a very fetching backless gown from the house of NHS, and two, Tristan, or rather Tristan's spirit, is standing in front of me looking decidedly unhappy.

This can't be good.

"What the fuck are you doing out there?" I exclaim in shock.

"Me?" Tristan hisses. "What the fuck are you doing in there?"

I wince. "Um, it was an accident... sort of."

"An accident?" His voice rises with incredulity. "An accident? No, when a goat wandered into a random cave in Jerusalem causing a shepherd to discover the two-thousand-year-old Dead Sea Scrolls, that was an accident. When Dr Alexander Fleming went on holiday and forgot to clean his Petri dishes and came back to find he'd invented penicillin, that was an accident. When the Titanic crashed into an iceberg and sank, that was an accident."

"Actually, I think that one was gross negligence," I muse.

"What is not an accident is deliberately possessing someone's body while they're unconscious," he snaps.

"Wait a minute, you're a..." I swallow in disbelief. "You're a–a ghost!"

"Y'think?" He glares.

"Oh my god! I'm totally freaking out right now." I flap my hands in panic.

"You're freaking out?" Tristan scowls. "You're wearing my body like a sock puppet."

"I'm so sorry," I say with complete sincerity.

He pinches the bridge of his nose like he's searching for the last bit of his patience. "Just get out of my body so I can get back in."

"Um..."

"What um?" His sharp gaze lands on me. "No um... I don't like the sound of um..."

"I may be... temporarily... stuck in here," I admit reluctantly.

"What?" He blinks and stares at me.

"It was completely unintentional and to be fair, I thought you were stuck in here with me."

"Well clearly, I'm not." He frowns. "Christ, it's like *Freaky Friday.*"

"The Jodie Foster or Lindsay Lohan version?" I ask, then hold up my hands as he fixes me with a dry stare. "Just wanted to know how much leeway I've got while I'm temporarily in charge of your body."

I see a blur materialise in the corner of the room and squint. Reaching for the locker beside the bed, I grab Tristan's glasses and slide them on. Suddenly everything comes into sharp focus.

"Tristan, your eyesight really is terrible," I remark.

"Oh, I'm so sorry your current accommodation is not up to standard. Maybe you should leave a review on TripAdvisor next time you decide to hijack someone's body."

"I'm detecting a note of sarcasm," I say mildly, to which he simply stares at me.

I glance over to the corner of the room and realise that the blurry blob that had appeared was, in fact, Delores. Spotting Tristan standing next to the bed, she looks across to me as I lie on the bed also looking like Tristan, and I really do feel for the old bird. Not only is she currently stuck spending her afterlife in a perpetual state of confusion, but now she probably thinks she's seeing double.

She sidles up slowly beside Tristan and tentatively reaches for his hand. When she finds she can touch him, just like she could with me, she beams up at him widely.

"Beau," she announces happily.

"Yes, I know," Tristan sighs. "But one problem at a time, please, Mrs Abernathy."

I look across the room at the sound of the door handle and before I can utter another word, the door swings open and a very dishevelled Danny enters, looking as if the poor man hasn't slept a wink, but when his tired gaze falls on me staring at him silently, he lets out a gasp of relief and rushes across the room.

"Tristan! You're awake. I was so worried."

Before I can formulate a response, he's cupping my face in his hands and pressing his warm lips to mine. Giving a squeal of surprise, I scramble back, breaking his grip on my cheeks as I fumble the blankets off my legs, but I misjudge how close I've moved to the edge of the bed and roll off, landing on my hands and knees to break my fall. Unfortunately, the gown is barely held together by two flimsy laces and gives a bird's eye view of my gloriously naked bum.

"Wow," Tristan murmurs. He stares down at his own naked backside as I struggle to my feet, closing the gown behind me with a flush of embarrassment. "You're about as graceful as I am. At this rate, he'll never suspect a thing."

"Are you alright, Tris?" Danny asks in concern.

"I'm fine," I say as I edge across the room, keeping the back of the gown closed in my fist. "I'm just... you know, desperate for the loo, so I'm just going to..." I hike a thumb over my shoulder as I back toward the door. "Go and find the toilets."

"I believe I can help you there, Mr Everett," a business-like voice announces behind me.

Giving a startled yelp, I turn and step out of the way as a small plump middle-aged nurse marches in—honest to god, marches in like the gunnery sergeant from *Full Metal Jacket*, pushing what looks like a wheelchair, until she stops abruptly. She lifts the lid and, to my abject horror, inside is an adult-size potty.

"What the hell is that?" I say flatly.

"It's a commode," she replies briskly. "There's a privacy

screen just behind you." She points to a curtain mounted taut across a wheeled metal frame. "Do you need some help?"

"No, I do not," I declare indignantly.

"I suggest you empty your bladder, Mr Everett. We gave you a lot of intravenous fluids last night to help flush any foreign substances from your system."

That would certainly explain why my bladder feels like an overfilled water balloon that's about to explode.

"Christ, what is this, the Dark Ages?" I glance at the wheelchair slash port-a-potty. "I'm not peeing in that."

"Come now, Mr Everett, don't be such a baby."

"Absolutely not," I insist adamantly. "I'm going to use the loo like a civilised person although there is also no way I'm walking barefoot across an NHS toilet."

She lets out a loud huff of impatience, rolling her eyes and retrieving something from a nearby dispenser. What she hands me is a pair of paper foot coverings, the type you'd wear over the top of your shoes at a crime scene.

"Really?" I drawl. "You couldn't have just got me a pair of slippers?"

"What do you think this is, the Hilton?" she replies, pursing her lips and folding her hands across her waist and under her ample bosom. "It's that or the commode."

"Thank you, Nurse Betty." I give her a sarcastic smile as I primly grasp the back of my gown closed to cover my naked bum, or rather Tristan's naked bum. I lean down awkwardly, pulling the blue paper booties over my bare feet. "I'll be right back," I tell Danny in a softer tone.

"Down the corridor, second door on the left," the nurse says with a rather unimpressed brow raised. "Mind the red pull cord or you'll set off the alarm."

"Thank you," I reply with a frosty smile as I sail regally from the room.

I'm halfway down the corridor and almost to the toilet door when I realise Tristan is right beside me.

"I can manage to go to the bathroom by myself you know, I–" I stop talking as my gaze falls on Delores, who's tottering along behind us like a homing pigeon.

"Oh for—" Tristan shakes his head. He holds out his hands and takes hold of her gently, manoeuvring her onto the little row of plastic chairs lined up against the wall. "Sit... stay," he says slowly as he holds up his hands and backs away carefully. "Ah." He holds up a finger when she tries to stand. "No," he tells her firmly. "Sit and wait." She sits back down in the chair, watching him as she grips the handle of her handbag tightly and settles it on her lap. "Okay." He lets out a breath and turns back to me. "We need to talk."

Seeing another nurse pushing a patient in a wheelchair down the corridor, I open the door and step into the toilet. I reach for the pull cord and hope it's not the one for the patient alarm system. Fortunately, the room is flooded with a dim light, and I lock the door behind me. I stop in front of the toilet and lift the hospital gown out of the way.

"You know, you really do have a very nice looking penis, Tristan," I ponder as I look down and aim.

"Oh god." Sounding mortified, he rubs his forehead as if he's in pain. "Can you not look?"

"Not really, unless you want me to pee up the wall," I reply. "Really, honey, there's no need to be embarrassed. I've seen so many cocks it would make your eyes spin like a fruit machine."

"That's not really a ringing endorsement, Dusty," he replies. "And to be honest, it makes you sound a little slutty."

I find myself laughing despite the ridiculous situation we are currently in. I glance across at Tristan and see his mouth curving into a reluctant smile.

"What the hell are we going to do, boo?" I give a little shake as I finish peeing for England. Seriously, how many bags of fluids did they give me last night? And I flush the loo, turning to wash my hands as Tristan watches me thoughtfully in the mirror. "Danny's waiting in that room to fuss over his boyfriend, but instead he's getting me packaged as you. This is a whole avalanche of awkward."

"It can't be helped," he sighs in resignation. "Until we can figure out how to switch me back into my body, you're going to have to pretend you're me."

I can feel my eyes widen as I turn toward him sharply. "You don't mean I have to... you know..." I make a ring with one hand and stick my finger through the hole.

"Classy." His tone is droll as he raises his brows. "And no, absolutely not. No sex whatsoever. You're about to have a lot of headaches, so get used to it."

"Oh please." I roll my eyes. "I'm sure I can come up with a better excuse than that." Another thought occurs to me. "Fuck, what am I going to tell Bruce?"

"Let's not borrow more trouble, Dusty," he says as I ball up the paper towels I've just used to dry my hands and chuck them in the overflowing bin. "We'll cross that bridge if and when we come to it."

"I suppose we better go back and deal with Danny," I sigh.

"Just be gentle with him," Tristan says quietly. "I imagine what happened yesterday was a big shock for him. He thought I'd be safe, and I'd bet my collector's edition steel book of *Lord of the Rings* that he's blaming himself."

"Don't worry, boo." I blow him a kiss. "I haven't just got your back... literally. I got your man's back, too. We're going to figure this out, I promise."

Tristan nods slowly and I unlock the door and step out into the corridor. As we pass by the row of plastic chairs, Delores rises obediently and takes Tristan's hand. At least with him herding her along, she might be less inclined to wander off.

Upon reaching the room, I draw in a breath. I can totally do this. I can convince a clever and sweet detective that nothing weird is going on and that I am, in fact, the cute, kinda awkward, marginally sarcastic pathologist he's in love with. I've got this.

I walk into the room and take one look at his face.

I so haven't got this.

Thankfully, the evil nurse with the port-a-potty is nowhere to be seen. Danny immediately rises from the visitor's chair where he was perched and reaches for me, his face so filled with concern my heart almost breaks. He takes my hands as if I am literally the most precious thing in the world to him and draws me over to the bed and helps me sit down, then lifts my legs, carefully removes the paper booties, and tucks me under the thin hospital-issue blankets.

"Better?" He plumps up my pillow.

"Much, thank you." I smile for him and it's genuine.

I'm so glad Tristan has him. This is a very strange position to be in though. I've watched him and Tristan interact with each other for months. It's plain to see they love each other deeply, but seeing it... feeling it from Tristan's perspective has me pausing.

I've only ever had superficial relationships. I'm sure a shrink could dissect why—losing my mum at such a young age, my issues with my father growing up—but the truth is, I was just never interested in anything serious. Life was for living and believe me, I did a hell of a lot of living in the thirty short years I had a pulse. I never felt like I'd missed out on anything. I have no regrets—other than being murdered, of course.

But now, seeing the way Danny looks at me, or rather Tristan, I can't help feeling a little envious, and with that foreign feeling comes a startling realisation that maybe I do want something more.

My thoughts are immediately drawn to a dark-haired

rugby player that haunts a certain bookshop, and I wonder for the first time if more has been under my nose this whole time.

"You seem really deep in thought." Danny draws my attention back to him.

"Yeah, I guess I'm still a little out of it," I say.

"Knock knock," a familiar voice sing-songs from the doorway, followed by an actual knock on the open door.

I look across to see Chan back to her glamorous self and I relax. She's rocking her signature bodycon dress and killer heels. Her makeup is dramatic and flawless, and her shiny black hair is tied up in a complicated twist on top of her head and anchored with ornate hair-sticks.

"I brought breakfast." She holds up a tray of Starbucks cups and a paper bag. "I've got croissants and lattes, semi-skim, two sugars, and hold the sedatives."

Danny chuckles and shakes his head.

"Too soon?" She sashays across the room and drops them down on the table at the foot of the bed. "Tris, honey." She skirts around the bed and leans in, dropping a kiss on my cheek.

"Hey, princess," I say quietly, and her eyes widen fractionally as she realises I'm still in the driving seat. She glances around the room, almost as if she's searching for the real Tristan even though she can't see spirits. She hands Danny a coffee first, then me, before settling in the other visitor's chair on the other side of the bed from Danny.

"So, what did I miss?" Chan takes a sip of what I know is probably a cappuccino. "You're finally awake then?"

"I was just about to ask Tris about yesterday." Danny sips his coffee and hums in appreciation. "Thanks for this, by the way. I've been drinking that rocket fuel from the vending machine all night and it's probably going to keep me awake for the next two days straight."

"You're welcome," Chan replies. "Besides, I'm still trying to get back on your good side after what happened yesterday."

"Chan, I know it wasn't your fault," Danny says. "I was worried, yes, but I never held you responsible."

"And I appreciate that." She furrows her brow. "But I still feel terrible. I was only gone for a few minutes."

"Can you tell me what happened, Tris?" Danny turns his attention to me, and I glance covertly at Tristan.

"Was I drugged?" Tristan asks and I repeat the question to Danny.

"You were." Danny nods, his expression darkening. "Your blood tests revealed a massive dose of sedatives in your system. They don't think it's caused any lasting damage, but it knocked you out cold for several hours."

"But that doesn't make sense," Tristan says to me. "Why would someone drug me?"

"Can you tell me what happened at the community centre after Chan left the room?" Danny asks seriously.

"I was coughing and, without thinking, I picked up a cup and drained it," Tristan says, and I dutifully relay it to Danny.

"Was it your cup?"

"I don't know. Honestly, I wasn't paying attention. It was either mine or yours, but I couldn't say for certain which one." Tristan continues to feed me answers which I parrot back to Danny.

"So the drug could have been intended for either you or me." He scratches his jaw thoughtfully, tugging slightly at the growth there since he hasn't had time to go home and shave. "I made them myself from the urn of hot water and sealed individual tea bags, so if it was dosed it had to have happened at the table, which narrows the suspect pool exponentially. It had to be one of the ladies at the table."

"I can't believe I got roofied by a pensioner," Tristan says sullenly.

"It's possible it was intended for me," Danny muses. "After all, they all know I'm a police officer and that I am investigating Delores' murder. It's possible the murderer panicked and slipped something in my drink, which you then inadvertently picked up during your coughing fit." He looks at me.

"But it doesn't fit the M.O. Why go from arsenic to plain old sedatives and what the hell was it going to achieve?" I think out loud. "It's not like sending you off for a jolly with the Sandman is going to stop the investigation."

"I don't know yet." Danny sips his coffee again, "But I'm going to start with the person nearest me who could've had access to my drink while I wasn't looking."

"Ivy." My eyes narrow. "That scheming little Mata Hari."

"I'm going to investigate every single person at that table one by one, and I have a gut feeling it may lead us back to Delores' murderer."

"Just be careful," I tell him fervently.

The last thing we need is another disembodied spirit wandering around with unfinished business, especially if it winds up being Danny. Tristan will never forgive me.

"I'll figure it out." Danny reaches out and squeezes my hand. "I promise, but the most important thing is that you're here and you're safe."

I hate to burst his bubble but he's wrong. The most important thing right now is figuring out how the hell to get Tristan back in his body.

15

Tristan

It was hard seeing Danny with Dusty yesterday, even though she is technically me. Well, in Danny's eyes, at least. Holy crap, this is all so crazy. How is this my life?

I find myself idly wandering around my flat. It's weird, not needing to sleep and not feeling hungry. Mrs Abernathy has planted herself neatly on the sofa, back straight and her ever-present handbag resting on her knees as she grips the handles like someone's going to steal it from her any moment. She's staring at the TV avidly even though the screen is blank.

I'm killing time until Dusty wakes up. I've never known anyone to sleep so much, it's like she's catching up on the last six months. She took another nap in the hospital while they kept her... I mean me... in for observation. It's a toss-up whether all the sleeping was just an aftereffect of the sedatives or her way of avoiding awkward conversations with Danny.

My attention turns to the bedroom as Dusty, wearing brightly coloured silk pyjama pants and a matching robe which flutters around her as she moves, sails regally out into the hallway and heads toward the kitchen

"Dusty, what are you wearing?" I follow her into the kitchen with a frown. "That's not mine."

"Chan left a bag last night with a few essentials." Dusty yawns and reaches for the kettle, filling it under the tap before flipping the switch on.

"Essentials?" My eyes narrow on my hand as she reaches up into the cupboard to get a cup. "Is that nail varnish?"

"You really are very short, aren't you?" She shakes her head as she places the cup on the counter.

"I am not," I reply with a huff of indignation. "You're just used to wearing heels that could double as scaffolding." She turns to look at me consideringly. "Don't you dare," I warn.

"I'm just saying"–she shrugs innocently–"maybe a cute little pair of Cuban heels."

"I'm not bloody Prince," I reply dryly.

"Mm-hmm," she hums as she turns back to the kettle and makes herself a coffee so strong and sweet you could stand a spoon up in it.

"Don't 'mm-hmm' me. I mean it, Dusty. While you're in my body you'll abide by my rules." I cross my arms. "And why are you wearing nail varnish?"

"I've been telling you for months you need more colour in your life, boo." She lifts the cup to her lips. "Besides, I thought you liked it?"

"I do on occasion, but usually blues, black, dark green, sometimes black cherry. What on earth is that?"

She smiles. "Coral sunrise."

"Oh sweet baby Jesus." I close my eyes and sigh. "I can't wear that for work."

"It's just as well you're not at work then, isn't it?" she points out with a raised brow.

"Dusty," I warn. "They may have given me today off because we just got out of the hospital, but I'll still have to go back tomorrow. And if you're still encamped in my body, it means you have to go."

"What?" She blinks rapidly. "Oh no... no, no, no." She waves her hand. "I'm not cutting up any dead bodies. I don't even like to handle raw meat."

"That's not what I've heard," I say dryly.

"Touché," Dusty sniffs. "But the fact remains, I'm not slicing and dicing anyone. Unless you've forgotten, I'm not actually a doctor despite those amateur clips on PornHub."

"PornHub?" I stare at her. "Really?"

"It was a phase." She shrugs. "But the facts remain the same, I don't think some previous kinky role-play qualifies me to cover for you. I'm not a doctor, I don't have a medical degree, and I can't perform a post-mortem."

"It's not brain surgery, Dusty. I'll be there talking you through it and besides, look at it this way, your patient will already be dead. It's not like you can kill them again."

"That's a big fat nope." She sips her coffee again, staring at me over the rim of her cup.

"Oh come on, Dusty, my job is really important to me," I whine. "Just this once."

"Sorry, Sweeney Todd, still nope." She continues to sip thoughtfully and watch me. "We need to figure out how to switch back, then you can do your own hacking up of corpses."

"I'll have you know there's no hacking involved. It's a post-mortem, not a dismemberment. I'm a professional, not a trainee serial killer."

"Still, the quicker we can get you back in your body the better." Dusty chews her lip.

"So what do you suggest?" I cross my arms. "An exorcism? Because I hate to break it to you, but I'm not Catholic. In fact, I'm not even religious."

"I don't think being Catholic is a prerequisite for an exorcism and anyway, I don't think that would work." She taps her fingers against the side of the cup. "I hate to say it, but I think we need to go back to see Evangeline." She grimaces.

"I thought you liked Evangeline?"

"I do, but if we go back to the bookshop, that means I'm going to have to tell Bruce what happened."

"I'm sure he'll understand," I say softly.

"Maybe," she murmurs.

"You really like him," I blurt out with the realisation. "I mean *like* like him, as more than a hookup."

"Can we not talk about grown-up relationships?" She rolls her eyes. "It's too early in the morning for me to be breaking out in hives."

"It's okay, you know, to want more," I say as I watch her. "Even in the afterlife, you're allowed to be happy."

"Tristan, what did I just say?"

"Fine." I raise my hands in surrender. "By the way, you'll need to feed Jacob Marley before we go anywhere. His food is in that cupboard."

"Tris, honey, I've been practically living with you for months. I know where JM's food is, just like I know where all your sex toys are hidden."

If I still had my physical body, I'm sure my face would be the colour of a lobster right now. Instead, I clear my throat innocently.

"I don't know what you're talking about and besides, my bedroom is off-limits, that was the agreement."

"That was before I ended up babysitting your body." Dusty smirks. "I found them this morning when I went into your bottom drawer. I have to admit I'm impressed, Tris... it's always the quiet ones." She winks at me.

"Ugh." I press my palm to my forehead, wondering if the ground can open up and swallow me. Only, if that happened while in my current disembodied state, I'd end up in my neighbour's flat below. "Can you just feed my cat, please?"

She chuckles heartily as she grabs Jacob Marley's bowl and begins to fill it.

"Where is JM, anyway?" Dusty asks. "He's usually skulking around here somewhere, but I haven't seen him since last night."

"I think we've traumatised him." I wince.

We'd walked through the door last night, and Jacob Marley had taken a single look at me—and I mean my physical body that Dusty's currently wearing like last season's Prada—and then he'd looked across to the insubstantial ghost form of me, and I swear that if he'd been a cartoon, his eyes would've popped out of his head on stalks. He gave a shrill yowl and darted from the room, and I haven't seen him since.

"Just fill his bowls and leave them on the floor. Hopefully, he'll come out once we're gone," I say.

She's just set his water bowl down on the floor when there's a knock at the door. She goes to answer it and I follow behind, hoping it's not Danny. Not because I don't want to see him, I do. I missed sleeping wrapped up in his arms last night, but Dusty managed to convince him to go back to his flat. I knew he wanted to stay and make sure I was okay.

This whole situation just plain sucks.

The door swings open and there's Chan standing outside holding a garment bag, which I'm not sure I want to know the contents of, in one hand and a takeout bag in the other.

"Oh," Dusty gasps, eyes bright with excitement. "Please tell me that's a triple bacon, sausage, cheese, and egg sandwich from Julio's?"

"It is." Chan grins as Dusty snatches the bag with a squeal, planting an enthusiastic kiss on Chan's mouth before turning back around and dashing into the kitchen.

"Hey, Tris." Chan walks in, glancing around. Even though she can't see me, she knows I'm here and I appreciate the acknowledgement.

She closes the door behind her and hooks the garment bag on the coat hooks by the door. She looks totally different, I realise with a jolt. She's wearing a bright shocking pink dress with padded shoulders which wraps around her body like a second skin. Instead of her standard elegant thin needle heels, she's wearing chubby platform ankle boots in the same eye-watering pink. Her long black hair is wrapped in a complicated braid and hanging over one shoulder. But the crowning glory is the large and elaborate hat pinned to her head at a jaunty angle.

The first time I met Chan was at Dusty's funeral and every time I've seen her since she's always looked flawless, but I didn't realise until this moment quite how much losing Dusty had dulled her shine. She not only looks a lot more flamboyant and definitely more colourful now, but there seems to be a lightness to her that wasn't there before.

She heads into the kitchen, and I follow. Dusty is now planted at the small kitchen table with a bottle of ketchup, and she's spread out the wrapping from her sandwich on the table, not bothering with a plate as she begins to separate out the layers and add ketchup.

"And you said you'd be no good at a post-mortem," I mutter as she looks up at me and grins. "I can feel my arteries hardening from over here. Will you please treat my body with a little respect?"

She doesn't answer and instead lifts the thick reassembled sandwich to her mouth and takes a huge bite. As half the filling is pushed out the other side of the soggy bread and drops to the packaging with a wet thud, her eyes roll back in her head, and she lets out the most obscene and borderline pornographic moan I've ever heard.

I watch as she chews like a little chipmunk, humming in pleasure and almost dancing in her chair like a child would. Thin stripes of ketchup smear from the corners of her mouth to her cheeks, making her look like the fast-food version of the Joker.

"I'm getting heartburn just looking at that," I say with a wrinkle of my nose.

"Ohhh, soo good." The words are slightly muffled due to the amount of sandwich she has crammed into her mouth, or I should say, my mouth. At this rate, when I get my body back, I'm going to be ten pounds heavier.

"You know, Tris," Dusty says around another mouthful of food. "I didn't realise how much I'd missed certain things. For the most part, I'm more than happy being dead. I've gotten used to it now plus, you know... Bruce... he's just a big shiny bonus. But I can't deny missing certain things, like hugging Chan and hanging out with her or, you know, eating and sleeping. If we figure out how to switch bodies, maybe we could make this a regular thing. You know, like I could book your body for a week at the end of July."

"I'm not a caravan park in Devon, so no, you bloody cannot."

"It was just a thought." She grins and I'm pretty sure she's just messing with me.

"So what's the plan?" Chan asks as she makes herself a cup of tea.

Dusty swallows and wipes her mouth. "We're going to the bookshop in Whitechapel. There's a ghost there, Evangeline Crawshanks, who might know how we can switch bodies back. It's worth a shot anyway."

Chan nods slowly, turning around and leaning against the counter as she sips her tea. "It's been so good having you back. I don't want it to end but at the same time, I feel awful for Tris. I adore him and this has got to be really hard on him, especially considering how awkward it was yesterday with Danny. I wish there was some way I could keep you both."

"Hey." Dusty reaches out and grasps her hand, squeezing

affectionately. "We'll figure it out, I promise. I have to give Tristan back his body, but I'll find a way for us to be close again, even if we have to use a damn Ouija board."

"No, absolutely not," I say firmly. "We will find a way for you and Chan to stay close, but you are not using one of those filthy boards. You know both Evangeline and Bruce told us that they only attract the lowest, most base earthbound spirits. Let's not borrow more trouble. We've got our hands full as it is."

"Fine." Dusty rises, patting her stomach happily. "Right now I'm going to get dressed. Chan, are you coming with us?"

"Oh, I wouldn't miss this." She grins.

I leave Chan to finish her cup of tea in peace; it's not like I can have a conversation with her anyway. I check in on Mrs Abernathy, who is still randomly watching the blank screen of the TV, but whatever, it's keeping her quiet and in one place so I'm not going to disturb her. Dusty has disappeared into the bedroom to get showered and dressed, and I find myself once again wandering aimlessly. I kind of get it now. No wonder Mrs Abernathy is always wandering off. Being a spirit is really boring. I can't touch anything, I can't talk to anyone... well, anyone living.

I stop in front of the window and stare out onto the street miserably.

My thoughts are once again drawn back to Danny. The next few days are going to be rough on him, and there's nothing I can do to change that. Until I get my body back, Dusty is going to have to try and avoid him as much as possible to avoid sticky situations, but there's no way for him to take that anyway other than as a rejection.

He looked so dejected when he left the flat last night. It almost killed me to see that look on his face. It's not like we can tell him the truth. It's going to be hard enough convincing him I can see ghosts and not sounding completely nuts, but add in a freak body swap and it's tough to see how that's not going to completely mess up our fledgling relationship.

I love him more than anything and I know he loves me, but sometimes love isn't enough. These days my life is insane. Displaced spirits looking for closure, weird dark wraith things floating about all over the place, and now a dead drag queen in charge of my body while I roam untethered, not living but not dead either.

Life is not supposed to be this hard.

I'm going to have to tell him the truth. I want a life with Danny, I'm pretty sure I want to grow old with him. I want to spend my old age hiding each other's false teeth and laughing at each other's incontinence pants. I can't do that if I'm not completely honest with him. I can only hope he'll accept all the weird parts of me as well as the good parts.

I really don't want to lose him, but I can't share a home with him and constantly try to hide every conversation I have with spirits. It's exhausting just thinking about it. No... I'm going to do it. I'm going to tell him the truth... I'll maybe just wait until I have my own body back.

"Okay, I'm ready, let's go," Dusty says from behind me, and I turn.

"No, absolutely not, go and change." I shake my head slowly.

"What?" Dusty looks down at her outfit innocently.

"What?" I repeat as I stare.

She's dressed my body in the tightest pair of jeans ever invented. They might as well be painted on. Not only that, but they're bedazzled with lines of rhinestones running up the seams.

And I wish the jeans were the worst of it.

The t-shirt isn't so bad, but the jacket... It's a military style with double rows of tiny buttons, enormous shoulder pads, and enough bling on it to cause a migraine.

She's at least acknowledged my wishes and not worn heels, instead opting for my trusty Doc Martens, although she's switched out the black boot laces for bright purple ones. Seriously? Where did she even get those from?

As I stare into my face, which is wearing Dusty's trademark smirk, my eyes look bigger somehow, my eyelashes full, like little feathered fans, and my lips look plump and shiny.

"You're wearing makeup?"

"Just a tad." She holds up her thumb and forefinger. "A mere smidge. A little mascara and lip gloss."

I'm pretty sure it's more than that, but then another thought occurs to me.

"Dusty, where are my glasses?"

"Relax, they're safe, boo," she says, tapping her pocket.

"Why aren't you wearing them?" I frown. "You won't be able to see anything without them on."

"But it ruins the whole aesthetic." She waves her hand over the outfit as if to prove her point.

"No, I think you'll find it's the outfit doing that." My frown degenerates into a full-on scowl. "You are not letting me go out dressed like that. Go and change."

"You're not my dad," she pouts.

"You look... I look like one of Janet Jackson's bloody backup dancers." My eyes narrow. "Everyone will take one look at me dressed like that and think I've had a breakdown. Either that or I'm auditioning for the reunion tour of Rhythm Nation."

"I think you're overreacting, Tris, honey." Dusty fluffs my hair which seems to be gelled or sprayed into an artfully swept mess.

"And what's up with those jeans? You're going to need a surgeon to get me out of those." I narrow my eyes even more. "Are they cutting off circulation to my balls?"

"Relax, hun." Dusty winks. "The boys are just fine."

"Probably because they've crawled up into my body to hide," I mutter sourly.

"Look, we're wasting time." Dusty waves her hand. "Do you want to get your body back or not?"

"Is that a trick question?" I reply. "And I'd preferably like to get it back as I left it, not looking like one of the cast members from *Strictly Ballroom*. You look like you're about to show me your paso doble."

"Come on, Tris. Just this once. Pretty please?" She grips her hands together in a begging gesture.

"Fine." I roll my eyes. "But you better pray we don't see anyone. I don't know how the hell I'll explain it."

"Are you two done arguing or whatever you're doing?" Chan waves a hand vaguely in our direction. "Because this is really difficult to follow with only one half of the conversation. Isn't there anywhere you can go to learn to be a medium or whatever? Because honestly, my life would be so much simpler if I could hear what was going on."

"Sorry, don't think so, babe, but next time I'm checking in with the Higher-ups I'll ask. That is, if I don't get fired from my job as a spirit guide in training for illegally commandeering Tristan's body."

"Do you really think you'll get in trouble for it?" Chan frowns.

Dusty shrugs.

I glance down when Mrs Abernathy sidles up beside me. She smiles widely at me and offers me her handbag.

"Very kind, but no thank you." I force a smile. "I think I look ridiculous enough for one day," I mutter under my breath as I take her hand.

"Shall we go then?" Chan asks.

"Beau?" Mrs Abernathy says firmly as she offers me her handbag again, and I shake my head.

I hear the front door open and then a loud thump followed by a faint... "Ow."

"Dusty, will you just put Tristan's glasses on before you fall down the stairs and break his neck?" Chan says in amusement.

I let out a long and exasperated sigh as I turn to follow them. I have a feeling it's going to be a long day.

16

Danny

"You look like you're a million miles away." I glance up to find Maddie hovering over my desk with two mugs of coffee. "Want to talk about it?"

I take the mug she offers me and sip gratefully, my head pounding. I barely got any sleep last night. Not only because I've gotten so used to being curled up with Tristan wrapped around me like a gangly octopus and my bed felt incredibly cold and empty, but because I can't stop thinking about the past forty-eight hours.

Tris was acting very strange. I mean, he's always been a little quirky, but this was odd behaviour even for him. I could've sworn... and this is going to sound really weird... but there was a moment when I looked into his eyes, and I could've sworn it wasn't him looking back at me.

Shaking the ridiculous thought from my mind, I take another gulp of my coffee, almost burning my tongue in the process. This isn't *Invasion of the Body Snatchers,* after all; he'd just come around from being drugged. I'm sure there's nothing more complicated to it than that.

"Christ, Danny. I can practically hear the gears grinding

from over here. What's going on? If you can't trust your partner, who can you trust?"

"It's nothing." I shake my head again. "I'm being stupid or paranoid. To be honest, I'm not sure which."

"Well, I know for a fact you're neither, so if something's bothering you, it's for a legitimate reason. So spill."

"It's Tristan." I release a slow breath, wondering how to explain when I'm not really sure what the problem is.

"Okay." She pulls up a chair and plants herself next to me.

"It's going to sound stupid."

"Quit stalling and spit it out, Danny." She leans back in the chair comfortably and sips her coffee.

"Tristan is being... well, not Tristan." I frown when I realise how dumb that sounded.

"Huh?"

"He's been all cagey and pulling back from me. In the hospital, it was awkward between us, and it's never been like that. From the moment we met, we just clicked. There was this connection between us so tangible you could feel it, and yesterday it was just... I don't know."

"Can I be brutally honest here, Danny?" I nod and she continues. "Stop being a baby and give the poor guy a break. He was just given enough sedatives to drop an elephant according to the docs. His eggs are probably going to be a bit scrambled for a few days."

"I really don't know how you get through life weighed down by your mushy and sympathetic bleeding heart."

"I think you're mistaking me for my wife." Maddie grins.

"Isn't that the truth," I huff in amusement before sobering. "I guess I was just surprised that he didn't want me to stay last night. He said he just wanted some space."

She winces. "Ouch. Do you think he's having second thoughts about you two moving in together?"

"Well, now I am," I say in alarm.

"Relax." She holds up her hand. "It's probably not the case. I'm sure his noodle's just a little baked. Like you said, it's been a weird couple of days. He maybe just needed to decompress. He's had a lot thrown at him in a short space of time and if he was feeling rough, maybe he really just did want some space to sleep it off. He probably felt like he wouldn't be good company."

"I didn't need him to be good company, I just needed—"

"To take care of him?" She cuts me off, finishing my sentence. "Danny, you're one of the good ones, and I've never been into guys but even I can see that. But let's be honest here. Are you sure this isn't more about you than Tristan?"

I watch her silently, afraid to admit she might have a point.

"You got your feelings hurt. What happened to him the minute your back was turned scared you. Knowing you the way I do, you've probably got a good hefty dose of guilt mixed in with a little sting of rejection that he didn't immediately fall into your arms and let you make it all better."

"That's not exactly it," I say sulkily.

"There's nothing wrong with wanting to protect and take care of the guy you love, but you've got to remember he's a person too, and sometimes people just need a little breathing room."

"You think I'm suffocating him?"

"Not at all. I'm just saying, in those moments when he just needs to take a tiny step back and find his balance again, don't take it as a personal rejection. You guys have only been together what, six months?" I nod again. "You're still figuring out how you fit together, but that's something that only comes with time. I do get it, Danny, I really do. After what you told me about your family and how they reacted to you coming out, I know rejection is a tender spot for you, but trust me. Eventually, you'll feel secure enough in your relationship with Tris to let him take a step back to centre himself, secure in the knowledge that he's not going anywhere. He loves you, it's so easy to see, but you need to remember that being in a long-term relationship is new for him too."

"When did you become a relationship expert?" I smile slowly as I ponder her words.

"Since I've been in a relationship with the same woman for over ten years. Trust me, whatever you're feeling right now, me and Sonia have been there, done that, got the t-shirt and matching coasters. We figured it out, you will too."

"Thanks." I blow out a breath. "I guess I needed to hear that."

"You're welcome, I'm happy to tell you you're being a big baby anytime you need it." I chuckle quietly. "Now I've told you everything you're doing wrong. Do you want my advice?" She tilts her head slightly as she studies me.

"Do I have a choice?" I reply with a smile.

"Nope." She drains the last of her coffee and sets her empty mug on the edge of the desk. "I was just being polite. What you need to do is talk to him, be honest. Tell him you understand if he's feeling a little shaky and needs some space, but that you're here for him when he's ready."

I nod. "I can do that."

"Good." She slaps my knee companionably. "Now are we going to do some actual work, or do I need to start billing you for all this therapy?"

"I get the feeling I can't afford you."

"And you'd be right." She grins. "How are you doing with your share of our suspects?"

I glance down at my notes and sigh. When we realised what had happened to Tris, we divided up the list of everyone that was sitting at or had access to that table between us and started running background checks.

"Nothing." I shake my head. "I've checked Trudy Wells,

Birdie aka Margaret Forester, and Vera Ashworthy. They all came back clean, nothing out of the ordinary."

"There's not much my end either. I checked Phyllis Grover and Violet Hardy, they're both clean too. I checked Ivy Chappell and although nothing stood out, I still think she's the one who had the easiest access to your drink. "

"I think we should start by questioning Ivy, see if we can shake anything loose." I scratch my chin contemplatively.

"Everything else is a bit of a dead end, so it can't hurt." Maddie shrugs. "Although there is one more thing that's a bit odd."

"What?"

"There's one more person in their unholy little circle that has piqued my curiosity." Maddie's eyes narrow. "Maeve Landon."

"What about her?" I ask. "I thought she came back clean?"

"Not exactly." She shakes her head. "I hit a dead end."

"What do you mean?"

"I can only trace her records back to the early nineties," she replies. "Before that, there's nothing. Mrs Abernathy's niece seems certain she'd mentioned being married."

"You think she's using a different name?" I tap my fingers rhythmically on the desk. "I think I know someone who can help."

"Who?"

"He's a friend from up North and was on the force with me until he had to leave for... various reasons, but he was one of the best investigators I've ever worked with. He's a PI now. I'll contact him and see if he can help."

"I don't know, Danny. I can't see how he'd be able to do anything we can't do ourselves with enough time."

"Exactly, time. He doesn't have the caseloads we do, plus he's not bound by the same red tape and paperwork we are," I explain.

"Fine, do it." She nods as she climbs to her feet, pushing the chair out of the way as she reaches for her jacket. "In the meantime, I think we should start by having a little heart-to-heart with Ivy."

"Sounds like a plan." I tap out a quick email and shoot it off with some of the basic information about what we're looking for before pushing out of my chair and joining Maddie.

Ivy lives in a little one-bed retirement bungalow in Clapham, and as I pull up to the pavement and park along the edge of the road outside her property, I see the fussy floral net curtains twitch slightly.

"Are you ready to be mauled by a hormonal OAP?" Maddie sniggers.

"Very funny," I reply dryly as we climb out of the car and head toward the front door.

Before I can even raise my hand to ring the doorbell, the door is flung open and Ivy stands there, fluttering her eyelashes at me.

"Detective," she exclaims delightedly. "What a surprise!"

"Sure it is," I hear Maddie mutter behind me, drawing Ivy's attention.

Her smile dims. "I see you've bought *her*," she says sourly and I turn to look at Maddie.

"Her?" She mouths in amusement.

"Mrs Chappell, may we come in?" I say politely.

"It's Miss Chappell." She smiles coyly at me. "But you can call me Ivy."

"May we come in?" I ask again.

"Of course." She beams at me, but as her gaze sweeps over to Maddie, her tone cools. "I suppose you can come in too," she tacks on just for Maddie.

She turns and heads back into the bungalow, leaving us to follow along behind her. The second we're in the door, I'm hit with that musty, floral, old-lady scent. The bungalow is neatly kept with worn floral carpets in garish colours and silky wall-paper which may once have been white but is now a kind of cream colour from age. We walk along the short hallway, trying to avoid looking at the rows and rows of ornamental china plates mounted on the walls, each decorated with rural cottage scenes and flowers.

"Would you like a cup of tea?" Ivy asks as she stops and turns toward us.

"No thank you," Maddie and I chorus.

Ivy turns and heads toward her sitting room rather than the kitchen, seating herself in an armchair with lace doilies draped over the arms.

"Please take a seat." She inclines her head toward the two empty chairs.

"Actually," Maddie says, "may I use the bathroom?"

"I suppose so," Ivy says, her demeanour ungracious until she realises that means she'll have my attention all to herself. Then she brightens somewhat. "Second door on the left."

As Maddie leaves the room, I turn my attention back to the eccentric old lady.

"Ms Chappell," I begin.

"Ivy," she corrects.

"Ivy, I'd like to ask you some questions regarding an inci-dent at the afternoon tea after Mrs Abernathy's funeral."

"Oh if you're talking about the spiked brownies, there was no harm done." She waves her hand. "None of us want to press charges. After all, it wasn't poor Kevin's fault. There was a mix up in the kitchen and we got his special brownies by mistake."

"Spiked brownies?" I repeat. "You mean the brownies served at the afternoon tea were laced with–"

"Weed," Ivy supplies helpfully. "Or whatever they're calling it these days."

"Cannabis?" I blink, shaking my head. What was it with this

particular community centre? First arsenic, then sedatives, now cannabis.

"Did anyone ingest the spiked brownies?" I ask.

"Oh yes," she giggles. "The ladies were quite out of sorts."

"But no one suffered any adverse effects?"

"Not unless you count the amount of bags of crisps Birdie got through." She claps in delight. "I believe the young ones call it getting the munchies."

I shake my head. We're getting off topic, but the brownies and Kevin is something we'll definitely be circling back around to.

"That isn't actually the incident I was referring to," I say. "I'm referring to Tristan."

"Tristan." She puckers her wrinkled lips as if in deep thought. "Isn't he the nice young man who took a nap at the table? He did seem very tired."

"He wasn't sleeping," I reply flatly. "He was drugged with some kind of sedative."

"Oh," she says innocently as she smooths her skirt. "You don't say. I wonder how that happened. Are you sure he didn't have one of the brownies?"

"No, he didn't," I reply. "And I think you know that."

"I'm sure I don't know what you–"

She breaks off as Maddie walks back into the room, smiling.

"Oh, I think you do know what my partner is talking about, Ms Chappell," Maddie states as she raises her hand holding a small plastic prescription pill pot which she gives a little shake. The rattle is loud in the suddenly quiet room. "Diazepam prescribed to Ms Ivy Chappell."

"It's just to help me sleep," she says defensively.

"Ms Chappell," Maddie says coolly. "You do realise that this is the exact benzodiazepine found in Tristan Everett's blood-stream when he was admitted to hospital."

We don't know that, of course. The hospital hadn't been able to confirm anything but the fact it was a type of sedative medication; there's no way in hell to track it to a specific prescription, but Ivy doesn't know that. Her eyes dart to me nervously, and I'm guessing I'm playing the good cop again, even though I'm not feeling it at the moment. I'm still enraged that someone drugged my boyfriend.

"Look, I'm sure you didn't mean any harm." I soften my voice and school my expression into one of understanding.

"I don't..."

"Ms Chappell, this is your chance to tell us your side of it before we officially enter this medication as evidence," Maddie bluffs, laying it on thick.

"It was an accident." Her eyes shift between the two of us. "I didn't mean to hurt the young man."

"Then why did you do it?" I try to keep my voice even.

"I was just trying to be friendly, but you were so uptight and tense, I thought I'd help you relax. So I slipped a couple of my pills in your tea when you weren't looking, but honestly, it wasn't even that much. It usually only helps me relax and get a little mellow. It helps with anxiety."

"Jesus, she must have the tolerance of a rhino," Maddie murmurs.

"You had no right," I snap, my temper finally getting the better of me. "Do you have any idea how dangerous that was? What if he'd had an allergic reaction to it? What if you'd put in too much? You could've killed him."

"I'm sorry, I didn't mean to hurt him," she says contritely.

"No, just to drug me." I scowl at her. "You are in very serious trouble, Ms Chappell."

"Look, I'll apologise to the young man. Tristan, was it? I'm sure he'll be very understanding."

"Well, I'm not," I say coolly. "And I'm sure Mrs Abernathy wouldn't be either, if she were here."

"Delores?" She frowns. "What does she have to do with this?"

"Are you telling me you didn't poison her?" I accuse. "After all, you've proved you have no conscience when it comes to drugging innocent people."

"I had nothing to do with Delores' death," she says indignantly.

"I'm afraid we're going to have to continue this conversation down at the station." I stand slowly, looking down at her. "And I suggest you find yourself some representation."

"What, like an agent?" She frowns in confusion.

"He means a solicitor," Maddie states.

"No, I don't think so." She folds her hands on her lap and shakes her head stubbornly. "I'm not going anywhere. You can't make me."

"Actually, we can. We have evidence and a confession, so we can charge you for drugging Tristan and attempting to drug me. Whether we'll be adding murder to those charges is yet to be determined."

"Murder!" Ivy gasps. "I didn't murder anyone!"

"Well then, you can get a solicitor and tell your side of the story," Maddie offers bluntly.

"No," Ivy snaps. "I'm not going with either of you."

"Look, Ivy," Maddie says mildly. "We can do this the easy way or the hard way. You either get your jacket and your handbag and accompany us to the station under your own volition, or we can call a squad car to your quiet little cul-de-sac, lights and sirens blazing, and march you out of here in handcuffs in front of all your neighbours. But either way, you're coming with us."

"Fine." Her eyes narrow calculatingly. "But I'm an eighty-two-year-old pillar of the community. There's not a jury in the land that's going to convict me."

"Wanna bet?" Maddie stares at her flatly. "You broke the

law. This isn't Monopoly, there is no get out of jail free card just because you're old."

I watch as Maddie helps Ivy out of the chair and she pulls her coat on, reaching down to pick up her handbag while glaring at Maddie.

I don't know, I've got a strange gut feeling about this. There's no doubt in my mind she absolutely is responsible for what happened to Tristan, but I'm not convinced she's responsible for poisoning Delores. I guess time will tell. Although I'm hoping sooner rather than later before anyone else gets hurt.

17

Tristan

"God, I hope this works," I breathe as we stand outside the bookshop.

"It will," Dusty says firmly as she reaches for the handle, swings the door open to the chiming of bells, and steps inside the shop. "Evangeline will know how to fix this mess, trust me. She's been around so long she knows everything. She's like Yoda in a cardigan with a bag of knitting."

I follow in behind Dusty and Chan, holding onto Mrs Abernathy's hand. I'm barely inside the shop when I stop sharply, feeling a powerful wave of dizziness pass over me. I rock back on my heels slightly and blink.

"Hey? Are you okay?" Dusty asks in concern.

I swallow. "Yeah."

There's a strange buzzing at the back of my skull, and it feels like my skin is rippling with static electricity and my hair is standing on end. In fact, I'm pretty sure if I was to look in a mirror, my big hair would look like I'd just stepped off the stage at a Country Music Awards.

But the weirdest thing is the strange pull I feel. It's like something is tugging me in the direction of a solid wall. Only I know it's not a solid wall; behind there is a doorway to the spirit world. Fuck, is that what I can feel? It's potent.

"Tris?" Dusty says softly.

"I'm okay, just a little dizzy."

"I forgot about that," she murmurs as she studies me. "The first time you experience this place can be a little... intense. The first time we came in here, it almost knocked me on my arse."

I take a deep breath, even though I'm technically not breathing on account of being incorporeal, but the action is calming, nonetheless.

I nod. "I think I'm okay now."

As we approach the counter, Madame Vivienne glances up and does a double take so fast I'm sure she's given herself whiplash. Her eyes widen as she looks first at me and then at Dusty wearing my body. Vivienne rummages under the counter and pulls out a half empty bottle of gin. She fumbles with the lid, hastily screwing the cap off as she lifts the bottle to her lips and glugs shamelessly, her eyes never leaving us.

She finally lowers the bottle as she sucks in a breath.

"Nope, not dealing with that," she decides aloud and without further ado, she gathers up her gin bottle, a stack of tarot cards, and several books, and scurries behind the beaded curtain, which swishes and clatters in her wake.

"Is she always this welcoming?" Chan remarks with a raised brow.

"My goodness," a familiar voice says mildly. "You two have got yourselves in a bit of a pickle, haven't you?"

I turn to see Evangeline sitting quite calmly on the sagging sofa, her knitting needles clacking comfortingly.

She gives Mrs Abernathy a kindly smile. "Hello, Delores, dear."

"Beau?" Mrs Abernathy shuffles over to Evangeline and offers her handbag.

"No thank you, dear. That's not for me." Evangeline shakes

her head before turning her attention back to me and Dusty. "I can't wait to hear what happened, I imagine it's a fascinating tale."

"Actually it's pretty boring and straightforward." I scratch my head. "I accidentally got drugged and while I was unconscious, Dusty jumped into my body to protect me. Then when I woke up, I was out here. She's in there and wedged in tighter than those jeans she's shoehorned me into."

"Indeed." Evangeline sets her knitting in her lap, folding her hands neatly as she studies us. "Tristan, were you injured in any way?" she questions.

"No, just temporarily knocked out," I clarify.

"Well..." she hums.

"Please tell me you know what's going on and how we can fix this," I plead desperately.

"I do know what's going on." She clucks her tongue as she regards us thoughtfully. "I believe you have yourselves a case of spectral displacement."

"Special what?" Dusty blinks.

"I suspect that when you jumped into Tristan's body, you accidentally displaced him," she explains. "As for what to do about it, that's a little more complicated."

"But there is a way?" My eyes widen fearfully. "Please tell me there's a way."

"I've only ever heard of one other similar case of spectral displacement, and I believe you'll find all the details in Uncle Cornelius' book."

"Great," Dusty mutters sourly. "So once again our fate rests in the hands of a drug-addled guide to the dead."

"You want to look up the chapter on a man by the name of Bertram Phineas," Evangeline continues.

"Who was he?" I ask curiously.

"A man with whom Uncle Cornelius crossed paths in his later years. Bertram was a very unlucky fellow. Got blackout drunk one night at a pub called The Drunken Duck and woke up the next morning to find a mischievous spirit had stolen his body while he was passed out. Poor chap ended up in Bedlam. His friends and family thought he was mad as a hatter, but the truth was some complete stranger was in control of his body and he was doomed to follow them around."

"What do you mean?" I frown.

"You're still connected to your body, Tristan, by an invisible umbilicus. It was the same for poor Bertram. The connection between soul and body can only be severed by death, but in both cases you and Bertram were unconscious, not dead. Therefore you are still bound to your earthly remains, even though someone else has taken up the residence. Wherever it goes, you go."

"So how do we get Dusty out of my body and me back in?" I ask.

"I'm not entirely certain of the mechanics of it, but I believe a shock is called for," she muses.

"What kind of shock?"

"Like I said, you'll have to refer to the book. All the details are in there," she says decisively and then picks up her knitting once more, effectively considering the discussion concluded.

"Beau?" I look down and once again Mrs Abernathy has appeared by my side and is offering me her handbag.

"No thank you," I say politely.

"Did you know some people who practise witchcraft actually like to dance around naked in public?" Chan emerges from between two bookcases with a book open in her hands.

"So do people from The Wildcard, that club in Soho..." Dusty clears her throat. "So I've heard." She claps her hands together and rubs them purposefully. "Right, we need a plan. Let's go back to the flat and get *Crawshanks Guide*."

"Er yeah... about that." I offer an awkward and apologetic smile. "It's not actually there."

"Well, where is it then?" Dusty fists her hand on her hip.

"It's in a drawer."

"Yes?" she replies expectantly.

"In my desk."

"For fuck's sake, Tris, this is like pulling teeth."

"At the mortuary." I wince as she fixes me with a flat stare.

"Urgh." She rolls her eyes. "Of course, it bloody is."

"Sorry, I meant to bring it home, but I just forgot about it. How was I supposed to know I'd need it to perform a body swap?" I reply.

"Come on, then." Dusty swaggers toward the door. "Chan, are you coming?"

"Where?" She looks up from scowling at her phone.

"We have to go to the mortuary where Tristan works."

"As creepy and not fun as that sounds," she pouts, "I'm afraid I'm gonna have to take a rain check. Ginger is having a crisis. Honestly, I don't know what's got her dick in a knot, but you'd think she was pregnant by the way she's carrying on. It's always drama with that one."

"That's why she's such a great drag queen." Dusty smiles fondly. "She really nailed that Shirley Bassey number in the end."

"She did," Chan says quietly as she approaches Dusty. "Look, I just want to say now, in case you figure out a way to switch bodies back, which I'm absolutely supporting, by the way. It's not fair for Tris to be kicked out of his own digs, but I wanted to say... no matter what happens, I'm so glad we had this time together. That yesterday we got to say all the things left unsaid when you died."

I watch as Dusty cups Chan's face and I can feel the love between them. I wish there was some way for them to have this without involving my body, but I can't come up with anything. If only Chan could see spirits too. Okay, she wouldn't be able to touch Dusty, but she could at least talk to her.

"Love you, princess." Dusty wraps her arms around Chan.

"Love you too, Dusty Bun." Chan smiles as she squeezes tightly.

"Urgh." Dusty rolls her eyes, pulling back with a smile. "I knew I should never have let Tristan make you watch *Stranger Things*."

"I could sing *Never Ending Story* for you if you like." Chan grins.

"I love you more than anything, princess, but we both know you're better off lip-syncing."

Chan laughs even though her eyes are wet. "Saying goodbye a second time is harder than I thought."

"Then don't say goodbye." Dusty wipes away the tear sliding down Chan's cheek. "We'll always find each other. We're forever, never forget that."

Chan steps back and nods. "I'll see you soon, Tristan," she says to the air, not sure where I'm standing.

I don't answer, there's no point, but even if I did, there's nothing I can say that will make her feel better. I watch as she lets herself out of the shop, leaving the door open, and disappears down the alley.

"Poor dear," Evangeline says as she concentrates on her knitting. "But it will work itself out, these things often do."

"What do you mean?" Dusty stares at her intently.

"Close the door on your way out, dearie, you're letting in a draught," she says calmly and disappears in the blink of an eye.

"I hate it when she does that cryptic shit." Dusty huffs out a frustrated breath. "Come on, let's get out of here before Bruce appears and I have to explain why I'm wearing you like a masquerade costume."

We step out onto the street and the door slams behind us in a loud jarring ring. Mrs Abernathy links her arm in mine and the three of us head down the alley together.

"Dusty?" I say after a moment's contemplative silence. "Can

I ask you something?"

"Sure."

"Over the past couple of days, I can't help but notice how close you and Chan are, how you're always kissing and touching. I guess I just wondered if... um... you and Chan... did you two ever...?" I leave the question hanging.

"Have sex?"

"Sorry, that's really rude and intrusive. You don't have to answer, I'm just trying to understand your relationship."

"It's complicated," Dusty sighs. "She's my best friend, my ride or die, my confidant, my life partner... my person. Like, if I accidentally murdered someone, she'd be the one handing me a shovel as we wrapped the body in a shower curtain. I don't think it's possible for two people to be closer. But in answer to your question, yes, we did sleep with each other a couple of times when we were younger, but it wasn't... It was about affection and comfort. I know that probably sounds weird. We felt safe. We love each other, we're just not in love with each other."

"Despite how confusing and scary this has been for me," I say quietly. "I'm glad you and Chan had this time together."

"You're such a sweet man, Tristan." Dusty smiles affectionately at me. "For what it's worth, I'm sorry for all the trouble I've caused."

"For what it's worth"—I smile—"thank you for jumping in to try and save me. It may have backfired spectacularly, but I know you were trying to protect me."

"Come on," Dusty says. "Let's get to the mortuary, but just remember what I said. I am not cutting up any dead bodies."

"Oh Tristan, thank god you're here." My friend and colleague Henrietta hurries to intercept me as I walk in the door. "I know it's your day off and technically you just got out of the hospital... again." She gives me a reproving look as if choking on an ice cube or getting drugged by a potentially murderous group of old ladies was in anyway my fault.

"What can I do for you?" Dusty says uneasily.

"What on earth are you wearing?" Her brows shoot up into her brightly coloured hair as she slowly eyes the outfit Dusty dressed me in. "Crikey, are you joining the cast of Riverdance?"

"I'm trying something new," Dusty says primly. "It makes a statement."

"Is that statement, 'I'm Michael Flatley's stunt double'?"

"Was there something you wanted?" Dusty rolls her eyes, and I'd kick her if I could. She is supposed to be pretending to be me.

"Yes, hun. I know it's a massive pain, but Gerald Delford is here from *The Journal of Forensic Medicine and Pathology*, wanting to see a post-mortem. He's really interested in your double-stitch method."

"He's not supposed to be here until next week," I hiss although Hen can't hear me.

"I-I thought he wasn't coming until next week," Dusty stutters.

"His schedule got moved up. I've been trying to call you all morning." Hen blows out an agitated breath. "He's got the place in quite an uproar. Even Mr Baxter hasn't had his usual midday nap."

"Mr Baxter?" Dusty blinks.

"My boss," I explain quickly. "He doesn't actually do any work around here; he usually splits his time between reading the Angling Times or napping."

"Anyway," Henrietta continues, "we have a couple of cadavers being stored here which were donated by the families. We were going to send them over to the university, but I don't suppose anyone will mind if you use one of them, they're just going to get butchered by medical students anyway."

"Butchered?" Dusty murmurs faintly, looking a little pale.

"Oh god, here he is now... smile," she hisses under her breath and Dusty pastes on her wide stage smile, although on my face it looks rather maniacal. "Mr Delford, we were just coming to find you. This is Tristan Everett." She shoves Dusty forward.

"Ah, Everett," he booms jovially as he reaches out and grasps Dusty's hand, giving it a firm pump. "So good to meet you. I say, that's a very... interesting jacket."

"It brings all the boys to my yard." She grasps her shoulder and massages lightly as if that handshake had knocked something loose.

"Quite," Mr Delford rumbles. "Well, I've heard a lot about you. I must say I'm very much looking forward to seeing your signature double-stitch method."

"What can I say?" Dusty gives a reluctant smile. "I'm a fan of Buffalo Bill... and lotion."

"Indeed," he replies in confusion. "Well, shall we?" He lifts his hand toward the corridor toward the post-mortem room. "I believe your charming colleague has procured a volunteer cadaver for us."

"Oh, I don't think–"

Hen cuts her off and grabs her arms forcefully steering her toward the back. "Come on, Tristan. Let's get you ready, shall we?"

"I really–"

"Just this way, Mr Delford. If you want to go on through to the room I showed you earlier, we'll be right there." Hen smiles at him widely as she shoves Dusty into the changing room just off the main post-mortem room.

"This is a huge mistake–"

"Tris, hun"—Hen grabs a gown and roughly pulls it over Dusty's clothes, spinning her around and tying it off at the back —"I know you've just got out of the hospital and are probably feeling a little"— she studies my face as Dusty blinks those full eyelashes at her—"not yourself, but I really need you to take one for the team here. Getting a mention in a scientific journal will go a long way to getting the funding we need for this place. I can't go another winter with that boiler, Tris. The building was like the Arctic last Christmas, and don't even get me started on the fridge for the staff room. So you're going to go out there. You don't even need to showcase a full post-mortem, just show him some of your techniques and you can be home by teatime."

"But I–"

"Thanks, hun." She pats her cheek fondly. "I knew I could count on you."

She disappears back through the door as Dusty turns to stare at me.

"Well, you're no bloody help, are you?" she hisses.

"What do you want me to do?" I raise my hands helplessly. "They can't see me!"

"Fuck." She lets her head drop back and sucks in a breath. "You owe me for this." She finally meets my eyes as she reaches for a pair of blue latex gloves and yanks them from the dispenser roughly.

By the time she steps into the main room, she's fully gloved and gowned. She's also insisted on wearing a blue paper hairnet and a surgical mask.

"This isn't the CDC, you know," I say as I follow her into the room.

"I'm not touching that thing unless every inch of my body is covered," she sniffs.

"It's called a cadaver, not a thing, and it's not your body," I point out. "It's mine."

"It doesn't mean I want to smell like a funeral director."

"I don't smell like a funeral director," I say defensively.

"No," she relents. "Admittedly, you smell lovely..." Her voice trails off as the table comes into view. "Okay, that's really a dead body."

"Look, Dusty," I tell her. "If you really don't want to do this, you don't have to. Just tell them you don't feel well. We can grab the book and go home."

"No." She takes a fortifying breath. "I've got this. Hen wants a new fridge for the staff room, and far be it from me to deny a woman fresh milk in her tea." She nods. "I can do this."

"You don't need to touch any of the internal organs," I say quietly, even though Hen and Mr Delford can't hear me. "Just cut through the top layers of skin, and I'll talk you through the stitching. Just imagine it's one of your stage costumes."

"A costume? Yeah... if I was Ed Gein." She grimaces. "Okay." She straightens her spine. "No digging for buried treasure, just some fancy cross-stitch, no problem."

She steps up to the table and looks down at the naked man on the table with his pale waxy skin.

"Here you go." Hen hands Dusty a scalpel.

"The head bone's connected to the neck bone... the neck bone's connected to the..." Dusty hums under her breath.

"Tris, what are you doing?" Hen whispers.

"Just distracting myself." She swallows as Hen moves to stand next to Mr Delford on the other side of the table.

Dusty leans over the body, her hand trembling as she holds the scalpel.

"I think I'm going to faint," she mutters.

"Just breathe through your mouth." I move to stand directly behind her. "I'll talk you through it."

"I-I..." Suddenly, her eyes roll back in her head, and she falls backwards, stiff as a board, the scalpel clattering to the floor. All I see is the back of her as she topples toward me and then blackness.

I blink slowly as I become aware of a throbbing pain in the back of my head. My body feels heavy and somehow too tight, like a shirt that's gone through the dryer and shrunk. I can't quite lift my arms without it pulling snug.

"Tristan, good gracious," a loud voice rings out, echoing across the room, and I recognise the familiar tone of Judy, who works up in the office and pretty much does Mr Baxter's job for him. "Are you alright? What on earth are you doing here working? I told you to take today off."

Slowly, it begins to register that I'm back inside my body, even though it feels really weird. But where the hell is Dusty?

"I-I think I'm fine," I croak.

"Oh my god! What happened!" also bursts out of my mouth, and in a moment of dread I realise one thing. That wasn't me that spoke.

"Dusty?" I think loudly.

"There's no need to shout, Tristan. I fainted, I'm not in a coma. Where are you anyway?"

"Okay, don't freak out, but I think we're somehow both stuck in my body."

"WHAT!!!!"

"I said don't freak out."

"How can I not freak out? I haven't been enclosed with someone in a space this small since I played Spin the Bottle and ended up in Charlie Braithwaite's understairs cupboard when I was thirteen with his tongue stuck in my mouth. Urgh, he'd been eating Twiglets too, and I can't stand marmite. Put me right off."

"Are you okay. Tris?" Hen asks in concern.

"I think he hit his head harder than we thought. Maybe we should—"

"No more hospitals," I blurt out, cutting Judy off. "I'm just going to go to my office for a moment and sit down, then I'm going home."

"Very well." Judy looks up at Mr Delford. "Why don't you come with me, Mr Delford? I'm afraid Tristan's not up for a demonstration today, perhaps tomorrow."

"Certainly." He passes by me and pats me on the shoulder. "Rest up, lad. Maybe next time."

Judy and Mr Delford exit the room while Hen hovers over me in concern.

"I'm so sorry, Tris. It's just you looked fine, so I thought–"

"It's fine, Hen. Why don't you go grab me a bottle of water? I'm going to go sit in my office for a bit. Get my feet under me before I call for an Uber."

"Of course I can. I'll be right back." She disappears through the door, and I wait until she's out of sight.

"Okay, let's get this bloody book and get out of here," I say aloud to Dusty.

"Took the words right out of my mouth," she replies and it's so weird to hear both of our words coming out of my mouth, it's like I'm talking out loud to myself.

Fuck this for a game of ping pong, I want my body back. If I thought it was weird before on the outside looking in, that was nothing compared to how it feels sharing my consciousness with Dusty.

I push myself upright, but as I go to step forward with my right foot, I think Dusty tries to step with my left, and instead we end up stumbling and falling flat on my face.

"Ow," I mutter against the cold tile.

"Whoops." Dusty winces.

"Ok, Dusty." I draw in a breath. "One of us needs to be in charge of motor functions. So just don't... do anything."

"Fine," she sulks.

I push myself back to my feet and take a couple of stumbling steps toward the door, only one goal in mind. Retrieve *Crawshanks Guide* from my desk and get back to the safety and privacy of my flat so I can work out what the hell is going on. I didn't think my life could get any more complicated but, oh boy, was I wrong.

18

Danny

I find myself staring mindlessly at my screen, once again at a dead end. None of the leads so far have panned out, and I'm no closer to figuring out who poisoned Delores Abernathy. Ivy Chappell had been another of those dead ends. She admitted to drugging my tea, which Tristan had ended up drinking by mistake, but so far we've found no evidence that ties her to the arsenic poisoning.

As much as I love my job, this really is the unglamorous side of police work. It's nothing like it is on TV; instead, it's hours, days, or even weeks of painstaking investigation that most of the time don't pan out. This case has been one massive frustration from beginning to end. Why use something as dated as arsenic? Why kill an old lady with dementia who had no money and at best only had a few more years left anyway?

I need a break, I think as I rub my forehead in frustration. And not a quick run to the shitty coffee machine on the next floor. I mean a real break, maybe a weekend away with Tris, no work, no interruptions. Just the two of us.

My phone vibrates across my desk, and I see the name Samuel Stone flash across the screen as I pick it up and answer.

"Sam," I greet. "That was quick. I wasn't expecting to hear from you so soon."

"Yeah, well, what can I say? I'm very good at what I do," a deep familiar voice answers, one heavily laced with a Yorkshire accent, and for a moment I feel a fleeting pang of homesickness. Even though I'm happy in London with Tris and would never go back up North, it reminds me of my family, something I really don't particularly want to think about.

"You found something?"

"More than just something," Sam rumbles. "Let's just say finding Maeve Landon's real name is just the tip of the iceberg. You're not going to believe the shit I dug up on her."

"Well, don't keep me in suspense."

"Not over the phone. Can you meet me?" he asks.

"You're not in Leeds?" I remark in surprise.

"I'm in London, have been for some time."

"Why didn't you say something?" I ask, slightly hurt that he didn't tell me we were both in the same city again.

"I..." He goes quiet for a moment. "I had some stuff I had to work through first, but that's part of the reason I'd like to see you face-to-face... there are some things I need to say."

My stomach drops a little, wondering what it is he has to say to me. "Okay, where are you?"

"I'm at Charing Cross at the moment. I have something I need to do first, but can you meet me in Covent Garden in about an hour?"

"Sure," I answer, checking my watch. "Where?"

"There's a coffee shop called The Black Penny on Great Queen Street."

"I'll find it." I nod even though he can't see me.

"And Danny?"

"Yeah."

"I'm looking forward to seeing you. It's been a long time," he says reflectively.

"Yeah, me too," I say quietly.

We mumble our goodbyes and I hang up the phone. Rising from my seat, I unhook my jacket from where it's draped across the back of the chair and pull it on. I probably should include Maddie if Sam has information about our case, but I don't. There's unfinished personal business between me and Sam. I haven't seen him since I left home and moved down South to London. I tried to stay in contact, to check in on him and see how he was doing, but it was clear at the time what he wanted was space, and as his friend, all I could do was respect his wishes.

I shoot Maddie a message and manage to navigate my way out of the building without running into her. Not that she wouldn't have understood, but I guess I've got some mixed feelings seeing Sam after all this time, especially after what happened to him.

By the time I've made my way to Covent Garden, I'm pretty much bang on time. Bustling my way through the crowds of tourists, past museums and market stalls, I manage to find The Black Penny and head inside. It's got a nice feel to it, urban and laid-back, with blackened wood cladding, exposed brickwork, and Edison-style lightbulbs hanging from the ceiling on long black wires.

As if drawn by a lodestone, my gaze lands on the man tucked at a wooden table towards the back, his head down as he stares at something on his phone and ignores the coffee cup tucked next to a manila file beside him. I wander along the long gallery-style counter, ignoring all the salads and sweet treats, and instead opt to just grab a plain coffee.

After thanking the short hipster guy sporting a cartoon villain moustache and standing behind the counter, I head toward the table. Almost as if sensing my presence, Sam looks up, and I draw in a slow breath and force my feet to keep moving. He looks so different from how I remember him but a hell of a lot better than the very last time I'd seen him, lying broken in a hospital bed.

"Danny," he says quietly as he stands.

I set my cup down on the table and stare at him, wondering how I should greet him. Fuck it, I decide, pulling him in for a hug. He stiffens for a moment and then relaxes, his arms coming up tentatively as he presses his palms to my back.

"Sam," I whisper, pulling back to get a better look at him.

He was always well-built, if a little on the soft side around the middle. It's clear he's lost a lot of weight in the time we've been apart and not in the *I'm on a fitness buzz* kind of way but more of the *I drink far too much coffee and forget to eat* variety. But it's his face I study, his once clean-shaven jaw and short, almost military-esque hairstyle having given way to dark stubble and pitch-black shaggy hair that hangs to his collar and is badly in need of a cut. But the thing I can't help noticing is the nasty jagged scar puckering his skin, slightly dragging down the corner of his eye and running down his cheek.

"It's good to see you," I tell him honestly.

"Yeah." He pulls back as we both take our seats on opposite sides of the bench table. "You too. You look good."

"Thanks," I smile.

"London agrees with you." He studies my face with as much scrutiny as I'd mapped his.

"I guess it does."

"Or maybe it's the cute pathologist you're practically shacked up with." His mouth curves at the corner, crinkling his scar further.

I raise a brow. "And how would you know that?"

"Because I'm very good at what I do." He chuckles. "Did you really think I'd come to London and not look you up?"

"No, but I'd kind of expected a phone call or a message at the very least," I reply frankly.

He nods as he reaches for his coffee. "I had some things I had to work out first."

"You look good," I say after a moment.

"I look like shit, I think is what you meant to say," he says quietly as he toys with the handle of his cup.

"Nah. Add a trench coat and a fedora and you're one Maltese Falcon away from passing for a hardened film-noir PI."

"Well, I certainly have the name for it," Sam snorts. "All I need is a twenty a day habit and a penchant for whiskey sours."

"Here's looking at you, kid." I raise my cup and toast him playfully before taking a sip.

He shakes his head, a small smile playing on his lips. "I'd forgotten about your film obsession."

"How are you really, Sam?" I ask seriously. "I'm sorry I had to leave before you were fully discharged from the hospital, but my job started pretty much straight away. I sometimes think getting the job was less about my qualifications and more the fact they were desperate for staff."

"I'm not surprised they offered you the job with an immediate start," Sam replies, his dark eyes sincere. "You're a hell of a detective, you know you are."

"So are you," I remind him.

"Once maybe," he murmurs, staring into his cup. "But I'll never work for the police force again."

I nod. I completely understand why he'd feel that way. "I'm sorry I didn't get to say goodbye properly though," I say, my voice tinged with regret.

"I probably wouldn't have agreed to see you anyway," he admits. "I wasn't in a good place at that point. My recovery... " He pauses. "Well, let's just say it took longer than expected."

"And are you? Recovered?"

He shrugs. "My broken bones are healed, and I'm more or less back to normal, just slightly less pretty and missing a spleen."

"I didn't mean physically," I say.

"You mean, have I gotten over the fact I was attacked and almost beaten to death for being gay?" He sighs. "My life changed in ways that I couldn't have possibly imagined that night," he murmurs in quiet contemplation. "My life is... different now. I'm not the same person you knew, not even close."

"I'm so sorry, Sam." My heart hurts when I think about how badly he suffered, not just from the sheer hate and brutality of the attack or the physical scars he was left with, but from the way people we'd known for years—friends, colleagues—all turned on him. I know that some of them even thought he'd deserved it, although they hadn't been stupid enough to say that to my face.

"Don't be. I don't need your pity," he says in a firm voice. "It took me a long time to get my head straightened out and adjust to my new reality, but I'm content. I like it here in London and my business is doing well."

"I'm glad."

He looks me directly in the eye. "Part of the reason I wanted to see you rather than talk over the phone was because I wanted to say thank you."

"Thank you?"

"I know what you did for me, and I know what it cost you," he says.

"It's nothing." I shrug uncomfortably.

"Danny." His voice almost dares me to disagree with him. "It wasn't nothing. You were the first to come to the hospital to check on me, and after it all came out about my sexuality and the tongues started spewing venom, you stood up publicly and not only called them out but came out yourself in solidarity. Don't think I don't understand how hard that was for you. I know your family stopped talking to you after that."

"To be fair, they were hardly talking to me before." I stared down at my cup. "I didn't just do it for you, Sam. I'm no martyr, so don't go putting me up on a pedestal. I couldn't live like that anymore. I wasn't ashamed of who I am, and you shouldn't have had to be either. We shouldn't have to hide, worried about what could happen if we misread a situation or misjudge someone's interest. What happened to you was wrong, but what came after made me ashamed of everyone around us."

"You and me both," he sighs. "Still, what's done is done. I won't be going back."

"You know, I'd love to introduce you to Tristan. Maybe we could grab dinner one night," I offer.

"I'd like that." He smiles slowly. "Although I wouldn't have pegged him as your type. You always went for the built, athletic types, not cute little twinks. They were always more my type."

"No, your type was snarky with a tongue so sharp you could cut yourself on it." I chuckle. "And why am I not surprised you know what he looks like."

"I'm good a–"

"At your job," I finish his sentence with a roll of my eyes. "I see you're still as modest as ever."

"Speaking of being good at my job." He picks up the manila folder and slides it over the table to me.

"Your suspect. Maeve Landon aka Peggy Johnson aka Iris Carter aka Harriett Walker... I could go on."

"What?" I reply as I open the folder curiously.

"She's a black widow." He shrugs. "At least, that would be my guess. I haven't got to the bottom of all of it yet, but the more I uncovered, the more there was. Her birth name is Edith Anderson, born in Letchworth, October 8th, 1936. She married in '56, and he died two years later of unknown causes. She then changed her name and remarried in '59, then husband number two died too. It's her MO. She marries, husband dies, she changes her name and moves on."

"How the hell did you put this together so quickly?" I frown as I flip through the paper trail.

"Let's just say I have access to certain resources that you don't," he says carefully.

"I'm almost afraid to ask."

"Then don't." Sam shakes his head. "Now this is the important part. Edith had an older brother, now deceased, but he was arrested in 1984 and charged with multiple counts of fraud and forgery for which he served time."

"He was a forger?" I say as I stare at a couple of passport photos of a younger version of the woman currently calling herself Maeve Landon.

"A very good one by all accounts, but found amongst the things in his flat was a ledger of all the identities he'd created for his clients. Honestly, I don't know why he felt the need to document everything, but it certainly made the prosecution's case easier."

"So he had a list of all his sister's aliases?" I guess.

"Yep, but get this. Before she got married to husband number one, she worked as a chemist's assistant."

"Did she now? Do you think the brother knew she was bumping off her husbands?" I scan down the list of names on the paper in front of me.

"I would imagine he did, or at least suspected, if he was creating new identities for her every couple of years," Sam replies. "But I doubt he had much of a conscience. He lived in Bethnal Green and apparently had ties to the Krays."

I scratch my chin thoughtfully and look up as Sam chuckles. "What?"

"You always scratch your chin like that when you're trying to puzzle something out." He smiles and shakes his head. "I'd forgotten you did that."

I return his grin. "I suppose as bad habits go, there are worse ones."

"Anyway," he draws my attention back to the notes, "here's where it gets interesting. When the brother was arrested, the police were running down the names on his list to build a case and came across Edith in her then-current alias, Harriet Walker. They dug a little further and found her husband had died only a few weeks earlier under suspicious circumstances, but before they could arrest her, she disappeared. It seemed her brother had already created her new identity but hadn't listed it. I went back through all the death certificates and reports for the dead husbands, and although a couple of them were listed as deaths from unknown causes, most of them came back death by poisoning. Do you want to guess her poison of choice?"

"Arsenic?"

"Bingo." He raises his brows. "And you know what poisoners are like, they find an MO and they stick to it like glue, even at the risk of getting caught. It's like a compulsion."

"Jesus Christ, that would make her a serial killer." I sit back in my chair. "But why Delores?" I chew my lip, deep in thought.

"It's possible she was just an easy target," Sam replies. "Just because Edith stopped marrying her victims, doesn't mean she went dormant. If you start looking, the bodies will probably start piling up."

"Are you sure you don't want to come and work with me?" I ask. "I know they'd snap you up in a heartbeat."

"No thanks." He shakes his head. "I'm happy doing what I do. Like I said, this"—he nods at the file—"is only a very rough outline. There's a lot more legwork on this case. It's probably going to take quite some time to unravel all the details."

"Thanks for this, Sam," I say earnestly. "I'm seriously impressed."

He shrugs. "You'd have got there eventually, I just sped up the process."

"I need to call my partner." I drain the last of my coffee and tidy all the paperwork back into the folder.

"Ah, the fiery, red-haired Detective Madeleine Wilkes."

"Will you stop spying on me?" I roll my eyes. "If you want to know what's going on in my life, pick up the phone and ask."

"Can't help it, force of habit." His mouth twitches.

I push myself up from the table and pick up the folder. "Thank you again, Sam. I owe you."

He stands as well. "Trust me, you don't owe me a damn thing."

"Okay, but at least let me buy you dinner soon and then you can meet Tristan."

"It's a deal." His mouth curves.

"Well, I need to get going." I tuck the folder under my arm. "We need to pull the original investigation into Edith Anderson, and we need to track down Maeve Landon and invite her to join us for a chat."

"A chat?" Sam repeats in amusement.

"Did I say chat?" I reply. "I meant arrest her bony arse."

"Mind if I tag along?" Sam grins. "I have no intention of joining the Met, but I'm curious to see how this all plays out."

"By all means," I offer. "Be my guest."

19

Tristan

"This is so freaking bizarre." My hand lifts and my eyes are drawn to it as if I'm studying it.

"Dusty, do you mind?" I blow out an irritated breath. "I'm trying to read this."

"I do not like this at all," Dusty says, and even though I can't see her, I can feel her pout on my lips.

"You and me both," I answer. "But if you'd let me concentrate on this book, then we can figure out how to separate us and give me back sole ownership of my body as quickly as possible."

"Urgh," she says sulkily, "but that book is so boring, and it makes no sense at all."

"Dusty," I warn.

"Fine." She throws up my hands dramatically and the book tumbles to the floor. "But I still don't understand how we both ended up wedged in here. Honestly, it's like when you're a kid and you try to see how many of your friends you can squeeze into a photo booth."

"I'm not really sure how it happened," I muse as I lean down to pick up Crawshanks Guide and settle back on my worn sofa. "Best guess, when you fainted you were technically unconscious, and when you fell backward, I was standing in the way. I mean, that's kind of what Evangeline said, wasn't it? That if someone's unconscious, then a spirit could theoretically take possession of the body, which is how you ended up in me in the first place."

Dusty sniggers. "That still sounds so dirty."

"Focus," I sigh. "Honestly, you have the sense of humour of a pubescent child."

"Okay, sorry," Dusty says and rolls my eyes. "I get the whole unconscious possession thing, but what I don't get is, when I fell backwards and you ended up back in your body, why wasn't I just pushed out of the other side. What did Evangeline call it? Special dismemberment."

"Spectral displacement," I correct absently. "That's a good point. I can't say for certain, maybe it was just bad timing. Like a glitch, the moment I pushed inside–"

There's another snigger in my head.

"Dusty..."

"Sorry."

"Maybe at the exact moment I ended up back in my body, you also started to wake up, and we somehow both got squished together. Like Jeff Goldblum in *The Fly*."

"First of all... ewww, and secondly, that makes no sense." She shakes my head.

"Nothing about this entire situation makes any sense, but it's the best I've got. Only right now I'm less concerned with how this happened and more concerned with how the hell we fix it."

"What if you knock me out?"

"How am I supposed to do that?" I say, exasperated. "We're both stuck in here. All that would happen is we'd end up knocking both of us out, and quite frankly, I think my poor body has taken enough punishment."

"Alright, fair point," Dusty concedes, and my hands lift the book. "What does Corny Crawshanks have to say?"

"Alright, let me see." I skim through the pages until the name Bertram pops out at me. "Hang on, I think this is it," I mutter as my gaze skims across the paragraph.

On concerning the afternoon of the 4th, it was then I happened, quite perchance, upon a sorry fellow by the name of Bertram Phineas, a stout, swarthy chap, very much enamoured of more than the odd pint, and well known by the patrons of The Drunken Duck. A rather affable drunkard who on more than one occasion became so inebriated, he was unable to find his way to the doss house he frequented on Limehouse Street and would oftentimes sleep it off in the local graveyard amongst the moss and bones.

For most, this would present as a rather unseemly pastime and nothing more, but for one such as myself this presented a much darker invitation. I believe it was during one such time of overindulgence that Mr Phineas fell asleep and was happened upon during this time of deepest slumber by an errant earthbound spirit.

Seizing upon such an opportunity presented, the malcontent creature did then impose itself upon poor dear Mr Phineas and take up an uninvited residence in his physical form. Mr Phineas himself was summarily put out as one might shoo out a stray cat that has wandered over one's threshold.

Being neither a stray nor a feline, Mr Phineas found himself suddenly as insubstantial as the wind but still quite firmly anchored to his body. The spirit found this all to be a great amusement and was in no way inclined to return Mr Phineas' form to him.

Now, unfortunately, the spritely creature began to behave in a very unseemly manner, sparking the attention of those who were quite used to Mr Phineas' usual antics. The doctor was called for and declared Mr Phineas to be of unsound mind and summarily dismissed him to the tender mercies of the orderlies of Bedlam.

During his protracted stay at this stalwart institution, Mr Phineas, that is to say, the spirit who had infested Mr Phineas' body, found himself to be the recipient of a rather new and exciting medical breakthrough, whereas the staff would introduce electricity through the patient's brain via two conductors attached to either side of the skull.

The resulting shock pushed the spirit from Mr Phineas' body, at which instance he was able to regain possession. The aftereffects did linger, and Mr Phineas found himself to be suffering with frequent headaches to which I offered him cocaine to ease his discomfiture.

The staff, believing Mr Phineas to be cured of his ailment, released him with fourpence for the night's lodging. He went immediately to The Drunken Duck and proceeded to become intoxicated, whereupon he then passed out in the very same graveyard. As one might imagine, the threads of fate are fickle, and Mr Phineas once again found his body infested with another spirit, one who was quite obsessed with seeing the world. Using Mr Phineas' physical form, he signed up with the captain of a merchant trading vessel and was last seen sailing for the West Indies, and so thus ends the cautionary tale of poor Bertram Phineas.

"Oh." My brows draw together.

"Oh what?" Dusty says in a bored tone of voice.

"Didn't you pay attention to any of that?" I reply.

"Hmm." She rolls my eyes. "Something about a boat and cocaine. If I'd wanted to know about that, I would've watched Love Island. Honestly, I got to the part about graveyards and tuned out."

"Then you missed the part when Cornelius said it took a shock to get the spirit out of Bertram's body so he could get back in?"

"A shock? Seriously, that's it? What? We're just supposed to have someone jump out on us and shout 'Boo'?"

"Um, not that kind of shock."

"What other kind is there?" she asks blankly.

"The electrical kind."

"What, like static electricity?" Dusty wrinkles my nose.

"Because that happened to me the one and only time I wore Uggs and pressed the button for an elevator. Let me tell you, that shit stings, my hair was standing on end for an hour."

"No I mean as in several volts, Bride of Frankenstein, kind of... *It's Alive!* electricity."

"Yeah... no thanks." Dusty tosses the book across the room.

"That's really mature, Dusty, but it's not like we have a lot of options." I push myself off the sofa and walk across the room. Well, I try to walk across the room, but it ends up being more of a sassy hip-swaying strut. I shake my head and breathe out slowly. I can't wait to have my body back to myself.

"Do you mean they just wired that guy to the mains and zapped him?" Dusty asks in horror.

"Kind of. I mean, electricity was a shiny new toy back then. They thought it could be applied as a cure for most medical ailments," I reply. "They were electrocuting people for having ingrown toenails."

"Bloody Victorians," Dusty mutters. "You're not actually serious about recreating that, are you? Because even I can tell that would be an epically bad idea."

"No," I answer with a frustrated huff as I open the book once more. "But I could really use some help right now." I lift the book and something flutters from the pages and lands on the floor. As I lean down to pick it up, I frown in confusion.

"What's that?" Dusty asks, turning it over in my hand.

"It's a blank business card," I respond as I stare at its shiny holographic surface. "I found it... I was outside the bookshop, and I ran into a stranger. This fell from his pocket."

"Why did you keep it?" she asks. "It's got nothing on it."

"That's just it. I didn't, at least not intentionally," I muse. "I shoved it in my pocket, meaning to throw it away, but I forgot. I haven't worn that jacket since then. It's still in my room, so how did this card end up inside the book, in my desk drawer, at the mortuary?"

"I've given up trying to figure out this weird shit." Dusty flips my hand negligently.

I tilt the card in the light and watch in surprised fascination as a silvery swirly script appears before my eyes.

Harrison Ames - Witch.

For all your magical needs.

I turn the card over and sure enough, on the back there's now an address which is in Islington, not that far from here.

"This is it, Dusty!" I exclaim excitedly.

"Really?" Dusty raises a perfectly sculpted brow. "What's he going to do, chant and burn some sage? I think we need something a little more substantial than some New Age hippie in tie-dye."

"There's a lot of stereotyping in that sentence." I shake my head. "Look, what have we really got to lose at this point?"

"Oh, I don't know, your dignity?"

"That went out the window with you holding my penis and peeing for me," I answer. "Anyway, this is technically my body, I've got seniority, and I say we're going."

"Fine," she huffs. "But don't come crying to me when he tries to sell you tarot cards and incense sticks."

Grabbing my jacket and keys, I head out of my flat eagerly. Last night we'd had to come up with a lame excuse once again for Danny to not come over. It had been awkward enough when Dusty was in charge of my body and I was on the outside looking in, but with both of us currently crammed in here, it would have got a little cramped in the bed with Danny too.

I miss him like mad. I've kind of been ignoring messages from him because I just don't know what the hell to say. We had a real moment the other night when we decided to move in together and add another layer to the relationship we're building, then all of a sudden, from his perspective, I start ghosting him. Which is ironic given the situation.

Twenty minutes later, I find myself climbing out of an Uber

outside the address on the card. It's a small shop, like really small, tucked away from the main High Street. Taking a breath, I open the door and step through. The space is tiny but bright and clean. Instead of the type of dust-covered clutter Madame Vivienne has in her place, this one is meticulously clean with glass display cabinets lining the walls. I wander along them slowly and mentally catalogue the contents. One contains expensive-looking amulets and jewellery along with deep bowls filled with gemstones of every colour. The next case is filled with tarot cards and runes, another holds some extremely old and rare books. There's also wicker baskets filled with fragrant dried herbs.

I'm so caught up in all the fascinating objects I almost miss the handsome red-haired man sitting on a chair in the corner and watching me, the same man I'd run into outside the book-shop in Whitechapel.

"Oh, hello." I smile nervously. "Um, Harrison Ames?"

"That's me," he says. His gaze drops to the card I'm still holding in my hand and his eyes narrow. "Where did you get that?" He points to the card.

"I, uh..." I step closer. "We ran into each other outside Whitechapel Occult Books & Curiosities the other day."

"I know."

"Yes, well, um, you dropped this as you were walking away. I tried to call out to you, but when I looked up you were gone," I explain.

"That's impossible," he scoffs. "I didn't have any of those cards with me that day. They're very special. I don't just give them to anyone."

"Um, I don't mean to be rude but... you're a witch?" I blurt out, not sure if I intended that as a question or a statement. "I need some help."

He studies me closely, his head at a slight tilt and his full lips pursed. "You don't need a witch, you need an exorcist."

"Excuse you!" Dusty busts out indignantly and I grimace. Although it's my voice she's using, her tone and inflections are completely different from my demeanour. I can only imagine I come across as someone with a multiple personality disorder.

"You have someone in there who doesn't belong, Mr Everett," he says calmly.

"How do you know my name?" My eyes narrow in suspicion.

"Does it matter?" He raises one perfect eyebrow.

"To be honest, I don't really care," I reply, feeling utterly wretched. "I just want my body back. This whole thing with Dusty was just bad luck, bad timing, bad everything, and we don't know how to separate ourselves. She was just trying to protect me."

"I see," he murmurs as he continues to study me.

"Please," I say quietly.

"You are a curious one, aren't you?" he murmurs.

"What does that mean?" I reply in confusion.

"Look here, Ginger Spice," Dusty snaps, shoving me into the back of my mind. "Are you just going to talk in riddles all day, or are you going to help us? I know that you don't know us, and you've no reason to help, but Tristan is the kindest, sweetest man you could ever meet. None of this is his fault. He helps people... okay, dead people, but they're still people. He's patient and loyal and really funny."

"Do you want me to help him or date him?" Harrison replies with a smirk.

"Very funny, but I don't think his sexy-as-hell detective boyfriend would appreciate that," Dusty says flatly. "We kind of got caught up in a situation where I had to make a quick judgement call, which may or may not have been a dumb-arse thing to do. If you don't help us, Tris won't be able to get his body back and move in with his super-hot boyfriend. Delores won't be able to resolve her unfinished business and go into the light.

The mortuary won't end up in the stupid science journal because of the stitching thingy. Henrietta won't get her new fridge for the staff room, and I'll have to explain to Bruce that I'm stuck in someone else's body, and we're supposed to be going on a date for Dia de los Muertos. His family are expecting us and trust me, his abuela is not going to be happy if we're a no-show."

"Dusty, is it?" She nods. "Brace yourself."

"What?" she replies, a bit baffled.

He rubs his hands together like he's the Karate Kid, and I swear I see tiny little microbursts of lightning lick across his palms. He suddenly presses his hands to my chest, and it's like I've been hit with a defibrillator. The sudden shock of power hits me so forcefully, it throws me back, taking my feet out from under me. I hit the floor hard, knocking the air from my lungs.

For a second I lie here, stunned as to what the hell happened, while trying desperately to suck in some air, but I'm severely winded. I slowly see Harrison's face appear above me, studying me appraisingly before nodding in satisfaction. He extends a hand and I reach up and grab hold. Once on my feet, I straighten up shakily. I feel like my skin is tingling and my hair is standing on end, but otherwise I feel... normal. My body no longer feels like an overstuffed sausage that's going to burst any moment.

I hear a pained groan behind me and as I turn to look, I see Dusty sit up on the floor, her eyes wide and her hair enormous and smoking slightly.

"What the hell was that?" She blinks. "Did we get hit by a bolt of lightning?"

"You're welcome," Harrison says easily.

"Thank you so much." I turn to him and pat my body down like I'm looking for something. "I can't tell you how good it feels to be me again. I don't know how I can ever thank you enough."

"Just try not to let your body get hijacked again. The Higher

Powers don't like things like that. It messes with their grand plan."

"What grand plan?" I ask, but he just shrugs before reaching out and gently grasping my chin with his cool fingers. He tilts my head as if to get a better angle to peer at my face.

"You've been marked," he mutters.

"What?"

"Someone or something has taken a very definite interest in you," he states.

"Who?"

"Well, that's the question now, isn't it?" He licks his bottom lip slowly.

"I saw..." I hesitate for a moment, wondering if I should admit what I'd seen first in the care home and then at the community centre. Then again, this man seems to know far more than he's letting on. "I saw a reaper, twice now. It looked straight at me. It was almost like it was watching me and then it disappeared."

"A reaper and yet you live?" He seems genuinely taken aback by my words, although not surprised at the concept of a reaper. "No one has ever seen one twice, and it couldn't have been looking at you if you weren't its target."

"What do you mean?" My stomach trembles with a strange mixture of fear and fascination.

"Reapers only go after those they're assigned to escort into the afterlife. Any other living being is simply white noise to them. It shouldn't have even been aware of your presence, and you should not have been able to see it." He pinches his lip in thought.

"What do you think it means?" I ask.

"I have no idea," he says, and he seems to be genuine. "I've never heard of anything like it."

"Oh." I struggle not to sound too disappointed.

"Anyway, I have things to do, so run along. Try to stay out of trouble and tell your friend to stay out of other people's bodies..." He lifts a brow and I see a fleeting glimmer of humour. "Unless, of course, it's consensual."

Dusty cackles in delight behind me as Harrison returns to his chair in the corner, picking up a book he was obviously reading before we came in.

"Thank you again," I say gratefully. "I really do owe you."

"And I might just collect one of these days," he says as he opens his book and begins to read. "Oh, and Tristan," he calls out as I'm about to head towards the door. Without looking up, he points to the corner of the room. "Take that with you, please."

I turn to see Delores standing there, looking as lost as usual.

"Come on, honey." Dusty takes her hand and leads her out of the shop. I follow behind them, staring at Dusty's still-smoking hair as it fills the air with the curious scent of extinguished birthday candles.

We step out onto the pavement and the door closes behind us.

"Well, I have to say, Tris"—Dusty shakes her head politely as Delores offers her handbag—"as fun as it was being alive for a hot minute, I'm glad to have things back to normal."

"That makes two of us." I smile in relief.

"What's the first thing you want to do? Have a latte? Grab something to eat? Take a nap?"

But I know exactly what I want. Or rather, who I want. I grab my phone from my pocket and dial Danny's number. It barely rings twice before he picks it up.

"Tristan, is everything alright?" he asks, and I hate that I've worried him so much over the last few days that those are his first words to me.

"I'm fine, nothing's wrong. I'm actually feeling loads better and I wanted to see you," I say honestly. "I miss you."

His voice softens. "I miss you too."

"Where are you right now?" I ask.

"Just about to head out to Northwold Community Centre."

"What? Why?" I reply worriedly. "We haven't exactly had the best of luck there," I remind him.

"I know but long story short, we know who is responsible for Delores Abernathy's murder."

"WHAT? WHO?" I burst out.

"Tris, I'm sorry, I can't talk right now. We're on our way to arrest her. I'll call you later."

"No, wait!" But it's too late. He's already hung up. I grab my phone and pull up the Uber app.

"Where are we going?" Dusty asks, holding Delores' hand and patting it comfortingly.

"Clapham," I say worriedly. "Danny found the murderer."

20

Danny

"Have you found anything?" I look up as Maddie enters the room. She throws me a frustrated look and shakes her head.

"What about you?" She nods towards the old-fashioned cherry wood sideboard I'm currently rummaging through.

Closing the drawer and moving down to the one underneath, I continue to search. "Nothing so far," I mutter. "There must be something here."

It had taken a favour pulled in from one of Maddie's friends who worked over at the magistrates' court to get us seen so quickly but once we did, there was no problem getting a search warrant for Maeve Landon aka Edith Anderson's tidy little two-bedroom house in Clapham Common. Sam may not have had much time to look into Maeve, but what he found was more than enough to convince a judge.

I think we all have a vested interest in seeing how this plays out. Not only could we possibly close Delores Abernathy's case, but we may end up wrapping up a whole load of cold cases too, possibly even uncovering more.

I have an uncomfortable feeling in my stomach, a gut

instinct that tells me we've barely even scratched the surface of this woman's crimes.

"I don't know what to tell you, Danny, but the officers upstairs haven't found anything yet and there's nothing in the kitchen. This place is meticulously kept, not so much as a speck of dust or a coaster out of place." Maddie sits down in one of the chairs.

"We need something more concrete." I chew my lip thoughtfully as my gaze scans the living room. "She's a clever woman. She has to be to avoid being caught for this long. She's not just going to leave anything out in the open that would trip her up…" I scratch my chin as my mind works furiously. "I know there's something here, there has to be. What do we know about the house itself?"

"Victorian semi-detached." Maddie pulls out her notebook and flips through a couple of pages. "Owned by Charles Landon, Maeve's name isn't on the deeds. Looks like he bought the place back in 1967, way before he met Maeve. Records show they married in 1994 at the local registry office. Her name was Maeve Bennett at that point."

"That must have been the identity her brother created for her in '84 right before he was arrested."

"Landon was older than her, by thirteen years or so. He would've already been 71 years old when they married according to the marriage certificate your friend Sam unearthed."

"Did I hear my name?" Sam strolls into the room with his hands casually tucked in his pockets and looks around the room.

"We were just talking about Charles Landon," Maddie says. "There's no death certificate listed for him." She raises one gloved hand and points a finger at him. "You'd better not be touching anything without gloves." Sam grins and pulls one out to show off the blue latex.

"So where is he?" I lift a brow, already suspecting the answer.

"I think we all know what's most likely happened." Maddie scowls. "If he were still alive, he'd be nearly a hundred years old. Maeve's still drawing his pension and all the bills are paid, but there's no sign of a man living here at all."

"We can probably add theft and fraud to her list of charges then," I say darkly.

"Poor man." Maddie shakes her head. "The sad thing is, no one seemed to notice he'd disappeared. Maeve certainly picked well. An older man who kept to himself, didn't have many friends. A confirmed bachelor most of his life, no living family, no children."

"We have to find something." I glance down at my watch.

Maeve wasn't here when we arrived to execute the search warrant, and while we have enough to arrest her once we find her just based on what Sam uncovered, it might not be enough to convict her. We need a smoking gun... or rather a bottle of arsenic with her fingerprints on it.

"We had old Victorian terraces like these back on the street where I grew up in Leeds," Sam says as his gaze deviates to the doorway. "A lot of them had original features that were boarded up when the houses were modernised."

"What—like fireplaces?" Maddie frowns.

"Like cellars," Sam points out.

"You think it's possible?" Maddie turns to me.

I close the drawer to the sideboard and stand. "Maybe. We don't have time to track down blueprints to these houses, even if they still exist, but if a cellar existed at some point, the entrance would have most likely led off either the hallway or the kitchen."

I head out of the living room, motioning Maddie and Sam to follow along behind me. Even though technically Sam shouldn't really be here, Maddie seemed happy for me to let him tag along, especially given his invaluable help on the case so far. The fact he has police training as a former detective with the South Yorkshire police probably doesn't hurt either, but I can't deny I've missed him. We always did make a good team.

I can still hear a couple of the officers we brought along searching upstairs but I ignore them. The hallway doesn't really reveal anything.

The front door leads into a narrow passageway with a straight staircase to the right and a coat rail attached to the wall on the left. The wallpaper is a faded rosebud pattern, yellowing with age. There's a small cupboard door on the right near the end of the corridor, which upon quick inspection reveals nothing more than a hollow triangular space underneath the stairs filled with an old-model vacuum cleaner, a carpet sweeper like my grandmother used to have, and several cleaning items.

Once we enter the kitchen, I'm struck again with reminders of my grandparents' house. Although meticulously clean like the rest of the house, it's extremely dated. There's an Aga instead of a regular cooker, and the cabinets all date back to at least the 1950s. Beside the back door, which leads out into the garden and old coal shed, there's another door which I know from earlier inspection is the door to the pantry, an old-fashioned cupboard which housed food and kept things cool before refrigerators became commonplace. I have a vague recollection of my great-aunt having one back home.

I'd only given it a cursory glance earlier, dismissing it out of hand, but now I reopen the door and take a much closer look. It's shelved along each wall, and each of those shelves contains canisters of sugar and flour, cereal and tinned foods. I step further into the cupboard and rap my knuckles against the walls behind the condiments and packets of food. Two of them are solid brick, as you'd expect of a house over a hundred years old, but the back wall of the cupboard gives a hollow echo as my knuckles tap against it.

Shoving all the packets and tins aside, I study the wall carefully until I find a small hole, just large enough to slide a finger through. I feel around inside the hole and sure enough, I discover something metal.

"What is it?" Maddie asks in fascination.

"I think it's a latch of some sort." I wiggle my finger awkwardly and suddenly the metal mechanism shifts, and with an eerie creak, the whole wall opens outwards, shelves and all, revealing a small passageway and a set of very narrow stairs leading down into pitch blackness.

"Uh, you first," Maddie says weakly as she leans her head around the concealed doorway and looks into the darkness.

"Afraid of the dark?" I quirk a brow in her direction.

"Not especially, but I've seen enough Indiana Jones films to know there's probably some giant spider webs draped across that very narrow... creepy... possibly boobytrapped..."

"Do you want me to go first?" Sam asks impatiently. "Or are we going to stand here until the old woman comes home?"

"I got it." I shake my head, pulling my phone from my jacket pocket to use the flashlight function to light my way. After all, I don't think Tristan would be too happy if I accidentally broke my neck falling down the stairs in a serial killer's murder cellar.

I head along the short passageway to the top of the stairs and begin to descend. Although it's not as obsessively clean as the rest of the house, this passageway leading down into the cellar is far from disused. I can hear Maddie and Sam behind me, and as I reach the bottom step I see an old-fashioned light switch mounted on the wall beside me. I flip the switch and the room is bathed with dim light from a bare bulb suspended from the ceiling.

I glance around curiously. I'm not sure what I was expecting, but it just looks like an old cellar used for storage. Racking and industrial shelves line the walls, many of them containing storage boxes. In one corner is a huge black trunk with reinforced metal corners and a few more boxes. All in all, it doesn't look like much.

"Well this is a little disappointing," Maddie muses.

"What were you expecting to find down here?" I snort quietly. "Frankenstein's laboratory?"

"Is it too much to ask?" she replies.

"Hey, you guys." Sam draws our attention to the corner and I realise he's already rooting through one of the boxes. He pulls something small out and tosses it to me.

As I catch it, I look down and realise it's an outdated passport. Flipping it open to the correct page, I see a photograph of a younger, middle-aged version of Maeve, and the name on the passport is Harriet Walker.

"Bingo." I smile as I look back at Sam. "Is there more in there?"

"See for yourself." He steps aside and opens another box. Before long, all three of us are pulling out all kinds of documentation, including things in the names of all of Maeve Landon's former identities and a few we didn't know about.

"It's like an archive," Maddie muses.

"I do appreciate a serial killer that keeps meticulous records," Sam remarks as he pulls out another box.

"What do you think is in there?" Maddie asks as her gaze lands on the dark trunk.

"Only one way to find out." I crouch down in front of it, and as I do I see a small padlock securing the latch. "It's locked. I don't suppose you've seen a key anywhere?" I ask hopefully.

"Don't worry, I got you." Sam kneels down beside me and produces a small leather wallet with small needle-pointed lock picks from his pocket.

"Do I even want to know where you got those or how you even know how to use them?" I raise a brow.

"Probably not." He grins as the lock springs open.

Unhooking it, he sets it on the floor beside us and reaches for the latch, then flips it open and lifts the lid. A sharp, pungent, chemical-like odour wafts from the open lid, forcing all three of us to cough unexpectedly. Blinking back the tears, I raise my forearm to cover my mouth and nostrils with my sleeve.

"What the hell is that?" I mumble.

"It looks like salt." Maddie reaches for it without thinking.

"No!" I bark out, grabbing her wrist before she can touch it. "It may look like salt," I say, softening my tone as Maddie freezes, "but from the smell of it, it's mixed with god knows what other chemicals."

"What do you think it's for?" she asks in consternation.

I glance around and see an old walking stick propped against the racking and grab hold of it. I use the curved handle to sift through the top couple of layers like I'm shifting sand. As I dig a little lower, something dark brown and leathery appears, and suddenly I hear Sam swear softly under his breath and Maddie gag behind me.

As the leathery shape is slowly revealed, I realise with a sickening feeling that it's a shrivelled and desiccated human head. It looks like the mummified remains of what seems to be a male victim.

"How much do you want to bet we've just found Charles Landon?" I say a little sickly.

"Jesus, he looks like beef jerky," Sam mutters. "Poor guy must've been down here for quite some time."

"Fuck," Maddie exclaims behind us. As I turn, I see she's moved away from the corpse in the trunk and is staring at another one of the shelving racks on the other side of the room.

"What is it?" I cross the room to stand beside her, where I see what has caught her attention.

It's rows and rows of glass canisters, jars, and bottles which wouldn't have looked out of place in a macabre museum or in an old apothecary's. My eyes graze along the handwritten labels, reading slowly.

Arsenic... Cyanide... Strychnine... Aconite... Lead... Mercury... Nightshade... Hemlock...

"We need to go, now!" I say urgently, grabbing Maddie's arm and towing her back to the stairs. "Sam, move!" He rises and follows without question, leading me to believe he's just arrived at the same conclusion I have.

I leave the light on as we climb the stairs quickly, then hurry along the passageway until we're back in the kitchen, where I open the back door and the kitchen window for ventilation.

Maddie frowns. "What was all that about?"

"That was a bunch of extremely lethal poisons to inhale as well as ingest, not to mention whatever that cocktail of chemicals was in that trunk that prevented Charles Landon from fully decomposing, all in an enclosed, unventilated space. It's not safe down there."

"Maeve Landon seemed to do just fine," Maddie replies.

"She's a trained chemist. Not only does she know what's down there, but she knows how to handle it safely. We don't," I tell her. "We need to call Poison Control and get them to clear that room as well as remove what I'm assuming are Mr Landon's remains. His post-mortem will have to be handled very carefully once we know what he was preserved with."

"Why do you think she did it?" Maddie swallows loudly. "Kept him like that?"

"Probably to not arouse suspicion," I guess. "I've had the misfortune to be around a corpse that had reached the putrefaction stage and trust me, there's no way the neighbours wouldn't have noticed the stench. She would have needed to maintain the illusion he was still alive so she could continue to cash his pension and live in his house."

"Just when I think it can't get any worse." She blows out a breath. "I'm guessing we've got enough on her now."

"And then some," I agree.

"Now we just need to find her." Maddie purses her lips thoughtfully. "Do you think she knows we're onto her? Maybe she's made a run for it."

"I doubt it." I shake my head as I look down at my phone. "Wait a minute. It's the first of May, isn't it?"

"Yeah, why?" Sam asks.

I glance at the calendar Sellotaped to the wall and see today's date encircled in red.

"I know exactly where Maeve is," I realise.

"Where?"

"Trying to win first place for her jam tart," I reply.

"What?" Maddie blinks.

"She's at Northwold Community Centre because today's the day they host their annual Jam Tart Society Social."

"Okaaay," she says slowly. "I don't even want to ask how you know that."

"Trust me, we'll find her in Clapham," I say confidently.

"Fine." Maddie grabs her own phone just as mine rings. "I'll call Poison Control and let the officers upstairs know what's going on, then we can head out."

I nod as I answer my phone, frowning in concern when I realise who is calling me. "Tristan, is everything alright?"

"I'm fine, nothing's wrong. I'm actually feeling loads better and I wanted to see you," he says, and I relax a little. I've been a bit on edge ever since he ended up in the hospital.

"I miss you too," I tell him softly, ignoring the fact that Sam, the nosy git, is listening to every word with interest.

"Where are you right now?" Tristan asks.

"Just about to head out to Clapham Community Centre," I tell him, trying not to give too many of the details away.

"What? Why?" he answers and I can hear the worry in his voice. "We haven't exactly had the best of luck there."

"I know, but long story short, we know who is responsible for Delores Abernathy's murder."

"WHAT? WHO?" he bursts out.

"Tris, I'm sorry I can't talk right now," I tell him as Maddie walks back in the room. "We're on our way to arrest her. I'll call you later."

Hanging up the phone, I turn to Maddie.

"I've told the others no one is to go down into the cellar until Poison Control has cleared it, then we'll get forensics in to clear out everything else."

"Good." I turn to Sam. "You tagging along?"

"Are you kidding?" He grins. "I haven't had this much fun in ages."

"You have a very strange idea of fun," I mutter as we head out of the house and towards the car.

Next stop, the Clapham Senior Ladies Social Circle and Jam Tart Society's annual Jam Tart Society Social.

21

Tristan

I see Danny the minute I jump out of the Uber with Dusty and Mrs Abernathy appearing beside me. He's already striding purposefully to the door of the community centre with a grim and determined look on his face, flanked by Maddie and another guy with black hair and a trench coat that I don't recognise.

I hurry after them as they enter the building, but they're already inside by the time I reach the door. Pushing it open, I step inside and see banners strung up which announce The Jam Tart Society Social.

"Oh god, here we go again." Dusty rolls her eyes. "For the love of god, Tris, don't touch anything, don't eat anything, and definitely don't drink anything."

"You don't need to tell me twice," I mutter. I cast a quick look in the direction of the toilets where I'd seen the reaper and shiver involuntarily.

Pushing open the door into the main room, I skid to a halt as the wall of noise hits me. The Jam Tart Social is obviously a big hit because it looks like the whole community has turned out. It's even more packed than Bingo Bonanza.

Once again, all the tables and chairs are set out and covered with cake stands and pots of tea. Up on the stage sits a long table packed with various pies and tarts. The bingo caller from the other day is also on the stage, standing in front of a microphone. Hopefully, this time he's learned how to use it correctly without attempting to perforate our eardrums. He's wearing a brightly coloured, garishly patterned tracksuit, and a sliver of his ample paunch peeks out from the bottom of his t-shirt. His only concession to formality is a bow tie which seems to be decorated with slices of pie.

Lined up alongside him are Phyllis who is waving to the crowd, Birdie who looks like she's just tasted something sour, and Maeve who stands at the front, beaming widely as she's handed a first place rosette. She pins it neatly to her cardigan, then lifts her tart and smiles as someone takes a photograph.

From the corner of my eye I can see Danny and Maddie at the side of the room. They are flanked by two uniformed officers who've arrived without my notice, or maybe they were already waiting there for Danny to arrive. Either way, I'm not the only one who's noticed their presence.

Maeve's eyes lock on them, narrowing calculatingly as they inch closer to the stage. The guy on the microphone says something, but I'm not listening to him or the applause that follows. My interested gaze is too busy tracking the person I assume, judging by Danny's laser-focused and insanely hot I'm about to arrest you vibe, is the one responsible for Mrs Abernathy's death.

It seems Maeve may have come to the same realisation because suddenly she launches her prize-winning tart in their direction. Turning sharply, she shoves the guy with the microphone out of the way and hurries past him, toward the steps that lead off the stage and down into the community hall full of people.

Caught off guard, the poor guy on stage loses his balance,

windmilling his arms uselessly as he falls backwards onto the long table, which collapses at one end and ends up acting like a catapult. Dozens of pies and tarts are fired into the air and, for a moment, time seems to slow as they arc gracefully toward the crowd. People look up in astonishment, mouths falling open, then suddenly there's a loud screeching sound as chairs are shoved hastily aside and everyone scrambles to get out of the way.

The action is too late. The pies and tarts land with unnerving precision, detonating like little sweet fruity grenades that explode pie crusts and fillings everywhere. In the crowd, I catch a glimpse of Trudy Wells, always so prim and well put-together, standing with her eyes wide in shock as blackberry filling drips ponderously down the side of her face and a big glob plops onto her pristinely pressed cream-coloured blouse.

It's chaos everywhere. The children present scream in delight, thinking it's a brilliant game, as they pick up any cake or pastry they can find and start throwing them, all while clapping and dancing like savages. Chairs topple, tables are knocked askew, and tiered cake stands fall.

For a moment, I'm struck by how much this carnage reminds me of when a massive pie fight ensues at Fat Sam's in the final scene of *Bugsy Malone*. I almost look over at the piano pushed against one of the walls, expecting someone to suddenly belt out, *You Give Little Love*.

"Damn," Dusty remarks mildly. "She's spry for an eighty-year-old."

I follow Dusty's gaze and see Maeve navigate her way down the stairs exiting the stage but when she reaches the bottom step, her way is blocked by the stranger in the trench coat who was with Danny earlier. Without missing a beat, Maeve raises her handbag and clocks him squarely on the side of the head, sending him sailing into the nearest table.

"What is it with old ladies and their handbags?" Dusty

watches the spectacle unfold avidly. "I wish I had some popcorn," she mutters, almost as an afterthought.

Maeve, seeing her chance, scurries between the tables and heads for the exit. Suddenly a table shoots across the floor, barring her way. I turn to Dusty, raising a brow.

"Don't look at me." She holds her hands up. "I didn't do it."

We both turn to Mrs Abernathy, who is looking in Maeve's direction, but the action only holds her attention for a moment. Losing interest, she turns to Dusty and offers her handbag.

"Not right now, Delores." Dusty lowers her hands and puts her arm around the little old lady. "I think the person responsible for your death is about to get her just desserts."

"Really, Dusty?" I throw her a dry look and she grins.

Maeve, who wasn't that fast in the first place and is now blocked by the table, finds herself suddenly surrounded by Maddie, Danny, and the two police officers, who are all covered in various splotches of cream and fruit fillings and lightly dusted with sugar.

I hurry over to meet them as Danny carefully pulls the old woman's hands behind her back and cuffs her as gently as possible.

"Tristan, what are you doing here?" He frowns when he sees me.

"Making sure you're okay," I reply honestly. "I had no idea how wild and dangerous these old ladies are."

"You're not kidding," Maddie scoffs before turning to Maeve.

"Edith Anderson, aka Maeve Landon, aka Harriett Walker, aka Peggy Johnson, aka Iris Carter, you're under arrest for the murders of Delores Abernathy, Albert Walker, Gavin Johnson, and Peter Carter. You are also under arrest for fraud and theft." Maddie looks up as Danny's friend approaches with a neatly folded white handkerchief pressed to his temple. "And assault," she adds for good measure. "I have no doubt we'll also be adding a murder charge for Charles Landon."

"What?" I stare at them.

"Edith here is a black widow." Maddie looks at her in disgust as she finishes reading the old woman her rights. "She likes to poison her husbands, then change her identity and move on."

"But I don't understand." I frown as I look at the old lady staring belligerently at Maddie. "Why kill Mrs Abernathy? She was the sweetest, most harmless lady."

Maeve turns her attention to me and I have to admit it's unnerving how cold her eyes are.

"She was a cheat," she hissed. "She should never have been allowed to enter the Jam Tart Society Social last year, let alone win it. She had one of her carers at the home bake it for her."

"What the actual fuck?" I exclaim in absolute disbelief. "Are you seriously telling me you killed her over a bloody pie contest?"

"She was a cheat," Maeve says stubbornly. "So was the foreign girl."

"The foreign girl? Oh god, you mean her carer Polina, don't you?" Maddie's eyes narrowed. "You poisoned Polina on purpose, didn't you? She didn't get sick because she ate Mrs Abernathy's scone by accident."

Maeve tightens her lips and glares.

"Wait." I lift my hand, shaking my head as I try to assimilate all the information. "So her name isn't Maeve?"

"No, her real name is Edith," Danny says, looking down at the woman with a scowl. "And I don't care how long it takes to unravel all the details of her crimes, I'll make sure she answers for every single life she's destroyed."

"Thought you were going to get away with it, didn't you?" Maddie glares at her.

"I would've gotten away with it if it wasn't for you fuc–"

"Holy shitballs, it's just like a Scooby-Doo ending," Dusty cackles in delight next to me.

Not exactly, I think to myself, my cheeks colouring at the language coming out of the old woman.

"I'll take it from here," Maddie tells Danny as he passes Edith to the waiting officers. "I'll ride with them back to the station and get her booked in." She turns to me and winks. "Tristan."

I offer her a warm smile as they head out of the room, then turn my attention to Danny and the man standing next to him.

"Who's the sexy side of beef?" Dusty eyes him in appreciation. "He's like the super-hot version of Columbo."

I'm not even sure there can be a super-hot version of Columbo, I want to say, but I can't, not out loud, although as the words fall from Dusty's mouth, I swear I see the stranger's mouth curve slightly.

She's right about one thing though—he is sexy. There's a scar running from the corner of his eye down his cheek, but it doesn't in any way detract from his handsome face. In fact, it would make him look somewhat dangerous and even intimidating if not for his relaxed body language, the playful amusement dancing in his eyes, and the soft curve of his mouth which wrinkles that scar.

"Tristan," Danny says, drawing my attention, "this is my friend, Sam Stone, from back home."

"It's nice to meet you." I offer my hand.

"Likewise." He grasps my hand and I smile at his accent, so like Danny's but a few degrees lower.

"Are you okay?" I ask as he removes the handkerchief from his temple and I see a smear of blood.

"I'm fine." He shakes his head with a rueful smile. "Although I don't know what she had in her handbag. That thing felt like it was filled with bricks. My ma used to say all a woman's secrets were hidden in her handbag. Bit worried as to what a black widow killer would be carting around in hers."

I stare at him for several long moments, dropping my hand as his words shift something in my mind. I turn to Mrs Abernathy, who's hovering alongside Dusty, and my gaze drops to the bag clutched tightly in her bony claw-like hands. The same bag she's been trying to give to me and Dusty for days.

Like Dusty, finding the killer and solving Delores' murder wasn't enough. Even when unable to directly communicate with us, she's been trying to tell us all along what she needed to resolve her unfinished business and be free from the death cycle she's locked in, first by humming the Ella Fitzgerald song and then by telling us Beau's name, but the one thing she's been adamant about is that we take her bag from her... The very bag she'd been clutching when her body was discovered lying in her bed in the care home, I realise with a jolt.

My gaze shoots to Dusty and I can see in her eyes that she's come to the same conclusion.

"Delores, honey." Dusty smiles at her gently. "Shall I take that for you?" She holds out her hand and Mrs Abernathy stares at it for a moment before offering her the bag.

Dusty wraps her fingers around the handle as Mrs Abernathy drops her hand, but seconds later the bag disappears from Dusty's hand and reappears in Mrs Abernathy's.

For a second I'm reminded of when Dusty stood in my kitchen locked in a death cycle of her own, unable to change anything about her physical appearance. To demonstrate this to me the first time when I didn't understand, she flicked her one remaining shoe at me across the room. Only instead of hitting me in the head as its trajectory would have suggested, it simply reappeared back on her foot. It must be the same with Mrs Abernathy's bag. Which means whatever she's trying to show us we can't access... unless...

"Tristan, are you okay?" Danny asks in concern. "You kind of zoned out."

"I-I'm fine." I shoot another fleeting glance at Dusty as she takes Mrs Abernathy's hand, but as I turn back I notice that Sam's eyes are fixed on Dusty.

"Oh my god, can he see me?" Dusty whispers. "He's looking right at me."

"Tristan," Danny says again, drawing my gaze away.

"I think I'll just go and check everyone's okay, see if they need a hand cleaning up," Sam says to Danny. "Tristan, it was nice to meet you." His gaze flicks to Mrs Abernathy and his mouth curves. "I have a feeling you're a fascinating person to get to know."

Before I can say anything, he turns and walks away, grabbing a toppled chair and setting it upright before helping a young woman nearby pick up some broken crockery. Pulling my gaze away from him, my stomach rolls over and not in a good way, more in a slightly nauseous, *I feel like I've done something wrong*, kind of way. Danny's watching me with worried eyes, his expression somewhere between confused and hurt.

"Tris, what's going on?" he asks quietly. "You've been acting strange for a while now, and I don't know... you seem to be pulling away. Did I do something wrong? Did I push you too fast when I asked if you wanted to move in together?"

"No." I rush forward, taking his face in my hands, not caring who's watching. "No, please don't think that." I press my lips to his, kissing him softly. "I love you, Danny. I love you so much I could spend the rest of my life telling you that and it still wouldn't be enough times." I pull back enough to stare into his eyes. "I want to live with you, I want to spend the rest of my life with you. You haven't pressured or rushed me into anything. I can't wait to go flat hunting with you, to find a home that's going to be just ours. I know it sounds crazy, but I really want to go pick out curtains with you and a new set of plates and maybe one of those funny soap dispensers for the bathroom. I want to do all of those things to make it our home. Not yours, not mine... ours."

"Then why–"

"Have I been acting so weird lately?" I breathe heavily and close my eyes, knowing that the time has come. If Danny and I are going to have any kind of future together, I have to tell him the truth about me, even if it makes me sound completely crazy. But not here, not like this. "There are some things I have to tell you." I trace my fingertips along his jaw. "And I will. I'll tell you everything but"—I glance at Mrs Abernathy—"there's something really important I need to do first. Will you trust me?"

He studies me silently, his eyes searching my face, and I feel utterly stripped bare and not in a sexy, *I'm about to have a mind-blowing orgasm,* way. Finally, he nods and I can tell that, although he believes I love him, he's holding a part of himself back and I don't want that. I don't want anything to come between us ever, especially not this, it wouldn't be fair. I have to believe we can figure this out and come out stronger.

Because it would be the ultimate irony if that fateful night so many months ago gave me both Danny and my gift but meant I could only have one at the expense of the other.

"Will you come to the flat tonight?" I ask, my heart thudding dully in my chest with a mixture of nerves and worry.

"Okay," he replies quietly.

I lean in and kiss him again, wanting to stay with him but knowing I have a responsibility I can't ignore.

"I'll see you tonight." I kiss him one last time and reluctantly pull away. "I promise."

Turning abruptly, I head out of the room with Dusty and Mrs Abernathy close behind me.

22

Tristan

I raise my hand to knock on the door as I dance impatiently in place. I glance down the street, then down at my watch before knocking again. The door suddenly swings open and Larry stares at me in confusion.

"Tristan? Can I help you with something?"

"Actually you can," I reply. "I need to ask you a question and it's probably going to sound a little weird."

"Okay..." Her voice is hesitant and I don't blame her.

"The night your aunt died, I was in the room just after they found her and she was laying on her bed, fully dressed and holding onto a handbag, a black leather one."

Larry nods. "I know which one you mean. She took it with her absolutely everywhere, wouldn't let it out of her sight."

"Do you have that bag by any chance?" I ask.

I have this weird feeling churning in my belly. It's a kind of sense of urgency laced with excitement at the thought of unravelling the mystery of why she kept trying to give us a bag she never let out of her sight. At this point I'm not even sure what we're going to find in there. A lost Fabergé egg? George Washington's false teeth? A packet of cough sweets and a bus timetable from 1988? Who knows, but I'm curious as hell to find out.

"You want Aunt Delores' handbag?" she asks with a baffled frown. "Why?"

"It's a bit hard to explain." I shove my hands in my pockets and rock on my heels awkwardly. "I think she hid something inside it, something important."

"Like what?"

"That's just it. I don't know, but it was important enough for her to never let the bag out of her sight," I reply. "Do you have the bag?"

"Yes," she answers. "Somewhere. I picked it up with the rest of her things from the home, but I haven't gone through it all yet."

"Could we take a look?" I ask.

"Is this really necessary?" Larry sighs as she looks down at her watch. "I really need to get to work and if I don't leave soon, I'll miss the bus."

"I'll pay for an Uber if that happens," I offer. "Please, Larry, just a quick look."

"Fine," she relents, stepping back so I can cross the threshold. Closing the front door behind me, she leads me into her living room. There are several cardboard boxes stacked in the corner of the room that hadn't been there last time I visited.

Crossing the room, she picks one of the ones labelled 'clothes' and slides it over to me.

"Check this one," she says before pulling out another similarly labelled box, unfolding the flaps at the top and rummaging through the neatly folded contents.

I do the same, vaguely aware of Dusty and Mrs Abernathy hovering nearby, watching us. I've just got the box open and am carefully checking through the contents, hoping it's not full of underwear, when Larry pulls out a black object wrapped in a clear plastic bag.

"Here it is." She pushes the box out of the way and carries the bag to the table.

She unties the top of the plastic bag and reaches inside, pulling out a shabby leather blob that's identical to the one Mrs Abernathy is carrying around and has been trying to give me and Dusty for days.

Unzipping the handbag, Larry upends it carefully and spills the contents over the table's surface. It's a strange mishmash of assorted objects, just as I suspected. There's a tiny little clutch purse containing several twenty pence pieces and a King George halfpenny. An embroidered handkerchief with the letter 'B' monogrammed in the corner. And a TV remote control, possibly from the care home, which Larry chuckles at as she sets it aside.

She sifts further through the contents to find a pair of nail scissors, a ball of string, a packet of Polos, a loose domino, and several teabags.

"I don't know what you're looking for, Tristan, but I don't think it's here." Larry shakes her head as she moves aside a teaspoon and one green sock. "Jesus, she was like a magpie." She chuckles affectionately as she picks up an empty tube of toothpaste.

"May I?" I point to the now empty bag.

"Sure." She picks it up and hands the limp leather blob to me.

I look inside and, not seeing anything, I stick my hand in, cringing at the crumbs and god knows what else pooling in the bottom. I run my fingers carefully over the worn interior and feel something flat beneath the lining.

Exploring further, my fingers stumble upon a tear in the seam. Easing them carefully through the gap, I manage to grasp the flat object, which feels very thin and fragile, and pull it free.

"What's that?" Larry whispers in surprise.

I look down to find it's a very fragile piece of paper, and as I gingerly unfold it, mindful not to tear it, I see it's actually an old envelope addressed to a Miss Delores Emerson and dated 1944. I glance across to Larry, who is staring at it in wide-eyed fascination.

"Emerson was her maiden name," she explains. "Open it."

Sliding my fingers inside, I pull out a worn letter so delicate it looks like it will fall apart if I breathe on it too hard. The folds in the paper are weak, as if it's been read over and over, to the point where the whole thing is almost in pieces. So as not to damage it any further, I lay it out flat on the table and begin to read aloud.

"Dearest Deedee, I don't have very long, the transport is waiting outside for me, so please forgive my rushed words. You know I will write again as soon as I'm able. They tell me you're being reassigned and once again we must be kept in the dark as to our locations. I cannot tell how far apart we are, you could be as distant as the moon or you could be on the same continent as me. It's torture not knowing that you're okay. Charlie has promised me he'll get this message to you come hell or high water. I think I'll have to ask him to be my best man after all of this.

I dream about you every damn night and I wake aching for you in my arms. I long for the day this is all over and we can be together. I can't wait to show you my home, my ma and my sister are going to love you just as much as I do. Texas may be very different from the life you're used to in London, but I promise you're going to love the ranch. I'll teach you to ride the horses just like I promised. I can't wait for the life we'll have, Deedee, with my ring on your finger and the children we'll make together.

They say it'll be over soon, we only have to wait a while longer. Remember what we promised? We'll meet in Hyde Park by the band-stand where we danced the night we met. I think of that night so often, it's one of my most treasured memories. I'll wait there every day if I have to. I'll wait forever...

All my love, Beau x"

Larry sniffles and I look up to see her pluck a tissue from a nearby Kleenex box and dab her eyes.

"Poor darling, they were so in love." She sniffs loudly. "I wonder what happened to him. I wonder why they didn't meet up?"

"He died," I mutter, staring back at the letter. "They both worked in intelligence for their respective governments, so all they had were stolen moments together. Judging from Beau's note, I expect neither of them knew where the other was most of the time. They must've moved around a great deal, that was probably why he suggested they meet in Hyde Park after the war was over."

"It's so sad." Larry wipes her nose.

"She never knew what happened to him exactly." I turn to look at Larry. "I asked Trudy and she said all your aunt was ever told was that his plane went down and he was lost. They wouldn't tell her where or how. It was deemed classified by the War Office and because she wasn't his widow, she had no chance of getting any information."

The small carriage clock on the mantelpiece chimes and Larry glances across worriedly.

"I'm going to be late for work." She glances at me apologetically. "I'm so sorry but I have to go." She very carefully folds the paper and places it reverently back in its envelope, crossing the room and tucking it in a drawer for safekeeping.

"It's fine," I reply as we head toward the door and step out onto the doorstep. "Thank you for indulging my curiosity."

"No, thank you." She gives a melancholy smile. "Because of you, I have another little piece of her I didn't have before." She reaches out and squeezes my arm gratefully before turning and hurrying down the path.

"Wow." Dusty releases a loud breath and I turn to see her glancing down at Mrs Abernathy. "He really loved you, didn't he, Delores?"

"Beau." She blinks up at Dusty.

"What are we going to do now?" Dusty asks me.

"We're going to reunite two people who've waited a lifetime to be together."

"Have you been watching Titanic again?" Her eyes narrow suspiciously as she fists one hand on her cocked hip.

I roll my eyes. "That's beside the point."

"How exactly do you propose we do that anyway?" Dusty asks pointedly.

"Because I think he's still waiting," I murmur.

"What?"

"I think Beau is still waiting for his Deedee," I say determinedly. "We're going to Hyde Park."

"Hear that, Delores, honey?" Dusty squeezes her hand warmly. "We're going to get your man."

She beams widely. "Beau."

By the time I climb out of the Uber at the entrance to Hyde Park, I already have my phone in my hand and directions pulled up on Google Maps.

"According to this, the original bandstand still exists," I say quietly as we wander along the path. It's getting late and the park is fairly quiet. "It was originally built in Kensington Gardens but moved to Hyde Park in 1886. The famous trumpeter Harry Mortimer played in the bandstand in 1944."

"And you really think Beau's there? That he's waited all this time?" Dusty asks.

"I guess we're about to find out." I glance at her teetering across the grass on five-inch platform heels while Mrs Abernathy wanders along beside her, holding her hand. "The bandstand is just up ahead."

In the distance I can see a hexagonal bandstand surrounded by grass and trees. A low, pale pink fence flanks the steps leading up to the stage and encircles the structure, which is painted a glossy black. The two-tiered pointed witch-hat roof is held up by thin supports. It's plain, with no flowers or decorations surrounding it, and I can imagine it lit up with fairy lights while soft music dances on the night air. I make a mental note to see if there are any live events scheduled for here that I can bring Danny to on a date.

"Bloody hell," Dusty gasps and stops dead.

I follow her line of sight, and my eyes land on a man wearing a military uniform and standing by the steps. His eyes are locked on us, and as his face breaks in a smile, he removes his hat and smoothes down his hair nervously.

Dusty and I both turn to Mrs Abernathy, who is standing between and just slightly behind us. I have to blink twice for my brain to register what my eyes are showing me. The doddering little old lady in the tea-cosy hat and mismatched socks is gone and in her place stands a young woman.

She's beautiful and fresh-faced, her deep chocolate brown hair swept away from her face and caught in two rolls pinned at her temples while the rest of it falls in smooth waves to her shoulders. She's wearing a pretty floral tea dress and a coat that tapers in at the waist and falls to her knees, and on her feet is a pair of dark green suede chunky heels.

No longer confused and trapped in the prison of her mind, she smiles, her dark eyes clear and intelligent. She turns first to Dusty, rising up on her toes and placing an affectionate kiss on her cheek.

"Thank you, Dusty," she says, her voice sweet and warm, before turning to me. She reaches out, and as she strokes my cheek, I swear I can almost feel her touch. "Thank you both for taking care of me."

"You're very welcome," I whisper, unable to help the smile that tugs at my lips.

"Will you look in on Larry from time to time?"

"Of course," I promise and she nods in satisfaction, turning her attention to the gorgeous dark-haired G.I. waiting patiently for her.

She takes a few steps towards him, then suddenly stops and turns back to look at me.

"Be careful, Tristan," she says softly. "The witch was right, something has taken an interest in you, but just remember, things aren't always as they seem."

Before I can open my mouth to ask her what she means, she smiles and turns back toward the bandstand. Dusty and I watch as she flat out runs towards Beau, who rushes to meet her, his face filled with joy and longing. She leaps into his arms as they collide, their mouths fused together for several long moments before he swings her around, her feet swaying above the ground and her delighted laugh filling the air.

Finally, she slides down his body as he sets her on her feet and they both turn back to us. She gives us a joyful wave and he raises his hand and salutes us warmly. Then they join hands and turn towards the bandstand, and as they take a step forward, they disappear.

I swallow the lump in my throat, blinking back happy and sentimental tears as my thoughts turn to Danny. I want my forever with him but there's a part of me that's afraid he won't understand or he won't believe me when I tell him the truth. I turn to Dusty as she wipes her eyes and blows her nose on a tissue that promptly disappears.

"Come on, boo." She smiles at me. "Let's go home."

"Dusty," I say quietly, "I need to tell Danny the truth. Will you help me?"

"Of course I will," she replies. "Don't you know by now, Tris? I'd do anything for you."

"Thank you," I whisper as she links her arm through mine. I jolt in shock.

"I can feel you?" I gasp.

"Yeah." She grins. "I suspected you might be able to. I think there's kind of a weird connection thingy between us now because of the whole body-swap thingy."

"We're connected?"

"Well, I have been inside you." She winks as I shake my head in resignation. "Come on." She tugs me and we start walking back down the path. "I'm going to help you get your man..." She stops suddenly, her eyes widening. "Oh my god, this is totally like the moment in *Grease* when Sandy asks Frenchie to help her. Oh! Does this mean we get to do a makeover?"

"I'm not dressing like a slut to get my man." I roll my eyes as we start walking again.

"And his name's Danny too! Oh this is too perfect, are you sure you don't want a makeover?"

"Dusty?" I say quietly as we move further away from the bandstand.

"Yeah?"

"I really do love you," I tell her impulsively. "Don't ever change."

"Right back atcha, boo." She grins. "Right back atcha."

23

Danny

Feeling uncertain, I look down at the keys in my hand. Tristan gave them to me months ago when I began sleeping over so often. With us both finishing work at different hours it was easier to let myself in. It's always been so easy with him. We just fit together from day one, but now... I don't like feeling this way. I know he loves me and I know he said I hadn't rushed him and that he really did want to move in together but...

I'm freaking out about whatever it is he wants to talk to me about. I've got this awful gut feeling it's something big, something that could make or break our relationship, and I guess I'm scared. I don't want to lose him, he's the best thing to ever happen to me.

We need to talk. The sooner we clear the air the better, and standing on his doorstep having a meltdown is not the answer, but I can't help it. All these crazy things keep running through my head.

I grip the keys tightly, knowing I should just use them and let myself in like I have a hundred times before. It's not a big deal.

So why does it feel like such a big deal?

I lift my hand to knock but pause, knuckles inches from the door. This is so stupid. I drop my hand down to my side again and close my eyes, inhaling slowly. Hearing the door open, I open my eyes and see Tris staring at me in puzzlement.

"Why are you standing out here?" he asks with a small frown marring his brow.

"I..." No words. I literally have none. I can't tell him I've been standing outside his door for ages having an internal debate on whether to just let myself in.

His eyes soften as he steps out onto the landing in his favourite pair of thick socks. He wraps his arms around me and, as I look down into those gorgeous green eyes of his, he pushes up on his toes and presses his mouth to mine. His lips are soft, his kiss full of love, and something inside me begins to slowly uncoil.

I feel his fingertips dancing along the nape of my neck above my collar as he pulls back. He places one more reassuring kiss on my lips and takes my hand, pulling me into the flat and closing the door behind me.

He leads me into the living room and indicates for me to take a seat on the sofa, then rubs his hands on the thighs of his jeans. I can tell he's nervous about something, and that just sets all my alarm bells ringing again.

"Do you want me to get you a drink or something?" he asks.

"No." I shake my head, my voice sounding a lot calmer than I feel. "I want you to tell me what's going on. You've been acting strangely for days, first pulling away, then kissing me like nothing's changed. You say you don't feel that I'm pushing you too fast about moving in together, but maybe I am and you're subconsciously taking a step back."

"No!" he says firmly. "No, I swear that's not it." He gives a little frustrated growl under his breath, which would be cute if I wasn't so worried. Instead, I watch as he fists his hands in his hair, making his curls wilder than usual. He breathes deeply as he fixes his gaze on me. "This is harder than I thought. I have so much to tell you and I'm not even sure where to start, and no matter what I say I'm going to sound like a completely crazy person."

"I'm sure that's not true," I reply.

"Okay." He holds his hands up. "I'm going to start at the beginning and it's a bit of a long story, but I need you to have an open mind and also for you to remember that no matter how nuts this all sounds, I can prove it."

"Okay," I agree as he rambles, and it's so authentic Tris that something eases inside me, allowing a curl of curiosity to seep through my worry.

"Okay," he repeats, as if calming himself. "It all started when we met at The Crown, the night of Seamus' leaving do. When I embarrassingly choked on that ice cube and ended up technically dead."

"I remember," I murmur, trying not to think too much about what would've happened if I hadn't been able to revive him.

"When I woke up, something was different... I was different." He licks his lip nervously and I keep quiet, letting him get it all out. "I didn't realise until the next day when you walked into the mortuary with a murder case."

"Dusty Le Frey," I interject, thinking back to the attractive drag queen who'd been friends with Chan and Tristan.

"Yeah, um... well, the moment Dusty was wheeled into the mortuary I discovered I could see the dead."

I stare at him, not really understanding what he's trying to tell me. Sensing my confusion, he hurries on.

"I mean I can see their ghosts, their spirits, souls—whatever you want to call them. I see dead people. I'm talking full-on Haley Joel Osment, dead people popping up all hours of the day and night trying to talk to me."

I blink slowly, my brain trying to comprehend his words, but they don't make sense. Tristan is one of the most scientific, empirical people I know. I would never have guessed for a second that he would believe in this kind of paranormal stuff, let alone claim to be able to see ghosts.

"I'm getting ahead of myself a bit." He waves his hand. "It all began with Dusty. The truth is, I never knew her. I'd never met her before she was wheeled into my post-mortem room. I didn't know Chan either. The first time I met her was at Dusty's funeral."

"I don't understand." I frown. "You knew all those details about Dusty."

"I knew them because she was standing right next to me throughout the whole investigation." He gives a defeated sigh. "I know this is a lot to take in, but it's the truth. After my near-death experience, my perception was altered. It woke up a part of me that had been dormant. Ever since then I've been able to see spirits. They come to me for help."

"Help?" I repeat.

"Some of them need help crossing into the light, particularly those who have died before their time and are locked in a death cycle like Dusty was. She was murdered and tethered to the earth, stuck looking exactly as she did at the moment of her death. She couldn't move on until her unfinished business was resolved. At first, we thought solving her murder would free her but it didn't. It turned out it wasn't finding her killer that brought her peace. It was resolving all the things unsaid between her and her father."

"You gave him a box of letters," I mutter. "Dusty's father."

"Yes." He smiles faintly. "She told me where to find them, and they said everything that she wanted to say in life but didn't. Do you remember that I told Dusty's dad to close his eyes and imagine that Dusty was right in front of him?"

I nod.

"Well, she was," he says. "It was hearing him say he loved her just the way she was, unconditionally, that allowed her to move on."

"So you're saying she went..." I can't believe I'm actually about to say this. "She went into the light?"

"Yes and no." He smiles in amusement. "Yes, she went into the light but she didn't stay. She convinced the Upstairs Management to let her come back as my spirit guide. She's been with me ever since. Well, when she's not at the bookshop with Bruce."

"Bruce?" My brows raise in confusion.

"That's a story for another day." He shakes his head. "The important thing is Dusty chose to come back for me, and now she helps me to help other spirits."

"Other spirits?"

"Ever since Mrs Abernathy died, she'd been attached to me," he explains. "It's really difficult trying to figure out the unfinished business of an old lady with dementia when you can't have a straightforward conversation with her. But the good news is we did—figure it out, I mean. Me and Dusty. Delores Abernathy is now packed off safely into the light with her true love who'd waited nearly eighty years for her. It really was a Titanic moment. You know, right at the end, when Rose goes back to the ship and Jack is waiting by the clock. It was exactly like that... well, except minus Leonardo Di Caprio... and the boat... and the iceberg."

My brain feels like it's stalled. I can't quite wrap my head around the calm matter-of-fact way he's talking about ghosts as if they're real, reconcile it everything I've known up until now.

"You don't believe me," he says with a sigh. "It's okay, I get it. I wouldn't believe me either, but in this case I can prove it. Are you ready?"

"For what?" I ask in confusion.

He turns and looks at the corner of the room. "Dusty?"

I open my mouth to say— well, I'm not sure what—when suddenly the coffee table in front of me starts rattling and banging. I fall back against the sofa, eyes wide, absolutely speechless, as the table actually levitates a clear two feet off the floor. It doesn't stop there though. The lights throughout the whole flat flicker on and off rapidly, and the TV clicks on and cycles through the channels. Books start flying off the bookshelves, spinning madly in the air.

"Jesus, Dusty," Tristan hisses. "I said a small demonstration, not full-on The Conjuring. And will you stop the banging? Unless you want Mr Grumpy in the downstairs flat banging on the door and complaining about the noise..." He pauses for a moment, about the same amount of time it would take for someone to reply to him. "Well I won't be bloody moving anywhere if you give Danny a heart attack. I said help me convince him, not make him feel like he's on the set of Poltergeist... What? Actually, it is pretty impressive. Have you been practising?"

The lights settle down, the TV flicks off, and the books reorder themselves neatly on the shelf as the coffee table lowers gently back down to the ground. I'm still staring speechlessly as he turns back to the corner.

"I think we might have broken him," Tristan says in concern. "What? No, I'm not telling him that." He waits a beat again before rolling his eyes. "Fine, thank you, and tell Bruce I said hi." He turns back to me, wincing apologetically. "Sorry about all that." He waves his hand behind him. "It's the drag queen in her, she's all go big or go loud, doesn't know the meaning of the word subtle."

I'm still staring at him. I open my mouth, but no words come out.

"Please say something," he says quietly. "I know this is a lot, it was for me too. I may have had six months to get used to it, but I still have days when I struggle, or I see things I wish I hadn't. I wasn't given a choice. And apparently the gift is non-returnable." He tries for a joke but his heart isn't in it. His eyes fill with tears at my prolonged silence. "This is who I really am, Danny. I knew it might change how you look at me, that it might change the way you feel about me, but I couldn't spend the rest of my life lying to you," he says as he bites his lips, quickly wiping away the tear that slid out from under his glasses, and I realise how stripped bare he is right now.

He risked everything to show me the truth so that we can have something real between us, something solid, something we can build on. It just isn't in Tris to create this elaborate kind of prank. Deep down in my gut, something is telling me this is real. Am I a little freaked out to find out ghosts are real? Yes would be a gross understatement. Does it change the way I feel about Tristan? Not a chance in hell. If anything, I'm a little in awe of him, of the bravery it took to not only embrace this gift he had thrust upon him, but also to open himself up to me, to make himself completely vulnerable, knowing I could reject him.

"Say something," he whispers as another tear slides down his cheek.

I push myself up from the sofa and cross the room so I can take his face in my hands and kiss him gently, pouring all my love into that kiss.

"Danny," he breathes against my mouth as we break the kiss.

"I love you, Tris." I hold his face firmly, tilting his jaw up slightly so his eyes meet mine and he can see the truth of my words. "I love you just the way you are."

"I was so scared that–" He swallows tightly as his voice breaks slightly.

"That I wouldn't understand?" I finish his sentence. "That I would leave?" He nods mutely. "Tris," I sigh. "I've held back so many things I wanted to say to you because I was afraid I was pushing you too fast, but I don't think we can gauge our relationship by some perceived timeline of what we think we should be doing or not doing. And for that to work, I think we need to be completely honest with each other. Do you agree?" He nods again. "You're it for me," I whisper. "I hope that doesn't freak you out, but you are literally the air that I breathe, Tristan Everett. I can't imagine my life without you in it."

"You're it for me too," he says as he turns his head and places a soft kiss to my palm. "I never thought I'd have this with someone, especially not with all the responsibilities I had with work and my dad, but then you turned up, saved my life, then turned it completely upside down in the best way. I don't want a future without you in it, but you have to understand life with me isn't going to be easy."

"I don't want easy," I tell him honestly. "I want real."

"Oh, Danny." He blinks back the tears.

I smile slowly. "I want to grow old with you, Tris."

"I want that too," he says quietly. "But what about all...?" He lifts his hands and makes a little circular motion. I assume he means the whole seeing-the-dead and helping-them-find-the-light business.

"It's okay," I tell him softly. "I mean, it's going to take a bit of getting used to, I'm not going to lie, but it's kinda cool."

"Really?" That one word is filled with hope.

"Yeah." I wrap my arms around him and draw him in close. "In a completely and utterly terrifying way."

He wraps his arms around my neck, rising up on his toes to kiss me. "Don't worry," he says, smiling against my mouth. "You protect me from all the crazy murderers, and I'll protect you from all the ghosts."

"Now that sounds like the perfect partnership," I mutter as I take his lips. Kissing him deeply, I sink slowly into the headspace where only he exists. All I can feel and taste is him, he surrounds me and fills all the spaces inside me until I want nothing more than to drown in him. I skim my hands up his sides, sliding under his sweater to feel the heat of his skin, when a thought suddenly occurs to me and I pull back.

He gives a little whine of protest and chases my lips.

"Are there any ghosts around now?" I ask.

"Nope." He kisses me again. "Dusty's gone to see her boyfriend Bruce, only don't tell her I said that because she won't admit he's her boyfriend."

"Her boyfriend?"

"He's dead too," he mutters and chases my lips again. "Danny," he breathes against my mouth between kisses, "take me to bed. I need you."

Helpless to resist him, I pick him up, and he wraps his legs around my waist. I carry him into the bedroom and kick the door shut behind us.

"There's no one in here, is there?" I ask worriedly, not really wanting an audience for what we're about to do.

"Nope." He bounces slightly as I toss him on the bed. "Bedroom's off-limits, especially when you stay over. Dusty knows the rules," he says a little breathlessly as he strips his socks off and tosses them on the floor before shimmying out of his jeans and briefs.

"Have they ever caught us before?" I ask curiously as he rises up onto his knees and strips his sweater off, leaving him gloriously naked in front of me.

"Um," he grimaces guiltily, "not exactly."

"What do you mean not exact–" I break off and I suddenly know. "The other day when you had my dick in your mouth and then you suddenly rolled me up in sofa cushions and hustled me into the bedroom?"

He squirms slightly. "They didn't see anything."

"They?" My eyes pop.

"Dusty had her hand over Mrs Abernathy's eyes. Honestly,

she didn't see anything." Tristan begins stripping me out of my clothes.

I help him because I really don't want to think about it anymore, I just want Tris naked and as close to me as humanly possible. It's felt like a distance has been growing between us lately, but now that everything's out in the open, I need him more than I've ever needed anyone in my life. I need to feel the connection between us.

"It feels like forever since you've been inside me." Tris wraps his arms around my neck and presses his long lithe body against me, letting me feel every inch of his warm naked skin.

"It's not been that long." I skim my palms down his spine, cupping his perky little arse.

"I guess it just feels longer since Dusty possessed my body." He brushes his lips against mine.

"What?" I pull back and stare at him.

"Uh, never mind, long story with a happy ending... forget I said anything... conversation for another time when we're not both naked and hard."

"It's a conversation I'm going to want to revisit," I tell him firmly.

"Scout's honour." He grins.

"You were never a scout," I remind him and he shrugs, pulling me onto the bed with him.

I roll onto my back as he straddles my hips. Pulling off his glasses, he tosses them on the bedside table and retrieves the lube. His beautiful cock is pointing at me, and I can't help but wrap my fist around the hot silky length of him and give a slow lazy slide from root to tip. His head falls back on a gasp as he thrusts into my hand, my own aching cock resting against his arse.

He fumbles the cap open on the lube, drizzling some of the cool liquid onto his fingers as he reaches behind, and I know he's as desperate as I am, but I don't want to rush this.

"Let me," I murmur as I reach behind him and slide my fingers between his cheeks, feeling the slick glide of the lube. He leans forward and kisses me deeply as I slide my finger into the hot heat of him.

He's like a fevered dream, moaning into my mouth as I slide my fingers in and out of him.

"Danny." He tears his mouth from mine and drags in a shaky breath. "I need you... please."

Pulling my fingers free, I lift him slightly and press the sensitive head of my cock to his opening, pushing inside him as we both groan loudly.

He pushes himself up into a sitting position, the change of angle forcing my cock deeply inside him until I'm seated to the root. His eyes lock on mine as he slowly begins to ride me, his hips undulating, my fingers digging into his skin.

I'm utterly bewitched by this man, my love, my life. He holds my beating heart in the palms of his hands, and I don't even think he knows it. Doesn't know the power he holds over me.

"Danny," he gasps, throwing his head back and arching his spine as I groan. "So deep," he moans as, judging from the helplessly pleasured cries falling from his lips, my swollen cock exquisitely rubs the little bundle of nerves deep inside him.

I can feel my orgasm building, hopelessly overwhelmed with my desperate love and need for this complicated man. Pushing myself up into a seated position, I wrap my arms around him and take his mouth while I roll him underneath me and thrust inside him hard.

He cries out into my mouth and I swallow the sound, swallow his pleasure as I pound into him. His fingers rake my skin, marking me, and I can't get enough of him. He's everything. I want him to know that but I can't form the words, so I just keep thrusting into his body, feeling his legs wrapped around me tightly. Our skin is burning with heat and slick with sweat. The scent of our bodies fills the humid air, cocooning us as his taste lingers on my tongue.

His body tightens, his hole clamping around my cock and milking me as I feel the hot slick burst of his release between us. Unable to stop myself, I bury myself deeply and let go, my cock pulsing inside him, filling him with my cum and marking him in the most primal way possible.

We collapse in a sweaty heap, bodies still joined, our hearts thumping and our breathing ragged. Both of us are trembling with the sheer intensity of what we brought to each other. It's always been explosive between us, the chemistry off the charts, but this... this is a whole other level I didn't even know existed. It's like the layers we both built around ourselves to protect us from the world are being slowly stripped away, and for the first time we really see each other.

I can feel his fingers trace lazy circles on my back. No, not circles, I realise after a moment with an exhausted smile against his chest. He's drawing little love hearts on my skin.

"I love you, Tris," I whisper quietly.

"I love you too, Danny, always," is his soft response as I drift into sleep.

Tristan

The light is so bright it's almost painful, and I hold up my hand to shield my eyes. I don't know where I am or how I got here. There's a moment of panic followed almost immediately by a curious sense of calm. It washes over me as gently as a lapping tide. A dreamy kind of lassitude I can't explain, but it banks the anxiety.

Slowly, the harsh white light begins to recede, and a blur of colour and movement surrounds me. The dainty clink of china and silverware fills my ears and as I glance upward, I notice an elaborately painted ceiling and a rather ostentatious crystal chandelier.

With a frown of confusion, I drop my gaze back down and turn in a slow circle, taking in my surroundings. There's a sea of round tables shrouded with ruthlessly pressed white table-cloths. Upon each table, the silverware is polished to such a shine it almost makes my retinas ache in protest. Nestled amongst the heavy crystal glasses are rather fancy centrepieces of some sort of greenery and tiny white flowers.

The tables are filled with customers in very expensive clothes, dripping with jewellery, I imagine by Tiffany and

Cartier. You can practically smell the money in the room. The servers all have that same haughty expression as they melt seamlessly between the tables, delivering impossibly tiny portions of food smeared across fine china plates.

I look down and it's only then I realise I'm wearing the pyjamas Hen bought me last year for our office Secret Santa, they have little dancing grim reapers on them. Honestly, I don't even know where she finds this stuff. I'm also wearing Danny's old police hoodie and my feet are bare. I glance around again in alarm, but nobody seems to be paying any attention to me at all. It's as if they can't see me.

This is one weird-arse dream. I've never been anywhere this posh in my entire life, I can't imagine what I'm doing here now. There's a strange sort of prickling awareness skittering down my spine, followed by the curious sensation of being watched.

My gaze scans the room once more until it snags on a table by the wall. There's a man sitting there, and he seems to be staring in my direction. I turn to glance behind me and then back to him. I point to my chest uncertainly and he smiles.

Holy crap, he's gorgeous.

Before my brain can register what I'm doing, my feet are carrying me in his direction, sinking into the plush expensive carpet with each step. He's wearing an expertly tailored suit of dark grey with a crisp white shirt open at the collar, exposing the line of his throat. His hair skims his shoulders, so black it almost has a bluish hue to it, and his eyes, when they meet mine, are a strange aqua colour, as pale as arctic ice.

"Tristan," he says calmly as I reach his table, his voice deep and commanding. "We meet at last."

"Huh?" I say rather obtusely.

This really is a very strange dream.

"Please." He indicates the seat opposite him, and after a second's hesitation, I slide down onto the padded cushion.

"Would you care to sample anything from the menu?" he offers smoothly.

I shake my head as I note the logo on the menu.

"This is White's of Mayfair." I cast a quick glance around the restaurant again.

"Indeed." He smiles as he lifts a glass of white wine that I swear hadn't been there a moment ago, taking a sip as he watches me. "Are you sure I cannot tempt you?" His mouth twitches. "Perhaps a cup of tea?"

No sooner than the words leave his lips, I'm suddenly desperate for a cup of tea. I open my mouth but before I can utter a word, a delicate china cup filled with tea in just the right shade of caramel is set in front of me. I lift it to my lips and hum in satisfaction. Two sugars, just the way I like it. I take another polite sip and set the cup carefully back in its saucer, my gaze never leaving the stranger seated opposite me.

He studies me silently for several drawn-out moments, his long, elegantly tapered fingers tapping against the table linen in a thoughtful staccato. "You and I can no longer afford to ignore each other, Tristan," he finally says.

"Ignore you? I have no idea who you are." I blink. "How can I be ignoring you when we've never met before?"

"Maybe not formally as yet. We have crossed paths more than a time or two, but perhaps you don't recognise me." He grazes his thumb over his lush lower lip in consideration. "Maybe this will help."

His form shifts into a hazy black smoke and suddenly I'm staring at a dark, deeply cowled reaper, his robe and hood rippling as if he's floating underwater.

I gasp loudly and his form once again solidifies into the handsome suited stranger.

"You're... you're the one. I mean, the reaper I saw in the care home the night Mrs Abernathy died and then again at the community centre during Bingo Bonanza."

"I was surprised you were able to see me in my true form." He sets his elbows on the pristine tablecloth and steeples his fingers in front of him, his eyes flaring with interest. "Every other time we've crossed paths I've appeared in mortal form, as you see me now."

"Are you sure you're not confusing me with someone else?" I frown. "We've never met. I mean, I'm pretty sure I'd remember someone who looks like you."

"Hmm, perhaps a little help then." Before I can ask what he's doing or jerk back from the unexpected movement, he reaches across the table and presses those long, elegant fingers to my forehead. "Remember," he whispers.

I stare at him as a fragment of a memory slowly trickles through my consciousness, followed by another, then another. "You were at my mother's funeral," I gasp with quiet realisation. "And Dusty's funeral too. And... and... oh my god." My breath leaves me in a rush. "You were there, that night in The Crown, the night I met Danny at Seamus' leaving do. You were standing in the crowd, looking down at me as I came around from choking on that bloody ice cube."

"Tristan," he says simply. "I'm the one who sent you back."

"What?" I suck in a breath so sharply I start choking on my own spit.

The handsome stranger simply hands me his water glass, watching as I try to sip, my eyes watering as the coughing fit subsides. He leans back in his seat, his intense gaze sweeping leisurely across the restaurant. "You humans are strange creatures."

"Who are you? Are you God?" The words tumble from my lips before I note how ridiculous they sound.

He simply huffs in amusement. "I certainly wouldn't presume to fill those shoes," he scoffs. "Let's just say, I was around long before he appeared, and I'll be around long after he's nothing but a memory."

"I don't understand." My brows crease. "What's going on here?"

"I've been watching you for a long time, Tristan," he says, his tone matter-of-fact.

"You do realise how creepy that sounds, right? Not to mention slightly sinister," I reply, my tone just as flat, and his mouth twitches again. "Is this the part where you kidnap me and cut me into pieces which you'll then store in a freezer in your cellar?"

He stares at me quietly for a moment. "You've been watching the crime channel again, haven't you?"

"Danny's a fan of unsolved mysteries."

"Of all of them, you've always been my favourite." He gives me a lazy smile.

"All of who?" I reply in confusion. "And does being a favourite come with house points or gold stars? I work well with stickers as an incentive."

He chuckles and it's a strange sound. The air shimmers around us like it's reacting to him somehow.

"What are we doing here? What's going on?" I ask, wondering if I'm going to remember this very vivid, extremely weird dream when I wake.

"I'm here because things are about to change," he says quietly.

"Wow..." I raise my brows. "Can you vague that up for me?"

"A body is about to be uncovered and it's someone I believe you are very familiar with," he answers, his pale arctic eyes filled with enough seriousness to make my flippancy dissolve into a scowl.

"Who?" I see him hesitate and a ball of annoyance curls in my gut. "Don't clam up on me now. Weird dream or not, you can't just tell me someone I know is going to end up in my mortuary and not give me a heads-up on who it is."

"They won't be arriving at your place of work." He gives a

graceful shrug. "They will be brought to a colleague of yours, a forensic anthropologist by the name of O'Hara."

"O'Hara?" I stop to think for a moment. "Roger O'Hara? Then it's not a corpse, the body is just bones. That must mean it's a cold case," I reason. "But who...?" The sentence dies on my lips as the answer comes to me. "Bruce." I glance across at him sharply. "I'm right, aren't I? The remains that are going to be found are Bruce's. Dusty told me his body was never recovered."

He sighs. "I had hoped his remains would stay buried for a few more decades at least. The timing is very inconvenient."

"I'll be sure to let him know how inconvenient his murder is. I'm sure he'll be mortified," I reply dryly.

"Don't be obtuse, Tristan," he mutters absently as he toys with the stem of his wine glass, the inside of his signet ring tapping against the crystal in a soft repetitive *chink chink*. "You need to intercept his remains before they're identified."

"What? Why?" My mouth falls open.

"They're what's keeping him tethered to earth. It's his unfinished business."

"Surely finding them is a good thing, then? It means he can cross over now, he can finally find peace."

The beautiful stranger shakes his head. "You don't understand, Tristan. It is imperative you stop him from crossing into the light," he says bluntly.

"Why?"

"Because he is needed here, whether he realises it or not. His fate is now inextricably bound to the astral portal."

"You mean the magic door in the bookshop?"

"Must you oversimplify everything, Tristan?" He sighs as he rolls his eyes.

I shrug. "It saves confusion later on."

"Yes"—he arches a brow, his tone slow and deliberate—"the portal in the bookshop."

"So let me get this straight. You want me to wait until his bones are discovered." I begin to tick the items off my fingers. "Then you want me to steal them from the forensic anthropology department before they can be identified as a cold case murder. Then you want me to hide them so Bruce can't solve his unfinished business and can't cross into the light and find peace."

"Yes." He gives one decisive nod.

"You're an arsehole," I conclude.

"I've been called worse."

"How can you ask me to do that?" I glower at him. "You're asking me to go against everything I believe in, everything I've trained for. Not to mention, commit a crime. You do realise my boyfriend is a detective at Scotland Yard, right?"

"I had noticed."

I continue without stopping for a breath. "But putting all that aside, how is any of this fair to Bruce? Because I'm pretty sure guarding a magic door for all of eternity wasn't part of his career plan."

He sighs in exasperation. "Will you please stop calling the incredibly powerful and ancient inter-dimensional portal a magic door?"

I ignore him. "I bet he doesn't even get a pension plan or paid holiday. Do spirits have some sort of union? Because I'm pretty sure what you are talking about is illegal."

"Mortals," he mutters as he pinches the bridge of his nose and breathes deeply.

"Oh come on," I huff. "Really, what's the worst that can happen if Bruce quits?"

"All the creatures of the Hell dimensions will use the portal as a conduit and spill out and destroy Earth," he replies.

"Ah." My mouth falls open. "Well as reasons go, I have to admit that's a pretty solid one, but why does it have to be Bruce?"

"It's complicated. Let's just say his soul is bound to the portal and it responds to him."

"So he's like the key?"

"Again with the oversimplification." He clicks his tongue disapprovingly.

"Did it not occur to you to... I don't know... just ask him? Maybe give him some sort of incentive? You know, I've heard happy workers are vastly more productive and loyal than ones that have been lied to. I know he'd stay if he knew the truth."

"I take it back, you're not my favourite," he says flatly. "Even Nostradamus wasn't this much trouble."

"That's probably because he had his hands full with the Medicis," I reply sweetly, "or the plague, take your pick."

"I'd rather not." He frowns.

"Look—" I blow out a breath—"I'm not even sure why I'm arguing with you. This isn't real, it's just some weird dream where I'm sitting in the middle of one of London's most exclusive restaurants. So exclusive, I heard they once kicked out the prince of Monaco for not using a napkin, but here I am, sitting in my pyjamas and bare feet, having a cup of tea served to me in bone china. You won't even tell me who you are. So no. Just flat-out no. I will not do what you ask. Even if any of this were real, I wouldn't do that to Bruce because I believe in free will. I don't believe the end of the world will come about just because one sweet man wants to find his peace."

I finish my rant and find him sitting back in his seat, watching me consideringly.

"Very well," he says suddenly.

"What?" I stare at him with suspicion.

"You've convinced me." He stands slowly and smooths down the front of his impeccable Savile Row suit.

"I have? I did?" My eyes narrow. "Of what?"

"That Bruce deserves a choice." He rounds the table and lifts his hands, adjusting his expensive diamond cufflinks. "His bones will be uncovered and events already set in motion can no longer be stopped. This path leads to only two outcomes. Either Bruce continues to guard the portal or he crosses into the light and inadvertently causes the end of the world."

My eyes narrow even further. "You don't seem too concerned."

"It's not my world." He shrugs as he reaches into his pocket and retrieves a rather old and battered fob watch, a complete contrast to his pristine attire. "You mortals are not the only ones in existence, no matter how much you like to think you are." He snaps the watch shut with a small metallic click and tucks it safely back in his pocket. "Listen very carefully, Tristan, because I dislike having to repeat myself. From the moment Mr Reyes' bones are unearthed, you have exactly sixteen days until the end of the world. The only way to avoid your destruction is to convince him to stay and guard the portal, but how you achieve that end is entirely up to you. Tell him the truth, offer him a choice, or lie to him and bury his bones so deep they will never again see the light of day. As you're so fond of free will, that particular choice is yours. But mind my words. If he abandons the portal, nothing will prevent the end from coming. Do I make myself clear?"

I nod my head mutely and he turns away from me.

"Hey, wait!" I shout and he pauses, glancing back over his shoulder. "Will you at least tell me your name?"

"I have been known by many names," he murmurs as he stares at me in consideration. "But"—those sinful lips curve—"you may call me Death."

I sit bolt upright in my bed, a thin trail of sweat trickling unpleasantly down my spine as my heart hammers in my chest and I breathe heavily.

"Hey." Danny's warm comforting rumble soothes as I feel

the bed shift and the warmth and weight of his hand stroke my back. "Bad dream?" he asks, his voice barely more than a whisper in the darkness of our bedroom.

"I..." My voice sounds croaky to my ears and my throat is dry.

"What's that?" he asks as the moonlight filtering through the crack in the curtains catches something metallic and glints.

It's only when the bed shifts again as Danny leans over and clicks on the bedside lamp that I realise I'm clutching something in my hand. I blink rapidly as my eyes adjust to the sudden soft light flooding the room. Looking down, I slowly unfold my fingers, and a small gasp escapes my lips when I see, nestled in the palm of my hand, a small, battered fob watch.

COMING SOON!
Dead Serious
(COLD) CASE #3 Mr Bruce Reyes

CRAWSHANKS GUIDE TO THE RECENTLY DEPARTED

El Dia del Amor

VALENTINE'S PLANS

Dusty

What's it like being dead? Well, it's not semi naked men lazing around on clouds playing harps, not that I would say no to a bare assed, harp plucking, loin cloth clad cherubim, but death... it's actually more like being stuck in a room full of tourists. No one speaks the language, and they're more interested in staring at the world through their phones than actually looking at what's going on around them.

No one sees me anymore. I used to walk into a room and, honey, I owned it. Now, I'm invisible, looking through the window to a party I'm no longer invited to. Other than that, not much has changed, except I no longer have to shave my legs, and I have a limitless wardrobe, which frankly was a prepubescent Dusty's wet dream.

Death has been an adjustment, and to be honest, I'm still adjusting.

"Dusty, I look ridiculous, why did I let you talk me into buying this?" Tristan draws my attention as he stares at his reflection in the mirror, twisting this way and that to better see himself.

I glance up from laying sprawled on his bed and grin. He

looks fucking adorable in his black skinny jeans and trademark Doc Martens. I managed to talk him into a black, short sleeved shirt scattered with little red love hearts. In addition, he's wearing red braces attached to his jeans and the cutest little black bow tie. His wild dark hair is a riot of loose waves and curls and perched on his disgruntled nose is his thick, dark framed glasses.

"What?" I scoot around on the bed until I'm lying on my stomach with my chin propped in my hands. "You're like the hottest nerd I've ever seen."

"You don't think the bow tie is a bit much?" He frowns.

"Honey, bow ties are never too much." I smile wickedly. "Especially when worn with nothing but the underwear I picked out for you."

I watch as his adorable cheeks flush.

"Um..." Tristan clears his throat.

"You are wearing them, aren't you?" I cock a brow questioningly. "Come on... it's Valentine's Day, boo, if you can't wear lacy, fire engine red knickers today, when can you?"

"But what if Danny doesn't like them? What if he thinks it's weird?" Tristan turns to look directly at me.

"Oh, please." I roll my eyes. "What happened at Halloween when Chan got you to wear them under your costume and Inspector Delicious saw them?"

"Um... he liked them." Tristan blushed again.

"Er... understatement," I snort loudly. "I saw what happened to the flat when you two let loose on each other that night. Trust me, wear the knickers, and I guarantee Detective Dreamboat will have you coming before you've got them past your knees."

Tristan chuckles slowly. "What about you? What are you doing tonight?" he asks conversationally.

"I'm heading to The Rainbow Room." I grin. "It always gets

wild on Valentine's Day. Chan and Ruby are going full on Moulin Rouge for the stage show tonight."

"Sounds like fun. Maybe Danny and I should stop by after dinner." Tristan smiles.

He's become very close to Chan since Halloween and I'm grateful for it. I really worried about her after my death.

"You should stop by, but I get the feeling you'll be very busy... and very naked." I wink.

"You make it sound like we have no self-control." Tristan sighs.

"How long has it been since you two spent the night together?" I ask pointedly.

"Okay, fair point," Tristan concedes. "Danny's been stuck on night shifts a lot lately."

"I know." I wave a hand airily. "I mean, if only the good citizens of London would stop committing crimes after dark so you can get laid."

"I know, right?" he snorts softly. "It's not too much to ask, is it? Besides, I think it has less to do with the crime rate and more to do with the new DCI who's taken over... homophobic arsewipe," he adds under his breath.

"Want me to go haunt him for a few days?" I offer blithely. "I could move some shit around, rattle the windows... appear at the foot of his bed in a shroud, moaning and wailing?"

"Knowing you it would be less moaning and wailing and more working your way through a killer show tune medley... plus you wouldn't be caught dead in a shroud... literally."

"True," I ponder. "But I could still go scare the crap out of him for you. Oooh, I could dress up as a bride... totally creepy. There's only one thing scarier and that's little girl ghosts, but I really don't think I could pull off the Victorian urchin look."

"That's sweet." He smiles at me. "But I'm not sure that was what you were sent back here to do."

"They were a bit ambiguous on that." I shrug. "It's not like they sent me back with an instruction manual. I'm pretty sure it's a grey area."

"Probably best not." He shakes his head as a loud knocking at the front door echoes through the flat.

"That'll be him. Go on, off you go," I shoo him from the room. "Have fun and don't do anything I wouldn't do."

"That's a pretty low bar." Tristan pauses by the bedroom door, turning back to me with a slight furrow between his brows. "Dusty, are you sure you'll be alright tonight?"

"Absolutely." I smile widely. "You know me, I'm always alright."

He nods slowly and heads out of the room. A few moments later I hear the front door open and close, and once again I'm alone. I climb off the bed and turn to look at my reflection in the mirror.

"I'll be fine," I mutter into the stillness of the room.

STANDING ON THE OUTSIDE

Dusty

One of the up sides of being dead is instantaneous travel. No more taxis, Ubers, tubes, or buses. I simply think where I want to go and the next thing I know, bam! I'm at Tristan's, or the mortuary, or The Rainbow Room... and once... Tom Holland's bedroom. Okay, don't ask me how I managed that one because I haven't been able to recreate that particular fluke no matter how hard I try and, boy, have I tried.

Tonight, however, I find myself at The Rainbow Room and it's like coming home. Every inch of it as familiar as my old flat, which has now been let to a sweet young couple just starting out. All of my things are gone now, given away or sold, but it doesn't matter though, I mentally shrug, even if it did hurt like hell there was nothing else to do. It's not like I can use it anymore.

Brushing away the familiar heaviness in my chest, I look up at the crepe paper bunting, strings of lights, and hearts and balloons exploding over every inch of the club. I know for a fact there are loaded confetti cannons concealed everywhere. The one thing I can say for Ari is that he isn't afraid to spend money as quickly as he makes it, and when it comes to events and holidays, he always goes all out hoping to outdo rival clubs.

The club is already full, and Ramone is behind the bar flirting outrageously as he concocts the wildest cocktails he can dream up. Brandy is holding court at one of the tables, her plastered foot propped on a chair while her broken bones heal, and she's looking very sour that she's not up on stage.

Ginger, bless her, is still the baby of the club, but at least she's starting to grow into her look, and I'm pleased for her. She'd come from such a strict, religious background, her family wouldn't accept that she was gay, let alone understand why she would want to dress in what is deemed female clothes. She was so timid when I took her under my wing. I'd spent hours showing her make-up techniques, letting her try on my costumes and wigs, and teaching her how to perform on stage. Now, watching her smiling confidently in a gorgeous 1930's style fringed dress and strutting around on five-inch heels like she'd emerged from the womb wearing them, it makes my stomach warm and chest fill with pride. It's like watching my little baby bird take flight.

As for me, I'm fully embracing my inner Britany Spears tonight. I'm talking full on *Oops! ...I Did It Again*, skin-tight red PVC bodysuit, red knee-high go-go boots on four-inch heels and platforms. My blonde hair is scraped back into a high, tight ponytail... that's another up-side of being dead. No more itchy wigs, my hair is whatever I want it to be whenever I want it.

As the music blares out across the club, I strut to the dance floor to shake my booty, slipping through the gyrating bodies and ignoring the fact that they're sliding through my insubstantial form as if I wasn't even there.

Suddenly the music switches, and the unmistakably primal beat of Eurythmics, *Sweet Dreams* begins. I stare up at the stage as it rotates and watch as Chan and Ruby appear. They're a mirror image of each other, seated on matching thrones, legs spread, hands folded in front and resting on the pommel of a shiny black walking cane. Chan's wearing a black corset, cute little frilly knickers, stockings, and boots laced up to her knees. Her signature jet black hair is tied back into a tight bun at the nape of her neck and a tiny top hat is pinned at an angle on her head.

Ruby is dressed much the same but in blood red, my signature colour. They're both surrounded by lithe and tightly muscled dancers in tiny leather pants and heavy eye make-up. I watch transfixed as they run through their number, lip syncing to the gorgeous tones of Annie Lennox. The choreography is sharp and dramatic and up on stage they're simply breath taking.

Even as I enjoy the sheer deliciousness of their act my heart thuds dully in my chest, and I feel a strange sinking feeling behind my rib cage. Six months ago, that would've been me and Chan up on the stage together. As *Sweet Dreams* gives way to Lizzo's *Good as Hell,* the confetti cannons explode over the dance floor. I can't even feel it as it falls straight through me and scatters across the floor at my feet.

I turn away, and as the crowd parts my breath catches, under the sparkling lights is my sweet little Benny. He's dressed up in a tux, bless his heart, and in front of him is a girl about his age, who is also Down syndrome. She's dressed in a pretty chiffon dress with a sparkly clip in her curly hair. They're dressed like they're at prom rather than a drag club. She's smiling up at him with her hands settled on his shoulders, his at her waist, and almost a foot between them as they innocently sway, stepping from foot to foot.

I swallow past the lump in my throat, my eyes burning with sentimental tears. My sweet boy has found himself a girlfriend, and he looks so happy. I glance across the dance floor to Ginger and watch her glance up shyly at a cute dark-haired guy as he wraps his arms around her. My gaze tracks across to the bar where Ramone is holding a pretty femme's hand and kissing it with a wide grin. I glance back up at the stage and see Chan and Ruby smiling widely as they perform.

A sinking feeling in my chest begins to burn all the way down to my stomach where it sits like lead in my belly.

In that one moment, I come to a slow and devastating realisation... everyone has moved on.

I don't belong here anymore.

A GRAVE INVITATION

Dusty

I stare at the brass plaque, its surface covered with beads of misted rain. The memorial garden is silent, as it should be at almost midnight on Valentine's Day. Everyone is out celebrating with their loved ones, partners, and crushes.

Our Beloved Dusty, never forgotten and forever in our hearts...

The words etched into the plaque are mocking me as I sit on a bench in the drizzling rain. They have forgotten me, or at least, that's what it feels like. I've been dead barely six months, and it feels as if I never existed at all. Was I really so forgettable?

The cold February rain begins to hammer down harder, clattering against the pavement with spiteful fingers, mirroring my bleak mood, but I can't even feel it. I can't feel the cold, I can't feel the wetness against my skin, saturating my hair and clothes... because it doesn't, it simply falls straight through me.

Like I'm nothing, like I don't exist.

I blink rapidly but everything looks blurry through my tears, and there's a hollowness inside me that I just can't shake. After a long moment, I become aware of a bright red blur through the haze of grey. I blink again to clear my vision and see a single, perfect red rose in front of me. My gaze slides down to the wide masculine hand gripping the long, thorn free stem and I take in the golden skin and neatly trimmed nails. My gaze tracks slowly to my left, up a long firmly muscled arm and across a broad torso to a smiling face. His honeyed skin and deep brown eyes glow in the dim light.

"Bruce?" I sniff. "What are you doing here?"

"I'd have thought that was obvious." He smiles softly. "I'm here for you." He waves the rose under my nose with a little enticing wiggle. "Be my Valentine?" He smiles as I take the rose with shaky fingers and give a watery smile.

I sniff again loudly, wiping my nose. "You left the bookshop?" I say randomly.

"I do get the night off every now and then you know," he chuckles. "And tonight is special."

"For some maybe," I mutter looking back toward my memorial plaque.

"Hey." His fingers skim my jaw lightly and draw my gaze back to him. "What's wrong?"

I shake my head, breaking his soft hold on my jaw. "Nothing, it doesn't matter. I'm just being a drama queen."

"Dusty, drama queen is your default setting. I'd be worried if you weren't," he says softly, and I find I can't look away from the quiet intensity in those dark eyes.

"They've all forgotten me," I whisper as the words catch in my throat.

"Ah," Bruce replies knowingly. "I wondered when you'd reach this stage."

"What stage?" I frown.

"Dusty." He takes my hand gently, entwining his thick blunt fingers with my long tapered, red tipped ones. "They haven't forgotten you, they're moving on."

"But I've only been dead six months." I swallow back a fresh flood of tears and look up blinking as I blow out a breath.

"Do you want them to be miserable?" he asked.

"Is that too much to ask?" I pout and he stares at me pointedly. "No." I sigh. "I don't want them to be sad, but what am I supposed to do? I feel lost... like I'm stuck in limbo, which is dumb because it's not like I wasn't given a choice. I chose to come back, but now..."

"It happens to all of us who stay behind." He squeezes my hand reassuringly. "The pull to the things that are familiar to us is so strong, but inevitably we come to the realisation that life, for the living, moves on and we no longer belong with them. It's their natural progression, and we have to let them go, otherwise the only ones we hurt are ourselves."

"But what am I supposed to do?" I sigh. "Go through the rest of existence not being able to experience all the things I love."

"Such as?"

"I don't know." I let out an exasperated breath. "Everything! Eating, drinking. The smell of the rain, the warmth of the sun on my skin, the beat of music pounding in my chest. All those human experiences I took for granted, and it's the worst kind of torture because now I can't feel any of those things anymore. It's like living in a two-dimensional world. I can see it, but I can't feel it."

"Well, that's easily fixed." He stands up and moves in front of me. It's then that I realise he's not wearing his rugby kit but instead is dressed in a tuxedo, which he fills out to perfection. I stare at his hand as he holds it out toward me.

"What?" I blink in confusion.

"Trust me." He smiles.

I reach out and take his hand as I rise to my feet. "Where are we going?"

He grins boyishly. "I'm taking you to a real party."

TIERRA DE LOS MUERTOS

Dusty

The wet, dark drizzly memorial garden blurs and disappears around us. Bright swirls of colour like carnival ribbons swirl and swirl around us, and I feel a ripple of a warm breeze across my skin and the faint sound of music. As the notes become louder and clearer, I can make out a complicated rhythm of guitar strings, violins, and trumpets accompanied by deep male voices.

When the spinning finally slows to a stop, I glance up, my mouth falling open in wonder. I have no idea where the hell I am, but I'm surrounded by an endless vista of colour and sound. There's a clear starry night above us and spread out ahead like an ocean is an unending celebration. There are tables and candles everywhere, garlands and garlands of brightly coloured flowers heavily scenting the air.

"Oh," I gasp as I breath in. "I can smell the flowers."

"They're beautiful, aren't they?" Bruce smiles. "There are campasuchil, which you know as marigolds. There's also Terciopelo Rojo, Crisantemo Blanco, Nube."

I feel the warm summer night's breeze ripple across my skin, and as I look down, I notice I'm no longer wearing skin-tight PVC but instead a black figure-hugging dress decorated with embroidered multicoloured flowers and with ruffles around the fishtail skirt and across my chest and upper arms, leaving my shoulders bare. My hair is scooped into an intricate loop at the nape of my neck and more flowers are tucked into the side.

"How?" I glance up at Bruce as he winks at me.

"I know how much you like to match your outfit to the occasion." He smiles.

"Where are we?" I look back out at the vista filled with hundreds, even thousands, of people celebrating.

"Tierra de los Muertos," he replies. "The land of the dead."

"You're Mexican?" I murmur curiously as I study him. I've always thought he was gorgeous from the moment I met him with his dark hair, warm gold skin, and chocolate-coloured eyes, but I never really stopped to consider his heritage.

"Half, my mum was English," he replies easily. "But my papa was Mexican."

"But your name is Bruce," I say stupidly.

"Papa was a fan, what can I say?" He chuckles.

"Springteen or Willis?"

"Forsyth." He grins. "He loved the Generation Game."

"So did my mum," I reply softly in remembrance, and it occurs to me I've never asked him any questions about his life before the bookstore. Most of the time we just find a quiet, uninterrupted corner to fuck. I don't even know his last name.

"It's Reyes," he says.

"What?"

"My last name." He laughs warmly.

"How did you know?" I frown.

"Your expression, sometimes I can read you like a book, Dusty." He squeezes my hand again. "And you're just now realising how little we actually know about each other, but that is something we can remedy." He tugs my hand, and we start moving, descending a stone stairway with glowing lights leading the way surrounded by flower gardens and a rich heady scent.

We reach a wide plaza upon which dozens of round tables sit, each with crisp white linens and fat candles guttering in the warm air. The air is filled with the exhilarating and joyous sound of Mariachi, complex notes played on harps and guitars.

"What is all this?" I ask as he leads me through the maze of tables and dancing couples.

"El Dia del Amor, the day of love." He glances over his shoulder to catch my wide-eyed gaze. "This is how we celebrate Valentines in the realms of the dead."

"This is amazing," I mutter.

"Abuela!" Bruce calls out waving with one hand while still holding onto me with the other. "Abuela! Come meet Dusty!"

My body stiffens nervously as a short round woman turns toward us. Bruce must sense my tension, offering me a reassuring smile as he tugs me closer to the old woman. She's wearing a full round dark skirt decorated at the hem with large flowers, her white blouse has the same wide ruffle across her shoulders and her iron-grey hair is scraped back in a severe bun, revealing tiny gold hooped earrings.

"Abuela." He grins breathlessly as he leans down and drops a kiss on her cheek.

"Mijo." She smiles indulgently. "I was wondering when you would arrive. Hector was looking for you."

He nods and pulls me forward presenting me to the little old woman. "This is Dusty... Dusty, this is my Abuela, Guadalupe Reyes."

"Hi," I squeak and thrust out my hand awkwardly. "It's nice to meet you, Mrs Reyes."

Her dark eyes scan me from head to toe, and for a brief moment, I wonder whether she just sees a skinny boy in a dress. I'm beginning to sweat a bit under her intense scrutiny, and just when I think I'm going to pass out from the stress, she nods.

"Hm," she hums. "My grandson speaks of you often. You may call me Lupe or Abuela if you wish." She reaches out and grasps me, pulling me in and hugging me tightly, and damn, she has a hell of a grip for a tiny little old lady.

I open my mouth to speak when she cuts me off, yelling loudly. "Alejandra, come meet Bruce's girl."

"Oh, I'm not–" The breath whooshes out of me as I'm spun and hugged tightly by a beautiful middle-aged woman with grey shot hair spilling down her back and wrists filled with jangling bracelets.

"It is nice to meet you, Cariño," she exclaims in her musical accent. "I hope you and my nephew will be very happy."

"Oh, um... we're not–"

"Tio Miguel!" she yells loudly cutting me off again. "Come meet Bruce's girl!"

"But I..." I find myself spun around again and embraced by a tall well-built man. His glossy hair is black with silver wings, and he engulfs me tightly.

"Welcome to mi familia! We hope you will be very happy!"

"Thank you, but I–"

"Tio Roberto!" he yells loudly. "Come meet Bruce's girl!"

A short round man with a wide smile and a bushy moustache embraces me tightly, but he's so short his face ends up crushed to my chest.

"Welmosneifiijikdjki..."

"What?" I pull back.

"I said, welcome to the family, Mija." He pats my bottom a little too familiarly, and I stumble back.

"Um, that's very kind, but–"

"Tia Carmen, Tia Yolanda! Come meet Bruce's girl!" he bellows and before I know it, I'm being embraced by two identical older women.

"Welcome!"

"We hope."

"You'll be."

"Very happy!" They beam in unison.

"Don't mind them, they're just one person with two mouths," someone says from behind me, spinning me around and hugging me firmly with a hearty slap on the back, which nearly knocks my teeth loose. "I am Tia Josefina, and this is my daughter Adriana."

I stare at the older woman and her middle-aged daughter standing next to her.

"You're Bruce's girl?" Adriana grins.

"Yeah, sure." I sigh in defeat, with a shrug. "Why not."

I'm passed from person to person, hugged and kissed and patted fondly. Old, middle aged, young, men, women. Pedro, Santiago, Juan, Maria, Silvia, Luisa, Eduardo... I literally lose track until finally I'm deposited in a chair at a table, and when I look up, Bruce is sitting across from me, grinning wildly in amusement.

"Here." Abuela Lupe slides two plates onto the table. "I make enchiladas... you try my tamales too."

I lean forward and my taste buds begin to sing. I inhale the scent deeply, and for the first time since I died, my stomach rumbles. Picking up my knife and fork I cut a small piece and slide it into my mouth groaning loudly while Abuela pours the wine.

I haven't eaten since my death. There was no need, and I didn't feel hunger. My body, no longer corporeal, had no way to process food or drink, but here in the realm of the dead, I can feel and touch and taste everything.

"Oh my god!" I scoop up another mouthful.

"Good?" Abuela demands.

"So good," I groan with my mouth full.

She huffs in approval and walks off.

"Here." Bruce hands me a glass of wine and I sip it, feeling the burst of flavour ripple across my tongue.

"Oh my god, I can taste it!"

"In the mortal world we can't consume food or drink as our bodies are incorporeal, but here in the land of the dead, it's a whole different set of rules. You can do anything here, experience anything you want."

"This is amazing." I grin as I sip the wine, reaching out and squeezing his hand across the table. "Thank you," I say sincerely.

"You're welcome." He smiles in return, his eyes softening.

"Can I ask you something?" I glance back up at him as I chew another mouthful of Abuela's heavenly enchiladas, and when he nods, I continue. "Why does everyone have Tio or Tia in front of their name?"

"Tio means uncle and Tia means auntie," he explains. "They are all great aunts and uncles and cousins on my papa's side, and they're way more fun than the English side of the family who like to sit around primly sipping tea like they're at Royal Ascot."

I chuckle softly as I glance around. "I can't believe this place." I shake my head with a smile. "It's incredible."

"I'm glad you like it." He picks up the basket holding the bottle of wine and tops up my glass. "Like I said, you're not bound by the same rules here. You can do anything you want."

My smile stretches into a grin, and I feel my eyebrow quirk. "Anything?"

TANGO FOR TWO

Bruce

I chuckle delightedly as I lean back in my chair, bathed in the soft glow of lamplight. I lift my glass and sip the wine slowly as I watch the entertaining spectacle unfolding in front of me. Dusty is up on stage singing with the band, and I have to hand it to her, I've never heard a mariachi version of *Its Raining Men,* but the absolute highlight for me is when they hit the chorus and five burly Mexican men with thick, bushy moustaches and wide black sombreros with silver edging burst into *Hallelujah... it's raining men... amen...* in their heavy accents.

Best. Night. Ever.

I lift my glass to my lips, but as I take a sip, I find myself snorting into my glass and spraying the wine up my nostrils as I watch Dusty execute a perfect high kick before sliding her leg down the side of one of the guitar players. I watch as she spins and bends, rolling up and rubbing her gorgeously rounded bum against the trumpet player, flicking her arm and knocking his wide hat askew.

I set the glass down, chuckling quietly as I wipe my mouth.

"I haven't seen you smile like that in a long while, Mijo," a warm and familiar voice murmurs beside me.

I look up and watch as Abuela slides into the seat next to me before turning her attention to the stage and to Dusty who now has a tambourine and is slapping it against her thigh with a cheeky smile... where the hell did she get a tambourine?

"You like her," Abuela states.

I turn to look at my grandmother, her dark eyes hold mine steadily, and I find myself unable to look away. I barely remember her from my childhood. I have a faint recollection of being taken to Mexico when I was six to visit her. All I remember is a frail old woman with papery skin and a warm smile. She passed not long after. I've gotten to know her so much better since I died.

"Mijo?" She prompted and I glance back to Dusty.

I bark out a laugh, my pensive scowl rippling into a wide grin as I watch Dusty. I'm pretty sure that's not what you're supposed to do with maracas... My gaze slides across to my assorted cousins, aunts, and uncles who are standing transfixed with mouths hanging open.

"Sí, Abuela." I turn back to her with a smile. "I do like Dusty a lot, she..." I break off searching for the words to explain. "She's... it's like I didn't know I was standing in the dark until she started shining, and she was so bright I couldn't look away."

Abuela stares silently, her dark eyes searching my face. Unable to stand the intense scrutiny I turn back to Dusty to find her wrapping those siren red lips around the mouthpiece of a trumpet and I chuckle.

She's like no one I've ever known before. I died back in the 1980's in the peak of my prime. Most of the men I'd been involved with in my short time had been much the same as me. Burly, thickly muscled, questionable facial hair. Although I've always been clean shaven, all my previous lovers had sported the Freddie Mercury signature moustache. The world I'd known had been a far less tolerant place. Many of us forced into underground clubs and meeting places to score a partner, and at the height of the AIDS epidemic, it was a difficult time.

After I died, I resigned myself to being alone until Dusty walked into the bookstore. It was like the moment in the *Wizard of Oz* when the door opens, and everything changes from sepia to glorious technicolour. I'd never met anyone like her before. She's just so... unapologetically Dusty. There's no other way to describe her. I hadn't realised how dull and monotonous my existence had become. Nearly four decades had passed in the blink of an eye, like a disjointed dream where time has no meaning, that is until a gorgeous gay man in a bloodstained blonde wig, a gold dress and one stiletto had sashayed into my life.

She'd touched my hand and it was like a jolt of electricity. Of course, then she'd put her mouth on me, followed by every inch of that sinfully gorgeous body of hers. It hadn't even occurred to me that as spirits we could still have... um... relations. I knew we could touch each other, but I didn't know my body still worked that way until she had my dick in her mouth and I was coming for the first time in nearly half a century, in fact the last time I'd orgasmed at all, Duran Duran were still topping the charts.

I fix my attention on Dusty, a smile playing on my lips. Her skirt is hiked scandalously up to her thighs, revealing those ridiculously long smooth legs I've had wrapped around my head more times than I can count. She's sitting astride a harp, wearing one of the guy's sombreros and singing her heart out to the mariachi rendition of what sounds suspiciously like Madonna's *Papa don't Preach*.

My gaze darts across to Tio Fernando, and sure enough, he's staring at Dusty with his eyes practically popping out of his skull. I snort loudly and pick up my glass of wine once more.

I stand by what I said. Best. Night. Ever.

"Have you told her?" Abuela asks, and for a moment, I'd been so caught up in Dusty I forgot she was there.

"Told her what?" I ask absently.

"Why you are not allowed to come home," she replies seriously.

"No," I reply after a moment. "We don't really talk much I guess," I admit, suddenly realising it's true. I guess we got so caught up in each other, in knowing we could touch and feel pleasure, it drowned out the loneliness, and we kind of forgot everything else.

"You should try having an actual conversation," Abuela states, her brow quirking pointedly.

"Sí, Abuela," I agree, not really wanting to talk to my dead grandmother about my relationship with Dusty or the insane chemistry we have, or that thing she does with her dic—

"What is she doing with Mama Luisa?" Abuela frowns in confusion.

"Uh," My eyes narrow thoughtfully as I glance up to find that Dusty has in fact pulled my great grandmother up on stage with her. "I think Dusty said it's called twerking."

"Dios mio." Abuela blinks. "It's just as well Mama no longer has a physical body, or she'd break a hip." She sighs deeply. "I better go get her before Papa Miguel disincorporates from shock."

"Don't worry." I grin. "I've got this."

I slide out of my chair and weave through the tables, crossing the dance floor as Dusty's eyes lock on me and her mouth curves. When I reach the edge of the stage, I reach up and hold my hand out to her. Instead of taking my hand, she slides her arm around my neck and drops off the stage, sliding down my body until her feet are settled firmly on the floor.

I drop a brief kiss on those fiery red lips before spinning her onto the dance floor. She twirls out into the centre of the floor, and when she stops, she's no longer wearing her black fishtail dress but a scandalous, strappy red number that skims her body like a coat of paint and slashed to the thigh, revealing creamy skin and a mile of leg.

My mouth curves as my brow quirks, and I stalk slowly toward her.

"You think that's impressive, then you should've seen my rapid costume changes on stage at The Rainbow Room." She grins.

I reach out and draw her in to press against me and skim my palm down her bare back to the edge of her dress at the base of her spine.

"Do you know the Argentine tango?" I whisper.

She smiles, slowly raising her leg so high her ankle hooks over my shoulder, then leans back, sinuously arching her back as I hold her. Reaching out she grabs a single long-stemmed rose from a nearby table.

"Three years of sneaking out after school for ballroom dancing classes, and I watched Strictly Ballroom so many times I nearly wore a hole in the DVD." She grins as she drops her leg and reaches for my hand. "And I always danced the girl parts," she whispers as she places the rose between her lips and winks wickedly.

There's something to be said for the intensity and seduction of Latin dance. The feel of her long lean sinuous body slide against mine to the beat of the music, spinning and dipping, her gaze never leaving mine.

I can feel my cock twitching as I run my hands along her warm smooth skin. Seeming to read my arousal as we near the edge of the dance floor, she grabs my hand and pulls me into the crowd. She laughs in delight as we weave through the tables and people, keeping a tight hold on my hand as she tows me along in her wake. We end up in a quiet courtyard.

She glances around quickly and drags me behind a row of thick shrubs and heavily flowering bushes.

"Dusty, what—"

She pushes me up against the stone wall behind me and seals her lips to mine, her tongue plunging into my mouth. I feel her deftly unbuttoning my shirt and running her long fingers through my chest hair.

"Mmmm," she hums against my mouth, trailing her lips down my throat as my head falls back and thuds dully against the wall.

She trails her hot mouth down my chest, dipping her tongue into my belly button as her hands cup my rock-hard dick through my trousers.

"Dusty," I moan quietly. "We shouldn't... not here. We could get caught."

"That's half the fun." She smiles up at me, her gaze locked on me as she slowly unzips my trousers and slides them down over my thick thighs. "Do you really want me to stop?" she asks slyly.

I'm unable to even utter a single syllable as she grasps the waistband of my boxers in her teeth and lowers them, dragging them over my throbbing dick. I watch helplessly in her thrall as she leans in, burying her face in my crotch and inhaling deeply before licking a hot wet swathe over my balls and up the length of my brutally rigid cock. I'm almost panting like a dog as she sucks me down into the warm cavern of her mouth, hollowing her cheeks and sucking hard as she withdraws almost to the tip before swallowing me again.

I hear a sudden burst of laughter and look up with wide eyes as a tall, dark-haired man, and a petite woman enter the courtyard. I freeze as they cross the flagstones moving closer. Only my head and shoulders are visible above the bushes as Dusty continues to devour my cock with single minded intensity. I try to pull back as they near, but she grips my hips and swirls her tongue around the head before taking me to the back of her throat.

A gasp escapes my lips as the couple pass by, glancing up at me and shooting me a strange look.

"Evening," I squeak and feel Dusty chuckle around my dick.

They hurry past and exit the other side, disappearing into the festivities. My eyes roll back in my head as she grips my dick firmly, lifting it and sucking my balls into her mouth one at a time.

"Sweet mother Mary of all that is good and holy and pure," I mutter, and the next thing I know she's grabbing me and pulling me to the ground behind the bushes so no one else can see.

Stradling my legs, she sucks harder squeezing my balls and rubbing her finger along my taint. Unable to help myself, I grip her hair and thrust deeper into her mouth.

"Do it." She pulls off and pants. "Fuck my mouth the way I like it."

Unable to do anything else, I thrust into her mouth, feeling lightning shoot down my spine and my toes curl. My balls tighten, and before I can utter another word, I explode into her mouth. She swallows each pulse until I'm wrung dry.

"You," I gasp, grabbing for her and dragging her up my body. She straddles my hips, and I shove her dress up frantically reaching for her lacy red knickers and desperate to get her dick in my mouth. I shove my hand into her knickers, and I've just got my hand wrapped around her throbbing wet cock when I hear a throat clear loudly.

Dusty and I freeze, staring at each other.

"Bruce Manuel Reyes," a familiar voice states firmly.

"*Manuel?*" Dusty mouths to me.

"*Shut up,*" I mouth back.

"I know you're in there," the voice says dryly.

I groan as I shove my spent dick back in my boxers and button my trousers. "*Sorry,*" I mouth to Dusty as she tries to shove her aching dick back into her knickers and smooth her dress down over the obvious bulge.

We climb to our feet bashfully and peer over the top of the bushes to see pretty much my entire family lined up like the cast of a west end show on a second encore. I can only imagine what this looks like to them.

After having her fingers dragging through my hair, it's probably sticking up in all directions. I can taste her red lipstick smeared over my mouth. My shirt is open but still buttoned at the collar, which is sticking up at one side with my bow tie wrapped messily around my throat. Dusty isn't in much better shape as she tries to fix the straps of her dress, her hair has come loose from her bun and is sticking up, and her lipstick is smeared up to her cheek bone.

"Um, Bruce was just helping me look for my earring." Dusty clears her throat.

"The earring that you're wearing?" Abuela raises a brow.

"Yes..." Dusty states slowly with a nod. "Yes... we found it, thank you for asking."

"What were they doing?" Mama Luisa asks.

"Looking for something." Alejandra blushes.

"What were they looking for in a bush?" Mama Luisa replies in confusion.

"An earring Mama." Abuela rolls her eyes.

"What would an earring be doing in a bush? Is it like a treasure hunt, should we all look?"

"NO!" Several family members chorused with a mixture of horror and amusement as the little old lady hobbled toward the bush.

"Oh." She frowns. "It's been a long time since I played in a bush."

I elbow Dusty as she snorts loudly.

"Oh, would you look at the time," I exclaim loudly as I hustle to tuck Dusty behind me to hide her obvious erection. I really don't want to explain that one to Mama Luisa. I'm not entirely sure she realises Dusty isn't a girl.

"Why don't you show Dusty La Luna before you go?" Abuela says knowingly.

"I will." I nod. "It was good to see you all."

"It was nice to meet you all." Dusty waves as I tow her out from behind the bush and hustle her out of the courtyard in mortification.

A TRUTH AND A PROMISE

Bruce

"Oh my god, you should've seen your face," Dusty laughs softly.

"I am never going to live this down." I sigh as I hold out my hand to steady her.

She's walking barefoot along a low stone wall, her strappy heels dangling from one hand, the other holding onto my hand as we walk along companionably in the moonlight.

"I love this place." She breathes in the heady scent of flowers and warm air. "It's like I'm real."

"You are real, Dusty," I tell her seriously. "It's just that living in the mortal world is... complicated."

"I don't know how you ever leave this place," she says contemplatively. "I wouldn't."

"That's because you're not ready to move on," I tell her knowing it's the truth. "You're not ready to leave Chan and Tristan."

"True." She skips nimbly over a missing block of stone and lands lightly on the other side. "I don't know if I'll ever be ready to leave them. Which is kinda weird when you think about it. I mean I've known Chan most of my life so that's understandable, but I've only known Tristan for six months. Yet when I think about leaving him, there's this hollow feeling deep inside of me, and it just feels... wrong."

"That's because you were meant to find him," I explain. "There was an instant connection between you two and that usually means that your souls are bound to each other in some way."

"What do you mean?" She frowns in confusion.

"Just that your paths are somehow entwined." I shrug. "I don't know specifics, but I do know that you came into each other's lives for a reason, and only time will tell what that reason is."

"You're awfully knowledgeable about all this stuff." She glances over to me, her eyes soft and thoughtful.

"I've been around a while." I shrug.

"Bruce," she says softly, and I look up as I feel her lean down. Wrapping her arm around my neck and hopping easily into my arms, I find myself holding her bridal style as she kisses me softly. "Thank you," she whispers against my lips. "I've had the best night."

"It's not quite over yet." I smile. "Come on, I want to show you something."

She slides down my body until her feet are resting on the floor, and I take her hand, leading her up a set of winding stone steps. It's quite a climb, and we walk in companionable silence, winding further and further up until the steps open up into a small courtyard, and I hear Dusty gasp softly next to me.

"Wow," she mutters, as she lets go of my hand.

The small courtyard is contained by a low wall and on the other side, a sheer drop down the side of a mountain. Laid out in front of us is the whole of Tierra de los Muertos twinkling in the night like a jar of fireflies.

"This view is incredible," Dusty whispers, as she stares out across the endless land of the dead, which glows in a vast array of colors beneath the endless night sky. "Where are we?"

"La Luna." I turn to gaze behind me, and Dusty follows.

Behind us, butted up against the mountain, is an enormous house made of stone and carved with intricate designs with windows framed by wooden shutters and painted in brightly coloured pinks and blues. Vines of wild, heavily scented flowers wind up the house and coil around the windows.

"It's gorgeous." Dusty stares.

"Yes." I nod slowly. "It's mine, my home... or at least it will be... one day. It's not finished."

"When did you start building it?" she asks curiously.

"Nearly forty years ago." I shrug.

"And it's not finished yet?" Dusty's brow quirks. "The Taj Mahal took less time to build."

I sigh as Abuela's words echo in my ears, and I wander to the edge of the wall and look out over the land of my people.

"I'm not allowed to come home," I say quietly, feeling Dusty move to stand beside me.

"What?" She frowns. "Why the hell not?"

My mouth twitches at her enraged tone. I reach out, snaking a hand around her waist and sliding her in front of me so she's leaning back against the wall.

"I don't understand." She frowns. "I met your family, and they adore you, why won't they let you come home?"

"It's not up to them." I shake my head. "I'm not allowed to leave the mortal world."

She blinks up at me uncomprehendingly.

"Well... at least not permanently," I add seeing her confusion. "Some time ago, I figured out that I could sneak in for short periods of time to see my family, but it's a kind of Cinderella deal. I have to return by a certain time."

"But why can't you leave the mortal world?"

"Because of how I died," I reply softly.

She hops up onto the wall so she's sitting in front of me, her head tilting the way it does when she's trying to figure something out.

"What happened, Bruce?" she finally asks in a low, concerned voice.

"I was murdered," I answer simply. "You know yourself, being taken before your time throws up all kinds of complications and unfinished business that traps us there unable to move on."

"But you died back in the eighties." She frowns thoughtfully. "You said it yourself, you've been there nearly forty years, so how come you haven't resolved your unfinished business?"

"Because they never found my body," I explain.

"What?" she whispers. "Bruce, what happened to you?"

"Well, that's part of the problem, I don't remember," I admit.

"Nothing?"

I shake my head. "Not a single thing. The last thing I remember was playing rugby and then nothing. I found myself trapped, and for the longest time, I stayed around my family, I watched them grieve, watched them move on. No one could see or hear me, and I was so lonely. I didn't understand what was happening. Eventually I found my way to the bookshop in Whitechapel, and I found a way to be useful helping others."

"But isn't that hard?" she asks. "Helping other souls cross over into the afterlife and not being able to yourself?"

"Sometimes," I admit. "But I got used to it... and then I met you." I can feel the smile creeping over my face. "And my life got a little brighter."

"So..." She grins slowly. "You're saying I make the whole of existence better?"

I snort softly. "Something like that."

She reaches out and draws me closer, spreading her legs so I can step into the cradle of her thighs as she watches me.

"You know you're nothing like the guys I was involved with when I was alive," she muses, almost to herself.

"Is that a bad thing?" I ask.

"No," she murmurs. "Just different."

"What sort of guys did you go for before?"

"Older guys mainly." She shrugs.

"I'm way older than you." I grin. "Technically if I'd lived, I'd be in my seventies now."

"Not quite that old," she laughs. "Most of the guys I was involved with were around their forties or fifties, still fit and good looking."

"You had a type then?"

"Yes and no." She decides after a moment. "It's not like I was just physically attracted to guys that age, it was more the lifestyle. It suited me to have someone older, confident, and who was willing to spend money on me and have no strings sex. I didn't want a relationship, but I liked the attention. I know it sounds really shallow, but by them buying me expensive gifts, it made me feel... I don't know, wanted I suppose."

"I get it." I nod, thinking quietly. "Can I ask you a question?"

"Sure." She hooks her feet around my calves and draws me in even closer.

"Why me?" I wonder aloud. "That day you and Tristan walked into the bookshop, what made you choose me?"

"I don't know." She frowns. "I guess I've never really thought about it. I mean you're hot. All that golden skin and dark hair, and god, your arse and thighs in those shorts." She winks and I chuckle softly. "But the truth is, I felt a pull to you. I don't think I realised it at the time, but it was the same with Tristan, and I don't know what it means."

"I guess we'll figure it out at some point," I mutter as I slide my hands around her and grip her arse, massaging those sinfully plump cheeks as I lean in and taste her mouth. "I believe we were interrupted before." I grin between kisses, sliding her dress up her thighs and reaching into her knickers as I wrap my fist around her already erect cock. "Now where were we?"

She leans back on a long moan as I drop to my knees and wrap my lips around her dick, licking the salty drop of precum at the slit, suckling the head and then sliding her aching cock to the back of my throat. Its long and slim, the skin heated and silky as I slide up and down her length, dragging my tongue along the underside to the symphony of her pleasured groans. I feel her fingers tangle in my hair as I take her deeper and move faster. I don't have any patience tonight. I have this unexplainable need burning in my gut, and I know it's for her. I need Dusty.

I pull my mouth off her cock and stand, taking her mouth again desperately as I strip off my jacket, yanking off my tie and tossing it aside.

"Bruce," she moans against my mouth as her hands grapple with my trousers, opening them and shoving them roughly down my legs along with my boxers.

As I toss my shirt aside, kicking out of the rest of my clothes, as I reach under her skirt and drag her knickers down her legs and toss them aside.

She's panting heavily, her eyes wide, and her pupils dilated as I lift her easily off the wall and spin her around, bending her over the rough stone and sliding her dress up her body and casting it aside so that we're both completely naked.

"We probably shouldn't be doing this," she breathes heavily, her eyes rolling, and her head falling back against my shoulder as I press hot open-mouthed kisses to her neck, trailing down to her shoulder and nipping gently. "Your family have already caught us once tonight."

"No one will find us here," I growl against her ear as I cover her, pressing the length of my body to her back and reaching around to grasp her dick, I stroke her firmly. "It's just you and me."

I kiss slowly down the back of her neck, following the line off her spine until I reach the delicious curve of her buttocks. I love the way she looks with her long hair, her dresses, and heels, but equally I love her like this, completely naked and unabashedly male. Her long lean body is mouth-watering, with her shapely ass, flat chest, tiny rosebud nipples and long slim dick. I just want to lay her down and worship every inch of her skin.

I grip her cheeks and part them, running my tongue over her perfect little pink hole, relishing the loud groan as she bends further over the low wall, arching her back and pressing her arse further into my face as she unconsciously widens her legs.

"Please," she gasps.

Not needing to be asked twice I suckle at her opening before pressing my tongue inside. I love the cry that tears from her throat as she presses back again, riding my face as I rim her enthusiastically. My own neglected cock throbs and aches as I pleasure her mindlessly. All I can think about is getting inside that tight, wet heat and hearing her scream my name.

"Bruce," she moans. "More."

I pull back and spit into her hole as I hold it wide. Not that I need to, that's one of the perks of existing in a place where the rules of reality don't exist. It kind of eliminates the need for mundane things such as lube and condoms. There is no pain, no disease, only intense pleasure. I slide one finger into her, pumping slowly before adding a second and curling them until I reach the spot that drives her wild.

Within seconds she's bucking against me pushing her dick further into my fist and impaling herself on my fingers.

"Bruce," she pants out loudly. "Get your dick inside me now."

I grin against her skin, suckling at the spot where her shoulder meets her neck. I love how demanding she is. I've always had a thing for bossy little bottoms.

I pull my fingers free and line up the blunt weeping head of my cock and slide smoothly inside her in one slow thrust and dragging a satisfied moan from her.

"Fuck me hard," she whispers on a sharp breath. "I'm not going to last long. Everything is more intense here."

"I know, but we don't have to be back until dawn," I whisper into her ear, as I pull back and thrust into her deeply. "I'm going to fuck you over and over again... all night long."

"Yes," she cries out, as I grasp her hips and begin to ride her. "God, yes, do it."

My mind empties, and I can't think past the tight grip of her body, how deeply my cock is buried inside her, and how her dick in my hand throbs and drools her arousal over my fingers. We're animals, rutting in the stillness of the night, our harsh panting breaths and overwhelmed cries echoing off the silent, incomplete house behind us.

"Oh my god, I'm going to come," Dusty growls. "Make me come, Bruce."

I tighten my grip around her prick the way she likes and stroke her roughly, ploughing into her hole as she tightens. I feel her orgasm, warm cum spurting between my fingers and coating my fist as her insides squeeze and pulse around me. Unable to do anything else, I bury my face between her shoulder blades and moan loudly as I follow her down into oblivion coming deep inside her.

"Fuck," I whisper shakily. "You're right, it's so much more intense here."

"We should definitely visit more often." She huffs an exhausted laugh.

I withdraw slowly as my dick softens and turn her in my arms, cradling her face gently as I lay a soft, affectionate kiss on her plump lips. She smiles at me as I grasp her hand and step aside, watching as her eyes widen.

On what had been a small, dark, empty courtyard, there was now a thick down filled quilt laid out, scattered with plump cushions and surrounded by lit candles, lanterns, and fragrant flowers.

"Bruce," Dusty whispers in surprise.

"You deserve a little romance." I press a kiss to her cheek and lead her to the quilt. Dropping down between all the cushions, I settle her between my legs, her back nestling against my chest. I grab a blanket and wrap it around the pair of us, reaching for a full champagne flute and handing it to her.

She relaxes into my arms, letting out a deep sigh of contentment as we sip champagne and stare at the glittering stars above us.

"You're really something else, do you know that, Bruce," she mutters after a while.

I huff lightly against her. "You're just saying that because you love my huge cock."

She sets her empty glass down and turns in my arms, readjusting herself so she's sitting straddling my lap. I pull the blanket around her naked body once again, so she doesn't get cold, watching as she cradles my face, her eyes searching mine.

"I mean it, Bruce," she says softly. "I mean, yes, I do love your massive cock, that goes without saying, but its more than that." She frowns thoughtfully. "You're a good man, possible one of the best I've known, and I want you to be happy."

"I am happy." I grin.

She shakes her head, her expression serious. "Bruce, I want you to know I'm going to do everything I can to help you."

"Help me what?" I answer in confusion.

"Help you remember what happened to you," she says quietly. "It's not right that you're not allowed to go home. It should be your choice. I'm going to get Tristan and Danny to help."

"Dusty, it really doesn't matter anymore." I sigh. "There's very little chance of them finding my body after all this time. I've made my peace with it. There really isn't anything you can do."

"That's where you're wrong." She strokes my jaw soothingly with the pad of her thumb, her eyes filled with determination. "Bruce... I'm going to do everything I can to help you figure out how you died."

ABOUT THE AUTHOR

Vawn Cassidy is the MM pen name of author Wendy Saunders. She lives in Hampshire in the UK with her husband and three children.

She writes Supernatural and Contemporary Fantasy Fiction as Wendy Saunders and Romantic Suspense as WJ Saunders.

Suddenly Beck was her debut MM novel and was born of her love and enjoyment of MM Romance. She wanted to write something fun and light hearted, and as a quirky and unapologetic Brit herself, she wanted to set a story back home in the UK as opposed to her other fiction which is primarily set in the states.

With Dead Serious she returned to her Supernatural roots and her love of all things ghostly and preternatural with a good healthy dose of humour.

If you want to get in touch feel free, she's always lurking around on social media, or you can sign up to her mailing list here and also visit her website

www.vawncassidy.com

ALSO BY VAWN CASSIDY

Crawshanks Guide to the Recently Departed

Dead Serious Case#1 Miz Dusty Le Frey

Dead Serious Case#2 Mrs Delores Abanathy

Belong to Me

Book 1 Suddenly Beck

Book 2 Definitely Deacon

Book 2.5 Forever Finn (Novella)

Printed in Great Britain
by Amazon

12838018R00178